SECRET WEAPON

ELISE NOBLE

Published by Undercover Publishing Limited

Copyright © 2022 Elise Noble

v3

ISBN: 978-1-912888-55-9

Edited by Nikki Mentges, NAM Editorial

Cover design by Abigail Sins

www.undercover-publishing.com

www.elise-noble.com

There are no secrets that time does not reveal.

— JEAN RACINE

AUTHOR'S NOTE

I often have characters from one series pop up in another, but this is the first true crossover book I've written. In terms of timeline, *Secret Weapon* follows on from *Buried Secrets* in the Baldwin's Shore series and *Chimera* in the Blackwood Security series, but it's also a little bit of a sequel to *Ultraviolet*.

As a consequence, *Secret Weapon* contains huge spoilers for both *Ultraviolet* and the Baldwin's Shore series, so if you haven't read those yet, I'd strongly suggest doing so first in order to maximise enjoyment :)

1

EMMY

I was trapped in my worst nightmare.

No, not a poorly defended combat position with a battalion of heavily armed enemy soldiers circling—been there, done that, lived to tell the tale—but a small town in Oregon.

A small town with a big craft store.

And Bradley, my darling glitter-obsessed assistant, was currently in said craft store, and no doubt he was buying *everything*.

I should have pulled rank. I should have insisted we evacuate to Portland earlier this morning when we had the chance, but we were staying in a five-star hotel, and I'd been seduced by the idea of a massage and a breakfast buffet. Fuck knows, I'd deserved both. The last few weeks had been brutal.

First, I'd had to survive Bradley's festive vision, then I'd flown to Egypt to rescue a friend of a friend of a friend from a bunch of rogue smugglers and take a swim—involuntarily—in the River Nile. After Egypt, I'd spent two days dealing with corporate bullshit, which had actually been less fun than taking on the bunch of trigger-happy lunatics, and then my husband had asked me to assist with a little side project.

It had all started with a parrot.

An African Grey, to be precise, and a talkative one. Pinchy had been rescued from Animal Control by one pal and adopted by two others, and now he spent his days in an upscale Richmond apartment, begging for snacks and spewing curses. I'd always thought I swore like a trooper, but that damn bird gave me a run for my money.

He also had one particular catchphrase that intrigued us.

Don't shoot Mike.

Or, as it later turned out, *don't shoot, Mike.* Punctuation was important, kids.

A normal person would have embraced the expletive-ridden tirades and stocked up on parrot treats, but not my dear husband. No, Black wanted to know who Mike was and, more importantly, who hadn't wanted him to shoot. The bird must have copied the words from someplace, right?

And as the head of investigations for Blackwood Security, the global security firm we owned along with two other business partners, Black had been in the best position to find out where.

The "where" had led us from Charlottesville to Santa Clarita via Las Vegas. Initially, Black had been looking for a common or garden murder with a perpetrator named Mike, but of course, it wasn't that straightforward. When was anything *ever* straightforward?

First, he'd begun researching the habits of parrots. Turned out that when pet birds escaped, they didn't tend to go all that far because they had no clue how to care for themselves in the wild. Once they'd tasted freedom and found it was kinda rancid, they often tried to fly back home.

A call to Animal Control told us where Pinchy had been picked up, so Black had taped a large-scale map of Virginia to the wall of our shared office and marked the location with a big red X. Then he'd worked his way outwards, reviewing every suspicious death for the past year. We didn't think Pinchy would have survived longer than that on his own—the bird got crabby if he had to walk six steps to fetch his own almond. Hallie, who was Pinchy's joint owner and a junior member of Blackwood's investigations department, had assisted with the legwork, and Ford, her new boyfriend who also happened to be a cop in the Richmond PD, provided the occasional insight. After six weeks, the three of them had got absolutely nowhere.

No murder victim within a hundred-mile radius of Pinchy's final landing place had owned a parrot.

We began to wonder if Pinchy might have been stolen, if he'd once lived out of state and been dumped when his new family got sick of his potty mouth. Or if his owner had been shot but survived. Ford contacted colleagues in other police departments to ask about parrot thefts, and we widened our search to include gunshot injuries. Hallie approached local veterinarians to see if they knew Pinchy and drew a blank. Nobody recalled a foul-mouthed parrot, and trust me, once you met that bird, you didn't forget him easily.

The file almost made it as far as the cold-case pile, but not quite.

Why not?

Because Ford's former partner was an asshole, that was why.

Detective Duncan was as lazy as he was inept, and as Ford was about to leave the station on Christmas Eve, his new partner, a wet-behind-the-ears, freshly promoted newbie named Jayme Matassa—*call me Tass*—had found a pile of dusty files on her desk. Files that hadn't been there when she went to use the bathroom five minutes before. Also missing? Detective Duncan. Ford, being the gentleman that he was, had offered to take the files to the archive room so Tass could go home to her family. And Ford, being the nosy fucker that he was, had flipped the cover on the top file to see what was in it. That Duncan was listed as the lead detective hadn't been a surprise. The case was a suicide, now closed, a fifty-six-year-old antiques dealer named Sharona Cummings who'd downed a bottle of wine and then blown her brains out. Sadly, the situation wasn't a surprise either—too many people hit rock bottom and saw no other option. No, the surprise had been the bird sitting on her shoulder.

Pinchy.

Guess how Black spent Christmas Day?

After Christmas, one of Sharona's former neighbours had put us in touch with Sharona's daughter. Aubree Dobbs lived in Las Vegas with her husband and two kids, a perfect family in a McMansion on the outskirts of Henderson. Aubree worked part-time as a cosmetologist while the children were at school, and her husband was a pit boss on the Strip. Of course, we'd dropped by for a chat.

"If I'd known Mom was feeling that way, I'd have helped her, of course I would." Aubree accepted the tissue I offered. Yes, I'd been roped into visiting, but at least Black and I could spend a night or two in our Vegas apartment recovering from the festive season. Just the two of us. "But we'd grown apart, and...and I have the kids, you know?"

"When did you last see your mom?" Black asked. He had a pretty good bedside manner when the mood took him.

"L-l-last Christmas." And she'd died in April. "We h-h-had a fight."

"What did you fight over?"

"Over Mike."

Jackpot. But that did leave one big question...

"Who's Mike?"

"Her boyfriend. Ex-boyfriend now, I guess. My pop died

years ago, and Mom dated, but nothing serious until *he* came along."

"The file listed her boyfriend as Tony Spicer?"

"Michael is his middle name, and he always preferred it over Tony."

"The two of you didn't get along?"

Aubree shook her head. "Oh, he was smooth, but *too* smooth, if you know what I mean? Like it was all an act? The time or two I was on my own with him, he bordered on rude, and it was obvious why he was with my mom."

We both waited expectantly, although I could predict where this was going.

"Money. Mom had money from Pop's life insurance, and from her business, and Mike didn't even have a job, not a proper one. Oh, sure, he had ideas. He convinced Mom to invest in a wind power plant, and a real estate development, and a Christmas tree farm in freaking Arizona. Every time I asked her about Mike's 'portfolio,' about where the money was, she just said these things took time to turn a profit."

"Did you give this information to the police?"

"Of course I did! But the detective told me it was a clear-cut case of suicide. She even left a note."

And a neighbour had found Sharona dead, not Tony or Mike or whatever his name was. He'd shown up on the scene later, playing the part of devastated soulmate while the folks from the funeral home removed the body from the house. The note had been brief, just a couple of lines apologising for ending things that way, and if I recalled correctly, he'd been the person to identify the handwriting as hers.

"Detective Duncan, right?"

"You know him?"

"Only by reputation. What did he say about the money?"

"That if she'd given it willingly, then there was nothing they could do. Mike bled her dry, and the cops didn't think that contributed to her death? I'll never forgive him. *Never*." Aubree choked out a sob. "He lied about Captain too." Yes, Pinchy had once been named Captain, which explained his love of pirate language. "Mike said he rehomed him to a neighbour, but I'll bet he just opened the window and let him fly out."

"You didn't try to take him?"

"My son's allergic to parrot dander. Every time we visited Mom, he'd start sneezing. I mean, I did offer to find him a new home—Captain, not my son—but Mike said he'd already handled it." Another sob. "I'm s-s-so glad he landed on his feet in the end. Do you think his new owners might send me pictures?"

"I'm sure they will. But I'm curious—who taught Captain to swear? Your mom?"

An incredulous laugh burst from Aubree's throat. "No, oh gosh, no. Captain belonged to my little brother, but when he started working on a cruise ship, Mom took care of him. Mom hated Cody's job, *hated* it—she wanted him to become a doctor—but he always loved boats. That's where Captain got his name."

"Your brother's still working in the cruise industry?"

Aubree nodded. "He's a third officer now, sailing around the Mediterranean. He'll be thrilled to hear about Captain too."

"I'll make sure you get updates."

"And if you ever see Mike, tell him I hope he rots in hell."

Oh, we most certainly would.

Our quest to find Anthony Michael Spicer, also known as Michael Christopher Barclay, also known as Elwood John Michaelson, took us on a digital journey from Richmond, over to New York, and back to the West Coast. Now known as Mick Baker, Mike was shacked up with a wealthy widow in Santa Clarita, living off her investments and no doubt scamming her out of every cent possible. Sharona Cummings hadn't been his first victim, and if we didn't do something about the problem born as Michael Elwood, she wouldn't be his last, either. In the weeks before we touched down in California, we'd found six more women he'd taken advantage of. Three were dead—one "accident" and two "suicides"— and the other three rued the day they'd ever met the asshole.

The sun was setting as we rolled into Santa Clarita—me, Black, and my half-sister, Ana. Ana's boyfriend had taken their daughter to visit his parents, and since Ana did better in combat situations than social ones, she'd opted to join us for the fun instead. Vance Webber, a senior investigator from Blackwood's LA office, had done most of the legwork, so we knew Mike's current mark was celebrating a friend's birthday with a visit to a local spa. Mike was "working," otherwise known as binge-watching TV in his pyjamas while eating a family-sized bag of pretzels.

He wasn't amused when Black and I appeared in his living room. One could even say he was furious. But the anger soon turned to fear when Black shoved him back into his recliner and stood in front of him, arms folded. Black was a big guy— six feet seven with the muscles to match—and Mike stood a foot shorter. I pocketed his phone and took a wander around the house as Black educated him on the error of his ways. Mike's latest victim had done well for herself. She owned a small chain of upscale shoe stores, and judging by the contents of her walk-in closet, she tested out most of the merchandise. I found a handgun in a drawer on Mike's side of the closet and removed the ammo. Ditto for the pearl-handled revolver tucked away in his lady friend's bedside table. I mooched through the three bedrooms, the four bathrooms, the generous kitchen/diner, and the small study. According to Vance, the woman had remortgaged recently to release equity, and the proceeds of the loan had been transferred to Hillside

Wind Energy, Inc., which had a flashy website but no tangible assets that we could find.

By the time I finished my look-see, Black was wearing a faint smile.

"We're going to give Mr. Elwood a ride to the police station. He'd like to confess a few things."

"I need to change my clothes first," he whined. "You said I could change my clothes."

Black waved in the direction of the bedroom. "Be my guest."

We followed him along the hallway and waited outside the door while he got dressed. I had no desire to see his frank and beans. A moment later, Ana spoke through my earpiece.

"You called it. He tried to go through the window, but he's back inside now. Heading for the closet."

The door opened, and Mike stood before us, mouth set in a hard line as he aimed his semi-automatic at Black's chest. Oh, he tried to look tough, but his shaking hands gave the game away.

"Get out of my house."

Black merely sighed. "We've just established that this isn't your house."

"You broke in!"

"We didn't break a thing."

Both Black and I were proficient at picking locks. He'd done the honours this time.

"Ever heard of the castle doctrine?"

"Of course."

"So you know that I can use deadly force to defend my home."

"I'm aware of that."

"Then you'll understand this."

Mike pulled the trigger, and the gun clicked. *Click-click-click*. Yup, called it again. Sweat popped out on his brow as he stared at the useless weapon, unable to fathom why it wasn't working. Hadn't he noticed the change in weight when he picked it up? Clearly not. Dumbass.

Black picked him up and threw him back into the bedroom.

"You have five minutes."

Five minutes later, Black and I stared down at the mess in the bathroom. Blood leaked from Mike's wrists into the tub and trickled down the plughole. He was alive, but barely.

"Oh dear." By my estimation, he had a minute or two to live. "What a terrible shame."

Think I was upset? Think again. Why else would I have left the straight razor on the vanity?

Black was similarly distraught. "Overall, it's a good outcome for taxpayers. Ready to go?"

"Do you want Italian or Chinese for dinner?"

"Is that even a question?"

Italian. Black always picked Italian. With gloved hands, I reloaded the weapons in the bedroom, and we faded into the night.

Our plan had gone swimmingly up until that point, so we were about due for a hiccup. And the hiccup came the next morning when the subject of an investigation got spooked and ran, so Black headed down to LA with Vance to assist in locating him. Ana and I were preparing to travel back to Virginia on our own when Hallie called. Was anyone available to help with a teensy issue in Oregon?

Originally, Dan—Hallie's boss and a close friend of mine —had planned to go with her, but Dan's son had just been sent home from school with suspected tonsillitis. Since the Oregon case involved a kid, and kids puzzled Hallie and scared the crap out of me, Ana—who was a mom and therefore qualified to advise on parental issues—agreed to provide support. And we'd wrapped up the case in a pretty little bow. The end.

Or so I'd hoped.

Now we were in the tiny little town of Baldwin's Shore, although not for much longer. Hallie's case was closed, and we were finally ready to fly home. Or at least, we'd be ready as soon as we removed Bradley from the fucking craft store. My life was full of challenges, and this promised to be one of the toughest yet.

NINE

B aldwin's Shore was a town of two halves.
Half the people who lived there were running away from something, and the other half wanted to run but couldn't.

I was no different.

Living a lie, always looking over my shoulder to see if *he* had caught up with me yet.

My former boss.

My mentor.

My nemesis.

He was a patient man. A planner. A devil in human form who ruled his cold world with a leaden fist. A psychopath who never forgave or forgot.

Of course, he didn't get his own hands dirty, not anymore, although perhaps he'd make a special exception for me. After what I'd done. But he'd send his foot soldiers first. Then his son. His beloved daughter. From time to time, I wondered what had become of them. Whether Vik had grown to be as ruthless as his father, whether Nastya had been elevated to queen yet.

We'd been friends once, Nastya and I. Roommates for three years. But then our paths had diverged, and I'd ended up here. Burrowed into a life that wasn't mine. The rest of my team dead while I lived on borrowed time.

Bored.

Bitter.

Disciplined.

Ready.

Waiting.

Tomorrow was Sunday, which meant a predawn run, followed by a drive north to the forest in Douglas County for some target practice before work. The hardest part of this new life was training alone. Once, I'd craved solitude, but now I found that the most broken part of me missed those impromptu discussions about weapons over lunch, missed the sparring, missed the rivalry that had pushed me to improve every single day.

My team had been my anchor.

And now instead of being free, I was adrift.

Every day, I wore a mask, a mask that had become a second skin, but there were times when it felt as if my body were rejecting the organ.

Like today.

Paulo, one of the two retail assistants I employed, had bounced into the store at a quarter to nine, and he hadn't stopped talking since. Brooke was on duty too—all three of us worked Saturdays—and she'd shielded me from some of the cheerfulness, but I'd still developed a headache by ten a.m.

Then things got worse.

At ten thirty, the bell above the door jangled, and suddenly there were two of them. Two excitable men with outrageous hair getting excited over Swarovski cabochons and giant yarn. Personally, when it came to practicality, I preferred paracord. It had superior tensile strength, and it was far easier to knot.

I raised my gaze to the ceiling. *Lord, grant me the serenity not to shoot anyone today.* The blonde who'd followed Paulo's twin inside made a beeline for the gift section on the other side of the store, as far away as she could get, and who could blame her? She probably had a headache too.

"Does this yarn come in any other shades of pink?" the twin asked, holding up a two-foot-wide ball in bubblegum.

I forced a smile. "Sure does, hun. It comes in flamingo and fuchsia, but those are both special order."

"How long does it take to arrive?"

"They say two weeks, but it's usually a little faster."

He made a face. "Too bad. We're meant to leave today, and there's no way I can stretch it out any longer than tomorrow."

"You're staying at the Peninsula?"

"No, I was visiting a friend in Eugene, but I checked out the spa at the Peninsula this morning. The hot-stone aromatherapy massage is fandabidozi."

Figured. The Peninsula was the town's fancy new resort, and it catered to the type of person who could afford the outfit this guy was wearing. Designer jeans, designer shoes, designer sweater. I'd learned to size people up quickly in my former career, and this guy was a hummingbird. Colourful, harmless, and irritating when he fluttered around in the wrong place.

But he was a hummingbird with money, and money was a necessary evil. If he spent enough of it, I might finally be able to afford that new rifle I'd been coveting for so long. Those things didn't come cheap, especially on the black market.

The craft store wouldn't make me a millionaire, but it did turn a small profit, a reasonable achievement considering I'd started the place from scratch. Hell, four years ago, I hadn't known my Delicas from my drop beads, but I was a quick study. I had to be. And when I'd arrived in Baldwin's Shore with nothing—no plan, no cash, and no idea how I was going to heal my shredded soul—I'd needed weapons. A pair of good, thick knitting needles were handy in a fight, and after I'd taken the first available job—as a live-in nurse to Easton Baldwin Senior—they'd fit right in with my new life. It was entirely possible to kill a man with a knitting needle. Nastya had done it once. Plunged one of those suckers right through his eyeball. Anyhow, I'd learned to knit as a cover story, and I always had been good with my hands. Turned out that cross-stitch and beadwork and modelling with polymer clay weren't all that different from, say, assembling an IED. You just needed an eye for detail, steady fingers, and the ability to understand which parts went where. Of course, there was no *boom* if things went wrong with handicrafts, but I rarely got things wrong anyway.

Measure twice and cut once, as my mentor had been fond of saying.

Most of the time, he'd been talking about sliding a knife between a man's fourth and fifth ribs, but the same principle still applied to craftwork.

The bell jangled again, and I glanced at my watch to see if it was time for another painkiller. Sadly not.

The newcomer wasn't one of our usual clientele. Blonde, athletic, and a couple of inches shorter than me, but she walked with a confidence that made her seem taller. She didn't so much as glance at the shelves, just headed straight in our direction. I reached under the counter for my favourite knitting needles, a pair of size elevens that were a tiny bit sharper than normal. But the hummingbird was her target, not me.

"C'mon, champ. Time to go. We've got to get to Portland."

"Wouldn't you love to spend an extra day here instead?"

"No."

"But Alex will be tired after his race. Don't you think he deserves some R & R? We all know he wasn't built for running."

"Firstly, it's only a half-marathon, and secondly, he'll probably walk it. If he wants to sit in a Jacuzzi for an hour, he can do that at home. Do you seriously need more beads? Your craft room's bursting at the seams."

Who was the hummingbird to the blonde? Not a boyfriend—I'd put money on the fact that he was gay. A brother? An employee? She seemed to think she was in charge, notionally at least.

"I need beads and feathers for Easter."

"Easter? But we've only just finished Christmas."

"Proper planning and preparation prevents poor performance."

True. So true.

The blonde rolled her eyes. "Just hurry up."

3

EMMY

"I love the chunky yarn." Bradley hugged a ball of it to his chest. "But how do you knit with it? Do you need giant needles?"

"We keep those, or you can knit using your arms," the blonde behind the counter told him. Her name badge said Darla, her kaftan said crime against fashion. "I'm running a class at four o'clock tomorrow if you're interested in learning?"

Bradley turned to me, pleading with his eyes.

"No can do, ace. We were meant to leave an hour ago."

"Okay, okay. Give me five more minutes to pick out colours, and I'll have to find a tutorial on the internet." He beamed at Darla. "Do you know how to use Zoom?"

She gave him a horrified look, and her assistant snorted. Paulo, according to his own diamanté-embellished name badge, but I was starting to think of him as Bradley's brother from another mother.

"Last time Darla used Zoom, she turned on the cat filter and then she couldn't turn it off again. I've been slowly dragging her into the twenty-first century ever since I started working here, but if you have to plug it in, then it's best that she delegates the task to me. Apart from the glue gun. She's excellent with the glue gun."

Darla picked up the glue gun, aimed it at the dude's head, pulled an imaginary trigger, and giggled.

"He's so right. Give me a scrapbook and a pair of scissors any day."

"But we *do* have a selection of tutorials on our YouTube channel, filmed by *moi*. I'm sure we can find the time to make one for arm-knitting."

Give me strength.

What was I doing in a craft store, you ask? Apart from trying to leave as fast as possible?

Good question.

Bradley, my darling assistant, had spent the past week in Eugene with Felipe, an old friend of his who'd recently opened a clothing boutique. And when the time came to leave, Bradley had decided to hitch a ride back to Virginia on my jet. Which ordinarily wouldn't have been a problem because we could have driven straight to the airport and been somewhere over Iowa by now. But then Alex, my personal trainer, decided he wanted to fly back with us too, and since he'd lost a bet and been forced to sign up for a half-marathon in Portland, that meant hanging around in Oregon until he'd finished. And then Bradley had heard about the craft store from the masseuse earlier, and now my house was gonna be filled with giant yarn and feathers and glitter and fuck knew what else.

At least, Bradley *claimed* that he'd only heard about the craft store this morning. Now that I considered matters, he'd been awfully insistent that we all stay in Baldwin's Shore for an extra night instead of checking in to one of the many five-star hotels in Portland, and I had a sneaking suspicion that if I asked Mack to check his internet search history, the Craft Cabin would be lurking on the list.

Come to think of it, the Portland half-marathon had been Bradley's idea too. Originally, Alex had signed up to race in Florida last November, but that event had been called off due to a hurricane, and I might have forgotten about the whole dumb wager if Bradley hadn't announced last week that he'd secured a last-minute entry for the Portland half.

Had he really made Alex run thirteen miles just to engineer himself an extra shopping trip?

Honestly, I wouldn't have put it past him.

Dammit all to hell.

I should've stayed in the hotel spa like Bradley suggested, but somebody had to do damage control, and Hallie was too busy browsing model ships in the gift section. How had it come to this? I was a world-class assassin, I ran the special operations team at a global security firm, and today, I was losing an argument in the hick version of Aladdin's cave.

"Do you really need a giant blanket?"

"No, but I *want* a giant blanket. Don't worry; I'll knit one for you as well."

"I definitely don't need a giant blanket."

"Of course you do—you married Gulliver. And I'll make one for Alex too because that's only fair." Huh? Alex might only have been an inch shorter than my husband at six feet six, but he wasn't an arts-and-crafts kind of guy. Fairness didn't come into it. But Bradley had already turned back to Paulo. "So what I need is enough yarn to make, say, five blankets, plus matching cushions."

Five? Who were the other two for?

The bell above the door tinkled, and it was an actual bell. A tiny brass thing suspended from the ceiling on a piece of blue string. Low-tech. Darla had probably hung it up there herself. Ana slunk inside, head down as she checked her phone. Judging by the smile on her face, she'd received a message from either her boyfriend or her daughter. Tabby was four now, almost five, and texted faster than I did. Plus she'd mastered emojis and GIFs. The little psycho sent me pictures of pineapple-covered pizza every other morning, and Ana thought it was hilarious.

But today, the smile slipped off her face, and as quickly as she'd walked into the store, she left. What the hell? I turned to see what she'd been looking at, but there was only Darla, and she was showing Bradley a hot-pink ball of yarn the size of a small child. He did realise we were flying in a Learjet and not an Airbus 380, right?

I followed Ana outside. Bradley wouldn't be finished in five minutes, anyway. No chance. At first, I thought she'd done a disappearing act, but when she saw me, she materialised from the shadows beneath a spreading evergreen.

"You okay? You look as if you've seen a ghost."

"Maybe I did."

"What the fuck are you talking about?"

Ana moved off down the street, fast but not hurried, watching our reflections in windows as we passed. Nobody was following.

"Ana?"

She didn't stop until she reached a small park nestled between a café and a dental practice. Actually, "park" was being generous. It was nothing more than a scrubby patch of grass with half a dozen picnic tables and a yellow-and-blue swing set. A flock of birds was pecking at the ground at the far end, but apart from that, it was deserted. Main Street in Baldwin's Shore was hardly a hive of activity. Ana took a seat at the nearest table, but rather than swinging her legs over the bench, she sat sideways, in case she needed to get up in a hurry. I mirrored her pose on the opposite side. If Ana was worried, then I was worried.

"Sis?"

"I don't... Where do I start?"

"At the beginning?"

"The beginning... I hate thinking about the beginning." She sucked in a breath. Surreptitiously checked her gun and forced herself to relax. Her shoulders dropped, but if she clenched her jaw much harder, we'd have to pay that dental practice a visit. "In the beginning, I was twelve years old."

"Twelve? You're talking about your time in Russia?"

Ana had grown up there, first in Vladivostok and then in Siberia, the pawn of a madman who'd trained her to do his bidding. He'd stolen her childhood, part of her soul, and almost her life as well. But she'd won her freedom, and now she *never* spoke about that chapter of her existence.

"Yes. Siberia. When General Zacharov chose me for his program, and I became Seven of Ten." Ana's voice dropped until it was barely audible. "Ten little soldiers, torn into our component parts and rebuilt in his image. Ten little drones, taught to act without question. We were all broken in our own ways. One, Two, and Eight didn't make it through training. Two lost his head, quite literally."

Ana choked out a laugh, but she looked shaken.

Ana never looked shaken.

"I'm so sorry you had to go through that hell. But you made it out. It's in the past."

"Is it? *Is it*? Seven of us survived. Two girls, five boys. I was the youngest."

"Why are you telling me this? I mean, I'll always listen if you want to talk, but why now?"

"Because that woman in there, the one talking to Bradley?"

"Darla?"

Ana doubled over, her laughter turning hysterical. "Darla? *Darla*? That's what she's calling herself?"

"In the flowery muumuu?"

"Darla?" Ana said again. "I guess it works. *Da*, in the muumuu. She's lost her fucking mind."

I was beginning to think she wasn't the only one.

"Ana, you're not making any sense."

"That's Nine. Darla is Nine. *Gavno*. She's wearing fucking flowers."

Had I stepped into an alternative universe? Darla wasn't Ana Mark II. No way. She knew more about embroidery floss than Bradley did, and more importantly, she didn't *feel* like an assassin. Ana and I both knew it wasn't possible to retire, not completely. Sure, we could pretend to be a suburban mom and a billionaire's trophy wife, but long term, keeping up the charade was exhausting. It wasn't who we truly were. And there were always tiny tells that would give us away—a reaction that was a little too fast, a gaze that was a little too probing. Granted, I hadn't spent much time with Darla, but she didn't give off those vibes.

"Are you sure?"

"Darya Volkova is a chameleon. Call it a gift."

"Maybe Darla just looks similar? And it's been, what, five years since you saw Nine?"

"Six, but we shared a room for three years in the beginning. It's her."

Ana didn't have to add "trust me." We both knew that was a given. And was it really so far-fetched? Ana had escaped to America, and she'd played at being a waitress and a secretary before we teamed up. Was it possible that Darla—Darya, whatever—genuinely liked crafts? That was the part of this story that I found hardest to believe. What was the point of cutting things out and sticking them into scrapbooks? I just didn't get it.

"Okay, let's assume you're right and Nine's decided to swap her Glock for a glue gun. What are we going to do about it?"

"Nothing. We're going to do nothing. You need to get Bradley and I'll get the car and then we can all get the hell out of here."

"You don't want to speak to her? For old time's sake?"

"No!"

"Okaaaay. Maybe she wouldn't even recognise you."

"She would. Darya has a freakish memory, especially when it comes to faces. She only needs to see somebody once and she'll never forget them. And at breakfast, Bradley said the craft shop has been open for two years. When did we take out Zacharov? Just over two years ago. If Darya's been here in Baldwin's Shore for any longer, she might not know he died. She's hiding; she has to be. And if she sees me coming, she's going to shoot first and then run. I know that because if our positions were reversed, it's exactly what I'd do. This is a battle we don't need to fight. She's made her bed—let her lie in it."

I was hella curious, but logically, I knew Ana was right. Let sleeping dogs lie. Why wake Cerberus if we didn't have to? And to be fair, Darla-Darya was probably pretty cosy in her bed with seventeen throw pillows and a crocheted comforter.

"I'll get Bradley."

Or not. The scream that cut through the air sent a chill up my spine that had me reaching for my gun. Ana mirrored me.

Animal or human? If I had to put money on it, I'd say the latter, and it hadn't been a playful scream or a hey-you-surprised-me scream. Was somebody in trouble?

I lifted my chin towards the forest two hundred yards away, and Ana gave a weighty sigh. But then she nodded. We'd spent our whole lives training so that in situations like this one, we didn't have to turn away.

And once again, we headed into the unknown together.

4

NINE

My cat shot through the door of the break room like a Tsirkon missile, and a bad day suddenly got worse. Because Pickle was followed by a dog—where the fuck had that come from?—and they leapt onto a set of shelves. The free-standing unit tipped over, scattering beads and Pickle across the floor. Paulo made a grab for the canine and slipped over on a river of faux pearls, and a cacophony of yowling and barking and shrieking sent a battering ram through my already delicate head.

Pizdets.

Pickle scaled another set of shelves, and the dog attempted to follow, but it was flagging. Where had all the blood come from? I focused on Pickle, but she didn't seem damaged, which meant the dog must be the donor.

The dog...

Brooke ran in with Romi Mendez and Shauna Weaver following close behind, and I realised it was Shauna's unruly mutt that was currently wrecking my store. She never had been able to control it. More than once, it had bolted down Main Street in pursuit of a car with Shauna huffing and puffing along behind. Today, it was miraculously wearing a leash, so why wasn't she holding the damn thing?

I thought longingly of the syrette of tranquilliser I kept nestled in my bra, just in case of a little emergency. It was meant for humans, but it would probably take a dog down too. Or kill it. I sighed. Death would invite questions I couldn't answer, so this would have to be done the old-fashioned way.

Paulo's new friend had run to help him up, and the blonde who'd been browsing the gift section was puzzling over the red streaks on the tiled floor. Brooke and Romi were frozen, Shauna was crying, and didn't any of these coddled westerners understand the concept of action?

I shuffled toward the dog, keeping the soles of my feet in contact with the floor so I didn't make the same mistake as Paulo. The thing launched itself at Pickle again, but half-heartedly, which suggested that in the war of blood loss versus adrenaline, whatever injury the dog had suffered was winning. When the leash whipped past me, I caught it and yanked, and the dog fell to my side with a strangled bark.

I nearly snapped, "Hold this fucking thing," at Shauna, but I caught myself just in time.

"Hun, could you grab the leash while I try to catch Pickle?"

Shauna didn't move, but the blonde held out a hand.

"Here, I'll take it."

"I really appreciate that."

Back in Russia, I hadn't been a cat person. My tormentor, the man who'd shaped me into what basically amounted to a pet assassin, had hated animals unless they served a particular purpose. Tracker dogs? Okay. Pet dogs? Not okay. In all honesty, I'd never intended to have a pet in America either, but Pickle had walked into the store one day, nothing but skin and bone, and while the old me would have put her out of her misery, new me thought "fuck it" and took her to the veterinarian. She'd grown on me now. A small creature who gave affection when she felt like it and asked for little in return.

Apart from today. Today, there was no affection, only pissed-off hissing.

I grabbed a square of taffeta from the fabric bin and unfolded it. Pickle was normally friendly, but her claws were sharp, and thanks to Shauna's incompetence, she was in fight mode. People should have to take a test before they could own a pet. Question one: Can you stop the varmint from being a pain in the ass? Negative? Then no dog for you.

Pickle readied herself to jump to a higher shelf, and I tossed the taffeta over her before she could make the leap. Then I bundled her up and deposited her in the staff bathroom to cool off while I dealt with the rest of the chaos. *This* was why I preferred to avoid people.

Paulo was whining about bruises, and as I checked on the dog's status, it collapsed onto the floor in slow motion, scarlet pooling underneath. Bleeding often looked worse than it actually was, unless you used a stiletto knife, or an ice pick, or a neat little .22, but I had to concede that there was a significant volume of blood on the floor.

"I think he's hurt?" The blonde stated the fucking obvious as she knelt at the dog's side. "He's bleeding."

Shauna contributed by bursting into tears, which took Brooke out of the game too because one of us had to calm Shauna down and it wasn't going to be me.

"Somebody help Scooby," she wailed.

"What happened?" I asked. "How did he get hurt?"

Brooke answered for her. "She thinks it was a cougar."

A cougar? Not this near town, no way. Baldwin's Shore had thick forest on two sides, and there was enough food out there that mountain lions didn't need to risk coming near man.

The blonde gently probed through Scooby's fur. "I don't see any bite marks, but maybe they're on the other side?"

"Is the blood definitely his?" Romi asked. "What if he bit the cougar?"

Doubtful.

I turned to Shauna. "You saw the cougar?"

"N-n-no."

Give me strength. "So what *did* you see, hun?"

"Scooby made this noise like...like...like a scream, so I ran along the path, and Scooby was there, and he was hurt, and I saw this *blur* disappearing into the trees."

"And what made you think the blur was a cougar?"

"I guess... I guess it was a beige colour?"

"I called Luca," Brooke offered. "He's on his way, but he's down near Bandon."

Luca was her fiancé, a former Army Ranger and a current sheriff's deputy. At one time, I'd thought his profession might cause me a problem, especially when I'd carved up a guy who abducted Brooke, but Luca had remained delightfully oblivious to my extracurricular activities. And lately, it seemed he'd actually been encouraging them. Tsk-tsk-tsk.

Anyhow, he'd be at least half an hour, and the non-cougar would be long gone. "What about Colt?"

Colt was the other deputy, the one who'd rescued a princess at the side of the road and somehow ended up dating her.

"He has the day off, and he went sailing with Brie and Kiki."

Sailing. Which meant they'd be on Nico's boat, and hopefully, Nico was with them. The local hotel owner was a man I avoided whenever possible. I considered it unlikely that he'd recognise me—we'd met just a handful of times prior to his arrival in Baldwin's Shore, and under very different circumstances—but I only took risks when the potential upside outweighed the downside.

I heard the snap of teeth, and the blonde leapt back. She'd managed to roll the dog, something the dog hadn't appreciated in the slightest.

"Here's where the blood's coming from." She pointed at a wound on Scooby's neck. "But it doesn't look like a bite mark to me."

No, it wasn't a bite mark. It was quite clearly a knife wound, but I couldn't admit I knew that.

"Maybe someone should take him to the veterinarian?" And by someone, I meant Shauna because her crying was getting on my last fucking nerve.

Brooke spoke up, as I'd known she would. She had a kind heart, too kind at times because with that kindness came a naivety that had gotten her into trouble in the past.

She saw the good in people.

I saw the bad.

"My car's right outside," she said. "Paulo, can you help to lift the dog? We're gonna need a towel or a blanket to lay him on."

"The throw from the couch in the break room?"

"That's perfect."

Speaking of bad, who was running around in the trees with a knife? I'd admit to being curious, and perhaps a little scouting was just what I needed to blow the cobwebs off and liven up a dull day?

Paulo reappeared with the throw, a multicoloured woollen thing I'd knitted soon after I arrived in town. I'd been broken back then. Cracked down the middle with pain and anger and sadness spilling out. The only man I'd ever cared about was gone, and I was left with two options: return home to face the music, or run. Lieutenant General Zacharov didn't tolerate failure, so returning home would have been distinctly unpleasant, and if he ever found out that I'd sabotaged the operation, I'd have been dead anyway. What did I have to lose by running?

My sanity, as it turned out.

The first couple of years in Baldwin's Shore hadn't been too bad. As my fractured soul healed, I'd taken pleasure in the mundanity of everyday life. Working as a live-in nurse to East Baldwin had been a piece of cake compared to my former life, even when I had to deal with his family, who ranged from milquetoast to malicious to murderous. I'd taught myself to knit, learned to bake, and wheeled East along the seashore every morning with the wind in my hair.

When Nastya hadn't come, when Vik hadn't come, I'd begun to relax. For a while, I carried one knife instead of two and only packed a gun on special occasions, and I cut myself slack if I missed an early-morning run. Target practice became entertainment rather than necessity. Boredom crept up on me like a slow-rolling fog, and I couldn't find my way out of it. Wasn't sure it was worth the effort. What need was there for a spy-slash-assassin in sleepy little Baldwin's Shore?

Then Nico came to town, and everything changed.

At first, I'd been spooked. Now, I was ninety-nine percent sure his presence was a coincidence, a big cosmic joke. But there was still that one percent of me that asked *what if he knows?*

I'd started training again, hard, the way I always used to. And in the scraps of spare time I eked out, I began to have fun. To enjoy myself. They'd given me a nickname—the Bad Samaritan—but at heart, I'd always be Nine. Nine of Ten. Only seven of us had made it through the initial training. Three more died later. There were only four of us left now, or perhaps three if Ilya had let his greed get the better of him.

"We need to get the dog onto the throw," Paulo said, snapping me back to the present. "I don't want to get bit."

"Maybe Shauna could help?" I suggested. Scooby was her dog. If anyone was going to get tetanus, it should be the girl who couldn't tell the difference between *Homo sapiens* and *Puma concolor*. Me? I'd had my shots. Always be prepared, General Zacharov had drilled into us.

Scooby didn't have the energy to snap as we pulled him onto the blanket, and that wasn't a good sign. But the veterinarian was only a two-minute drive away, and Isaac Ward seemed competent from what I'd seen of him. The dog might pull through—anything was possible.

"Should I come too?" Paulo asked. "No, I should help to clean up the store. Someone has to rescue all of those Swarovski pearls."

"Oh, you go, hun. If Dr. Ward doesn't have an assistant there, they'll need you on one corner of the blanket again." I turned to the blonde and the hummingbird. "And I'm afraid you'll have to leave too. I really need to get these bloodstains wiped up." The hummingbird opened his mouth to protest, but I'd had enough bullshit for one day. "If you want to jot down your number, we can ship whatever you'd like at no charge."

"But the yarn—"

Good thing the blonde took the hint. "No shipping charge—that's a great offer."

"We should help to—"

She linked her arm through his and marched him toward the front door. "We really need to leave the lady to take care of her cat, okay?"

"I'll email you," he called back over his shoulder, and I dredged up a smile.

"I'll be looking forward to it."

The instant the door closed behind them, I threw the bolt home and headed for the rear exit. If there was some asshole with a knife in the trees behind Main Street, I needed to find out who they were. Kids walked there. Okay, so I didn't much like kids, but I liked assholes even less.

I strolled out the door, breathing deep to settle my headache. Peace and quiet and a little fresh air worked better than any painkiller. Blood drops led across the small yard at the rear of the store, and I followed them like breadcrumbs, one hand ready to grab the gun strapped to my thigh if necessary. There was a reason I wore a muumuu most of the time, and that reason had less to do with making a fashion statement and more to do with concealment. Luck was on my side today—I'd picked out a nice subdued outfit this morning instead of nuclear orange or mustard-gas yellow.

The path curved into the trees, and I slipped a switchblade into my hand.

Whatever came at me, I'd be ready.

And they'd be sorry.

5

EMMY

Welcome to the "nothing is ever easy" club.

The scream had come from the north, but undergrowth restricted visibility to a few yards in any direction. Spiky evergreen bushes grew beneath pine trees, and a carpet of leaves and needles meant few footprints and no obvious tracks. If someone had come this way recently, we weren't able to tell.

Ana was on a path to my left. I couldn't see her, and I couldn't hear her, but I could feel her.

We'd met late in life, barely known each other existed until a chance meeting in a frozen wasteland just over two years ago. Trust didn't come easily to either of us, but despite that, we'd clicked. We'd clicked, and now Ana was one of the two people I trusted most in the world to have my back. The other was my husband, but he was still in California.

And Ana's presence wasn't the only thing I felt. A prickle at the base of my spine told me someone or something else was lurking in these woods, and the meeting wasn't going to be pretty.

Up ahead, our paths converged, and I glimpsed Ana

through the trees, thirty feet ahead of me. What was out here? *Who* was out here?

Turned out I didn't want to know the answer.

Because a moment later, *she* was there.

Darla, Darya, Nine—whatever her name was—and now I knew that Ana had been absolutely right. Nine was still wearing the fucking muumuu, but she had a knife in her hand, and her stance said *hunter*.

Ana was about to become her prey.

They stared at each other for a heartbeat. Never had I seen Ana hesitate, not once, but today she did, which let Nine get the drop on her, and before Ana could recover, her semiautomatic was flying through the air. Ana went for Nine's knife, but she was already one point down in this battle, and I couldn't shoot the bitch myself in case I hit my sister.

Ah, fuck.

I hated knife fights. Somebody always got cut, but I began running anyway, and my own blade was already in my hand. An Emerson CQC-7B with a textured grip, so even if my hand was slick with blood, I still stood a chance of holding on to it.

Ana leapt back as Nine slashed with the knife, then grabbed the bitch's wrist with both hands to control the blade. But that left Nine with a free hand, and I was still ten feet away when Nine got Ana with a vicious chop to the neck. Ana fell to her knees. Was she out? Shit, she was out.

Five feet away, four, three, and Nine lashed out backwards with a boot and caught the side of my knee. I saw stars, but I grabbed the back of her dress and yanked, hoping to tighten it around her throat. Instead, I heard the *scriiiitch* of Velcro giving way, and the whole thing came off in my hand. And Nine really did believe in being prepared. Under the hideous top layer, she was basically Lara Croft, complete with thigh holsters and a tactical belt that had to be custom made. And I'd just given her better access to her toys.

Fuck my life.

She smashed her head back, and not for the first time I felt the crunch of cartilage in my nose. My plastic surgeon needed to offer a loyalty card—after nine rhinoplasties, the tenth came free. But I was also used to pain and fighting through it—thanks, Alex—so I wasn't about to back down.

If Ana was right, Nine had gone into this battle with the assumption that she was fighting for her life, and now so was I. She wouldn't stop until I was dead. But we had to be fairly evenly matched—she'd undergone the same training as Ana, and I'd sparred with Ana plenty of times, although, granted, we hadn't *actually* been trying to kill each other. Nine had two inches on me height-wise and probably a little weight too, but she'd also been working in a craft store for a couple of years. I had the advantage of endless hours of practice during that time, with Ana, with Black, and with Alex, to name but a few.

Nine came at me with the knife, but I ducked, grabbed an ankle, and upended her. She used her momentum to roll, and in a heartbeat, she was back on her feet, but not before I'd kicked the knife out of her hand. Another appeared in a blink of the devil's eye, and we circled each other, assessing. A second later, she was in the air, swinging one-handed from a branch above, aiming a boot at my head as she went. I ducked but lost sight of her for a second, then felt a hand on my wrist and punched her in the shoulder as she grabbed my knife. It slid under a bush as Ana groaned softly, and there... Nine glanced to the side, only for a fraction of a second, but it was enough. I gripped her wrist and drove the point of her blade into a tree, hard enough that it stuck there. There was blood on her, not mine, I thought, but hers. I'd nicked her somewhere with my own blade, but as I tried to get an arm around her throat, she bit me, and fuck, that stung.

"You bitch!"

"*Idi na khui.*"

Oh, we were speaking Russian now?

"*Khui tebe tozhe, suka.*"

An elbow to the stomach knocked the wind out of me, but I had her in a chokehold now, and I wasn't letting go. She clawed at me, stomped on my instep, but I propelled her forward into a tree and then she needed her hands to save herself.

Out of the corner of my eye, I saw Ana roll to her knees, and I aimed a silent "thank fuck" skywards. Then Nine used her legs to push off the tree and sent me stumbling backwards, cursing, and when we landed I was underneath, but she was still on her back, which didn't give her the advantage she'd hoped for.

She tried to twist; I hung on and wrapped my legs around her waist. My arms were getting shredded by her nails, but skin regrew, right? She tried to reach for my hand, and I bit her. Payback was a bitch, and so was I. For the thousandth time, I wondered why I did this shit. I was married to a billionaire. I could have been sunning myself on a beach somewhere, but oh no, I had to fight with a Russian assassin in the bloody woods instead.

Then I heard it. The most glorious sound in the world. No, not the hiss of a coffee machine but the crackle of a stun gun as Ana jammed it into Nine's armpit and held it there for three seconds, four seconds, five. Nine let out an unearthly yelp as she spasmed, then her grip loosened enough for me to heave her off.

"Hope you had a good fucking sleep."

Ana bit her lip, and I'd never seen her look spooked that way either.

"Sorry," she whispered.

"Just get her the hell away from me. Tie her up."

We carried flex-cuffs and paracord as standard, and by the

time Nine opened her eyes, we had her hog-tied and disarmed. Of course, she began struggling right away, spitting curses in Russian and English and calling us all manner of uncomplimentary names.

And now we had the problem of what to do with her.

"So..." I started, wiping away the blood that still trickled from my nose. "Any ideas?"

Nine had several, all of them unpleasant and some of them physical impossibilities. Safe to say she wasn't happy with recent developments. Admittedly my Russian wasn't fluent, but she seemed to be pissed about us stabbing a dog? Was that some kind of idiom? Ana knelt beside her and brushed her hair almost tenderly, then she shocked me for the third time in as many minutes when she leaned in close. And kissed the murderous witch. Not with tongues—our old-new friend would've bitten it off—but more than a chaste peck.

What the fuck?

M y jaw might have dropped, but Ana didn't see it because all her attention was on Nine.

"Dasha, we're not here to hurt you," she murmured. "And we don't know anything about a dog."

Nine didn't relax, but she did stop struggling quite so violently.

"Bullshit. *He* sent you."

"He? You mean the general?"

"Who else?"

"Zacharov is dead. Nobody sent us."

"Dead?" For the first time, uncertainty crept into Nine's eyes. "Men like Zacharov don't die. They just take a vacation in hell and come back even stronger."

"We killed him."

"You? *You?*" Nine's expression hardened again. "Now I know you're lying."

Oh, for fuck's sake... "She's not lying. We put two bullets through his head, one each."

"I don't know who *you* are, but *she* wouldn't kill her own father."

"Well, she did. But I'm curious as to how you found out he was her father when it wasn't common knowledge?"

Even Ana herself hadn't realised, not until seconds before Zacharov's death when he'd revealed all in an attempt to save his sorry arse. Nine didn't answer, just gave me a hate-filled glare, and possibly there was a hint of petulance on her part too. If she didn't want to talk, I couldn't make her. Literally couldn't. I'd been well-schooled in the art of torture, but a woman like Nine would merely grit her teeth and deal with it, and besides, Ana seemed fond of her, fuck only knew why.

And right now, my nose hurt like a mother, so I wasn't about to stand around chatting.

I poked Dasha with my foot. "I take it you didn't scream a few minutes ago?"

Silence, as expected.

"Ana, can you cope here while I check out that noise we heard?"

"I'm okay."

She wasn't, but we could have that discussion later.

"Good. I'll have a quick scout, then I'll round up the others and we can get out of here."

I'd briefly considered whether Nine might have done something to hurt Hallie or Bradley before she stepped out for a stroll, but I'd come to the conclusion that they were fine. Her shock at seeing Ana had been genuine, and no way would she have created a scene on Main Street when she was trying to keep a low profile.

"What about Dasha?" Ana asked. "We can't just leave her like this."

"We'll chuck a knife somewhere before we vamoose." I nodded into the distance. "By the time she's wriggled over to it and freed herself, we'll be in the air. Bradley's gonna be heartbroken when I tell him he can't mail-order the giant pink yarn."

Giving Nine his address didn't strike me as a great idea. The last thing I wanted was a Russian super-assassin appearing on his doorstep. Or climbing in through a window. Or swimming up from the sewer like an oversized rat.

I prodded the bitch again. "Smile—in an hour, this'll all be over and you can go back to your embroidery."

"It's cross-stitch," she growled.

"Whatever. We'll even let you keep your toys. And if you get the chance, take a gander at a satellite photo—the Russians wrote off the Base 13 incident as a munitions mishap, but if you look real close, you'll see one of the holes is where Zacharov's office used to be. Two years ago, we left his smoking remains at the bottom of that crater." I held up her utility belt and admired it for a moment. "No skin off my nose if you don't believe us, but living with this level of paranoia isn't healthy. You should learn to relax. Maybe wear clothes with a waistline again."

I collected my hardware and injected myself with a little something to take the edge off the pain Nine had inflicted, but not enough to erase it completely because I needed a clear head for the next part. Nine's arm was still bleeding, and I crouched to check out the wound.

"Ana, can you bandage that?" What was wrong with my sister? It was as if she'd gone into shock. "Ana?"

"I'll do it."

"Darya? That's your name, right? You're gonna need stitches. We'll patch up the damage for now, but I'd suggest a trip to the emergency room once we've left. Do you want painkillers? I presume you've got appropriate drugs in your belt of magic tricks?"

I figured she'd refuse out of sheer bloody-mindedness, but today was full of surprises. She nodded and muttered, "Rear pouch, off side."

She carried similar kit to ours, and I passed the tiny syrette over to Ana, who'd at least come back to life with enough sentience to assess Nine's wound.

"Give her this. Back in five."

I'd barely taken two steps before a voice stopped me in my tracks. And it wasn't Ana's, but Nine's.

"Wait."

I turned. Did as instructed. "Well?"

"There's someone out here with a knife. Other than me, I mean. Watch your back."

"How do you know?"

"A local woman ran into the store with her dog, and the dog had a knife wound."

If that was true, it went some way to explaining why Nine was out here. She'd come to look for the offender, only to stumble across us first. But was she lying? Nine was smart, and like me, she must have realised that Ana wasn't herself today.

As proven by Ana's next words.

"If there's someone out here with a knife, we can't leave Dasha tied up like this."

No, we couldn't. And we couldn't dump her back at the store either, because that would blow her carefully constructed cover. I was a bitch, but I wasn't enough of a bitch to ruin Nine's life. If Zacharov had treated her half as badly as he'd treated Ana, then she'd been through hell in Russia. She deserved her retirement.

And besides, there was a simple way to confirm Nine's story. I pulled out my phone, then swore under my breath when I saw the cracked screen. Dead as a desiccated dormouse. I had a spare in the car, but that didn't help right now.

"Ana, can I borrow your phone?"

She handed it over, and Hallie answered on the first ring.

"Hey, it's me."

"Emmy? I tried calling you, but your phone went to voicemail."

"It broke."

"Is everything okay? I was in the craft store, and this girl ran in with a dog, and she said it got attacked by a cougar, but the cuts looked more like knife wounds to me."

Okay, so Nine wasn't kidding.

"Where are the woman and the dog now?"

"Three of the people from the store took them to the veterinarian. And there was quite a mess, so the owner closed for the day, and we figured we'd find you in the car, but you're not here, and Bradley's freaking out. Where did you go?"

Of course he was freaking out. Bradley was a man who freaked out if he spilled coffee on his sweater.

"Just keep him calm. And can you quietly, quietly get out the first aid kit and changes of clothes for Ana and me? Oh, and the spare phone from the glove compartment."

I broke so many phones, I bought them in bulk.

"Did something happen?"

"Nothing serious. A few cuts and scrapes, that's all. We'll be back in a jiffy."

Fuck. Now we had a decision to make... But I could push that back to Nine.

"You've got three options. One, we can do as originally planned—leave you here to free yourself later. Two, same deal, but we load you into the trunk of our car and drop you off at a location of your choosing with your stuff. Or three, we keep your weapons and let you go now on the understanding that if you try any shit, I'm putting a bullet between your eyes."

Nine gave the slightest wince as Ana packed gauze over her wound. At least the cut was clean—a simple slice, no jagged edges. And the captured assassin was calm now. The adrenaline kick from the fight was wearing off, plus her anger had simmered down.

"Why are you in Baldwin's Shore?" she asked. "Why did you come here if not for me?"

"A follow-up on a completely unrelated missing persons case. And we only came to the craft store because my assistant loves shiny things."

"Then set me free. I have no reason to hurt you."

I met Ana's gaze and raised an eyebrow. She knew what I was asking—could we trust this woman? Ana knew her former colleague far better than I did, and the final decision would be hers.

She gave Nine a more thorough pat-down and found yet another knife, this one in her bra, plus a syrette filled with an unknown liquid. Some kind of tranquilliser if I had to take a guess. Then she cut through the restraints, and Nine was free. Only time would tell whether we'd made the right decision, but I thought we had. I hoped we had.

Nine stretched languidly like a cat, her movements smooth considering what she'd just been through, then examined the bandage on her arm. Seemingly found it to her satisfaction and velcroed her dress back on. The voluminous fabric covered most of the damage.

When she stepped closer to Ana, I released the safety on my gun, but Nine just cupped Ana's cheek in her hand.

"You look good, Nastya," she murmured before returning the kiss. "Or did you stick with Ana? Have a nice life."

Then she glided off into the trees, but in the wrong direction. She was heading *away* from the Craft Cabin.

"Wait," Ana called. "Where are you going?"

"To finish what I started before you interrupted me."

Ana hurried after her. "But you have no weapons."

"So? Unless it's another of the Ten out here with the knife, I'll be fine."

Another of the Ten? So there were more of the original group left alive? All these little secrets...

"We can search. You should go get stitches."

"This town is my home, not yours. *I* deal with the problems. But please, make even more noise. Scare off the *mudak* completely."

"We're coming with you."

7

EMMY

At first, Nine looked as if she was about to argue with Ana. But either pragmatism struck or she wasn't feeling quite as confident as she claimed, because she shrugged.

"Shhh."

If Ana was going, then I was going too. The three of us headed for the path Nine had been on when we originally stumbled across her, and after several steps, I realised why she'd chosen that particular route. She'd been following a blood trail. Not a particularly obvious one, just a drop or two every few yards, but it was there. From the dog? Had to be if she'd tracked it all the way from the store.

Well, this was an unexpected turn of events. Definitely not what I'd been anticipating when I woke up this morning. There'd been times when I'd wondered what happened to Ana's original comrades, but I'd never guessed we might run into one of them in rural Oregon. And Ana clearly hadn't either. Not once had she tried to get in touch with any of the original Ten.

Up ahead, I caught glimpses of Nine moving through the trees, and yeah, you could tell she and Ana came out of the same mould. Zacharov might have been the world's shittiest father, but he'd been a good trainer.

Nine stopped dead.

Held up a fist, and Ana repeated the gesture.

Freeze.

Oh, joy.

Why had I made that stupid bet with Alex? If he hadn't been ambling his way around downtown Portland under duress, we'd have been halfway home by now.

Nine motioned us forward.

But instead, here I was, getting my face smashed in and traipsing around a forest looking for— Oh, fuck... I ran towards the girl on the ground—at least, I assumed she was female. You couldn't tell from her face, but the parts of her sweater that weren't sticky and scarlet were candy-floss pink. Someone had done a real number on her.

"Is she still alive?"

Nine was already on her knees, checking. "Shallow breathing, faint pulse."

But for how long? The blood trickling from her eyes and ears wasn't a good sign.

"Where's the nearest emergency room?"

"Coos Bay."

Since Ana was allergic to cops, I borrowed her phone again and called 911 myself. Twenty minutes. To give this woman a chance, we had to keep her alive for twenty minutes before help came. And hell, we'd already wasted too much precious time fighting amongst ourselves.

Next, I called Hallie.

"We need the jump bag. Can you bring the SUV to the empty lot between the dentist and the café? Drive right through, as close to the treeline as you can get."

"I thought you said it was just a few scratches?"

"This is for somebody else."

"Uh, yeah. Yeah, sure I can."

"Good. Keep your gun handy and don't get out of the car. I'll meet you there."

"What happened?"

"There's someone nasty in these woods, and the dog wasn't their only victim."

"Okay." The engine started. Good girl. I heard the tension in Hallie's voice, but she kept her head. "Okay, I'm on my way."

"What's happening?" Bradley asked in the background. "What's going on?"

I left that for Hallie to explain and touched Ana on the shoulder.

"You okay here?"

A nod as she sliced clothing off the woman's body. How bad was the damage?

"*Da*. Go."

Ana had been off earlier, seriously off, and I didn't trust Nine, but without those supplies, the woman's chances of survival would drop even further. She needed urgent trauma care, and we had the necessary equipment in the jump bag. I jogged through the trees, keeping my wits about me, but I suspected Nine was right—if the woman's attacker had still been lurking when we had our coming together, we'd scared him off with the commotion. The fight hadn't exactly been loud, but it hadn't been quiet either.

And the dog... The knife wounds suggested it had gotten close to the mystery assailant, too close. Had it interrupted the attack? Quite possibly, and then our presence had stopped the guy from coming back for another try.

Hallie's eyes saucered when she saw me. "What the heck happened to your face?"

Guess it looked worse than I thought. "There was a small misunderstanding."

"Small? Your freaking nose is broken."

"Perhaps you could find me some ice?"

"Is there a cougar?"

"The only monster in those woods is human."

Bradley scrambled out of the car. "OMG, OMG! Your face is smashed!"

"Shit happens." I grabbed the jump bag from the trunk. "Hallie, find him a cookie or something." Hmm... A cookie. Breadcrumbs. "What do we have that I can use to leave a trail through the forest? There's an ambulance on the way, cops too, and I need you to direct them."

"I have spray paint in my craft kit?" Bradley offered.

"Perfect."

"Red? Yellow? Green?"

"Whichever's brightest."

"That would be the wild lime." A quick rummage, and he held out a can. "Here you go."

"Hallie, make sure the EMTs bring a spinal board."

Ten seconds later, I was running back to Ana and Nine, playing graffiti artist on the way. What kind of sick fucker beat a girl and left her for dead? This was only a small town. Did Nine know him? Had she recognised the girl? We'd need to get our story straight, too. Ana and me, that was simple—we'd go with the truth and leave out the fight part. I took a moment on the way to smooth out some of the evidence. My blood was on the ground if anyone looked hard enough, but I'd think up an explanation for that if necessary. Maybe I could say I tripped over a tree root?

"Is she still with us?" I asked when I reached the crime scene.

Nine looked up. "Holding on."

Ana had applied a tourniquet around the girl's left thigh, and she was pressing a pad against a wound just below it.

"This is the only deep wound. Pass the haemostatic gauze?"

"Here you go. What else do you need?"

"Do you have a supraglottic airway device?" Nine asked. "Her throat is swelling."

"A laryngeal mask airway?"

"Yes, and a cervical collar."

I found both in the right sizes, and I didn't bother to ask Nine whether she was familiar with how to fit them. That would have been an insult. Instead, I busied myself giving fluids. Sanitised my hands, put on gloves, applied another tourniquet, this time to the girl's arm, identified a vein, cleaned the site, inserted the cannula, hooked up the IV. We had a bunch of medical trash, including needles that would need to be disposed of.

"How's she doing?"

"Pulse and breathing are steady," Nine confirmed.

Ana had the thigh wound packed with a clotting agent, and the blood wasn't flowing so freely now. "The bleeding's no worse, and the rest... This was methodical. They bound her hands and feet and worked her over. See?"

She lifted the girl's sweater to reveal a row of cigarette burns, and I did see.

"Not a lover's tiff, more of a torture session?"

"*Da.*"

Which left three big questions—who was this woman, and what did she know? And more importantly, how much had she told her assailant?

"Do you recognise her?" I asked Nine.

"Hard to say, but nothing about her looks familiar. A lot of people pass through this town."

We'd stabilised the girl as far as possible in the field. Nine squeezed the ventilation bag, Ana monitored the bleeding, and

I made a loop out of paracord to hang the IV bag from a handy branch.

"It wasn't a robbery," Ana said. "She's still wearing jewellery, and that watch wasn't cheap."

I took a quick inventory, and Ana was right. The girl wore an entry-level Rolex, plus stud earrings that were either diamonds or good fakes. Her necklace was beaded—something Nine might have made in her Darla persona—but she had what looked like a vintage emerald on her middle finger.

Meanwhile, Ana was patting down her pockets.

"No driver's licence, but she has a credit card in the name of Leona Curran and a key card for the Peninsula. Dasha, have you heard the name before?"

Nine shook her head. "I don't spend much time at the Peninsula."

The girl's pockets yielded nothing else, and all we could do was wait. Thankfully, a siren soon sounded in the distance.

"Cavalry's here. Darya, do you have to modify your story? We'll go with whatever you need."

"I'll say I opened the store's rear door out of curiosity and heard the scream, same as you. And of course I'll get a lecture on the dangers of running into the forest alone because that's a man's job." She rolled her eyes. "But I've grown used to playing dumb. And you should say you fitted the LMA. I know nothing about field medicine, and I'm just squeezing the bag the way you told me to. Does that cover it?"

Ana reached out to tug down Nine's sleeve where the edge of a bandage was showing. "That covers it."

I heard voices, and Hallie soon appeared, leading a pair of medics and a dark-haired guy in a deputy's uniform. No Bradley, thank fuck. We didn't need a running commentary on bruises in shades of plum, sangria, and chartreuse, or analysis of the deputy's well-muscled thighs, which were admittedly quite nice.

"The deputy is Luca Mendez," Nine murmured. "New to the job, but smart. Former Army Ranger."

"Noted."

As the group got closer, Nine sort of...shrank into herself. The prickly aura disappeared, and grim determination was replaced by relieved desperation. She even conjured up a tear. Ana had been absolutely right—Darya Volkova was a chameleon.

At least the medics had gotten the message about the spinal board. The guy carrying it hooked a toe under a tree root and stumbled as he jogged towards us, and I tried not to smile. If he went arse over tit, that would only make my cover story more plausible.

Luca reached us first. "What happened?"

I figured I should do the talking. "Your guess is as good as mine. We found her like this."

"How long ago?" the first of the medics asked. Taller, older, more confident. He was the team leader.

"Nineteen minutes. She's been beaten by the look of it, plus she's got one deep knife wound and a number of shallower ones. We packed the deeper one with Celox..." I handed over the packaging in case they weren't familiar with that particular haemostatic. "And we've loosened the tourniquet we initially applied. Her airway was swelling, hence the LMA, and the collar's just a precaution. Over to you." I straightened and stepped back, giving them room to work, and the junior guy took over from Nine. "Let us know if you need a hand."

"Initial reports suggest a cougar might have been involved?" Luca said.

"This was no cougar."

Nine wiped her face with a sleeve. "Brooke only said that

because Shauna Weaver told her it was a cougar, but I don't think Shauna actually saw it."

She'd slipped back into character effortlessly. *Brava, brava.* If my nose hadn't been throbbing like a bitch, I'd have believed the act too.

"Why are you all out here in the forest?"

"We heard something that could've been a scream and decided to investigate," I said.

"All of you? Together?"

Nine sniffed and shook her head. "No, no, I was at the Craft Cabin when Shauna ran in, and...well, the dog made a real mess. Brooke and Paulo took them both to see Dr. Ward, Romi too, and I wondered if the cougar story was true—you know how Shauna exaggerates everything—so I opened the back door, just to see if...you know...if I could see anything. East always said there were cougars in the forest, but I've never heard of an actual sighting, have you?"

"Herb Pettigrew swears he came across one, but Herb exaggerates even more than Shauna. It was probably a kitten."

"Or one of Elmira's cats." Nine gave a nervous giggle, then glanced at the girl on the ground and turned it into a sob. "I didn't see a thing, not a cougar or a kitty, but I heard the scream too. And probably I shouldn't have come out here, but East always told me to carry bear spray, just in case, so I grabbed it, and then...and then..."

Bear spray? Nine didn't have bear spray. I'd searched her, and so had Ana. And yet she was clutching a can in her hand, her knuckles white. I patted my pocket. Not content with fracturing my nose, that bloody bitch had stolen my fucking bear spray, and while Luca checked his own pocket for a handkerchief, she sent a cocky smirk in my direction.

"Why don't you sit down?" Luca suggested. "There's a log over there."

I got the smirk; he got a teary smile. "I do feel a little faint now. Is that normal? There's just so much blood, and... That poor, poor girl. What kind of monster would do this to her?"

"That's what I'll be working to find out." Luca offered Nine his arm, and she gripped it rather than leaning on it—that slice I'd taken out of her had to sting. Plus she'd developed a limp. As they headed for the log, Luca glanced sideways at Ana and me, then lowered his voice. "Darla, you know these people?"

"They were in the Craft Cabin earlier with that girl"—she nodded towards Hallie—"and a guy who I swear is Paulo's long-lost twin. B-b-but I don't know them, not even their names. I th-th-think they arrived right before I did, and then the blonde lady ran back to her vehicle to get a first aid kit, and she told me to squeeze the bag every six seconds, and will the injured girl be okay? She didn't say a word, not one word, and...and..."

Crying sure was an effective way to avoid answering questions. Deputy Mendez gave Nine an awkward pat on the back and then set his sights on his next victim. Me.

"What's your name, ma'am?"

"Emmy."

"Emmy. And your friend?"

"Ana."

"You're new in town? Don't recall seeing you around."

"Just visiting." I checked my watch. Let him see me do it. "We're meant to be on our way to Portland right now."

"I'll try not to keep you for too long, ma'am. Did you get into an altercation?" He motioned at his nose. "You have a bruise there."

My turn with the nervous laugh. "I ran back to my car to get the first aid kit, and I guess I wasn't looking where I was going because the next thing I knew, I'd tripped right over a tree root." He'd confirm that with Nine, and she'd back me up. She'd have to. "Smacked right into a tree trunk, and my nose started bleeding, which means you'll find blood over in that direction." I waved a hand at the trees. "And that blood is nothing to do with your victim, so don't waste your time on it."

"Thanks for the information. Can you talk me through what happened from the beginning? You were first on the scene?"

"Sure, but it looks as if those guys need a hand." The EMTs were getting ready to move the girl onto the spinal board. "The ambulance is parked a distance away."

Luca followed my gaze. "Right. And you don't want to hang around in these trees. Are you staying in Portland?"

"We were staying at the Peninsula here in town, but we checked out earlier."

"They can wait with me at the Craft Cabin," Nine offered, wincing as she stood. "You could talk with us there once you're done?"

Go back to the Craft Cabin? Bradley would be thrilled.

But I smiled and nodded because it was the best option, plus I could pick up coffee and a donut from the café next door. And I couldn't deny being curious about Nine. There weren't many female assassins in the world, even fewer with the skills she obviously had. Now that she'd stopped trying to kill me, a conversation promised to be quite interesting.

"Sure, we'll all wait at the Craft Cabin."

8

NINE

After seventeen years spent doing the mad general's bidding, I'd always thought nothing could surprise me, but it turned out I'd been wrong. Of all the things I'd considered might be in the forest, Nastya and her murderous little friend hadn't even made the list.

Nastya... I noticed the second blonde, the tough one, called her Ana, but in the beginning, she'd been Nastya. It wasn't until we'd started learning English and the boys began calling her Nasty A that she'd stopped answering to the old nickname. They didn't call her Nasty A in front of the general, of course, or Nastya, or even Ana. He hadn't liked us to use names, period. To him, we were numbers, tools, barely human at all.

Seven of Ten.

Nine of Ten.

Could he really be dead?

I found it difficult to believe, but if he was alive, then how was I still breathing? Nastya could have slit my throat where I lay and melted away into her world of darkness, and all the Lucas and Colts in the world wouldn't have been able to find her. My death would have become nothing but a footnote in Baldwin's Shore history.

And who was the new blonde?

She walked on ahead as I leaned on Nastya's arm, faking a limp. In truth, I *had* tweaked my ankle when I kicked the blonde *suka*, though it was just a niggle, barely even Advil-worthy. But if I needed an excuse to take time off to deal with this...this *mess*, then it wouldn't hurt for Luca to believe I was injured. A few days in hand would give me a head start if I needed to run, or the space to hunt for Shauna's "cougar" without Brooke and Paulo breathing down my neck.

What was Nastya's game? Would she truly leave Baldwin's Shore as she'd suggested? Even if she did, the thought of her knowing my location left me twitchy. Should I disappear again? I was better prepared this time—I had money, a backup vehicle, a plan—but this town was my home now. If I left, where would it end? Would I still be running at sixty? Seventy? I'd wanted to believe those days were over.

I glanced at Nastya, but she was focused on our surroundings. A mistake, if I felt inclined to slice open her carotid artery. What's that, you say? I didn't have a knife? Beg to differ—Nastya and her friend had both missed the scalpel blade in my hair clip. Tsk-tsk-tsk. They should have known better.

Nastya... The baby of the team, although she'd certainly had to grow up in a hurry. I'd just turned fourteen when I was dragged into the cut-throat world of professional assassination, but she'd still been two months shy of thirteen. We'd all been kids. Ilya was the oldest, and also the biggest prick with the exception of the general himself.

My phone buzzed with a text.

Luca: Going to the hospital with our mystery victim. Can you keep an eye on the two strangers until I get back? Do you feel safe around them?

And that was why I didn't want to leave. I might not have close friends, but there were people here who cared whether I lived or died, and that was oddly comforting.

Me: They don't worry me. How long will you be?
Luca: Couple of hours? I'll keep you updated.

Good. That gave me time to fix my arm. An emergency-room visit was out of the question, as was stitching the wound single-handed, but I could probably do something with glue. This wasn't the first time I'd had to do running repairs on myself, and it wouldn't be the last.

We reached the rear entrance to the store, and I let us inside. Nastya had carried the jump bag, and as soon as we got through the door, the tough blonde began rummaging through it. She came up with a bottle of pills and swallowed a couple dry.

"Advil?" she offered.

"No thanks."

I wasn't ingesting anything provided by her.

"Pass them here?" Nastya asked. "I have a headache now."

The thinner blonde wasn't like Nastya and the bitch. She fidgeted from foot to foot before she finally spoke.

"Emmy? What happened out there?"

So Emmy *was* her real name? I'd figured there was a fifty-fifty chance she'd lied to Luca. She peered at her face in the full-length mirror Paulo had hung beside the couch, assessing the damage.

"A tourist got worked over by an unknown assailant."

"How do you know she was a tourist?"

"Firstly, Darla here didn't recognise her, and secondly, the woman had a room key from the Peninsula in her pocket. Did you happen to bump into anyone called Leona while we were there?"

"Not that I remember. How do you know her name?"

"She was carrying a credit card belonging to Leona

Curran, but it's entirely possible she nicked it. Could you do me a favour?"

"A favour? Uh, sure."

"Take Bradley out for lunch at the café next door, and bring back coffee and some kind of sugar-based product when you're done."

"Lunch? You want us to eat *lunch*? Shouldn't you go get your nose X-rayed?"

"Maybe later." She turned to me. "Any idea how long the deputy'll be?"

"A while."

She flashed the other blonde a smile. "Give us half an hour, okay?"

Clearly, she was used to being obeyed. There was a certainty in her voice, the words phrased as a question but definitely an order. The skinny blonde backed away, then left us to what promised to be an uncomfortable discussion.

"So..." Emmy began. "That was fun. Have you got any ice?"

I wanted to push her out the door, not give her ice, but thanks to Luca, that wasn't an option. And if her nose got smaller, perhaps it would invite fewer questions? Paulo liked ice cubes in his Kool-Aid, so he always kept a trayful in the little freezer, along with his ice cream and his microwaveable fries. Because Paulo was Paulo, the ice cubes were bunny-shaped, but Emmy didn't strike me as a woman who'd care about that. I emptied the bunnies into a ziplock bag and wrapped the whole lot in a dish towel.

"Here."

"Thanks."

"Help yourselves to coffee. I need to fix my arm."

I didn't have a fancy jump kit like Emmy and Nastya —*Ana, I should probably call her Ana*—did, not here at the store anyway, but the first aid box was well-stocked. I'd end up with a scar, but what did that matter? I had plenty of those already, which was another reason for my fashion choices.

"You want me to stitch it?" Ana asked.

In Siberia, I wouldn't have hesitated to accept, but so much had changed since those days. Now, an inbuilt survival mechanism made me view every act of kindness with suspicion. Hell, the first time Brooke had brought home-made cupcakes to work, I'd thanked her politely, then tossed mine into the trash when she wasn't looking. Years had passed before I'd begun to trust a handful of close acquaintances here, only for Nico Belinsky to show up and shatter my fragile equilibrium.

And now my old roomie had arrived in Baldwin's Shore too, which meant all those suspicions came rushing back. Emmy called it paranoia, but I preferred the term "healthy vigilance."

"I'll use glue."

"Wait a second..." Emmy went back to rummaging. "We've got these stick-on stitches. BandGrip. They're meant to be good for knife wounds, so the doc assured me."

She threw me a package, and I caught it out of habit. Stick-on stitches? Maybe they'd work as claimed, or maybe they contained a slow-acting poison that would lead to a painful death.

"Dasha?" Ana patted the seat beside her. "I know this isn't easy. When I left Base 13, I found it hard to trust people too."

Emmy snorted, then winced because snorting wasn't a great idea with a broken nose. "Left Base 13? That makes it sound like you handed in a resignation letter."

"Okay, fine. When I killed a guard and snuck into your vehicle."

Ana had snuck into Emmy's vehicle? Was that how they'd met? Who *was* Emmy? Getting to Base 13 wasn't a straightforward exercise, and if you were one of Zacharov's many adversaries, leaving alive was even more difficult.

But Ana hadn't been an adversary. She'd been his favourite, the only one of us to have a room in his private residence.

"Why did you have to sneak away?"

"Because I couldn't leave otherwise, not with my daughter."

The surprises just kept coming, didn't they? What daughter? How the hell did Ana have a child? The general once told me that if I made the mistake of getting pregnant too soon, he'd have the baby scraped out of me with no anaesthetic. Pregnant *too soon*. At first, I'd wondered why he didn't simply have us sterilised, but later, I'd come to realise his plan. The general thought long-term. Once we were too old to work effectively but still young enough to breed, we'd have been expected to churn out a new generation. Ana had broken the rules. She'd fucked with his timetable. But her daughter would have been Zacharov's granddaughter, so I had to assume he was too egotistical to murder one of his own.

"I didn't realise you had a child."

"He kept us hidden away. How long since you left?"

"Four and a half years."

Four and a half years since my heart broke. Four and a half years since I faked my own death and ran.

"You've been here the whole time?"

"Most of it."

"He didn't tell me you'd gone. Those later years, he barely told me anything beyond how disappointed he was that I'd chosen to be 'difficult.' *Difficult*." Ana spat the word. "He used my daughter as leverage to make me do his dirty work, and somehow, *I* was the difficult one. For him, isolation was a tool. He manipulated me. He manipulated all of us."

Did that sound like something Zacharov would do? Yes,

but Ana was *his* daughter, and I couldn't forget that she knew how to manipulate people too.

She stood and held out both hands. "We used to trust each other, Dasha. Remember when we said it was us against the world?"

"That was a long time ago."

Emmy took Ana's place on the couch, the ice held against her nose.

"So were you two a thing?" she asked, her voice slightly muffled. "Just wondering if bi-curiosity runs in the family."

My turn to snort. "Well, Vik would definitely be a top."

They both stared at me.

"Who the fuck is Vik?" Emmy asked at the same time as Ana said, "What the hell does that have to do with Vik?"

9

NINE

"Viktor is Ten," Ana told Emmy. "Or was Ten. He might be dead—I have no idea."

Yet another claim of hers that was difficult to swallow.

"You don't know whether your own brother is alive?"

"My *what*? What are you talking about? Vik isn't my brother."

"Fine, half-brother."

Although she did seem genuinely surprised at the news, which was interesting.

"Why the hell would you think Vik is related to me?"

"Because someone told me he was Zacharov's son. The same someone who told me you were his daughter, and that turned out to be true, so..."

Had Rad been right? He'd had no reason to lie to me, and I'd trusted him more than I trusted this new version of Ana. Fuck, I missed that son of a bitch.

Ana kicked the couch with one booted foot, a stream of curses slipping from her lips. She'd left a dirty smudge on the beige fabric, so I picked up Paulo's spray bottle of stain remover and a cloth and wiped it clean. Then asked myself what the fuck I was doing because in the grand scheme of things, who cared about a spot on the damn couch?

"Vik?" Ana muttered to herself. "You've got to be kidding me."

Emmy squeezed her hand. "It might not be true."

That was of course possible, but once you began looking, you could see the similarities between the two of them. Sure, Vik had dirty-blond hair rather than Ana's near-black, and he hid his true nature behind a perfect smile instead of a dark scowl, but the eyes gave it away. When their masks slipped, they shared the same intense gaze.

Plus there was a discrepancy in Ana's act. Emmy had given it away.

"If you didn't know about Vik, then why did that one make the joke about bi-curiosity running in the family?"

Emmy rolled her eyes. "Because 'that one' is her half-sister. And for the record, I don't know what she ever saw in you."

Emmy and Ana were related? The punches just kept on coming, although it did explain a lot. Mother's side or father's side? *The eyes. Check the eyes.* Emmy was Zacharov's. And despite all the general's lectures about birth control, he sure hadn't been able to keep it in his pants. I started laughing, then quickly stopped because Emmy had bruised one of my ribs.

"What's so funny?" Ana asked.

"How many more of Zacharov's spawn are running around in the world?"

"That's not something I want to consider."

"Did Zacharov know about her?" I quickly answered my own question. "No, of course not because if he did, she'd have been Eleven of Eleven and you'd still be stuck in Siberia."

I rolled up the sleeve of my dress and inspected the bandage. Ana had done a reasonable job, but blood was beginning to seep through. Should I try the stick-on stitches? I studied the package. Faster healing, less scarring, take a shower after only one day... If Ana and Emmy were going to harm me, they'd had ample opportunity, so I figured I was safe in the short term at least.

"Something else I don't want to think about," Ana said. "Dasha, give me those. Accept help for once in your life."

"Fine." I thrust the package at her, although it still felt wrong. For so long, I'd had only myself to rely on, and trust didn't come easy. "*Fine.*"

She unwound the bandage, her touch gentle. "You're sure about Vik?"

"As sure as I can be without a DNA test."

"Is he still alive?"

"He was when I left. Don't ask where he is now because I have no idea."

"How many of us are left?"

"No more than four."

"You, me, Vik... Who else?"

"Maybe Ilya."

Ana pulled a face, which summed up my feelings about Ilya as well.

"What happened to—"

"Can we just stop talking about this?"

Because if she asked about Rad, all those old wounds would open up, and they'd taken years to close. I still saw him in my dreams. That dumb, goofy smile he wore when we were alone, the last kiss he'd blown me, the shadow of him slipping into the home that was to become his tomb at the end. For me, that moment had been the beginning. The beginning of the rest of my life.

Except now I'd come full circle. Here I was with Nastya, wondering what fresh hell I'd be plunged into next.

The antiseptic stung, but I'd had plenty of practice at hiding pain because pain was weakness and weakness was a death sentence. And the stick-on stitches fixed me up faster than a needle and thread or superglue. The awkward silence that followed? Less comfortable. When Emmy's phone buzzed, I felt a momentary flicker of relief, but I should have known it would be short lived.

"Oh, for crying out loud."

"What happened?" Ana asked.

"Nate and Carmen got bored on vacation."

"What's new?"

"A week ago, Carmen swore she'd spotted Reed Dorrington in a restaurant, but Nate thought she was mistaken. Long story short, they need a plane to bring Dorrington back."

Okay, I'd bite. "Who's Reed Dorrington?"

And who were Nate and Carmen?

"He's a particularly nasty little shit who had a fondness for raping coeds while he was in college. Daddy's money helped to get him out of a couple of jams, but eventually, the inevitable happened and he killed a girl. Of course he got bail, and of course he skipped, and since Cuba declined to extradite, he's been living it up in Varadero for the past three years."

"And this Nate and Carmen—they're friends of yours? They'll bring him back?"

"Exactly. Which means we're stuck here until tomorrow unless we want to fly commercial."

"You have your own plane?"

Emmy held up two fingers. "But one's undergoing scheduled maintenance." First-world problems. My heart bled. "Guess we'd better see if we can get our rooms at the Peninsula back. Ana, are you done there?"

Hell, no. She wasn't leaving. "Luca told you to stay here."

"Aw, it's so sweet that you listen to cops."

"He's also a friend."

Ana choked on a laugh. "You're *friends* with a cop?"

"We have a mutually beneficial relationship."

Emmy's turn to snort. And wince again. Didn't she learn the first time?

"You're *fucking* a cop?"

Normally, I'd have tempered my reaction, but today, I was feeling more like my old self than I had in years. So I burst out laughing too.

"Are you insane?"

"So I've been told."

"He's engaged to Brooke—one of my employees—but as I said, he's new to the job, and sometimes he needs a hand."

Ana regarded me curiously. "So you've been *helping* the cops?"

"Somebody has to. They have a tendency to play defence rather than offence."

"A bad habit of theirs. But why break your cover?"

"I don't break my cover. They have no idea it's me." I blew out a long breath and admitted the truth I'd been trying so hard to deny. "I got bored, okay? I thought I'd be content living a cosy little life in the middle of nowhere, but it's dull, dull, dull. Quite frankly, I'm sick of pretending to be cheerful all the time. It's unnatural."

How did people do it? Just listening to Paulo chatter from dawn till dusk left me cold, and Brooke never snapped back at anyone, even when silence cost her dearly.

Ana nodded her agreement. "I understand the boredom thing. I only lasted a few weeks as a stay-at-home mom, and even now, I struggle at PTO meetings. Those women are asking to have their tongues cut out."

"*You* go to parent-teacher organisation meetings? Have you lost your mind?"

Ana pointed at a poster on the wall. "Says the woman hosting a coffee 'n' crafts support group?"

Firstly, Thrive was Brooke's project, not mine. I merely

provided the venue. And secondly, I didn't attend the meetings, not in person. No, I just listened in from time to time and made notes. Whenever I needed a little adventure to take the edge off, Thrive provided me with a ready-made list of targets. Though I had to be careful. The women talked, boy did they love to talk, and if all the men who'd hurt them went through unfortunate experiences in a short space of time, they'd smell a rat. So I had to pace myself, get creative when I brainstormed the assholes' fates.

"It's actually a support group for survivors of sexual assault and domestic violence. Brooke started it after her own experiences."

Emmy screwed up her face. "Ouch."

"A friend would support her, yes? So that's what I'm doing. Turns out that domestic violence is a big problem for women who weren't trained from the age of fourteen in a dozen different ways to kill a man."

"Only a dozen? No need to be modest. So, did you have a chat with the guy who abused your friend?"

"A chat? No, I didn't speak to him. I decorated him."

"Decorated him?" Emmy glanced toward the store. "With what?"

"A soldering iron and a Stanley knife."

And I'd been careful not to use Darla's cutesy handwriting when I burned the word "rapist" across his forehead. That episode had been my first foray back to the dark side. Both Colt and Luca—in his pre-deputy days—had proven to be spectacularly ineffective at catching the sick-minded stalker who'd assaulted Brooke, probably because they struggled to understand the man's mindset. They simply didn't know how to think like criminals. Rather than using their brains, they'd spent their days guarding Brooke and asking questions, questions, questions, whereas I'd simply hung back in the darkness and watched her. Watched *him* watching her, the way I'd known he would. He had a twisted mind. Too bad mine was truly warped.

Emmy gave a low whistle as she drained a cup of coffee. "Nice work. Ana, c'mon."

I pictured them driving off into the sunset. "You should stay."

"Relax. Tell your cop buddy we'll be back in five. We're just gonna make hotel reservations and maybe ask a question or two about Leona Curran. I'm curious. Aren't you curious?"

"Yes, I'm curious, but that's not how things work around here. The cops ask the questions, and then I get the gossip from Brooke or Paulo or one of the others. It's much easier to fly under the radar that way."

"We'll be subtle, I promise. Come with us if you're worried we might make a break for it."

"I try to avoid the Peninsula."

Emmy turned back. "Why?"

I could have spun a story about the locals disliking outsiders, which was true, but Ana would have seen through the lie in a second. We were both outsiders. We always would be, but we knew how to fit in when it mattered. All it took was confidence and the right attitude.

So I told Emmy the truth. "I have a history with the owner."

"As in...you danced the horizontal tango?"

"Is sex all you ever think about?"

"Sometimes I think about carbs too."

I looked her up and down. If she ate carbs, they didn't stick around.

"No, I did not fuck Nico Belinsky."

I'd fucked Nico's father, and then I'd killed him. Which had made Christmas dinner at Brooke and Luca's place something of an awkward affair seeing as Nico and I had both been invited. I'd made sure to sit at the other end of the table. Sixteen years had passed since I'd slipped a knife between Lev Belinsky's ribs, and I'd been masquerading as a high-class hooker at the time, but I'd had a couple of conversations with a young Nico while I finessed my way into Belinsky's inner circle. He'd spent most of the time talking to my breasts, but the human memory was a funny thing—I recalled our chats with stunning clarity, so what if he remembered them too? Why tempt fate by spending more time than necessary in his presence?

The set of Ana's jaw told me she recognised the name, and she could probably take a good guess as to why I was avoiding Belinsky Junior.

"Why don't you go to the Peninsula with Hallie and Bradley while I stay here with Dasha?" she asked Emmy. "You can leave Bradley behind in the spa."

"That...is actually not a bad idea. But is Belinsky dangerous?"

In the same way that I was dangerous. He could kill—*had* killed—but he'd only do it if he had a reason.

"Not to hotel guests."

"Good." She turned to Ana. "You'll be okay?"

What Emmy was really asking? Whether I would try to kill Ana again. And the answer was no, not unless she tried to harm me first. For three years, we'd been closer than sisters, and I'd missed her when our group got torn apart. Having her in my space again was weird, but not horrible.

Ana came to the same conclusion.

"*Da*, I'll be fine."

10

EMMY

"So, what's the story?" Bradley asked from his spot beside me in the back seat. I'd let Hallie drive for once, and now we were parked in the guest lot at the Peninsula. "How did you end up with two black eyes and yet another broken nose?"

"I tripped over a tree root."

"Do I look stupid? Actually, don't answer that. Of course you didn't trip—we all know you have special powers of levitation. Can you stop chewing?"

I swallowed the last bite of bear claw, then stayed still as he touched up the skin around my eyes. Bradley never went anywhere without a full case of make-up, and at times like this, his inability to pack light came in handy. I checked my face in the mirror—yes, my nose was still a little on the wide side, but the bruising was gone.

"Thanks, champ."

"Don't rub anything. Do I have time for an aromatherapy facial?"

"Sure."

Bradley peered at me suspiciously. "Why are you in such a good mood? Normally when someone gets the jump on you, you're in a snit for days."

"Are you getting a facial or not?"

He scuttled out of the car like he was headed for the Macy's sale, and I let out a heavy sigh. My mood wasn't exactly great, but it wasn't terrible either. It wasn't every day I got into a no-holds-barred fight, and this morning, I'd gone hand to hand with one of the world's most highly trained assassins and held my own. And Nine was one hell of an interesting woman. A cute little puddle of small-town charm on the surface, but if you tossed a pebble in the right place, ripples of darkness spread out. And she wasn't the only remnant of Zacharov's empire left kicking around. Maybe I had a half-brother too, and at this moment, I wasn't sure whether that was a good thing or a bad thing. *Viktor.* Whose footsteps had he followed in? Ana's? Or our father's?

Would Nine drop any more hints? Perhaps when she was alone with Ana, she'd let something slip. I only hoped I'd made the right decision in leaving them, but Ana had seemed happy enough. And there was a cop on the way. Nine wouldn't risk being caught with a body.

"Are we going inside?" Hallie asked.

"Yeah, we are."

"And you're sticking with the tree-root story?"

"All I'll say is that you should avoid being alone with Darla —she's not what she appears to be. And keep Bradley out of her way too."

"Right." Hallie sucked in a breath. "Okay, but if we're still here tomorrow, he'll want to go back to the craft store."

"There's a good chance it'll be closed. But if not, make sure one of the assistants is around—Brooke or Paulo. Darla won't do anything with an audience."

"Darla's really dangerous?"

"She's definitely not the kind of person you want to stumble across in a quiet forest."

The doorman waved us inside with a flourish, and he didn't blanch at the sight of my face, so I had to take that as a positive. The receptionist didn't give me any funny looks either. No, she was just puzzled.

"You definitely checked out already. It says so right here."

"Yes, I know we checked out, but our flight's been delayed, so we thought we'd spend another night in town if you have rooms available?"

The receptionist studied her computer. "Okay, ma'am. Do you want the same rooms again? Uh, 104's been taken, but we still have 102 and 103. And I could offer 109?"

"Perfect. And do you have an additional room as well?"

"So you want *four* rooms?"

"That's right."

"But you only had three before?"

"Yes, and now we need one more."

If Alex had made it around the half-marathon course without dying—or worse, fucking up his knee again—he might appreciate a session in the Jacuzzi, though he would of course deny he enjoyed such things. And when I'd sent Brett —Blackwood's senior pilot—to pick up Nate, he'd suggested that we might want to fly from Medford rather than Portland when he came back. It was an hour closer to Baldwin's Shore, and also nearer to California, which was bail-jumper-bro's final destination.

"Room 213 is also free? It's on a different floor, but..."

"We'll take it. And while you're looking things up, could you tell me if Leona Curran is still here? I borrowed a paperback from her, and I forgot to return it."

"Leona? She's teaching the lunchtime yoga class, but she'll be finished in fifteen minutes."

Huh? Leona worked here? And she was teaching a class? If that was true, she couldn't be getting wheeled into the emergency room right about now. Had our victim stolen her credit card? There was only one way to find out.

"Which way is the yoga studio?"

"Through that door over there. Just keep going until you reach the end of the hallway."

While we waited for Leona's class to finish, I texted Alex. The fact that he responded straight away suggested either he'd sprinted the marathon course and was now relaxing at the finish, or he was ambling around with all the time in the world to check his messages. I knew which option my money was on.

Alex: I'll take a cab. This doesn't excuse you from tomorrow's training session.

Oh, hurrah.

A dozen women in pastel sportswear exited the studio, chatting and laughing amongst themselves. They all carried rolled-up yoga mats, and most had matching water bottles too. When only one person remained, I walked through the door with Hallie.

"Leona Curran?"

"Yes? Are you looking for a class? I'll be teaching Pilates at four."

Well, whoever not-Leona-in-the-woods was, she hadn't been targeted in a case of mistaken identity. Leona was an athletic Black girl with an ass to die for and amazing bone structure. Not-Leona was a petite redhead who might have been pretty, but it had been hard to tell under all the blood and bruises.

"No, we're not looking for a class. Did you lose a wallet recently? Have a purse stolen?"

Her face creased into a frown. "No? Why?"

"Where's your credit card right now?"

"In my room. Are you the police?"

"No, we're on vacation, but we found your credit card in the forest behind Main Street this morning."

"Really? You're sure it was mine? But that would mean..." Leona gasped and covered her mouth with both hands.

"Somebody broke into your home?"

"I...I live here. Right here in the staff block. B-b-but..."

Fear flashed in her eyes, and she took off running. What could we do but follow? At a discreet distance, of course—this place had security on-site, good security for a hotel, and I didn't particularly want either of us to get accosted.

One of the guards was stationed by the rear exit of the main building, and I gave him a wave as we passed at a rapid jog.

"Forgot my guidebook."

The staff block was actually three blocks set in a horseshoe behind a row of trees in the south-east corner of the property. Each block was two low storeys, plain white stucco fronting onto a neatly mown lawn. There was none of the flashy planting that flowed through the rest of the grounds, but the area looked well-cared-for. Walkways ran along the front of each floor, six doors to each, twelve doors per block, thirty-six rooms in total. Leona headed for the block in the middle—bottom floor, second door from the right.

"Ottie?" she called.

Who the hell was Ottie?

And what had happened in her room? Hallie and I skidded to a halt in the doorway, and I took in the disarray. The room was more of a studio apartment, a generous double with a sitting area and a small kitchenette. And either Leona was shockingly bad at housekeeping, or it had been tossed. Systematically, comprehensively tossed.

She waded through the jumble of clothes and papers and broken crockery and flung open the bathroom door.

"Ottie?" No answer. "She's gone!"

"Leona, who's Ottie?"

Leona gulped in air as she peered into the bathroom again, a pointless exercise if ever there was one.

"My friend. She was staying here, her dog too. They're both gone."

"Maybe she took the dog for a walk?"

"No, no, I always walk Gidget. Ottie never goes out, *ever*." Leona looked around the room again. "But she's not here."

I stepped inside, checked behind the couch and down the far side of the bed because there was room to stash a body there. No Ottie. As well as the double bed at the far end, a folding cot took up most of the remaining floor space. Ottie had been sleeping on it? That meant her presence was a temporary arrangement, not a full-fledged room-share.

"Where did you leave your purse?"

"On the desk. Always on the desk."

"What colour hair does Ottie have?"

"Dark auburn. Why? Why does that matter?"

Well, shit.

"I might know where Ottie is."

Leona turned slowly, and when she faced me, I saw her eyes were glistening. "Where is she?" The fear returned, but this time Leona backed away. "Who are you? What have you done to her?"

"We haven't done anything to her."

"Get away from me!"

Footsteps approached, the soft squeak of rubber soles on the walkway, and the security guard we'd buzzed past earlier appeared.

"Ms. Curran? Are you okay?"

"Someone broke in, and Ottie and Gidget are gone. Gone! Then these people showed up, and...and..."

Tears came, and I swallowed a sigh. Just for once, couldn't a witness give a rational account of what happened? The guard turned his suspicions on me, and I threw my hands up, in frustration rather than surrender.

"Don't look at me. I only found a woman unconscious in the woods with Leona Curran's credit card."

The tears got louder. Great.

The guard looked slightly unnerved too. "Maybe I should call someone?"

"Good idea. Call Deputy Mendez—he's at the hospital with the woman right now. I'm just here for a manicure."

I moved to walk past with Hallie in tow, but a second guy blocked our way. Tall, dark, and handsome in a polished way—not quite playboy, not quite mafia, but something in the middle—and he'd forgotten to shave this morning. His aftershave was a mix of sandalwood, pheromones, and power.

"What's going on here?"

The accent hinted at the West Coast, but he couldn't hide the underlying Russian, so I was going to hazard a guess and say this was Nico Belinsky.

"Your yoga teacher's roomie's disappeared. Well, not

disappeared—she's probably in the hospital—but she's not where she's meant to be."

At the second mention of the hospital, Leona let out a wail, as if the news had finally sunk in now. Hallie turned back to assist her.

"Hey, why don't you sit down? Uh, not in here because it might be a crime scene, but maybe outside?"

Nico folded his arms. "I'm sorry, and you are...?"

"Emerson Black and Halina Chastain. We're staying in this fine establishment."

"And how do you know Ms. Marquette is in the hospital?"

"It's a long story, but the short version is that we saw the medics load her into the ambulance."

"She had an accident?"

"No, what happened to her was more deliberate, I'd say."

"Then we should call the police."

Nico pulled out a phone, but I held up a hand.

"Way ahead of you, pal. Deputy Mendez is already with Ottie Marquette."

"And Deputy...uh, Colt is out on a boat," Hallie added. "He *is* another deputy, right?"

"Yes, and Colt is out on *my* boat," Nico said. "I'll contact him. Leona, are you all right? What happened to your room?"

"I don't... I don't know. When I got back from my class, there was all this mess, and...and... Is Ottie gonna be okay? Where's Gidget?"

"What type of dog is Gidget?" I asked. The only mutt anyone had previously mentioned belonged to Shauna, but I could call Ana and get her to take a look around.

"Uh... Uh..."

"A small one," Nico supplied. "Something white with brown ears?"

"I think it's a papillon," the guard said. "My sister-in-law has one."

I raised an eyebrow, and Hallie shook her head. "It was a different dog."

"Could we start at the beginning?" Nico waved a hand towards the main building. "We can talk in my office. Trent, don't let anyone near this building. And radio Matthew—find out how somebody managed to get to Leona's room in the first place. The grounds are supposed to be secure."

"Yes, sir."

Nico was clearly a man who expected to be obeyed because he strode off without waiting to check we were following. Oh, what the hell... My curiosity had been piqued. I texted Ana on the way and noticed Nico sending a message too, presumably to Deputy Colt.

"How did you know about Colt?" I asked Hallie.

"Brooke mentioned his name when she was talking about Luca."

"Good spot."

Nico had picked his office furniture from the Fortune 500 CEO catalogue—a dick extension of a desk, a quartet of uncomfortable chairs grouped around a table too low to be of any practical use, and glass shelves full of books. Did the books even open? Once upon a time, I'd nosed around the office of a big-shot movie exec, and all of his books had been fake, just leather spines and wooden blocks, which made sense because he was the dumbest son of a bitch I'd ever met. Inherited his money and his job from daddy and drove his Porsche off a bridge during a cocaine-fuelled bender not two months after our chat. His kid's mom—our client—had to sue his estate for child support.

But when I peered closer at Nico's books, some of the spines were cracked. Leo Tolstoy, Ayn Rand, Franz Kafka, Marcel Proust in the original French... Nico Belinsky wasn't a fool.

He waved towards the seats around the coffee table, and

when an assistant hurried in behind us, he asked for refreshments and a box of tissues.

"Who wants to start?" he asked. "Leona?"

"I don't know what happened. When I left to teach my morning classes, Ottie was there, and then she wasn't, and all our stuff..."

Those tissues couldn't come fast enough.

"Ms. Black? Can you shed any light?"

"Call me Emmy. And we haven't actually been introduced."

"My apologies." He held out a hand. "Nico Belinsky. I own the Peninsula."

He had a sensible handshake—not too limp, not too firm, not too skeevy. Why did Nine avoid him? Knowing her profession, I had to assume death and destruction were involved somewhere along the way.

"Congratulations. My assistant's a huge fan of the spa. And the gift shop, and the breakfast buffet."

"And you?"

"I prefer the bar."

He chuckled. "Try the Beluga vodka if you haven't already. I can recommend it."

"Thanks. If the second half of the day goes as well as the first, I'll need the whole bottle."

"Care to tell us what happened?"

"We were outside the café on Main Street when we heard a woman scream in the forest nearby, and when we went to check it out, we found a girl we now believe to be Ottie Marquette. She was carrying Leona's credit card, and she had dark red hair."

"What happened?" Leona wiped her face with a hand. "How did she get hurt?"

"It looked as if somebody gave her a beating. I'm sorry."

Nico patted Leona on the shoulder, awkwardly, as if he wasn't accustomed to offering comfort.

"The sheriff's office will get to the bottom of this. How bad were her injuries?"

"I'm not a doctor, but she was still breathing."

"Ms. Marquette is in the hospital in Coos Bay?"

"I believe so."

"Leona, I'll arrange a car. You shouldn't drive while you're upset."

"I...I... What about my afternoon class?"

"Marcella can cover for you."

Before Nico could act, Hallie raised her hand like a kid in class.

"You have a question?"

"Uh, yes? Leona, you said earlier that Ottie never went out. Why is that?"

Another good spot, and an excellent question. This was a beautiful part of the world—why bother coming here to stare at the same four walls every day? And what did Ottie do for a living? Even if she was camping out in Leona's room, she'd need spending money.

"She...she..." Leona focused on her hands, probably to avoid her boss's probing gaze. I was guessing that whatever the problem was, neither of them had mentioned it to Nico. "I think she was having trouble with an ex."

"You *think* she was having trouble?" he asked.

"That's what she said."

"Why didn't you tell me?"

"I...I was worried in case you said she couldn't stay here. And she thought it would be okay. Like, if she just laid low for a while and kept out of sight, then he wouldn't find her."

"You should have—" Nico started, but I cut him off with a glare.

"What was the boyfriend's name? If he made threats, we should pass his details over to the police."

"I don't know if there were threats, exactly..."

"Ottie was scared enough to stay inside, and now she's in the hospital, so I'd say it's a fair assumption, wouldn't you?"

"I j-j-just don't understand why she went out, not after she swore she wouldn't."

"Could the dog have escaped?"

"Maybe, I guess? But Gidget was real good at staying inside when she was told to."

"I'll have my security team question the staff," Nico said. "We have a perimeter wall. Unless the dog ran along the beach, it can't just have disappeared, and the lifeguard would have radioed in if he saw it go past."

"Which leaves three options—either Ottie took the dog with her, or somebody stole it, or the lifeguard was having an off day."

Nico was already shaking his head. "My staff don't fall asleep on the job, and if a thief had walked out with the dog, one of the team would have noticed."

"What if the thief put the mutt in a bag? Do you have cameras here?"

"Of course."

"Can you check them?"

"I'll get somebody onto that."

"And presumably, the cameras would also have picked up Ottie if she left with the dog?"

"Unless she used the staff entrance. The camera over that gate is awaiting a replacement."

Typical. "When did it fail?"

"The day before yesterday."

How convenient.

So when it came to Ottie's assault, we might not only be looking for a psychotic lunatic, we might be looking for an *organised* psychotic lunatic. Although when I said "we," I did of course mean Deputy Mendez and his colleagues because Hallie and I were on vacation and therefore not about to start a full-scale manhunt. We were just asking a few questions to satisfy our curiosity, that was all.

"And how did it fail? Physical damage? An electrical fault?"

"I believe there was a problem with the lens, but wait a moment... Why so many questions? Are you a cop?"

"You think I act like a cop?"

"Yes?"

Ouch.

"I'm definitely not a cop. For one, I actually get things done. Hallie here is training as a private investigator, and I'm her boss." Which suggested I was also a PI without being an outright lie. I wasn't a PI. Licencing agencies demanded pesky things like fingerprints and background checks, and I wasn't fond of that kind of scrutiny. "Technically, we're off duty today, but old habits die hard."

"I see. So you'll be passing anything you find to the sheriff's department?"

"Absolutely. Just trying to speed things along. As I'm sure you understand, the first forty-eight hours is the most crucial time period in any investigation, and detectives seem thin on the ground around here. I'm sure Deputy Mendez will ask you for the camera footage when he gets back from the hospital, so all we're doing is short-cutting that process. And nobody wants a small dog running loose on its own after dark. I hear there are cougars around."

"I saw the camera," Leona volunteered. "The glass was broken."

"Which begs the question of who broke it. What's the name of Ottie's ex? Does he live around here?"

"I don't know."

"You don't know where he lives? Or you don't know his name?"

"Any of it." Where were those damn tissues? "I don't know any of it."

"But you were friends with Ottie? She was dating a guy, and she never even mentioned his name?"

"I... It's complicated."

"Please, do tell."

Nico leaned forward in his seat, hands on his knees. He wanted to hear the story too.

"See, before Ottie got in touch a few weeks ago, I hadn't actually spoken to her in years. We were best friends in high school, real close, but she graduated before me and went to college, then I travelled around Asia for a couple of years, and the internet out there wasn't so reliable, and we sort of...grew apart. But she knew I was back in the US, and when she called and said she was having some problems and could she sleep on my couch until she found someplace else, what was I supposed to say? I figured it'd be good to catch up, plus I wanted to help her out. What else could I have done? Said no?"

"She didn't have any family she could turn to?"

"Well, yes, but her parents are all the way over in Massachusetts. I just thought she wanted to stay on the West Coast."

"So she lived nearby?"

"Not nearby, exactly, but in California. Nico, I'm so, so sorry about this. I'll pay for any damage to the room, and—"

He waved a hand. "Forget the room. I'm more concerned about the woman in the hospital. She'll be okay?"

Who the hell knew? "As I said, I'm not a doctor."

"I'll drive Leona over there myself. We should talk later."

I shrugged. "Sure." Nico seemed like an entertaining guy. Whatever Nine's reason for avoiding him, it wasn't because he was a prick. "I'll be in room 103. We can chat over vodka."

12

NINE

"I need to look for a dog." Ana shoved her phone back into her pocket. "Do you have any sausages? Or cheese?"

"We already found a dog. Or it found us."

"Different dog. This one belongs to the victim. A papillon."

"She was walking it when she got attacked?"

That suggested terrible spatial awareness.

"Who knows? Emmy just said it's missing. The sausages?"

"I don't have sausages. Paulo keeps burger slices in the refrigerator, but I'm fairly sure there's no actual cheese in them. How about cat treats?"

Ana shrugged, and she'd confirmed that Ana was the name she went by now. Nastya had died back in Russia.

"Those would probably work."

I nodded toward the jar with *Pickle* written across it in pink glitter glue—more of Paulo's handiwork.

"In there."

"*Spasiba*. I'll be back soon."

"Do you want company?"

"I thought you were staying out of this?"

That had been my intention, so why had I even made the offer?

Deep down, I knew the answer—this would be my last chance to see Ana, perhaps ever, and once she'd departed, I'd go back to my regular, dull life, dying a slow, depressing death from boredom. I kicked out the panel under the snack cupboard and retrieved backup weapons—another switchblade and a small semi-automatic—then tipped my chin at the rear door.

"Lead or follow?"

"You know the terrain better."

"What does a papillon even look like?"

"A tiny white thing with hairy ears."

"You're a dog expert now?"

"My neighbour volunteers at a dog sanctuary. I listen."

I considered putting on a coat, but even in winter, Oregon was positively balmy compared with Siberia, and I didn't want to risk getting stuck in the dress. Having to wear such ridiculous clothing was bad enough already, and if the seams couldn't detach the way they were designed to, I risked ending up in trouble. I envied Ana for her oh-so-practical jeans and ski jacket. The jacket had a tear in it now, but give me a needle and thread and— *Enough*. I could forget playing seamstress today and simply enjoy myself.

"Just like the old days," Ana murmured as we set off. "Except without the battalion of sadistic Russian *mudaki* hunting us down."

"So you say."

I was still watching my back.

"You don't believe me?" Ana sounded a little hurt. "I'd lie to most people, but not to you."

"I guess I'm still struggling with the *why*. Why would you risk your life to take out Zacharov? Why not burrow under the way I did?"

"You think I didn't try that? He found me."

I was about to retort that she should have hidden better—wasn't she the golden girl?—but then I realised.

"The tracker? You didn't remove it?"

"You knew about the tracker?"

How the general had drugged us, then slipped miniaturised location devices under our skin? Yes, I knew. Four had found mine, and I'd found his. Tiny kinetic trackers implanted into our backs, electronic spies that sent our locations to the general and probably a whole bunch of other data too. I'd incinerated mine in Vermont. Removing it hadn't been pretty—I'd been forced to do it in a hurry, which had left me with yet another scar—but the feeling of liberation had been worth the pain. Now it seemed that Ana hadn't found hers soon enough.

"We all had them. Zacharov was a control freak."

"A control freak who took my daughter and then expected me to do his bidding if I wanted her back. But even if I'd completed that job, when would it ever have ended? Only with death. His or mine, and I chose his."

"Where's your daughter now?"

"With her father. He had a week off work, so they went to visit his parents. Now they're back, and Sam says Tabby wants to build a fort in the yard. I keep telling myself it'll be okay, that they won't make too much mess, but no matter how hard I try to deny it, I know I'll get home to a half-built moat and Tabby will be begging for a pet alligator."

I stopped dead. Turned. "Wait... You're living with her father? As in, you're in an actual relationship?"

"How we got there is a long story, but yes. Despite the general's best efforts."

Was I worried about chatting as we went? Not really. Whoever had attacked Leona was long gone, and if anyone happened to see us, walking and talking looked more natural than skulking around, weapons drawn. This afternoon, the forest felt empty, devoid of human presence.

And yet Ana's life was far from empty. She had what I'd always thought was impossible for women like us—a family. Had I loved Rad? I thought so. As far as I was capable of love, anyway, but our relationship had been far from conventional. He'd still been Four, and I'd still been Nine, and our lives had still been dictated by a madman. Fraternisation among the team had been banned. Our entire affair had been conducted in secret.

Ana and I reached the spot where we'd found Leona, the ground scuffed and spattered with blood. I hadn't seen any tiny doggy paw prints, but the forest floor didn't lend itself to tracks—too many leaves and needles, not enough mud.

"Do you know the dog's name?"

"I'll ask Emmy."

While we waited for a response, we checked out the scene, and I put myself into the mind of the assailant. Zacharov might have had the empathy of a landmine and the warmth of liquid helium, but I had to concede that he'd been a good trainer. Ruthless, but he'd taught us to get the job done by whatever means necessary. And one of his favourite sayings had been *If you become him, you can destroy him.*

What had Leona's assailant hoped to gain from the encounter? The beating had been brutal but also businesslike. Legs, arms, torso, and I'd noticed a couple of broken fingers too. Plus those cigarette burns... A jilted lover would have gone for something more intimate. Rape, sexual assault, and the burns would have been on her breasts rather than her stomach. Robbery? No. She'd still had her credit card and her jewellery. Those bruises... I'd seen similar from amateur interrogations, carried out by brutes who'd watched too many Hollywood movies but gained little experience at actually extracting information. Pain had its place, sure, but words were more important. Go too far, too fast, and the subject would tell you anything you wanted to hear, whether it was true or not.

What had Leona told her attacker?

Curiosity killed the cat, Dasha. I had Pickle to feed now. I couldn't afford to fuck up my new life.

"He left this way," Ana said.

"What do you have?"

"Broken twigs, pointing east."

A careless egress. The ground got muddier as we followed the attacker's path, and I compared his shoe size to my own. He wore a twelve, at a guess. A big guy. Distinct treads, new boots not old.

My phone buzzed.

Luca: Colt's on his way. Can you watch out back and let us know if you see anyone in the trees?

Me: Sure, I'll keep an eye.

"What is it?" Ana asked.

"Luca wants us to watch the forest."

"Well, we're doing that, aren't we?"

"*Da.*" After all, he hadn't said how closely.

The attacker's path looped around to the south, behind the hair salon, the coffee house, the dental clinic, and a little way farther out, past the feed store and the veterinarian. I saw Brooke's new car in the lot, a small blue Toyota that she'd bought to replace the older model she'd crashed last year.

The trail carried on, running parallel to the road that led to the Peninsula, and then it stopped.

Chyort.

"He had a vehicle waiting."

Maybe he'd come from out of town? If that was the case, and Leona Curran was a guest at the Peninsula, I wouldn't have any further responsibility once Ana and Emmy left. When I tinkered around on the edges of justice, it was to keep the inhabitants of Baldwin's Shore safe. They were the folks who'd taken me in, who'd accepted me as one of their own, even if the lifestyle wasn't entirely ideal. If Leona's assailant had driven here from Eugene or Portland or Boise or Sacramento, he wasn't my problem. Luca could write a report, I'd clean up the store, and small-town life would carry on.

Ana scouted about. "Not just waiting, but hidden out of sight behind these trees."

Still not my problem.

"We should head back. Look for the dog on the way."

As if on cue, her phone vibrated. "It's called Gidget."

"Who names a dog Gidget?"

"Your cat is called Pickle."

"Only because I had to think up the kind of dumbass name that the owner of a rural craft store would use."

We slunk back through the trees, calling softly as we went, but no dog appeared. Hardly surprising—the assailant had knifed Shauna's dog, and it was much bigger than the papillon. If Gidget had been with Leona, he-slash-she was either lying dead somewhere or running in fear.

Back at the craft store, I only just had time to shove the BandGrip packages to the bottom of the trash before Brooke, Romi, and Paulo walked through the front door. At least Emmy had taken the jump bag with her when she left.

"You didn't start cleaning up?" Paulo called. "That blood's going to stain if we're not careful."

"I was busy."

"Doing what? Because—" He stopped dead in the doorway when he saw Ana. "I thought the store was closed?"

"That's right, but I ran into Ana here out the back. She came in for coffee while she waits for her friend."

Paulo's hands flew to his cheeks. "Out the back? You went *outside*?"

"I heard a noise."

"But it's dangerous."

"I took bear spray."

"It wasn't a bear out there." Paulo lowered his voice to a conspiratorial whisper. "Isaac said Scooby got cut with a knife. A knife! Brooke tried to tell Luca, but the call went to voicemail."

"Luca's at the hospital, hun."

"OMG! What happened? What *happened*? Brooke! *Brooke*!"

Perhaps I could have worded that better. "It's okay, he's not hurt. Paulo! Sit down and breathe."

Brooke skidded into the break room.

"What happened?"

"Luca's in—"

Ana put a hand over Paulo's mouth, and I sent her silent thanks.

"A young woman had an accident in the forest, and Luca rode to the hospital with her. I'm sure he'll call you just as soon as he can."

Brooke's turn to gasp. "What sort of accident? Isaac said Shauna's dog got stabbed."

"Well now, I'm not sure, but they took her away in an ambulance. She had a lot of bruises."

"Who was she? Do you know? I thought I heard a scream when I was talking with Romi, but we figured it was kids."

Good to know a scream from out there was audible in the break room—that added credence to my "I heard a noise" story.

"I didn't recognise her."

Brooke slumped onto the couch beside Paulo. "What's happening in Baldwin's Shore? It always used to be so quiet around here, and now we've had three incidents in one day."

"Three? What was the third?"

"Isaac was already dealing with an emergency when we got

there. Someone's dog got poisoned over at the Peninsula. Isaac thought that maybe it ate rat bait, but I can't imagine Nico being careless like that, not with that beautiful cat of his roaming around, and Colt's Tigger too."

A poisoned dog, a stabbed dog, a beaten woman, and a car parked between the veterinarian and the hotel... I was beginning to get a bad feeling about this, and when I glanced at Ana, her tiny nod told me her thoughts had gone in the same direction.

"What's the dog's name?" she asked.

"Uh, Widget?"

"Gidget," Romi said from the doorway. "Gidget, like the movie. *A Little Girl with Big Ideas*."

"Gidget Curran," Paulo added. "Isaac writes the pet names on the board with the owner's surname. Isn't that cute? Vega Mendez, Tigger Haines, Chunky Monkey Bartlett, Sne... Snej... Whatever Nico called his cat."

"Snezhinka." But I was more interested in Romi and Aaron's new addition. "You named your puppy *Chunky Monkey*?"

Her cheeks reddened. "It was meant to be a nickname, but it kind of stuck. He's just a chubby little lump with legs."

Less than a month into their relationship, and they'd already acquired a joint creature. Was that normal? Caring for a living thing together seemed like a big step to me. Rad and I had once tried sharing custody of an Accuracy International sniper rifle, but we'd invariably wanted to use it at the same time, which had only led to bickering until I went out and acquired a duplicate. Damn, I missed that gun. Four and a half years on, and I was still bitter that I'd had to leave it behind. Yes, guns were only tools, but it had been a particularly nice one.

And who knows, maybe it would have come in useful someday?

"Did Dr. Ward say whether Gidget would recover?" I asked Romi.

"He said that he washed out her stomach, but she had another seizure while he was treating Scooby. So we're not sure."

"And how is Scooby?"

"Isaac's operating on him right now. Shauna's sister showed up, and the waiting room only has three seats, so we decided it would be better if we came back here."

Paulo jumped to his feet. "We need to clean the floor and tidy all the mess away. Otherwise, how will we open tomorrow? One of us can go check on Shauna and Scooby later. Should we take a card? Candy? A fruit basket? What about the lady in the hospital?"

"I'm sure Luca will get in touch with her family. Brooke, can you tell us if you hear anything? I don't like the thought of a maniac running around town."

"I'll call you with updates. Romi, we should walk Vega and Monkey together for a few days."

Good plan. "Maybe Luca could go with you, hun? Or Aaron? He carries a gun, doesn't he?"

"Not really? I mean, he owns a gun, but he doesn't use it much."

"Why don't you guys pay a visit to the gun club in Bandon tomorrow? Practice never hurt anyone."

"I guess I could suggest it."

And I'd wake up early and head out with my own guns, although I never ventured near the range in Bandon. A year ago, I'd invested in my own little piece of wilderness an hour's drive from Baldwin's Shore, four hundred acres of hillside with a long meadow that was perfect for target shooting and a ramshackle cabin I'd spent time fixing up. In an emergency, I could disappear there and live off-grid for months or pick up the money, weapons, and documents I'd cached and go farther afield. The Darla Lewis identity was my strongest, sound enough to pass a reasonably thorough background check, but I had two others that nobody was aware of, both good for international travel.

"Let's clean up, then we can all head home and get some rest. It's been a difficult day."

And little did I realise that it was about to get even more complicated.

13

NINE

I t was almost over.

If you didn't know about the dog, you'd never suspect the disaster that had happened in the store earlier. Despite Paulo's fears, the bloodstains had sponged off the floor easily, and the only lasting damage was a few smashed beads and one broken sculpture. I'd pay Deck for the piece anyway. Why should he suffer financially because Shauna couldn't hold on to her damn mutt?

Or because Ottie Marquette had dated the wrong man?

I'd sent Brooke and Paulo home an hour ago. Brooke had a dinner date with Sara Baldwin—something I'd encouraged in my Bad Samaritan persona because I thought Sara could use a friend—and Paulo had a dinner date with the wealthy New York businessman he pretended he wasn't fucking. Ana, Emmy, Hallie, and Bradley had stuck around to help with the last of the clean-up. At least Emmy wasn't holding a grudge for my earlier headbutt. An occupational hazard, she said.

Together, we'd worked out what had most likely happened to Ottie and her dog. According to one of the housekeepers from the Peninsula, Ottie had been in the habit of letting Gidget out onto the grass in front of the staff block to do her business—Ottie always picked up the poop, the woman assured us—and this morning, an as-yet-unknown subject had tossed the pooch a snack laced with rat poison. Ottie had freaked when the dog began convulsing and ran out of the staff entrance with the mutt in her arms, heading for the veterinarian, which was only a ten-minute walk, and probably faster on foot than waiting for a cab. The only cab driver in Baldwin's Shore was Selwyn, who prided himself on driving at the speed of half-baked lava.

Our working theory was that Ottie's felonious friend had waited for her in a vehicle, but he'd had to change his plans when Rodrigo, one of the Peninsula's porters, had seen her hurrying toward the clinic and given her a ride the rest of the way. Nico had told Emmy that Rodrigo was angry with himself for not waiting with her, but he'd been on his way to a meeting with his parole officer.

We'd leave that one for Luca to unpack.

Assuming Ottie's assailant wasn't Rodrigo himself—which was a possibility that couldn't be discounted right now—there'd been an attempted snatch as she headed back to the hotel. But something had gone wrong, and what should have been a simple operation had ended with a chase through the forest and a beating.

One of Nico's security cameras had been taken out two days ago, hit with a stick by a vandal who stayed below its field of vision. Again, Rodrigo had been one person with the opportunity, but as a suspect, he didn't feel right. If Gidget had fallen ill five minutes later, he'd have missed his meeting, and if the dog had been DOA, then Ottie would have left the veterinarian before he'd completed his parolee requirements and gotten into position. On the one hand, a parole meeting made an excellent alibi, but on the other... No, he'd have chosen a different day, and he wouldn't have come forward so readily when Nico questioned his staff.

So, who had done the deed?

That puzzle would have to wait for Colt and Luca's investigation.

Ottie was in a medically induced coma, breathing on her own at least, but she wouldn't be answering questions anytime soon and the deputies wouldn't be searching the woods until daybreak. Hell, they hadn't even interviewed Emmy yet because Elda Tucker decided to hold her husband at gunpoint after he left the toilet seat up and they had to deal with that drama first. I suspected the couple's issues ran much deeper than Old Man Tucker's bathroom habits, but having spent years living with a bunch of military men, I could quite understand the sentiment. Was it really that difficult to take the pubic hairs out of the plughole?

Anyhow, Ana and her buddies were heading home tomorrow after they'd spoken with Colt and Luca, and as the investigation progressed, I'd take a view on whether I needed to have any further input. Brooke would keep me updated. She always did, even if she wasn't technically supposed to.

I'd traded email addresses with Ana. Now that our earlier surprise at running into each other had subsided, we'd been able to have a proper conversation, and it might be nice to stay in touch. You know, like regular people.

Pen pals.

On balance of probabilities, I thought that Zacharov was indeed dead. Ana—and Emmy—could have killed me ten times over today, yet I was still breathing, and the only logical explanation for this was that the general wasn't. I'd still have to watch my back for Vik and Ilya because they were in the wind, and there was still a good chance Nico would try to slit my throat if he realised what I'd done to his father, but maybe in time, I'd sleep a little easier.

Overall, it had been a good day.

Perhaps I'd even open a bottle of champagne?

"You want to come for dinner with us?" Ana asked.

"I shouldn't, not around here."

Emmy rinsed the last of the soap out of a bucket and kicked it into the corner. "So we'll go farther afield. What time is it? We could drive to Coquille? Or Eugene? That's big enough?" She rolled her eyes. "I've lived in the US for nearly twenty years, and I still don't understand the cities here. Americans call Coquille a city, but in England, we have bigger villages."

"Then maybe I should have hidden out in England."

"I tried that once. It was...messy."

"Messy?"

"I wasn't in a good place mentally, so I ended up fucking some posh guy, and now he's married to one of my best friends. And his sister's besties with Bradley. *Messy*."

Her candour was...strange. I'd gotten used to the concept of TMI with Brooke and Addy—Brooke's motormouth of a friend—but Emmy was an assassin. We lived in darkness. We didn't fuck posh guys or have besties or hire sequin-loving personal assistants.

Yet Ana had a boyfriend and a daughter.

She went to PT-fuckin'-O meetings.

Or so she said.

What if she was lying?

What if they were both lying?

I sure lied a lot.

Was Emmy joking? Should I laugh?

Fuck, civilian life was hard to navigate. Being Nine of Ten had been far from easy, and calling Base 13 home offered many drawbacks, but at least I hadn't had to second-guess the true meaning of every damn conversation. I'd been able to walk around in comfortable clothes, carrying as many weapons as I wanted, and if General Zacharov told us we had a couple of hours to kill, there'd only been one appropriate response: who's the target?

"I see. *Da*, messy."

"So, Eugene?"

Fuck it—at least I could act like my true self for an evening.

"I'll make my own way there."

"Suit yourself. Bradley?" she called, and he appeared beside us a moment later with a basket full of craft materials. The moment everything was tidy, he'd picked up where he left off pre-Shauna and begun shopping again. Still, I couldn't complain—with the amount of shit he was buying, I'd be able to afford that new rifle. "Can you book a table for dinner in Eugene?"

"What does everyone want to eat? Felipe took me to a darling little Italian place earlier in the week."

I shrugged. Ana shrugged. Hallie shrugged.

Emmy grinned. "Guess we're eating Italian, then."

"Excellent. I'll make the booking and reroute Alex."

Who? "Alex?"

"Our personal trainer," Emmy said.

They had a personal trainer? Actually, scratch that question. Of course they had a personal fucking trainer. When Ana fell from grace, she sure had landed on her feet. Was I bitter? No, that was the wrong word for it. I was happy that two of us had managed to escape from Zacharov's clutches. But I couldn't help being slightly envious of her life compared to mine.

"Seven o'clock?" Bradley asked.

That would give me enough time to go home, wash the blood off, change my clothes, and load up with a suitable amount of hardware. Emmy still had my knife and my gun, and I wanted those back, but I'd leave it until after dinner to push for their return. No point in making things awkward.

But as I locked the door behind us, she slipped everything she'd confiscated back into my pocket.

"I'm sure you'll need these at some point."

"Do you want your bear spray?"

Offering was polite, yes?

"Nah, keep it. I've got plenty more."

14

EMMY

Asiago lay on the outskirts of downtown Eugene, and the name made me chuckle. When in Rome or Milan, had I stumbled across a restaurant named Velveeta? No, not once, but then again, America wasn't exactly renowned for its cheesemaking.

On the plus side, Asiago did have a private dining room at the back, and Bradley had booked it for the entire evening. And the place was blessed with a decent wine list. Ana had volunteered to be designated driver, so I planned to indulge in a glass or two, but I'd stay sober enough to stop Bradley from singing karaoke at one o'clock in the morning, as he was liable to do if nobody kept him in check.

Well, it had certainly been an interesting day. Pills had taken the edge off the pain radiating from my nose, and now I took a moment to reflect. I quite possibly had another half-sibling. Vik. Viktor... Hell, I didn't even know his last name. Although what did it matter? I didn't plan to look for him, not if he was a knock-off of my asshole of a father. Later, when we were alone, I'd grill Ana on what she remembered, but only out of curiosity. He must be older than us, I knew that much, but she'd never even mentioned his name before. Or Darya's.

Darya Volkova. I wasn't sure if I liked her, but I didn't hate her, and I sure as hell respected her. She'd been a first-tier assassin, and she'd stayed at the top of the game for over a decade. How many high-value targets had she taken out during that time? Before she retired? *Retired.* Fuck, she was wasted in Baldwin's Shore. Today, I'd felt the raw power in her, and she still had the right moves.

A waiter appeared and presented us with menus, poured water, and laid out baskets of breadsticks. I chewed on one absent-mindedly as I studied the wine list. Tonight, I'd definitely earned a drink, painkillers be damned.

My phone buzzed with a message.

Leona: Ottie's still asleep. The nurse says I have to leave now, but I'll come back in the morning.

I'd given Leona my number so she could keep us updated, plus I'd offered financial and logistical support if she needed it, although Nico seemed to have that covered. He'd told her to take the next week off on full pay, and if Ottie needed a specialist consult, he would fund it.

Me: She's in good hands. Make sure you get some rest.

Another buzz, and I expected to see a reply from Leona, but the screen was still dark. Someone had messaged my other phone. The one few people had the number of.

Mack: Call me ASAP. Secure line.

Mack was one of my long-standing friends—yes, the one who'd married my posh ex, although I harboured no bitterness. He wasn't a bad guy, just a terrible guy for me, and I wished them all the happiness in the world. Mack also happened to be Blackwood's cyber guru, and if she wanted me to call her on a secure line, there was a problem.

I gave the wine list one last, longing glance and cursed under my breath.

"What happened?" Ana asked.

"No clue yet. Bradley, do you have an RF detector in your purse?"

Of course he did. Why had I even bothered to ask? He wasn't a big fan of guns, but he loved gadgets, although he had a bad habit of buying bugs from the internet and installing them around my home because he liked to know *everything*.

"You want me to sweep the room?" he asked.

"Go for it, ace."

The sweep came up clean, as expected, but it always paid to check. I dialled Mack. She was working on several projects at the moment, plus I'd asked her to do a little research on Ottie earlier. Ottilie Melissa Marquette, born in Sanford, Maine, according to Leona. She'd also given me Ottie's date of birth and the names of her parents in the hope that we could track them down. She didn't have their numbers, and Ottie's phone was missing. They needed to know what had happened to their daughter.

"Hey."

"Can you talk?" Mack asked.

"The room's clean, but if the waiter comes back, I'll go silent. What's up?"

"Honestly? I don't know, but *something* is. I ran a few searches on your girl—"

"Ottie?"

"Yup. Just little nibbles around the edges, and somebody slammed the door so hard my ears are still ringing. Emmy, *who is she*?"

"You have as much information on her as I do. Any idea who slammed the door?"

"No, but they're connected. I routed my traffic through a twenty-four-hour internet café in St. Petersburg, and, well, *look...*"

The phone pinged, and I peered at the picture Mack had

sent. A high-res satellite photo, zoomed in on a dimly lit city street. Snow on the ground reflected the little light there was and allowed me to see the cops in black helmets surrounding the building. Two of them were dragging a guy out the door, heading for one of the cars slewed across the road.

"We're talking St. Petersburg, Russia, here? Not St. Petersburg, Florida?"

"Yup, and that happened a half hour after I got cyber-kicked in the face."

"Ottie Marquette has a connection to Russia?"

"Sure looks that way, but it was a US database I was looking at, so..."

"So either the Russians were watching you watch the Americans, or there's an international angle we don't yet know about."

Well, fuck.

Right now, news of Ottie's assault was mostly whispers around town, and it would stay that way until tomorrow morning when we spoke with Colt and Luca. Then they'd start asking questions. I'd have to give them some kind of heads-up, suggest they keep things low-key. Only Nico and the real Leona knew the true situation, but... Nico was Russian. Was there a link there?

"Can you keep digging?" I asked Mack.

"Very, very carefully. As in, on tiptoe. It might take days to get any meaningful information if everything's flagged or classified."

And Ottie Marquette might not have days. "Okay, do what you can, and I'll go with humint from this end."

Human intelligence. Mack might have worshipped her computers, but I still preferred to get out and talk to people. Darya would be here soon, and I could ask for her thoughts on Nico. Friend or foe? Maybe she'd be more forthcoming than she had been earlier? In the meantime, I sent a message of my own, one that mirrored Mack's from earlier but with a different recipient.

Me: Call me ASAP. Secure line.

"What happened?" Ana asked. "There's an issue with Ottie?"

I told her about the switch Mack had tripped, but Ana was as clueless as me. "She was clearly hiding at the Peninsula, but from who?"

"That's the sixty-four-thousand-dollar question."

Or, as it turned out, the sixty-four-million-dollar question, but as we ordered antipasti and bruschetta, we were still blissfully unaware of that little fact-ette. Or the war we were about to walk into.

The door opened, and for a moment, I thought a diner had taken a wrong turn. Then I did a double take, and fuck, Ana was *so* right about Darya being a chameleon. Actually, if we were going for animal metaphors, a Siberian tiger was more appropriate.

If I hadn't been expecting Darya to join us, I'd never have recognised her. Gone was the mousy brown hair, replaced with a blunt platinum-blonde bob. Blue eyes had turned green, and rings of black eyeliner and a slash of scarlet lipstick gave her a vampish look. Tonight, she wore skintight black jeans, a snakeskin belt with a flashy silver buckle, and a tight jade-green turtleneck. When she didn't remove the leather jacket, I assumed she had a weapon or two strapped to her back. Probably in her boots too—she'd gone for chunky heels rather than spikes, and those could hide a multitude of sins.

Bradley didn't look close enough. "Sorry, my darling, this is a private dinner. But I love your outfit."

She locked gazes with him, and he shrank back a foot. "I was invited."

Oh, the Russian accent had come out to play tonight as well. Guess she'd decided to let her hair down. Or tuck it up under a wig, whatever. I was reasonably sure the blonde was fake. If she'd been wearing a wig earlier, it would've come off during our punch-up.

When Bradley looked to me for help, I had to laugh. "Bradley, meet Darya."

"Who?"

For fuck's sake. "Darla. You just spent half the day buying yarn from her."

"What? No way."

Hallie's mouth had dropped open too, and I didn't miss Darya's smirk. Yes, she was having fun.

"Darya's an old friend of Ana's."

Bradley pushed his chair back. "Oh no. No! Now there are three of you?"

Darya took the seat next to Ana and poured herself a glass of water from the carafe in the centre of the table.

"*Nyet*. There are two of them and one of me. And if you mention a word of this evening to anyone, I'll hand-deliver your yarn personally and stuff it down your throat."

Bitch. "Bradley understands how to be discreet, as does Hallie. I wouldn't have told them otherwise."

"Just making my position clear."

"Trust me, it's crystal. If you want to spend the rest of your life crocheting bath mats, none of us are gonna stop you."

"Actually, a latch-hook design is much cosier." She smacked her head. "What the fuck am I saying?"

"Darla doesn't come with an off switch?"

"When you've lived as someone for so long, it can be hard to get out of character."

"Yeah, well, take your shitty mood out on me, not my friends. Are you drinking tonight?"

When her eyes narrowed, I thought her charming

disposition might make another appearance, but after a long second, she shook her head.

"*Nyet*, I'm driving."

"Suit yourself."

Where was Alex? I was starving, so maybe those of us present should order and I could just pick him out a nice steak, although if I did that, Sod's Law would dictate the dish was on the charred side of well done by the time he showed up. What if I got dough balls to go with the antipasti while we waited? I'd earned my carbs today, and what my nutritionist didn't know wouldn't hurt him. Unless Alex arrived while I was stuffing my face and told tales because—

Oh, he was here.

"We saved you a seat." Between Darya and Bradley, lucky guy. "How was the run?"

"Two hours ten."

Faster than I thought.

"Nice. You've earned a big basket of dough balls."

He didn't bother to answer, just walked to the empty seat, and I knew he was cursing because he had his back to the door. Well, he should have arrived earlier. You snooze, you lose.

But then something weird happened. As he sat down, Darya looked up at him, and she actually smiled.

"*Privyet*, Alexei."

Alexei? Yes, it was his name, but nobody called him that, not anymore. Not since he moved to the US. Most people assumed Alex was short for Alexander. *Wait.* Wait, wait, wait... Did Alex and Nine know each other?

15

NINE

The surprises just kept coming today, didn't they?

Alex.

Alexei.

I suppose I shouldn't have been shocked. *Da*, the world was a big place with over seven billion people, but when you looked at the microcosm of special forces, it really was quite small. Incestuous, even. At times, your old enemy became your new boss. A former Spetsnaz operative could easily find himself hunting pirates off the Somali coast, or playing bodyguard to rich Emiratis, or hired as a mercenary in Syria. Or, it seemed, working as a personal trainer to a vicious British assassin with a taste for donuts.

Alexei looked down at me, confused.

"Do we know each other?"

"We met once, a long time ago. Twenty years."

I never forgot a face. It was both a blessing and a curse. A blessing because two decades later, I still saw Alexei perfectly in my dreams, and a curse because those dreams invariably turned into nightmares where I relived Rad's death over and over and over again. Where I saw General Zacharov's sneer as he slapped me. Where I saw heads disintegrate, and blood, so much blood...

"Twenty years ago? In Russia?"

"*Da*, on a helicopter. You were on our extract team, and you gave me your coat."

I'd been fifteen years old, sent along with Pavel and Artem to rescue a hostage in the days before General Zacharov went rogue. Why me? Because the separatist leader who'd taken the hostage had a daughter my age, and with creative make-up, I looked enough like her to get into his stronghold. My entrance had gone smoothly, but the egress was a different story, mainly because the hostage had been an imbecile of the highest order. Damned politicians. We'd escaped in a hail of bullets, then hidden out in a virtual swamp while we waited for transport. When we finally made it onto the helicopter, I'd been on the verge of hypothermia, shaking, wondering whether it might be easier just to die next time. Pavel and Artem—who'd done twenty percent of the work—had been happy to take eighty percent of the praise, and I'd been stuffed in the back next to Alexei, teeth chattering. Miserable. Exhausted. And that was when he'd given me his coat. Pavel hadn't offered a thing, and Artem had handed me his soaking-wet scarf, but Alexei tucked his overcoat around me and made me drink and eat a little before I fell asleep.

I fell asleep.

I never slept near people I didn't trust. Never. I'd go forty-eight hours without sleep before I'd close my eyes around a stranger. Yet I'd practically passed out on Alexei. And I mean *on* Alexei. Head on his shoulder, hand on his thigh, our bodies pressed together. I'd woken long enough to register him carrying me from the helicopter to the plane for the next leg of the journey, and that was the last time I ever saw him.

Until now.

But I'd kept his jacket.

Sometimes I'd even worn it.

And of all the belongings I'd had to leave behind at Base 13, that old, unwashed coat was the thing I missed the most.

Ana's eyes widened. "Our Alex is your Alexei? Are you kidding me? You wore that jacket all the—"

I shot her a warning glare. She smiled, and Ana's smiles were as rare as my own.

"Darya, meet Alex Garin. He's our trainer. Alex, this is Darya Volkova. Dasha to her friends."

Alex held out a hand. "Darya."

Dasha. "Alex."

I was glad now that I'd made the effort to wear nice clothes tonight. Rad used to laugh at me for dressing up, but I hated to look unkempt. Being ugly on the inside was bad enough. On Base 13, Zacharov and his minions had made every effort to strip away my femininity, to debase me, so was it really any surprise that I liked to put on lipstick when I was able to? Lipstick was freedom. A tiny act of rebellion in a world where exercising personal choice was rewarded with punishment. Darla didn't wear lipstick. A therapist would probably say I was punishing myself for past wrongs, and maybe they'd be right? My sins were legion.

"I always wondered what happened to you," Alex said.

"You remember that night?"

"I'm surprised you do."

"The kindnesses were few and far between in those days."

Silence followed, and I became acutely aware that everyone was staring at us. Now I regretted driving because I really could have used a glass of wine or three. I picked up the menu and studied it, just your regular socially awkward assassin, no big deal.

Fuck.

Alexei was here.

Beside me once again.

"Do you have photos from the run?" Bradley demanded, saving me from further humiliation. "We need to see them."

"I have *a* photo. Unfortunately."

Alex pulled his phone from his back pocket, and I made the mistake of glancing down. The man had thighs like tree trunks and the ass of a— No, I was *not* going there.

The phone got passed around the table, and when it reached Emmy, she burst out laughing.

"I can't believe you wore it."

Bradley got indignant. "Hey, it was a *great* costume."

"It was a fucking sunflower."

A sunflower? "You dressed up? As a flower?"

Alex shifted in his seat. "Only for a bet."

"Plus he raised over a hundred thousand bucks for Live without Limits," Bradley said. "It's a charity that helps disabled children, and the people there do *amazing* work, which means we should definitely be drinking champagne this evening. Where's the waiter?"

Emmy took a deep breath. "Bradley, you can't turn everything into an excuse to drink champagne."

"What, you expect me to drink Prosecco?"

"Oh, the fucking hardship," she muttered. "One bottle."

The phone got as far as me, and sure enough, Alex was dressed up as a sunflower with leafy green track pants, a yellow shirt, and petals around his face.

"See? Isn't he cute?" Bradley leaned over. "I made the petals out of modelling foam and hand-painted them."

"An oak tree would have been more appropriate."

"An oak tree? The leaves would take forever to make, but I can bear it in mind for next time."

"There will be no next time," Alex growled.

"So you say." Bradley turned to me. "Can I get pre-made leaves, or will I have to shape them out of Worbla?"

Alex frowned. "How would Darya know?"

"She runs an excellent craft store. It stocks the entire range of La Coutoura textured yarn."

"A *craft store*? You swapped your Makarov for a glue gun?"

Not swapped, exactly—now I had both. I shrugged. "For the record, I preferred the SR-1 Vektor to the Makarov."

Thankfully, the waiter showed up, and eating soon took precedence over talking. This reminded me of the old days, except without Ilya's raging misogyny and Pavel's juvenile sense of humour. The food was better too. No shchi, no kholodets, and no dried herring. Between courses, we talked about weapons and politics and international relations, all subjects I'd been out of the loop on for the past several years, save for what I saw on the news. And before dessert, conversation turned to Ottie Marquette because Alex wasn't up to speed on that particular topic. The news of a possible Russian connection piqued my interest but also raised more questions than it answered.

"What if the police presence in St. Petersburg was a coincidence? Raids happen all the time. If a business owner doesn't hand over the required bribes..." I made a cutting motion across my throat. "They pay, one way or another."

"You really believe that?" Emmy asked.

"Coincidences happen. Or did you have an ulterior motive when you walked into my store today?"

"Point taken. The only ulterior motive was Bradley's need to own every craft product ever made. I definitely didn't intend to get my face smashed in."

Now Alex studied her more closely. "I thought your nose looked different."

Bradley had done a good job with contouring, and the

bruises were well-hidden, but yes, the bridge was still fatter than it should have been.

"Yeah, well, now we know what we need to work on in the gym next week."

"It was a headbutt?"

"Yes."

"That's twice in the last year."

Really? Twice? Then Emmy clearly should have learned from the first experience. Sloppy work. Although I hadn't exactly covered myself in glory either—by the end, I'd been a dying bug, stuck on my damn back as she squeezed the breath out of me. We both needed to train harder.

"What happened to the other person who broke your nose?" I asked. "Did you take him out for dinner too?"

"Not right away. I hired her first." The waiter reappeared while I was still processing her words, and Emmy's attention turned to a more important subject, to her at least. "Ah, tiramisu. My favourite."

And then it was over.

The waitstaff cleared the table, Emmy picked up the whole check, which I hadn't expected, and it was time for goodbyes in the parking lot. If you'd asked me earlier, I'd have said that seeing the back of Emmy's gang would be a joyous occasion, but instead, I felt...kind of sad? Seeing Ana again after all these years, and Alexei... Reconnecting with that small part of my past had been weirdly pleasant. I'd been able to lay old ghosts to rest.

Ana wrapped her arms around me, and for the first time in years, I didn't have to dodge a hug or plan it in advance because she was carrying as many weapons as me. A gun at the small of her back, a knife clipped to her belt, a small pouch that probably held paracord and syrettes and a comms system. My choices were much the same, except I'd ditched the comms system in favour of extra ammo. Who did I have to talk to these days?

I got another—more exuberant—hug from Bradley and a small wave from Hallie. I sensed she wasn't sure quite what to make of me, so she'd decided to err on the side of caution. Smart choice. Alex kissed me on the cheek, one hand on my back, and that little touch shouldn't have made me shiver inside, but it did. Underneath the hard shell, I was still human, and I'd thought about him more times than was healthy over the years. Wondered where he was, how he was doing. Whether he was still alive because Spetsnaz units had made a number of high-profile fuck-ups and not all of the operatives had walked away from them. But now I knew. Alex was alive and well and living in the US.

"It was good to see you again," he murmured. "If you're ever in Virginia, look me up."

"But I don't have your number."

He stepped back. Smiled. "Check your pocket."

"I'll call you."

Maybe.

A trip to Virginia was out of the question, though. I had a craft store to run.

Then it was Emmy's turn, and she didn't touch me.

"Well, I'd say it was good to meet you, but the jury's still out on that one."

"Likewise."

"I'm sure you'll be hearing from Bradley. Probably tomorrow morning, next week at the latest." She glanced toward her SUV. "As long as Ana doesn't murder him on the way back to the Peninsula. Hallie's gonna have to sit in the middle and play referee."

"Does Ana need a ride? My car's empty, and I can drop her off at the gates."

"Then why don't you take Alex? That way, he can slide the

front seat all the way back without kneecapping anyone, and I won't need to listen to him bitching about legroom the whole way."

Spend another hour with him? I figured I could cope, and now I felt like kissing Emmy after all.

"Sure, I can take Alex."

16

NINE

For the first time in my life—the Darla years excepted—I was driving under the speed limit. Emmy had long since disappeared ahead of us, but Alex didn't say a word when I lagged behind.

Not one word.

What were we meant to talk about?

I'd wanted him here, and now I had him, but my tongue was tied in knots.

"So..." he finally started. "How bad was the fight?"

"I've been in better ones."

"Emmy came off the worst?"

I pushed up my sleeve and showed him the damage. "Let's call it a draw."

"A regular conversation wouldn't have sufficed?"

"I thought they were there to kill me. It's a long story."

"We have an hour." He glanced at the speedometer. "Maybe an hour and a half."

"Unlike some people, I prefer to avoid tickets. Does Emmy get many?"

"She could wallpaper her house with them, and she lives in

a big house." A shrug. "But her bribery success rate is reasonable."

"I haven't tried to buy a cop recently." This time, I'd taken a different tack and made friends with the local deputies instead. Yet another strange facet of Darla's life. "I don't have the budget for it anymore, but Emmy doesn't seem short of cash."

Alex barked out a laugh. "She has more money than she'll ever spend. Fast cars aside, her tastes aren't that expensive. She'd rather eat a cheeseburger than a gourmet meal. Why did you think she'd come to kill you?"

"Because Ana was there, and I figured Zacharov sent them."

"Lieutenant General Zacharov? He's issuing orders from beyond the grave now?"

Alex's response gave me the certainty I'd been looking for. That I'd been *hoping* for. The general truly was dead. Gone. Kaput. Deceased. Which meant the tight band of stress that had been wrapped around me for most of my life finally loosened an inch.

"Until today, I didn't realise he'd died. Even after they told me, I still struggled to believe it. He was always so careful, so in control, practically immortal. And vindictive like you wouldn't believe."

"I believe it. I saw what he put Ana through." Alex touched me on the shoulder, just the slightest brush of his finger, and that shiver made another appearance. "Darya, he's definitely dead. I was there."

"At Base 13? You were part of the operation? But I thought you were a personal trainer now?"

"I train Emmy and Ana, but that doesn't mean I neglect to train myself. And occasionally, I still get my hands dirty. Not often, because I'm meant to avoid high-impact exercise, but if a job's important enough, I'll take the risk."

"What risk? What happened?"

He took my hand in his and ran it down his leg, which was taking a fucking liberty. Yes, I'd always kind of liked him, but I wanted to talk, not grope his admittedly substantial muscles. I was about to snatch my hand away when I felt the knee brace he was trying to show me. And it wasn't a flimsy little thing either.

"You got injured?" I whispered.

"Three months after we met. Not a direct hit, just shrapnel, but they sent me to a butcher rather than a surgeon, and that was the end of my military career."

"I'm sorry."

Although not too sorry. Back in those days, I'd have gladly taken a butchered knee over my own conscription.

"I've made peace with it."

"How did you wind up here? In the US, I mean?"

"I wasn't going to let a Russian cut me open again."

"You came here for surgery?"

"At that time, the best orthopaedic surgeon in the world worked out of New York. I had savings, not enough, but because I had no insurance, he agreed to lower the fee. So I came to America. My uncle knew a guy in Virginia, and he offered me a place to stay while I recovered so I could go back for the follow-up appointments. All I had to do was work a few hours in his gym, training assholes to lift weights, until it was time to go home to Smolensk."

"But you're still here?"

"*Da*. Because I married his niece."

Alex was *married*? That shouldn't have mattered, so why did it feel like a punch to the gut?

"Congratulations. I guess it's too late to send a card?"

He laughed. "I don't even know where she lives now."

"You're not together anymore?"

"We were hitched for five years, which was four years too

many. The day I signed the divorce papers, Bradley brought the champagne and I drank the whole bottle."

"So you already trained Emmy in those days?"

"*Da*." A chuckle. "Colette hated Emmy, and Emmy used to call her 'the toothache.'"

"How did you end up working for Emmy?"

"Her husband hired me to kick her ass when he went out of town."

"Wait, *Emmy's* married?"

"For sixteen years now. But in the early days, there was no love lost between the two of them."

"How did you meet him?"

"At a bar. Colette liked to spend money we didn't have, so I took a second job as a doorman. Black—Emmy's husband—used to go there with a buddy to pick up women."

"He hired you from a bar?"

"My job interview was dumping five punks onto the sidewalk."

Since my own "job interview" had consisted of putting a knife through my stepfather's heart—a feat I'd achieved more through luck than judgment—I figured I couldn't be too critical of Black's hiring process.

"You like the job?"

"Most of the time. Do you like owning a craft store?"

"I like being my own boss and not getting shot at on a daily basis. But do I like the actual crafts? Not so much. How can people get excited over folding paper and knitting blankets and making their own Christmas decorations? I mean, they clearly do because the store's doing well, better than I ever thought, but...Bargello."

"Is that an expletive? What language?"

No, but it should have been.

"It's a type of needlepoint."

"Right. So if you don't much like crafts, then I have to ask the question... Why?"

Should I trust Alex? What if all this was some elaborate sting operation? A carefully laid trap just waiting for me to—

Stop.

All the paranoia in the world hadn't saved General Zacharov, but what had kept Ana alive? Teamwork. And she looked far happier than I felt. Maybe letting someone in wouldn't be the disaster I'd always assumed? Especially if that person was Alexei. *He'd given me his coat.* Even in freezing temperatures when he must have been cold himself, he'd given me his coat.

"So I left my former employment in a bit of a hurry..."

Was it weird that I still had my hand on Alex's knee? Probably. Was I about to move it? No. And since he'd been the one to put it there, I figured he couldn't have too many objections.

Another chuckle. "You didn't work out your notice period?"

"We didn't exactly have an HR department."

"And then you ended up in Baldwin's Shore?"

I nodded. "With a gun, a couple of hundred bucks, and the clothes I was standing up in. The first night, I slept in my car, but it wasn't *really* mine seeing as I'd stolen it. I'd switched the plates, of course, but I didn't want to take chances."

If anyone realised I'd gotten away, it wouldn't only have been Zacharov hunting me; the whole of the FBI would've been on my tail. Probably the Secret Service too, and the police, and the NSA. Nobody liked it when members of Congress ended up in enough pieces to make Humpty Dumpty look like a coffee-break teaser.

"And the next day, I was hungry," I continued. "So I went to the grocery store, and there was a card on the noticeboard. Live-in help wanted. Duties to include personal care, running errands, helping with mobility, overseeing medication, and providing companionship. Not my dream job, but I was sick of shooting people, and...and...I was hurting. I'd just watched a colleague die. I watched him die, and there wasn't a damn thing I could do except kill the man responsible, but it was too late."

Alex twined his fingers in mine and squeezed. "Darya, I'm so sorry."

"Dasha. For fuck's sake, call me Dasha."

Then it happened. For the first time since I was thirteen and kneeling over my mother's body, the tears came. I wasn't meant to cry. I was Nine. I was the Bad Samaritan. I was a tool, not a person, and I *did not fucking cry*. Except today, I did. I took my foot off the gas, and the world went blurry, and Alex steered the car to the side of the road.

"W-w-what the hell is wrong with m-m-me?"

And then I was enveloped in his arms, and all the pain of my entire fucking life was soaking into his shirt.

Shit.

17

NINE

How long did we sit there? Ten minutes? Twenty? Alex just kept stroking my hair, except it wasn't really my hair, it was a wig, but it looked like my old hair before I dyed it brown and grew it long. And after what seemed like forever, I ran out of tears and got my breathing back under control.

I wanted to apologise. I wanted to tell him how sorry I was for acting like a weak-willed fool, but what came out was, "If you tell anyone about this, I'll cut off your balls while you sleep."

And what did he do? He kissed me on the forehead.

"From you, I wouldn't expect anything less. Want me to drive?"

"I'm not incapable."

"I know that. Let's trade seats."

"I can—"

But Alex was already out of the car and walking around to my side. And I just... I just didn't have the energy to fight tonight. So we traded, and he set off slightly quicker than I'd been going but not fast enough to attract the attention of the highway patrol. And I sat there in silence because there really wasn't anything I could do or say to fix this, was there?

When the lights of Baldwin's Shore came into view, I expected Alex to head straight for the Peninsula, but instead, he slowed when we hit the town limits.

"Where do you live?"

"Why does that matter?"

"Because in order to drive you home, I need to know where your house is."

"I can drive myself home."

"*Da*, you could, but I need to know you're safe."

"What, you think there might be an assassin hiding in my house?" I brought my hands to my cheeks in mock horror. "Whatever will I do?"

"Dasha, just give me this, okay?"

Was this another "regular people" thing? Where the guy had to check there were no bogeymen hiding in the shadows, even though the girl was arguably more qualified to do the job?

"Fine. *Fine*, take the next left."

My home wasn't flashy, but it wasn't shitty either. I'd spent two years caring for East Baldwin, and when he realised he didn't have long left, he'd made sure I was looked after. The Baldwin family were the area's biggest landowners—yes, the town was named after one of their ancestors—and East had offered me an empty property from their rental portfolio. Choice of four, just pick my favourite. I had, of course, selected the place with the largest basement. The majority of his family had been far from happy about me getting a minuscule piece of their inheritance, but the will was watertight, and East said I'd spent more time with him than any of those miscreants, anyway. Only Sara had bothered to visit. The daughter of East's dead son rather than the living one. I didn't mind her. The rest of the family were assholes, although the worst of them were in jail now. Rarely had I enjoyed my job in the past, but last month, I'd taken great delight in ensuring one of that clan got charged with murder.

So I had my house, and the upstairs rooms were comfy and homey and chintzy and frilly and everything a visitor would expect from a woman like Darla. The doormat said *Welcome!* and a framed cross-stitch in the hallway said *Come as a guest, leave as a friend.* The shotgun hidden behind the coat rack said *get the hell away from me.*

I opened the door for Alex so he could do whatever safety checks he felt were necessary before I drowned myself in alcohol. Who cared about the painkillers I'd taken? Tonight, I needed sweet oblivion.

"Please don't judge me from the decor."

He read the quote on the mirror ahead of us. "Don't worry, be happy?"

"So I don't take my own advice. Get over it."

"And Emmy accuses me of being the grumpy one."

"Grumpy?"

"I spent a long time being angry at the world, and my knee hurt constantly. So, yes, I grouched a lot." He rolled his eyes. "Plus I have to train Emmy."

"Okay, I get it. But you used the past tense—what changed?"

"Eighteen months ago, I had another surgery. New surgeon, new technique." Alex bounced on the balls of his feet a few times. "Much better now."

"What's next? A marathon dressed as a unicorn?"

He leaned in close. "If you suggest that to Bradley, I'll cut out your tongue as you sleep."

For a moment, our gazes locked, and suddenly, the house felt really, really warm. Was there a problem with the thermostat? I tried to voice the question, but no words came out, and I ran the tip of my tongue over too-dry lips instead.

Then Alex stepped back and the heat was gone, replaced by an odd hollow feeling I was unfamiliar with.

"Do you want a drink?" he asked.

"This is my house. Shouldn't I be the one offering?"

"Thanks, I'll have coffee."

"Asshole."

"Black, no sugar."

I jerked a thumb over my shoulder. "The kitchen's that way. Help yourself."

But he didn't. He followed me instead. "Where are you going?"

"If ever there was a day that called for liquor, it's this one."

The "Don't worry, be happy" mirror opened on a hinge, and I flipped the light switch to illuminate the stairs behind it. When Alex paused at the top, I turned and crooked a finger.

"Will you walk into my parlour, said a spider to a fly."

He didn't heed the warning, just trailed me down the steps until we reached my favourite room in the house. My basement lair. Part gym, part surveillance centre, part weapons locker. At the far end, I'd laid out mats and a weight bench with a treadmill in one corner. A punching bag hung from the ceiling, and I'd screwed mirrors to the wall so I could identify my mistakes and correct them. Opposite the stairs, a bank of monitors showed me every room of my home and the Craft Cabin, and sound was available too. People sure did say interesting things when they thought you weren't listening. A locked strongroom to the right of the stairs held my toys, some I'd bought and more that I'd retrieved from weapons caches when I judged enough time had passed. I'd emptied three so far. At another two, someone had beaten me to the punch, and I'd once thought that Zacharov had found them, but now I suspected Ilya or Vik. Or possibly Ana. Maybe I should ask her? Only the four of us remaining had known the precise locations.

A squashy leather sofa nestled beside the weapons locker because sometimes I liked to sit and read. Or sleep. Even with the silent alarms that I'd installed around the perimeter of the property watching over me, I felt safer down here than I did upstairs.

"Drink?" I offered my solitary shot glass to Alex. "I can drive you back to the Peninsula before I drown my sorrows."

"I can walk there."

"You're not tired?"

He just stared at me. Right. Spetsnaz. He didn't get tired.

"I have four kinds of horilka," I said.

"No Russian vodka?"

"No." Switching to the Ukrainian version had been another act of rebellion. My mother came from Kyiv, and she'd always told me that I had her spirit. Now I took it literally.

"Okay." Alex didn't question me further, and for that, I was grateful. "Surprise me."

"Didn't I do that already today?"

"More than once."

I poured medova z pertsem—traditional horilka with chilli peppers and honey—for Alex, then chose ternivka for myself. A bittersweet moment, and I wasn't talking about the flavour. When I was small, I'd spent summer days picking sloes with my mama so she could make her own ternivka, and even now, those memories hurt.

Block it out, Dasha.

"*Budmo.*" Let's live for the moment.

I held up the bottle in a toast, then drank straight from it. Poured the damn stuff down my throat. Why even pretend I was going to stay sober tonight?

Alex raised an eyebrow. "Is that wise?"

"I once jumped out of a plane without a parachute. A little alcohol poisoning won't hurt me."

"Do I want to hear this story?"

I shrugged. "My target jumped out with the only 'chute, so I killed him during free fall and took it." I swallowed another mouthful of horilka. "It really wasn't that exciting."

"Does *anything* get your adrenaline pumping?"

"Today's altercation did," I admitted. Or maybe it was the alcohol talking? "Emmy's a bitch."

"She'd take that as a compliment."

"I meant it as one." A groan slipped from my lips as I sank onto the couch. "I'm out of practice. No amount of solo training can replace a proper sparring session." I nodded toward the punching bag. "That doesn't hit back."

"What did Emmy come up with today?"

"A rear naked chokehold."

"*Da*, we practise that."

"Once, I could have gotten out of it. Hell, five years ago, she'd never have gotten me into it."

"Shoulders up, chin down, intercept one hand, trap the other, and wriggle to the under-hook side."

"You think I don't know this? But my muscle memory is gone."

"You still have muscle memory, but these days, you're using it for knitting instead."

"Shut up."

"Am I wrong?"

"No, and I hate that."

"You should work with a trainer."

"Oh, sure, I'll just join the taekwondo club in Coos Bay and get ready to answer lots of awkward questions. I don't suppose you offer Skype sessions?"

Alex swallowed his drink and sat beside me. Close beside me. When he took the bottle out of my hand, I began to wonder if he was going to make some kind of move. And he did. But not *that* kind of move. A second later, I was on my back again, this time with a pair of tree trunks wrapped around my waist.

"No, but I'm here now," he murmured as he snaked a hand across my chest. "Be careful of your arm."

And also my rib, but the painkillers I'd taken had done their job. Plus Alex was breaking me in slowly. Moving at half speed while I found my form. I tore his top hand away and trapped the bottom one under my armpit, then used the space to scramble sideways. Tried to turn the tables and pin him down. Failed. Found myself underneath him, but that was an easier hold to get out of. I bucked him off with my hips and rolled, then I was on my feet and my backup gun was in my hand, and if I'd felt so inclined, Alex would have had a third eye.

"Again."

He drilled me through the moves over and over until they began to flow once more, and I understood why Emmy had kept him for so long. He was a good trainer. A great trainer. Calm, knowledgeable, and tough. Plus he had two heads, which was sort of weird, but this whole day had been strange, hadn't it? I reached out to push him away, but my hands closed around thin air.

Fuck.

"Stop moving," I told him.

"I'm sitting still."

Was he? Then that must mean...I was moving? Or the floor, or maybe both? My stomach was doing something weird as well.

"I feel sick."

Alex rolled off me. "You're drunk. Where's your bathroom?"

"I won't actually puke. My stomach's cast iron. I ate..." Ah, fuck, was I giggling? "I ate maggot cheese once."

"There wasn't any other food available?"

"Vik dared me. The maggots were meant to be there because in Italy, it's a delicacy, and when I was in Cambodia, I ate a fried tarantula."

"Remind me never to go on vacation with you."

"I've never taken a vacation. Hey, where are you going? We're not done here."

"Tonight, we are."

"But—"

Alex scooped me up, and I wasn't sure whether to love that or hate it. All those liberties he took. The way he manhandled me. Why did it feel so...intimate? This evening, he'd been under me, on top of me, and around me, and that had been strictly business, but now...

He deposited me on the couch and stuffed a cushion under my head. Brooke had made the cushion for me, so fluffy and soft... Alex reached for my belt buckle, and I put a hand over his, but he shook his head.

"Relax, Dasha. I'm just taking the belt off. You can't rest with a gun holster strapped to your back."

"Wanna bet?"

He ignored that. Deft hands removed my weapons. Alex laid them on the side table and then covered me with the knitted blanket I used when I slept down here. I'd made that fucking blanket. Damn, it had been boring.

"I'll see myself out in a few minutes. Don't worry; I'll lock the door behind me."

"Okay." My voice was sing-song, barely mine at all. "I can call you?"

"You'd damn well better call me. Get some sleep, Dasha."

18

EMMY

"So, spill."

Ana slumped onto the couch in my room at the Peninsula. "What an ass fuck of a day."

"Ass fucking can be quite pleasurable with the right guy."

She raised one dark eyebrow. "Who? Black?"

Fuck, no. He'd split me in two.

"Alaric. But he's taken now, so don't get any ideas about ditching Quinn."

Plus Alaric was a tiny bit scared of Ana, while Samuel Quinn had somehow managed to navigate the mysteries of her mind and fall in love with her.

Ana just snorted. "So you think this day was pleasurable?"

"Not pleasurable, exactly, but certainly stimulating. And speaking of pleasure... You and Darya? Was there something between you?"

"There was a period of...experimentation when we were younger, but we both prefer men."

"And Vik? Is it true?"

"How am I meant to know? Zacharov told me nothing."

"But you spent time with Vik?"

128

She shrugged. "Maybe it's true."

"Tell me about them. I realise you hate discussing your past, but I need to know, especially after today's surprise with Darya. What if we run into another of your ex-colleagues? I'd rather be prepared next time."

"It's statistically unlikely."

"Is it? If they're working in the security industry in any capacity, it's entirely possible we'll cross paths at some point, and there's a good chance we'll be on opposing sides. You need to tell me more about them."

Ana didn't answer, just got up and walked to the minibar. I didn't say a word as she added ice to a tumbler and poured two miniatures of vodka over the top. If she needed time, I'd give it to her. But not too much time because I was meant to be meeting Nico in the bar in twenty minutes. He'd left a note at the reception desk, inviting me to join him for that drink I'd suggested earlier, and I figured why not?

In the daytime, the doors in front of the balcony gave me a view of the sea, but tonight, Ana stared out at an inky sky. Rain lashed against the glass, the storm no doubt washing away any remaining evidence in the woods behind the Craft Cabin. The deputies should have searched earlier, but like so many public services, the Coos County Sheriff's Department seemed to be understaffed and underfunded.

"There were ten of us to start with. One, Two, and Eight died early on in training, and then there were seven. Two girls —me and Dasha—and five boys. Viktor, Artem, Ilya, Radomir, and Pavel. Ilya was the oldest at sixteen."

"How old is Vik?"

"A year and a half older than us. Three months older than Dasha."

Which would make him thirty-five, assuming he was still alive. Old enough, experienced enough to be hellishly dangerous, and young enough to work for years if he chose to do so.

"Did you get along with him?"

Another shrug. "Vik was cold. Ice cold. And ruthless."

"Cruel?"

Ana tilted her head to one side, pondering, then finally shook it. "Not cruel. Who was it that said we can judge the heart of a man by his treatment of animals?"

"I'm not sure. Some philosopher, probably."

"I don't know either. Anyhow, there was a bear."

"A bear?"

"*Da*, a bear and a survival exercise. The general used to toss us into the taiga a hundred miles from the base and let us find our way home. It was okay. At least we were doing our own thing out there rather than being ordered around." She smiled a tiny smile. "Three was definitely doing his own thing. One time, his canopy got tangled in a tree, and we had to cut him down. Dasha said we should have left him there, but hindsight is a wonderful thing."

"You weren't fond of Three?"

"Three—Pavel—was an asshole. But that day in the forest, we carried on walking, and then we found the bear. Only a baby, with its leg crushed in a trap. Judging by the damage, it must have been there for days, and Vik put it out of its misery. Said that the innocent deserved a quick death. And then Dasha asked, 'What about the guilty?' and he just smiled."

Ana shuddered, which meant that smile must've been fucking creepy.

"So he didn't share Zacharov's sadistic streak, then?"

"You misunderstand the general. He wasn't a sadist. He was a power-hungry control freak. And yes, Vik did share his win-at-all-costs mentality, but to what extent, I can't say. Do you want to hear the end of the story?"

"There's more?"

"Where animal traps are concerned, there are always more. Why set one when you can set twenty, especially if you're a lazy son of a bitch who doesn't check them every day? I wanted to close them all so no more animals could get caught. Dasha wanted to gather them up and hide them. Two wanted to leave them as they were because who cared about a few animals? He died a month later. I didn't lose sleep over it."

"Proof that karma exists. What did Vik want to do?"

"He wanted to *move* the traps. We spent an hour combing the forest, and then we reset every trap we could find in a circle around the dead bear."

"Surely they could still trap stray animals? He realised that?"

"Every war has collateral damage," Ana mimicked in a deep voice. "It wasn't ideal, but the general encouraged us to think long-term."

"Then let's hope the plan worked, eh?"

"It did. The trapper made it to the hospital, but gangrene set in and he died a week later. The story made the local news."

Ana's story told me that Vik had been a leader. A sneaky, ruthless leader, but perhaps there had been an ounce of humanity hidden within his core.

"Darya said there were four of you left at most. The two of you, Vik, and possibly Ilya. Who's Ilya?"

"In the asshole stakes, Pavel would have taken silver while Ilya got the gold." Ana swallowed another mouthful of vodka. "I don't give a damn that Pavel's dead, but Rad and Art were okay."

"Was Ilya good at his job?"

"We were all good at our jobs."

Okay, that had been a dumb question. In light of my upcoming bar date with Nico, I decided to change the subject.

"Any idea why Darya's so touchy about Belinsky?"

"Do I know for certain? No. But I can take a good guess."

"Which is?"

"Years ago, maybe fifteen years, an oligarch named Lev Belinsky made it onto Zacharov's shitlist. The job was assigned to me, and I studied the file, but at the last minute, I got sent to the UK to silence a double agent who was considering talking. But Lev Belinsky wound up dead anyway, so I imagine the file got passed to Dasha."

"You think Lev and Nico are related?"

"Lev had a son named Nikolai."

I didn't need to ask whether Nico and Nikolai were the same man. Nine's behaviour had already given me my answer. It was likely the two of them had met before they moved to Baldwin's Shore, although having interacted with the woman in two totally different personas, I figured it was also a good bet that Nico wouldn't recognise her, at least without a nudge in the right direction.

Well, he wouldn't be getting that nudge from me. Nine had been reasonably friendly tonight, and I was beginning to warm to her.

"Go easy on the vodka—I'll be back soon."

As I strolled along the corridor, I took one of my two wedding rings off my necklace and slipped it onto my finger. I didn't always wear them because, with my lifestyle, they'd only end up getting destroyed, but I didn't want to give Nico the wrong impression tonight. He struck me as a bit of a womaniser. Both of my rings were from the same man, I hasten to add—we'd just had two wedding ceremonies.

Nico was waiting at a table in a quiet corner of the bar, a bottle of Beluga and two shot glasses in front of him. As I approached, he rose to greet me with a kiss to the cheek. Yup, definitely a charmer.

"Have you been back for long?" I asked. He was wearing the same suit he'd been in earlier, but he'd undone an extra button on the shirt.

"An hour."

When he tapped the bottle, I nodded, and he poured.

"How are Ottie and Leona?"

"No change in Ottie, so the doctors say. Leona's blaming herself for leaving Ottie alone."

"It's not her fault."

"I know." Nico drained his glass and poured himself another. "Maybe it's mine."

"Yours?"

"I hired Rodrigo. Took a chance on a man that perhaps I shouldn't have."

"You said earlier he had a record—what was it for?"

"Assault. But who among us hasn't stepped in when a reprobate decides to bother a young lady?"

I took a sip of the vodka. Not bad, but I'd have preferred a gin and tonic.

"His only mistake was getting caught, huh?"

"So I thought."

"Your instincts were probably right."

"Based on your PI skills?"

"That and Ottie's movements. Someone poisoned her dog and lay in wait for her when she took the mutt to the veterinarian. Rodrigo stopped him from intercepting her on the way, but he got her on the way back."

"Poisoned? You think this was pre-planned?"

"The evidence so far suggests it could have been."

"I see. And you've told Deputy Mendez this?"

"Not yet. He was otherwise engaged this evening. A hostage incident, apparently."

"A hostage incident? In Baldwin's Shore?"

"A lady named Elda Tucker had a disagreement with her husband."

"Oh, those two. I'm surprised he's still breathing. If Elda doesn't shoot him, liver failure will do the job."

"I'll chat to Mendez in the morning."

"Ditto. And I'll speak with the rest of the staff too. I can't believe nobody saw a thing, especially if the dog was harmed deliberately as you say."

"Can I make a suggestion?"

"Go ahead."

"Tread carefully."

"Is that a threat, Mrs. Black? You're more than just a private investigator, aren't you?"

"Sure, I'm a loving wife and a philanthropist."

"And the rest?"

There wasn't much information about me online—Mack took care of that—and the few snippets painted a picture of a billionaire's trophy wife rather than a special ops bitch. So, Nico still had connections, and he'd been working them.

"I'm a PI in the same way that you're a simple hotelier, Mr. Belinsky. And no, it isn't a threat. I've merely heard a rumour that Ottie Marquette might have run into bigger trouble than a jackass of an ex."

"I see. Then I'll take that under advisement."

"Leave this to the experts."

"Are you talking about the sheriff's department or Blackwood Security?"

"I'm flying home tomorrow." I flipped a business card across the table. "But if you need somebody to replace that camera, I'm sure we can assist."

"I have people for that. Is there anything else?"

"I do have one more question."

"Shoot."

Would he still have said that if he'd known I had a gun at the small of my back? Probably. I'd bet my last donut Nico was carrying a weapon too, and that he knew how to use it. The man gave off *vibes*. They hadn't been so evident earlier, but peel the charm back and there he was.

"Why build a hotel in Baldwin's Shore? Your other properties are in London, Paris, and New York. Why small-town Oregon?"

"I also have a lovely place on the beach in Croatia. You should give it a try if you're ever in that part of the world."

"I'll bear that in mind. But you dodged my question."

Nico barked out a laugh. "Okay, I'll answer. I took this land as payment for a debt from a jackass who'd inherited it."

"That tells me how you acquired the land. It doesn't tell me why you stuck a luxury hotel on it."

"Oh, you're good." Nico picked up the bottle again, and I nodded. Russian custom dictated it was rude to say no. He filled his own glass too, then grinned. "In truth, the land would have been a write-down in my portfolio if I hadn't caught my ex-girlfriend in bed with the jackass a month later. I built this place to spite them. Last I heard, he'd gone bankrupt, and she'd moved in with her parents." He held up the glass. "*Za pobedy.*"

To victories. I clinked my own glass against it. And it had been a victory for me too, a small one—I could set Darya's mind at rest as to why Nico had shown up in town. He hadn't been looking for her.

"*Za nashu druzhbu.*" To our friendship.

He smiled, and it wasn't the usual polite-yet-distant version. "You speak Russian?"

"Enough to get by." I rose, waited for him to do the same. Offered my cheek again. "Thanks for the drinks."

"Anytime."

When I got back to my room, Ana was still there, lying on the couch. She cracked an eyelid when I opened the door.

"How did it go?"

"No change in Ottie, Leona's upset, and Nico definitely didn't come to Baldwin's Shore in search of Darya."

"How do you know that?"

I stretched out on the bed and recapped the story. "And yeah, it's an odd place for a resort, but he's done a nice job with it. People come for a week to use the spa, take a bunch of yoga classes, and wander around town, then they bugger off home again."

"What do you think of Nico?"

"There's a lot hidden under the surface, but I think he's okay."

"His father was an absolute fucker."

"So was ours," I pointed out.

"That's true."

"I might swim in the morning."

"In the sea?"

"Only if Alex is in full-on slave-driver mode. The pool's heated. Want to join me?"

"I guess."

"Careful, don't sound too enthusiastic."

"Is that shit Bradley trowelled onto your face waterproof?"

An excellent question. "If it isn't, I bet he has a bunch of other gunk that is. We should get some sleep."

Ana rolled to her feet, graceful even with a few drinks inside her. "Goodnight, sister."

"*Spokoynoy nochi, sestra.*"

19

EMMY

That night, I dreamed of blood. Of a bloated face, of bruises, of the crunch of cartilage and flashing knives. I was almost grateful when my phone rang, pulling me out of a sweaty, restless sleep. *James.* Yes, it was five thirty in the morning, but it was eight thirty in DC and he'd made the effort to fit me in before his day started, a day that was bound to be busy. He was the President of the United States, after all.

"Hey."

"You wanted to speak? What happened to your nose?"

Damn video calls. And yes, James and I knew each other well enough for him to notice the difference in my face.

"It broke."

"Just like that? Who broke it? Not Sky again?"

"An old friend of Ana's. Probably the less said about that, the better."

James sucked in a breath and closed his eyes for a brief second. When we'd been dating, my job had been a bone of contention between us—he didn't like the danger I placed myself in, and I hadn't been a fan of his overprotectiveness.

Over the years, he'd become more accepting, but he still struggled on occasion.

"You're okay?"

"I'm absolutely fine. How's work?"

"We signed a new trade deal with Japan."

"Exciting."

"Necessary. Why did you message me?"

"I'm just curious. I'm going to give you a name, and I want you to tell me if you've heard it before. Maybe at a briefing or something."

"What's the name?"

"Ottilie Marquette."

Oh, he'd heard the name all right. I knew his face too, including the expression of shock-slash-surprise he tried to cover up.

Interesting.

"Why do you ask?"

"I bumped into her earlier, and she rang a few alarm bells. In St. Petersburg." This time, the surprise was absent. "Oh, you already knew about that."

"Where is she?"

"First, tell me why you want to know."

"We're not playing games here, Linny." He still used my old nickname when his wife wasn't around. Or my husband. "This is a matter of national security."

"Then tell me why you want to know."

I smiled. Waited. I was holding all the cards, and James understood that. He was far from stupid, which made a pleasant change from his predecessor.

"We're on a secure line," I prompted.

James sighed. "Ottilie Marquette is a scientist at the Sandy Peake Defense Research Laboratory. Specifically, she was involved in creating mission guidance software. A bona fide genius, so they tell me. Two years ago, she was seconded to a more...experimental team. Project Marshmallow was tasked with creating—"

"Project *Marshmallow*?"

"I didn't come up with the name."

"Now I'm hungry."

"Want me to send a care package?"

"I'll never turn down food. Project Marshmallow? What did it involve?"

"The creation of a non-lethal, medium-range weapon that could be used to clear an area in a hurry. Basically, it was designed to cause an immense amount of temporary pain. I can't claim to understand everything about the technology, but lasers, radar, and millimetre rays were involved."

"Millimetre rays?"

"Longer than X-rays, shorter than microwaves."

Yup, he'd been briefed. Hell, he'd probably asked the same question. James was a man who liked to know the answers.

"How far did they get with it?"

"They built a prototype, but there were teething troubles. It was too easy to cook a person."

"*Cook* them? As in medium rare?"

He nodded. "Silently. Invisibly. From a mile away."

"I see how that could be an issue."

"The bigger issue is that five weeks ago, the weapon disappeared, along with Ottilie Marquette. I don't think I need to tell you how big of a problem that is. If this thing gets into the wrong hands, thousands of people could die, and on the black market, it would be worth millions."

Well, shit.

"And you haven't found any trace of Ottie and the ray gun or whatever it's called?"

"Not until you called. We thought she'd gone to Russia."

"Russia? Why Russia?"

"The investigation team recovered several deleted emails

from the network at Sandy Peake, and they connected those messages to associates of President Markovich."

The head honcho in Russia. Now I got it. Kind of.

"If Ottie was such a genius, and she worked with software, no less, why would she be careless enough to leave deleted messages floating around in the system?"

"Precisely what I asked. She wiped out her other work, and that's gone for good, but it could be a double bluff. I took a chance and spoke with Markovich, and he swears he wasn't involved. He's also incredibly nervous in case somebody tries to pin the theft or any subsequent use of the weapon on him."

"So he says."

I didn't trust the Russian establishment, not even a little bit.

"He's walking on a tightrope. Members of the old guard aren't happy that he's rooting out corruption and building bridges with the West, and those that do agree with his politics are cynical about his motives."

Which was understandable. The Russian government was full of traitors and spies who'd stab a man in the back at the first opportunity. Lies were more common than the truth. Greed was so widespread that any hint of altruism was viewed with suspicion.

And Markovich hadn't even been elected as president. No, he'd been a puppet prime minister until his boss died and he inherited the job. There were many who'd like to see him suffer the same fate as his predecessor. But I had to agree with James that Markovich was the least bad option right now, and over the past three years, he'd been taking steps in the right direction when it came to both foreign relations and domestic policy.

"Are you one of the cynics?" I asked.

James hesitated for a long moment. "Yes, but I also believe this is the best chance we've had in decades to improve global stability, and we can't afford to squander it. If news of the Marshmallow theft gets out, it'll finish Markovich."

"Hence the raid in St. Petersburg?"

"Hence the raid in St. Petersburg. So, I ask again—where's Ottilie Marquette?"

"At this moment? In a medically induced coma." Oh, he hadn't been expecting that. "And before she checked in to the hospital, she was hiding out with a friend. James, I don't think she took the weapon. If she did, she'd either be sitting in a corner office in a Russian lab or sipping mai tais in a non-extradition country."

"How did she end up in the coma?"

"Yesterday morning, she was beaten to within an inch of her life. Her assailant got interrupted by a dog, which gave her enough space to scream, and Ana and I happened to be nearby."

"Why?"

"Why were we nearby?"

"Yes."

"We were waiting for Bradley to finish buying yarn."

"Yarn?"

"And also Alex was running a half-marathon in Portland. Did you sponsor him? It was for a good cause."

"Yes, I sponsored him. Can we stick with the subject at hand?"

"You were the one who changed it. And in answer to your next question, no, we don't have any idea who hurt her, but they planned it. Poisoned her dog so she'd leave the property she was staying at, and in all likelihood took out a security camera three days ago in an attempt to cover their tracks. How big is the weapon?"

"The size of an AR-15, but bulkier because of the power pack. But even the batteries aren't so big because they use new technology."

"If it was in the studio apartment she's been staying in, it's not there now because someone turned the place over. I can ask the friend tomorrow, see if Ottie brought any other luggage, but she didn't mention it." I thought back to the room, to the upturned drawers, to the slashed cushions and the torn books. Had the culprits been faking a burglary? Or searching for something small? My money was on the latter because if the weapon had been there, why announce their presence so blatantly when all they had to do was pick it up, zip it into a suitcase, and wheel it out the front door? "You want my take on this?"

"Always."

"Someone who doesn't much like Markovich took the weapon, and for whatever reason, they need something Ottie has to make it work. That's why they didn't just put a bullet in her brain when they had the chance. She had cigarette burns too. Whoever got ahold of her was trying to make her talk."

James cursed under his breath. "How bad are the injuries? Will she wake up?"

"I don't know, but I can find out more in the morning."

"It *is* morning."

"Barely."

"Where are you?"

"On the West Coast."

"I'll arrange a team to meet you."

"Not so fast, dude. Don't come steaming in. Think about it—whoever wants what Ottie has tried to get it today, and they failed. Sure as shit they'll try again, and the best chance you have of finding your marshmallow is to watch her. Discreetly. And she needs protection."

"That can be arranged."

"Good, but do it quietly. Don't have the Feds land a helicopter on the roof of the fucking hospital and go running in with their guns drawn. If our suspects are staking the place out, they'll melt back into the shadows and maybe you'll never find them."

"I'll make sure they come in cars. Plain clothes. Where's Ottilie now?"

"Coos Bay, Oregon. Someone needs to tell her parents. I believe they live in Massachusetts."

"We're in contact with the parents. Coos Bay? That's south of Portland?"

"A three-hour drive."

"Is that three hours with you behind the wheel?"

My driving was another thing James wasn't enamoured with. But I rarely hit anything unintentionally, unlike my friend Dan who mostly stuck to the speed limits and wrote off a car every other month.

"Traffic was light."

"So we're looking at a four-hour drive, plus a couple of hours to get a team together. Could you watch Marquette this morning to buy us time?"

"I could, but there's another problem."

James groaned. "You have no idea how much I hate those words."

"Ottie was camping out at a local resort. The owner knows her name, and so do the staff, and her friend, plus there are deputies sniffing around. Somebody needs to do damage control if you want to keep a lid on this."

"Dammit. Can you speak with the friend? Pay off the resort owner?"

"I can try, but the owner's the son of a Russian oligarch, so..."

This time, James let fly with a whole string of curses. Most unpresidential.

"Russian? You think he's involved with this?"

"I might edge towards a 'no,' but I'm not going to commit either way right now. And I don't have a clue whether he's a Markovich supporter. I'll get Mack to nose around."

"What's his name?"

"Nikolai Belinsky. The father was Lev."

"I'll have my people take a look too. Are you alone in Oregon?"

"Ana's with me, plus Alex and Hallie."

"Hallie's the new girl? The one dating the cop?"

"That's right."

"Can you send them to the hospital while you deal with Belinsky and the rest? It's only for half a day."

"We'll have to talk about the fee..."

"Send the invoice to the usual place, and we'll wash it through. I owe you one, Linny."

"Mr. President, you owe me hundreds of favours by now."

He blew me a kiss, and then he was gone.

And just like that, Ottie Marquette became my problem.

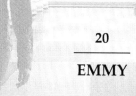

20

EMMY

"**W**here's Alex?"

Ana groaned into the phone. "How should I know? Probably asleep, same as the rest of us at whatever time this is."

"A quarter to six, and his phone's going to voicemail."

"The battery probably quit."

For crying out loud. Hadn't he heard of a charger?

"Get your arse over here. Ottie Marquette has turned into a headache, more of a migraine, actually, and we need to get to the hospital. I'll wake Hallie for a briefing."

But fifteen minutes later, after a hasty shower and a double espresso from the machine in my room, I was as worried about Alex as I was about Ottie.

"His room hasn't been slept in," I told Ana. "I checked."

"You're sure? He didn't just make the bed himself?"

Alex was a neat freak. Mrs. Fairfax, the housekeeper at the estate I owned with my husband, said that whenever he stayed at Riverley, he left his room tidier than it had been when he arrived. So it was a fair comment. But no, he hadn't simply made the bed this morning.

"Maybe he went for an early run," Hallie suggested.

"His bag isn't there."

I'd watched Alex dump his duffel into the back of Darya's compact after dinner last night. Bradley had handed him his room key, but he hadn't used it, and now I was getting worried. Because our new case had a Russian connection, and Darya was not only Russian but also deadly.

I gave Ana and Hallie a quick rundown of my discussion with James.

"So now Alex is missing, Ottie's in the hospital, and we've got a first-class Russian assassin tangled up in the middle of it all."

"Dasha wouldn't hurt Alex." Ana was adamant. "You don't know her the way I do. Alex—Alexei—was perhaps the first man in her entire life who showed her any sort of kindness. She used to fall asleep at night wrapped up in his fucking coat. In those days, it reached her knees."

"Then where is he? She was meant to bring him back to the hotel, and as far as he knows, we're leaving for the airport soon."

"Maybe he stayed at her place?"

"Firstly, Alex doesn't do hook-ups, and secondly, he'd have sent a message if he'd changed his plans. Where does Darya even live? Do you have a phone number for her?"

Ana shook her head. "Only an email address. She was cagey, but I know the hell she's been through. I didn't want to push her."

"You want me to try and find the address?" Hallie asked.

Hallie was young and not particularly experienced, but she was also smart and resourceful as well as gutsy, which was why we'd hired her to work for Blackwood in the first place.

"Go for it."

She slipped out the door, and I cursed under my breath. Ottie

Marquette was lying unguarded, and now we were wasting time. How did other people manage to take vacations? All I wanted was a couple of days of R & R, and shit just *happened*. This was my second attempt at a minibreak in as many months, and the second time I'd found myself doing anything but relaxing.

While Hallie did her stuff, I got ready for, well, anything. I had zero desire to go up against Nine again, but I would if I had to. Alex was more than a trainer; he'd been a friend for nearly two decades.

"Should we wake Bradley?" Ana asked.

"Let him get his beauty sleep."

Ten minutes later, Hallie came back.

"It's a pale-blue ranch-style home on Valley Drive. White picket fence, a single-car garage to the side, and a pink mailbox with flowers painted on it."

"Dare I ask how you know that?"

"They sell Darla's dresses in the boutique here, so I figured somebody must know her. And it's a small town. Everyone's real friendly. I told the guy at the reception desk that I'd borrowed her jacket yesterday and I needed to return it before I went back to Virginia, but I'd lost the piece of paper with the address." Hallie grinned. "He was pleased to help out. What happens now?"

"Now, me and Ana get to see if she's home."

"Should I wait here?"

"No, in the car. And if we don't come out within twenty minutes, you call the cavalry."

A surprise approach was almost impossible. I'd spotted three pinhole cameras watching us at the Craft Cabin, and there were probably more. I had no doubt Darya had electronic eyes all over the place, and she'd want to protect her home.

But we could make things more difficult.

As we approached the property, I switched on a jammer, which would take out wireless comms operating on any frequency but ours. What was lurking behind the floral curtains? The place lay in darkness, silent, no signs of life whatsoever, but Darya's red Honda was parked in the driveway. A decoy? Did she have access to another vehicle?

The residence sat on a good-sized lot with nice high hedges and no line of sight to the neighbours. Was that why she'd chosen it? For the privacy? If I'd been house-shopping in Baldwin's Shore, this place would have made the shortlist. Minus the twee decor, of course. A real estate agent would have described it as a "cosy family home."

"Garage has space for another vehicle," Ana said in my earpiece. She'd skirted around the south side of the house while I'd checked out the north.

"So she could have taken off."

"I still think you're wrong on this. Dasha's been in Baldwin's Shore for years. Ottie Marquette's been here for less than two months."

"Maybe Nine recognised her. Called an old acquaintance. You said yourself she's good with faces."

"Marquette stayed at the Peninsula, and Dasha rarely goes there."

"Rarely isn't never. Hallie said she sells her dresses in the boutique."

"How would she know people were looking for Marquette?"

"Neither of us knows what her network's like." What if she'd heard whispers, spotted the target, and seen the opportunity for an easy pay-off? Only for us to come sniffing around with the potential to upset her plans? Perhaps she'd been in the forest that day to finish Ottie off rather than save her? She could have snatched Alex as a distraction. "Call me cautious. Master bedroom's empty."

Darya hadn't rolled down the blinds, and her bed looked as cold as Alex's.

"Quiet on this side too. What do you want to do?"

"Is she likely to have booby-trapped the place?"

A long pause. "Probably, but the devices will be well-hidden. This was meant to be her long-term home, and she wouldn't have risked drawing attention to herself."

Great. "We'll have to go in." What other choice did we have? "Maybe we'll find a clue to her whereabouts?"

"Oh, you think? Dasha isn't a fool. If she's turned as you believe, she'll have sanitised the place."

"Well, what other leads do we have?"

Ana sighed in my ear. "Fine, we'll go in. Front, back, or window?"

"Window." If she'd set a trap, it would be easier to spot on a window. "I'll cut out the glass."

And I'd do it quickly because Ottie Marquette's hospital room was wide open right now.

21

NINE

At first, I thought the pounding in my head had woken me.

Where was I? The basement. I'd slept in the basement again. I took a split second to orient myself, then rolled to the side. And nearly stood on Alex. In sleep, he looked peaceful, stretched out on the floor with one arm crossed over his stomach and the other flung out across the floor. But why the hell was he still here?

And why was my smartwatch vibrating?

I glanced at the screen and saw the words I'd always dreaded.

Signal interrupted.

When I glanced over at my monitors, my extra eyes, all was well at the Craft Cabin and my rural hideaway, but the screens for my home were blank. They'd taken out part of my network. The feeds from the hardwired router were still running, but the local wireless cameras were dead.

And Alex was in my space. A virtual stranger. A virtual stranger I'd put on a pedestal in my mind, but still a man I barely knew.

Where was my gun? He'd taken it from me last night, and I'd thought he was being sweet, but now it was gone, and— It was still on the side table. I grabbed it, checked there was a live round in the chamber as there should be, and aimed at his head.

"Wake up."

Just for good measure, I gave him a kick, and his eyes flew open.

"What the—"

"Who are they?"

The console opposite the stairs began beeping. Another alarm tripped.

"Who are who?"

"Who did you lead to my home? Seven? That English bitch? Stay where you are!"

Alex had rolled to his knees, but at my command, he held up his hands. "Dasha, I don't know what you're talking about."

"Don't you call me that. To you, I'm Nine."

"You're not Nine, not anymore."

"So I thought, but it seems I have no choice. Lie on your front."

"I didn't bring anyone here."

"Then who jammed my cameras? You're in town, and Seven's in town. The bitch was right—there are no coincidences."

"You think Emmy is doing this? Give me my phone, and I'll call her."

"Nice try. There's no signal down here anyway."

"Then let me go upstairs."

"So it becomes four against one?"

Although I'd only count Hallie as a half. She was no operator.

"If Emmy's here, then she's probably looking for me. I didn't call in last night, and I should have."

"So why didn't she just knock on the damn door?"

"Because she doesn't trust people easily, and yesterday, you tried to kill her. If the positions were reversed, how would you respond?"

Okay, so I wouldn't have knocked on the door. And maybe I'd have used a jammer as a precaution.

"Do you have a landline?" Alex asked.

"Of course I do."

"Then let me call her. If I make any wrong moves, you can shoot me. I know you're capable."

"And if it's not Emmy?"

"Then there are two of us against whoever is upstairs."

Was Alex telling the truth? I really didn't want to shoot him. Disposing of dead bodies was a pain in the ass. But he was right—I'd do it if I had to. And then I'd get the hell out of Baldwin's Shore. The weapons locker doubled as a panic room, and there was a hidden trapdoor in the ceiling. I could stock up on hardware, then surprise whoever was waiting above before I left town.

"The phone is to the left of the screens. Move slowly. Keep your hands in the air until you get there."

He did as instructed, then lowered one hand to dial and switched the phone onto speaker.

"No secrets," he told me as it rang.

"Control room."

"It's Alex. I need to speak to Emmy."

"She's on radio silence."

"Then I need you to patch me through."

"She's in the middle of—"

"I know exactly where she is. Patch me through right now."

The next voice I heard was Emmy's. "Alex? Where the fuck are you?"

"I'm with Dasha. Everything's fine, and she'd like her cameras back."

"Everything's fine? How do I know you don't have a gun to your head?"

Alex gave me a weak smile. "I'd email a picture, but you're jamming the signal. Dasha wants to know why you didn't just knock on the damn door?"

"Because new information has come to light."

What new information? Alex looked at me, and I shrugged.

"Unblock the signal, and we can talk about this over coffee like civilised people."

"Where are you?"

"At Dasha's place."

"The house is empty."

"No, it's not. It just looks that way. Emmy, we drank too much liquor and fell asleep. There's nothing more to it."

A pause. "What's the name of my dog?"

I knew what Emmy was doing. Testing me. If Alex gave the wrong answer, I'd never know, but she would.

"Lucy."

A second later, the cameras blinked back on, and I saw Ana and Emmy standing by my dining-room window. Nice choice. The walls around it were clear, and they could climb down onto the sideboard. The sideboard itself had a built-in pressure sensor and was packed with enough explosives to level the entire house, but they'd only blow if I armed them. And today, I wouldn't do that.

"Now go and wait by the front door."

Alex hung up the phone, and I tucked my semi-automatic into my waistband.

"I'm sorry I pointed a gun at your head." Fuck, this was awkward. "And kicked you."

Alex held out a hand. "I think the lesson we take from today is that we all need to learn to communicate better."

"You're not mad at me?"

"I know why you reacted the way you did, so no, I'm not mad. But I'll be upset if you do it again. Come on."

He twitched his fingers, and I stared at his hand. Did I want to take it? Sure, I'd had my hands all over him last night, but this was different. It was also Alexei.

I took his hand.

"Better." This time, I got a proper smile. "I'll make you coffee."

"My head hurts. And my ribs."

"Your ribs? Did I injure you?"

"No, Emmy did."

"What? Why didn't you say anything? I was rolling you on the floor last night."

"So? Bruises are not a valid excuse for slacking." I shrugged. "And I needed the training."

Alex let out a calming breath, resigned. "We'll find you painkillers."

Ana and Emmy were waiting at the front door as instructed, and when Alex tugged it open, I glared at both of them.

"Haven't you ever heard of a doorbell?"

Ana rolled her eyes. "I said we should knock."

That, I believed. Emmy was the problem, not Ana.

And she folded her arms. "I'm sorry I disabled your cameras, okay? I was worried about Alex. He wasn't answering the phone."

He glanced at me. "There are issues with the signal in some parts of the house."

Now Emmy smiled. "Ah, so there's a basement?"

Pizdets, why did he have to give that away?

"I should have messaged you last night. That's on me, and it won't happen again."

"Good. Where's your bag? You need to get to the hospital."

"The hospital? Why?"

"The Marquette thing is bigger than we first thought." She locked eyes with me. "And then there's the Russian connection."

She just had to get the digs in, didn't she?

"Don't look at me that way. I'm not the only Russian in Baldwin's Shore. Try starting with Belinsky."

"That's where I'm going after I've dropped Alex, Ana, and Hallie at the hospital. Which reminds me..." She pulled out her phone and tapped at the screen. "I'd better tell Hallie to stand down."

"Have you noticed any other Russians in town?" Ana asked. "Apart from Belinsky?"

"Who didn't move here because of you, by the way," Emmy added. "He built the resort to get back at his ex's new beau."

"How do you know that?"

"Because he told me."

"And you believed him? What if he lied?"

"He had no reason to. I understand why your default setting is to assume that everyone's lying, and I've been known to fall into that pattern myself, but just occasionally, people tell the truth."

And sometimes, the truth hurt, especially when it came from Emmy's lips. I'd been manipulated my whole life, I knew that, and in turn, I'd done the same to others. The truth was a rarity in my world. At least, it had been until I moved to Baldwin's Shore.

"I've met four other Russians here in the last month. Two

female tourists who came to the Craft Cabin, a truck driver who delivered an order of embroidery floss, and Boris. But Boris has lived here for longer than I have, and he's in his late sixties, so whatever you're investigating, he's probably not involved. Will you tell me what's going on?"

When Emmy hesitated, Alex spoke.

"I know why you also find it hard to trust people, but Dasha isn't the enemy. Take a chance."

And that... Why was there a fucking lump in my throat? I'd been such a bitch to Alex earlier, and now he was defending me.

Emmy gave me a hard look, but then she sighed. "Ottie Marquette is a scientist. She worked at a defence laboratory in California, and she was involved in developing a really fucked-up weapon. And five weeks ago, both the weapon and Ottie went missing."

She'd stolen it? No, no, that didn't make sense. If she'd taken the risk of stealing a weapon, there would have been a buyer waiting with enough money for her to start a new life in a non-extradition country. Unless they'd double-crossed her. She'd been hiding in Baldwin's Shore, that much was obvious. But if her enemies wanted her dead, why hadn't they simply killed her? Why search her room? Had she held something back from the deal? Or was she innocent, and they needed her knowledge to operate their new toy?

Whichever, she needed to stay alive.

"You should get your things," I told Alex.

"*Da*."

He followed me into the house, and I closed the door to keep Emmy and Ana out. They'd violated my existence enough already this weekend. Alex's bag was still in my vehicle, but his jacket and his boots were in the basement. He put the boots on, but when I tried to hand him the jacket, he shook his head.

"Keep it."

Huh? "Why?"

"A replacement for the one you lost." He took my hand again and tugged me closer. "I like the idea of you wearing it."

Then he kissed me. Just a closed-mouth peck, but on the lips rather than the cheek, and I hadn't been prepared. Hadn't been prepared for the rush of warmth that would flood through me, or for the backflip my stomach did.

He leaned his forehead against mine. "And I *will* come back to Oregon."

"To see me?"

"Don't have any other reason to visit."

That stupid lump was back. *Alexei.* Once, he'd been the only person in my life who cared, even briefly, and he still cared.

"I'd... I'd like that. Do you want me to drive you to the hospital? The craft store doesn't open until ten. Then Emmy can go straight to Belinsky."

And I could spend another half hour in his company.

"You don't mind doing that?"

"Give me five minutes to change."

I'd have to go as Darla. Which might even be advantageous because some of the nurses bought craft supplies from me, plus I taught a children's creativity session at the hospital once a month, so maybe I could smooth a path into Marquette's room? Introduce Alex as a relative. Or Hallie, that would work better. She and Marquette shared the same waifish build and pale skin.

Under the wig, my hair was still presentable. Darla had never been the epitome of style anyway. I threw one of her baggy dresses over my jeans and turtleneck, then put my boots back on. One advantage of my new-found crafting skills was that I'd been able to modify the boots to hold all sorts of goodies that might come in useful someday.

My mouth tasted disgusting, so thank fuck Alex hadn't tried anything with tongues or I'd have put him off for life. I brushed my teeth for thirty seconds, then swallowed a couple of painkillers dry and jogged back through the house. The street was quiet at this time in the morning. The only person who got up early on a Sunday was Maggie Fothergill. She liked to take her cat for a walk on a little leash every day, come rain, come shine, even when the cat clearly hated the idea.

Alex was waiting outside with Ana and Hallie, and Emmy was nowhere in sight. Good. He didn't take my hand as we walked to the car, but he did open the driver's door for me, which was a first.

"Don't forget I owe you coffee," he murmured, too quietly for the others to hear.

My chest did some fluttery thing that reminded me of palpitations. Was I sick? Perhaps I could get the doctor to run an ECG while we were at the hospital?

"I never forget a thing."

22

EMMY

"It's seven o'clock in the morning, Mrs. Black. This had better be good."

"This is no more pleasurable for me than it is for you, I can guarantee that."

I'd woken Nico up. My call had gone to voicemail, so I'd let myself into his villa—its location was obvious by the "Private - Keep Out" signs—and roused him personally. To give him credit, he didn't try to throw me out or have his security staff do it either. But the two men I'd slipped past would probably get a stern talking-to later.

"Want me to make coffee while you put some clothes on?"

Turned out he slept naked, which was slightly awkward, but he did have nice abs.

"If you wouldn't mind."

He didn't bother with a shirt, just materialised in the kitchen two minutes later in a pair of grey flannel trousers and bare feet. Winter in Oregon, and his home was hotter than the tropics. Guess he didn't lose much sleep over global warming.

"Espresso? Cappuccino? Latte? You strike me as a latte kind of guy."

"Americano."

"Should I add a shot of vodka? You look as if you need it."

"Did you break into my home just to insult me, or was there another reason?"

"Usually I charge big bucks for a security audit, but I did yours for free. Sadly, it was a fail." The coffee machine whirred away. I slid his Americano across the marble breakfast bar and took a seat opposite. "But yeah, there's a reason I'm here."

"Which is?"

"Why did you leave Russia, Nico?"

"Now you want my life story?"

"Just curious."

The cogs turned, and I knew what he was thinking: *how can I get rid of this woman?* Fortunately, he decided that the fastest way was to answer the question.

"My late father had two hotels in his portfolio, and I soon realised the leisure industry was where I wanted to focus my time."

"You didn't want to follow in your father's footsteps? He was big in mining, right?"

Not coal mining, but nickel and copper. Blackwood's research team had emailed me a bio overnight. But although there was plenty of information on finances, it had been light on Belinsky family dynamics, and just for a second, I saw Nico's eyes cloud when I mentioned his father. A blink, and the darkness was gone.

"Mining didn't interest me. I sold off those holdings and all the other investments I didn't care for and began to put my own stamp on the business. Not many tourists have Russia on their bucket lists."

"You leaving had nothing to do with political changes?"

He seemed genuinely puzzled. "I stay out of politics."

"How do you feel about President Markovich?"

"I think all politicians are self-serving assholes, Markovich included. But perhaps he's marginally better than the last guy. We could have discussed the Russian government over dinner, Mrs. Black. You didn't need to stroll into my bedroom, although I'll admit I've been woken up in worse ways. If you weren't married, I can't say I'd be upset about that."

Ah, there was the playboy. I liked Nico. He didn't waste time on bullshit.

"If I wasn't married, then maybe I'd consider having the conversation over dinner, but I am, so..." I shrugged. "Yesterday, the situation with Ottie Marquette piqued my interest, and I made some calls. Turns out she might be part of something far bigger than we thought."

"And politics is involved?"

"Possibly. The powers that be would like to keep the events here quiet, which is difficult when Leona's upset and you've been questioning your staff."

"Let me guess—you want me to tuck Leona out of the way and spin a story to the staff?"

"You're more than just a pretty face, Nico. Would you mind?"

"What would I get out of the deal?"

"That's a question I've been asking myself. I get the feeling that bunging you a few quid under the table wouldn't work?"

He just laughed, as I'd expected him to.

"So how about a favour? I don't give those out easily, and I always pay up."

Nico took a sip of his coffee and walked to the window. He had a nice view of the gardens. Not as nice as the view from the other side of the house—the great room looked out over the ocean and his private dock—but there were definitely worse places to live.

"And when would this favour be available?"

"Anytime after I've finished dealing with the Marquette mess."

"Emerson Black... I looked at hiring Blackwood Security once, but I wasn't sure the company would be a good fit."

"Really? And why was that?"

"I thought a big firm like yours would be too rigid. Too black and white. But now that I've met you, I'm not so sure. You're fifty shades of grey, Mrs. Black."

"I'm not into spanking, if that's what you're asking."

"A shame. It can be extremely pleasurable." He took a sip of coffee. "I'm looking for a woman."

"Can't you just open your little black book and pick a number?"

"A particular woman. Her name is Kaylin."

"Is this the favour? You mislaid one of your harem?"

"Kaylin and I were never involved, not in that way. She was more of a...a sister, I suppose."

"You suppose?"

"My father had a relationship with her mother. She was his mistress. He had a lot of those, but Renée lasted longer than most. A model, an American model, and she had a child. I guess that when she gave birth, she couldn't have been much more than a child herself because she was in her early twenties when she was with Papa, and Kaylin was eight."

Nico Belinsky was full of surprises. He'd cared enough about a child that he wanted to use up a diamond of a favour on looking for the woman she'd become?

"How old is she now?"

"Eight years younger than me, so twenty-six. I've had a man searching for the past year, but he hasn't gotten anywhere."

Interesting, but where was the grey in this case?

"Isn't this a straightforward missing persons enquiry? Any number of good agencies would have taken it on. Unless of course she's wanted for murder or something."

"Funny you should say that." Nico smiled, but there was

no humour in it. Ah, shit. "I've only spoken to Kaylin once since my father got rid of her mother."

"When you say 'got rid of,' are we talking literally or figuratively?"

"I see you've googled Papa. She fell out of a window, and truthfully, I have no idea whether he was involved." But Nico didn't say it wasn't possible. Maybe Zacharov had made a rare good call when he added Belinsky Senior to his shitlist. "I read a news report online. *Model dies in midnight accident.* The article said Kaylin had gone to live with her grandmother in Virginia."

"My home turf."

"Indeed. Strange how the world works, isn't it?"

"You think she stayed local?"

"I have no idea where she might be."

"Tell me about the last time you spoke to her."

"I was leaving my lawyer's office in New York, and there she was on the sidewalk. And she looked so much like her mother that I just stared, and she must have felt my gaze on her because she turned her head, and then she recognised me. And she smiled. So I invited her to join me for lunch, then regretted it because I didn't need that reminder of the past." Nico kept his eyes focused on the window, but I could see him reflected in the glass. He looked anything but happy. "I went to a therapist once—just once—and she told me I wasn't responsible for the sins of my father. But she wasn't there, in Russia, and I was. I did things I'm not proud of, but I can't change the past."

"Only the future."

"The future... Kaylin had become a model, following in her mother's footsteps. She showed me her portfolio—all small stuff, but she seemed happy with the way things were going. Said she'd get her big break soon. I should have hired her, used her in an ad campaign or had her do some promo shots, but the guilt was eating away at me, so I paid the check and wished her well. And then I waved goodbye."

"How long ago was this?"

"Five years, give or take."

So the trail was nice and cold now. Fantastic.

"That was the last contact you had, and then you heard she'd got into a spot of legal trouble?"

"It was the last time I spoke to her, but it wasn't the last time she spoke to me."

"You'll have to elaborate."

"Before she left the restaurant in New York, I handed her my card. Said if she ever needed anything, she should give me a call." Finally, he turned to face me. "That was the guilt talking again. In truth, I never expected to hear from her. It was the sort of comment you make to a barfly on vacation—call me if you're in town, we'll hook up. You know?" He studied me. "Or perhaps you don't."

"I've never been one for bars or hook-ups. When did you hear from her?"

"A little over three years ago. She left me a message, but I was travelling at the time, and I didn't pick it up for twenty-four hours. When I got there, I found that I was too late."

"Got where? Too late for what? What did the message say?"

"That she'd run into trouble, and she didn't know who else to turn to. She sounded, well...terrified. She asked me to meet her in a hotel in Manassas, but by the time I'd chartered a jet and flown there, she'd gone, and the place was festooned in crime-scene tape."

"Who died?"

"An off-duty cop. They say she ran him over and left him for dead, but Kaylin wasn't a killer. Not the girl I knew. She was the only ray of sunshine in a house of darkness. When her mother was entertaining Papa, Kaylin was left to her own devices, and she'd follow me around, telling me stories and showing me drawings, and of course I acted annoyed, but she was always so cheerful about the small things that it was hard to keep up the pretence."

"People change as they get older."

"She didn't. The Kaylin I met in New York was still an eternal optimist."

"What's her last name?"

"La Rocca. Kaylin Marie La Rocca."

The case rang a bell. I'd seen the story on the news. An off-duty cop had left a family dinner to walk home one night, and his colleagues stumbled over him in the gutter the next morning with a tyre track across his chest.

"They found the car that hit him, didn't they? And it was registered to her?"

"So they say."

"You don't believe it?"

"I don't believe the story the police told, no."

"So what do you think happened?"

"I'm not a detective, Mrs. Black, but I'm a good judge of character. I can't give you a timetable of events that night, but I can say that the Kaylin I knew would have called an ambulance if she'd hit a man, not driven off into the sunset. And she contacted me—scared—before the incident, not after." Nico gave a weighty sigh. "I don't know whether she's dead or alive, but her fate has been weighing on my mind for three years, and I'd like some kind of closure. For her and for me."

"I'm surprised she didn't end up in Baldwin's Shore. Every other motherfucker on the run seems to."

He found that amusing. "So you've heard about Skip?"

"I was talking about Ottie. Who's Skip?"

"An armed robber who stole millions of bucks' worth of gold. He used to run a bar at the far end of Main Street."

"Applejack's?"

"The new owner changed the name. It used to be called Beer Me Up, and there was a flying saucer in the parking lot."

"This is quite an entertaining little town, isn't it?"

"The place keeps me amused. So, do you accept the favour? I'm not asking you to solve the mystery because I know that might not be possible, but I'd like you to review the case. If you find a lead and more work is needed, then funds are available."

One of the advantages of being married to a rich guy was that I could pick and choose the cases I took. I gravitated towards the more challenging jobs, the ones that made me think, and yeah, sometimes the more dangerous ones too. Cheating death gave an adrenaline rush like no other.

"No guarantees, but we'll take a look."

"Thank you." He took a seat again, and I got another eyeful of his chest. Luckily, I'd seen enough chiselled pecs not to get distracted, but he really was quite dishy. "How do you want to approach the Marquette situation?"

"Play up the villainous ex-boyfriend angle, play down everything else."

"If it helps, I asked her doctor to instruct staff on the front desk not to release her name if anyone enquired. Nice guy—he has a gym membership here. Anyhow, she's in the system as Jane Doe."

"If I wasn't married, I might kiss you for that."

Nico flashed me a pearly smile. "Yes, well, I thought that if whoever didn't kill her found out she was still alive, they might make another attempt."

"It's still possible they could do that."

Likely, even. If I were working for the other side, the first places I'd look for Ottie would be the hospital and the morgue. But Nico's subterfuge might have bought us a few hours. Long enough for backup to arrive and take over.

"She's in sight of a nurses' station."

Which wouldn't help much if someone showed up with a gun.

"Private room?"

"Of course, and I even arranged for an en-suite."

No doubt Ottie and her catheter would appreciate the thought.

"Are you looking for extra brownie points, Mr. Belinsky?"

He grinned. "Credit where credit's due. But in all seriousness, the new ICU unit in Coos Bay is a state-of-the-art facility. They're in the process of refurbishing the entire hospital."

"I'm sure it's very shiny, but a pro could get in there in a heartbeat."

Hospitals were an assassin's dream. Few cameras because of privacy, HIPAA, blah, blah, high staff turnover, visitors coming and going at all hours, and people were practically expected to die there. Kill a patient in the right way, and everyone thought it was a tragic accident.

"Are you including yourself among the pros?" Nico asked.

"No comment. Don't you have a tearful yoga teacher to influence?"

Nico rose. "I'll have breakfast with Leona. Steer her in the right direction. We're talking with Colt and Luca at nine."

"My chat with them is at eight thirty."

"Will you need to extend your stay again?"

"I'm not sure right now. If the acronyms show up on time, we might be able to leave. Are rooms available tonight if we need them?"

"I'll check. But if they're not, I have three spare bedrooms here."

"Your hospitality is much appreciated."

"Just make sure this person gets caught, Mrs. Black. Although if he stays in Baldwin's Shore, our neighbourhood vigilante might step in, which wouldn't necessarily be a bad thing."

"You have a neighbourhood vigilante?"

"Luca nicknamed him the Bad Samaritan." Nico chuckled. "I do believe he might think it's me."

Really? I didn't, not for a minute. Not because I didn't think Nico was capable, but because I knew exactly who the Bad Samaritan was. Darya and her fucking "decorating."

"And is it you?"

Another laugh. "No, but sometimes when the right man loses his head, it's tempting to send a thank-you card."

"He decapitated somebody?"

"Not decapitated, per se. He took a man out with a sniper rifle from eight hundred yards."

Oh, Darya had all the skills, didn't she?

"Ouch. What else has he done?"

"Scarred a rapist for life and forced a murderer to make a full confession."

"You want my advice? Forget the thank-you card and send chocolates."

Nico leaned in to kiss me on the cheek, and his lips lingered for a touch too long. "I'll have breakfast delivered to your room, Mrs. Black."

"Statistically speaking, it's usually the husband. Or the boyfriend. Do you know if he's local?"

Nico had provided a meeting room for my chat with Luca, plus coffee and pastries. After three espressos, I'd switched to regular old black, a move I was now regretting because I was in desperate need of a bathroom break.

Luca shook his head apologetically. In the end, he'd come

alone while the other deputy dealt with a missing goat. Baldwin's Shore really was a hotbed of crime.

"I'm afraid I can't comment on an ongoing investigation."

I shrugged. *Suit yourself.* "Well, according to Leona, Ottie had issues with the ex, so I know where I'd start looking. Is there any news on Ottie's condition?"

"There's been no change overnight."

"I guess under the circumstances, we should take that as a good sign. What about her dog?"

Now Luca smiled. "Brooke—my fiancée—spoke with the veterinarian first thing. The dog's vitals have improved, and it should make a full recovery."

"Thank goodness for small mercies, eh? Can Leona take care of it for a while?"

"If she can't, Brooke's offered. We already have one dog, and her boss won't mind her bringing an extra mutt to work as long as it gets along with the cat."

"Her boss is Darla, right? From the Craft Cabin?"

"Right. Did Darla seem okay yesterday? After the incident? I've been trying to get ahold of her this morning, but she's not answering the phone."

Mental note: ask Darya to speak with Luca. Nobody, least of all her, could afford to arouse his suspicions.

"She seemed a little shaken up afterwards. Maybe she had a sleepless night?"

"Brooke said you lent a hand with the clean-up at the store?"

"It seemed like the least we could do, and my personal assistant adores crafts. He was about to buy half the stock before yesterday's emergency, but I'm sure he'll make good before we leave."

"How much longer will you be in town?"

"Depends when we can get a flight. Can't say I'd be

heartbroken to stay an extra day or two—the spa here is pretty good."

"Well, I'll try not to take up too much more of your time. Could we just go through the events in the forest one more time?"

"Sure."

"You say you saw no sign of Ms. Marquette's assailant whatsoever?"

"He'd gone by the time we arrived. Perhaps the dog scared him off? Or bit him? Did you check with the local hospitals for dog-bite victims?"

"That's on my to-do list."

"My assistant said Shauna thought a cougar attacked her dog, so maybe the guy was wearing a beige coat? Or brown? What colour fur do cougars have, anyway?"

"Beigey-brown would be about right, ma'am."

"Emmy, please. Do you get many cougars around here?"

And so it went on...

Luca asked questions and I deflected for what I considered to be a reasonable amount of time, and then my phone rang.

Saved by the bell.

Or not...

23

NINE

As I strolled toward the nurses' station, the low-level buzz that hummed through my body gave me a taste of my old life. I was taking a risk coming to the hospital, of course I was, but not an excessive one. I'd missed this part of my job. The thrill of deception. Of convincing the world that I was a cute little pussycat when a Siberian tiger lurked beneath my skin. When I was eighteen, I'd roller-skated past a senator in hot pants and a tight little vest—that was me in the hot pants, not the senator, although I'd once run into another politician with that particular kink. Quite literally—I drove over him with a Mercedes sedan. Anyhow, while the senator was staring at my breasts, I'd hit him with the blow dart hidden in my lollipop. He thought he'd been stung by a wasp.

Five minutes later, he was dead and I was just another anonymous office worker, strolling along with a co-worker or perhaps a boyfriend, wondering what all the commotion was about. The man waiting with my change of clothes had been Vik—one of the few jobs I'd done with him.

Today, my team was mostly new. Ana and Hallie with me inside, and Alex in my Honda in the parking lot, watching for any unusual arrivals. The Craft Cabin didn't open until ten o'clock on Sundays, so I could hang around for an hour or two. We'd even stopped at the gas station to get Ottie flowers. Chrysanthemums and gypsophila, orange and white and slightly wilted. Alex had grumbled and said they were second rate, but it was the thought that counted, right? And my thought was that the nurses would see the flowers as a nice gesture, and wasn't it sweet that we'd dropped by to visit the poor girl. We'd picked up candy for the staff too. They were easily bought.

I didn't recognise the nurse on duty, and her name badge was handwritten. *Juanita.* Either a newbie or a temp. But I spotted the nurse manager with her purse slung over her shoulder, just going off duty by the look of it. *Shift change.* When she turned in our direction, I caught her eye and waved.

"Hey, Tracie. How are the kids?"

"Oh, hey, Darla. Alfie won a prize at the science fair on Friday, but Chloe's sick with the sniffles." She pointed at her own surgical mask. "Here's hoping I don't pass anything on. Are you here to see Mr. Studebaker? Because he's on the cardiac ward now."

"Earle had another turn?"

"The doctors want to put in a stent, but you know what he's like."

Da, too stupid to live, too stubborn to die. His arteries were blocked worse than an LA freeway, and still he ate a fried breakfast at the Steak and Shake every morning.

"Did Viola May call the ambulance again?"

Tracie nodded. "She switched out his bacon for the low-sodium kind and started frying his eggs in olive oil, but..."

She spread her hands wide. *What can you do?*

"I'll drop by to see him, but we actually came to visit with the poor girl who came in yesterday. We found her in the trees, and..." I shuddered for effect. "Miss Hayley here is a friend from her home town, and Miss Annabelle came for support. I know it's a little early, but the Craft Cabin opens at ten, and..."

I let the sentence hang, and as I'd hoped, Tracie took the bait.

"Since it's you. Really, she's only meant to have two visitors with her at a time."

"Oh, I'll just get these folks some coffee and be on my way. Is Miss Ottie allowed flowers? I thought that when she wakes up, she should have something pretty."

Tracie eyed the drooping bunch. "They might not last that long."

Which told me Ottie's condition hadn't improved any. I made a sad face—one the general had made me practise because sympathy didn't come naturally to me—and held out the box of chocolates.

"I know how hard you folks work. We'll make sure to keep out of your way." Juanita's eyes lit up, and no, she wouldn't give us any trouble. "If you see Marcia, could you let her know the stretched canvas she was waiting on arrived last Friday?"

"I sure will." Tracie squeezed my hand. "Miss Marquette's in the room over there. We'll take good care of her. She'll be having some tests this morning, but her friends can stay until then."

"We really do appreciate that."

Small talk was *so* tedious. Luckily, Tracie checked her watch and waved, and we were free to get on with our job. At least unconscious people didn't chatter endlessly.

Rooms in the ICU were set around the nurses' station, six private, four semi-private. Following a recent refurb, they'd gotten rid of the old curtains and replaced them with smart-glass dividers that could be turned opaque for privacy purposes, which made the place feel brighter, plus someone had painted the ceiling to look like the sky rather than the old greying tiles. I'd visited the hospital in Coos Bay many times in the past, not out of the goodness of my heart—I was heartless, I'd been told that many times—but because it never hurt to know your way around a medical facility. If you didn't look out of place, it was all too easy to don a pair of scrubs and inject potassium chloride into the IV of a wealthy businessman who'd complained of chest pain, for example. Plus a hospital was basically one big supply closet. Where do you think the contents of my first aid kit came from? And before you judge, these places charged fifty dollars for an aspirin—they could afford to lose a few Band-Aids.

Hell, even their coffee machine was a rip-off. Three bucks for a bitter cup of sludge?

But I needed the caffeine. My head still hurt, and being rudely roused by Emmy hadn't left me in the best of moods. The fact that I'd been made to skip breakfast had been the frosting on the cake. Not that I ate much frosting. It just wasn't healthy. Sometimes when Brooke brought cupcakes to work, I took one to be polite, but I tried to stay healthy the rest of the time, the occasional sip of horilka excepted.

I loaded three black coffees onto a cardboard tray. Did Hallie take milk? I didn't know, and I didn't much care either. Another vending machine sold "Happy Valley Breakfast Bars," whatever the fuck those were, and I figured they'd taste like shit but contain some kind of calories, so I added three of those too. Today, I was the Good Samaritan.

Beeping began as I headed toward Ottie's room, and a pair of nurses ran past me. Seemed that some poor bastard was coding out. Still, he'd picked the best place to do it. Close to the morgue—more environmentally friendly.

Why was Ottie's smart-glass frosted?

Hmm.

Inside, Hallie was on her feet, and I gave the two orderlies with the gurney my best Darla smile.

"Are you taking Miss Ottie somewhere?"

"We were just telling her friend that she needs to go for a scan."

Tracie had mentioned tests. But they wouldn't transfer Ottie to a gurney for that, would they? We were in the twenty-first century now. Hospital beds came on wheels. And the orderly... He was wearing a surgical mask, not unusual in a medical setting, but those eyes... I'd seen those eyes before. A thin scar bisected one brow, and he had a mole on his temple near the hairline. A bump on the bridge of his nose. The height fit. The build fit. And the scrubs didn't lie flat against his waist. He was wearing a belt under them.

The eyes...

Russian mercenary, second-tier, possibly third. I'd stumbled across him in Moscow six, maybe seven years ago. That day, he hadn't been my problem, so I'd let him walk.

Today? Today, he *was* my problem.

I tossed the coffee into his face. Boiling water made an excellent weapon, and it was the reason I always took my coffee black. Soaking someone with a soy latte, extra whip and a shot of syrup didn't have the same effect. I scored a direct hit—yes, I'd rehearsed that move many times before—then punched him in the mouth with the heel of my hand before he could yell. Followed up with a carotid strike, the same move I'd used to floor Ana yesterday, and kicked him in the balls as he fell. Problem solved, at least temporarily. But where *was* Ana?

I didn't have time to ponder the question because Moscow's buddy was coming for me, and this time, I'd lost the element of surprise. But I did have years and years of training on my side, so I grabbed the silenced pistol in his hand, spun back into him, and used my other arm to elbow the breath out of his lungs. Then I had the gun, and I turned it on him just in time for Ana to step out of the bathroom and wrap him up in a chokehold.

"Are you going to skip most of every fight this weekend?"

"I needed to pee, okay?"

"Did you stop to wash your hands?"

"*Idi na khui.*"

Hallie had pulled two sets of flex-cuffs out of her purse, but I waved her away. Too little, too late. I decided I'd been generous to award her half a point before. In a fight, she was worth a quarter at best. No matter, I had a syrette of tranquilliser in my hand now, and I split it between our two new friends. That should keep them quiet for a while.

"Are they dead?" Hallie whispered, glancing toward the door.

"Only sleeping."

For the moment, anyway.

24

NINE

"Should we call the cops?" Hallie asked, her face paler than Ottie Marquette's.

"Are you insane?"

I checked outside. The nurses' station was empty. Had our visitors caused the emergency? I considered it quite likely. After all, that's the course of action I'd have taken in the same situation.

"Then what should we do?"

"We should ask them nicely who they're working for."

"What, just ask them? Here?"

"Don't be ridiculous. This is a hospital. We'll take them somewhere quieter."

Which meant we needed a way to move these assholes. Could we stack them both on the gurney? Possibly, but even with a sheet over the bodies, their bulk would be noticeable.

"How? How do we get them out of here? Will they even fit in your car?"

A sensible question for once. We might be able to wedge them in, but it would be a tight squeeze. I should have bought an SUV instead of a fucking compact. How had *they* planned to get out of here? Or had they? Parts of the building were still being refurbished—they could have taken Ottie to a quiet corner and... No, I couldn't see it. There were workmen on-site. Sticking around would have been too much of a risk. They'd have a vehicle. And if they wanted to ensure she stayed alive, they'd have kept her on the gurney, which meant a *big* vehicle.

I dialled Alex. After he'd slipped me his number last night, I'd memorised it in a heartbeat.

"It's me. Don't talk, just listen. They got here first, and we have two of them alive. They'll have transport—a truck, a cargo van, something large enough to accommodate a gurney. We need it."

He didn't hesitate. "Then I'll find it. How long?"

"Five minutes."

I started the timer on my watch. A countdown. If we were still here in five minutes, we'd need bail money.

"Load one of them onto the gurney," I told Ana. "I'll be back." Then I pointed at Hallie. "You—wipe up the coffee."

Thanks to my previous visits, I was familiar with the supply closet, and I grabbed a set of medium scrubs from the shelf. Just my size. A moment later, I'd pulled them on and stuffed Darla's dress into a laundry cart. Also into the laundry cart went two more sets of scrubs and a package of surgical masks, plus half a dozen disposable scrub hats and a selection of bed linen. Hmm, my boots looked all wrong, but the scrub pants covered most of the black leather, and unless someone took the time to study me, they'd never notice. And they wouldn't study me. Cleaners were the invisible army, underpaid and underappreciated.

Two minutes gone, and I was on my way back to Ottie's room. The nurses' station was still empty, everyone focused on the ongoing emergency. Healthcare providers placed too much reliance on technology nowadays. If there was a problem, an alarm would ring, right? Not if you simply unplugged the machine. The one time I'd been hospitalised, I'd made Rad sit at my bedside until I was conscious enough to deal with my own shit again.

Fucking appendicitis.

Ana had moved the gurney into the bathroom as far as it would fit, and Moscow was sleeping peacefully on top of it. His friend—Moscow's Mule?—was wedged into a corner, out of sight in case a nurse reappeared. The coffee was gone. A tense Hallie sat in a chair at Ottie's bedside, gripping her hand, although I wasn't sure who was supporting who. Had Ana put Hallie there? Yes, I thought so. Seven was aware of the importance of appearances.

"Put these on." I held up a pair of scrubs. "In the bathroom."

At least Hallie followed instructions.

Together, Ana and I bundled the Mule into the cart, then Ana changed her clothes too. Checked my appearance the way she always used to and tucked a stray lock of hair under my cap. I returned the favour as my phone buzzed with a message from Alex. Aw, they'd brought their own ambulance? Cute. They'd need it.

"Our transport is an ambulance. The driver's immobilised. There's a side exit to the north—follow the signs for the morgue."

If you act like you belong, then you will. General Zacharov had given me that piece of advice at the beginning of my training, and I'd taken it to heart. If you looked confident, then ninety-nine percent of the time, nobody would ever question you.

We covered Moscow with a sheet—because nobody would let their gaze linger on a corpse—and Ana steered the gurney while Hallie pushed. I followed up with the Mule in the laundry cart. A nurse passed us, and Ana said, "Hi," and

Hallie said, "Hi," and I spotted the Portland Thorns keychain in her hand and muttered, "Rather be watching soccer," and she laughed, and then we were at the door.

Four minutes and fifty-three seconds.

And there was our transport.

Alex had been watching, and as Ana and Hallie approached, he swung open a back door. Five seconds later, Moscow was safely stowed on board, and it was my turn.

"Hey! You shouldn't be standing around here."

Oh, great. A bureaucrat. A woman in an ill-fitting suit strode in my direction, hands on her hips. Why was it always the pencil pushers who had time to stick their noses in where they didn't belong? Clearly, they didn't have enough real work to do.

If I needed to, I'd heave her into the back of that fake ambulance in one hot second, but for now, I just shrugged.

"They told me to come here and wait for the next ambulance. Some guy puked everywhere." A lazy genius had left a spray bottle of sanitiser hooked over the handle of the cart, and I held it out to her. "You wanna clean it?"

She took a step back. "Actually, you stay there."

"You sure?" I checked my watch. Five minutes, forty-seven seconds. "I'm due for a break."

"No, no... Uh, I have a meeting."

Annnnnd she was gone. I wheeled the Mule to the ambulance, Alex grabbed the front of the cart, and once we were inside, Ana slammed the rear door.

Six minutes.

That was okay.

"One of us should stay with Ottie." Who would be best for the job? "Ana."

Hallie raised a hand. "I could do that?"

"If there are more of these men, you'll be able to handle them, *da*?"

"Uh, I'll find Ana's regular clothes for her."

Hallie turned to rummage in the laundry cart, and I caught Ana's eye. She smiled back at me. Was she having fun? I was having fun today. Although I still needed coffee.

And I also needed to get to the Craft Cabin.

That meant we had approximately one hour to extract the required information from these assholes, and two out of the three were un-fucking-conscious. Alex had trussed up his prisoner with a selection of bandages and stuffed gauze pads into his mouth. Perhaps he'd know something, but Moscow was the team leader. This would be an interesting logistical challenge. What was I meant to do, leave the ambulance in the store's parking lot and poke at them between customers?

"Time to go," Ana muttered. "See you later?"

"Maybe."

Every time I prepared to say goodbye, something else went wrong, so I turned away instead.

"Give me your car key?" she asked.

Alex handed it over, and I could hardly argue. Ana using my vehicle made sense operationally, but it meant the farewell was out of my hands; I *would* see her later.

"Get back to Ottie."

We were on our way before Ana made it to the building, and I blew out a breath. After yesterday's fuck-up, and this morning's, I'd begun to doubt both my abilities and my instincts, but the takedown in the hospital had been textbook. Even Lieutenant General Zacharov couldn't have found much to criticise. As Alex put distance between us and the scene of the crime, I hauled the Mule out of the laundry cart and laid him on the floor beside the driver. It was standing room only in the back now. Wherever they'd found this ambulance, it was the real deal, and I selected a vial of ketamine from the range of goodies. The driver got a dose because he really didn't need to hear what we were discussing, and I kept the rest to replenish my own supplies.

"Should I sit in the front?" Hallie asked.

"Unless you want to deal with these gentlemen when they start to wake up."

"I'll sit in the front."

"Where are we going?" Alex asked. "Is there a plan?"

"Head south."

"We should call Emmy. And don't roll your eyes." *Pizdets.* He must have been looking in the rear-view mirror. "Communication, remember?"

"Fine, call her."

The phone rang twice on speaker, and then she picked up. "Hey."

"We have three alive," Alex told her.

"Hold on." A long minute passed. "Okay, I can talk now. You got three at the hospital?"

The sound of a stiff breeze told me she was outside. On the beach at the Peninsula? At this time of year, it would be empty in the morning.

"Dasha, Ana, and Hallie caught two inside, and I found the third in the parking lot. They wanted to take Ottie alive. We have their ambulance now."

"Well, fuck, and I mean that in a good way. How badly are they hurt?"

"Not hurt much, just taking a rest."

Moscow's face showed the only real damage, and his skin was starting to blister nicely. Maybe he'd have new scars to go with the old one?

"Nice. Where are you now?"

"On a road."

"The road between Coos Bay and Baldwin's Shore," I added.

"I'll need to update the powers that be, but I'd rather ask

our guests a few questions first. Darya, is there anywhere quiet we can do that?"

Two places sprang to mind, but I didn't want to invite them to my own piece of land. That was my secret, my sanctuary. Emmy had taken so much from me already this weekend, and I wouldn't give her that. Which left one place.

"There's an old cabin not too far from here. Nobody goes there, not anymore. I'll give you directions, and Alex can drop me off on the way."

"You're not coming?"

"I'm late for work."

"At the craft store? Couldn't you call in sick?"

"No, Miss High-and-Mighty, I can't call in sick. Only two of us are working today, and Paulo needs to teach his Sunday-morning watercolour class."

"I can send Bradley to help out."

"Bradley? Are you joking?"

"He's not the vapid shopaholic he appears to be. Underneath the glitter, he's smart, and he's also a team player."

"Tell me he doesn't have a gun."

"He wanted a gun, so we got him a gun—a Beretta Bobcat with pink grips—but he probably left it at home. Which is a good thing because his aim is terrible, although he's lucky enough that he could close his eyes and still shoot a man's nuts off."

"No shooting in the store. I hate disposing of bodies."

"A man won't die from losing his testicles."

"No, he'd just shoot back."

"Bradley won't die either. He doesn't even age. He's practically immortal, but if he ever does breathe his last, four-leafed clovers are gonna sprout on his grave like weeds. Do you want him to help Paulo or not?"

A part of me wanted to go sell yarn because the deeper I

got into this steaming pile of shit, the more likely it was that I'd lose everything I'd worked so hard to build. But I'd caught those men, dammit, so by rights, I should be the one to question them. Why let the English bitch take all the credit?

"I'll tell Paulo I have a headache. Bradley will have to make his appearance seem natural."

And I'd call Brooke as well. She wouldn't mind dropping by to check on the two glitterbugs later, just in case they needed adult supervision.

"Don't worry; I'll brief him. At least he won't have to fake his enthusiasm for macramé."

"Macramé is actually my favourite craft. If I tie a man up, there's no way he's getting loose."

"Glad to hear it, and I look forward to admiring your skills in person. Now, where's this cabin?"

25

NINE

The cabin in the forest had come to my attention last year after the Wicked Witch of Baldwin's Shore catnapped Pickle. If ever there was a candidate for ketamine, it was her, but I'd have to pay an after-hours visit to the veterinarian and pick up a cow-sized dose first.

But Pickle was safely back at the craft store now, and the cabin had been abandoned once again. Rumour said the place was haunted, a rumour that I'd never admit to starting, but I had to get my kicks somehow, didn't I?

The cabin was perfect for our purposes—completely off-grid and miles from civilisation, but the rutted driveway that led there from the main road was still passable. The cops had even pruned back some of the trees to get their own vehicles through during a recent murder investigation. Behold, our tax dollars at work.

"The floor in the far corner isn't good," I warned Alex.

"As evidenced by the hole?"

"I think the roof leaks. But the rest of the building is sound."

As were the sturdy old dining table and chairs pushed into

one corner. They didn't make furniture like that anymore. I lined up three of the chairs by the front window, backs to the glass, and positioned the fourth opposite. Yes. Yes, this was good.

"Let's bring them in. I can demonstrate my macramé skills."

"What should I do?" Hallie asked.

"Do you have someone who can trace calls?"

"Yes?"

One after the other, I tossed her the three phones I'd confiscated from Moscow, the Mule, and the driver, and she caught them with a little juggling. I'd unlocked them already —the beauty of today's super-secure facial recognition technology was that you could simply hold the device in front of an unconscious person and...voila. Oh, sure, there was meant to be protection against that, but a flaw in many biometric systems meant they struggled to process glasses. All I'd had to do was borrow the driver's spectacles and create a rudimentary pair of "eyes" using microporous tape and a Sharpie. Voila—their secrets were mine.

"Burners, I'm certain of it, but we need to find out who they called and when, and who called them. And when you have *those* numbers, trace their call histories too, and if you can, ping them and find out where they are right now."

"The signal's intermittent out here. I only have one bar."

"If you head south for half a mile, it gets better." From the way Hallie glanced around, it was clear she had no idea which direction south was. "And you can prepare. Find the numbers and go through the call histories. Check the messages. See if there's anything useful."

"Emmy will have a spare burner as well as a satellite phone if we need it," Alex said.

Of course Emmy would have a spare burner and a satellite phone. How long until she arrived? Ten minutes? Twenty?

Whatever, we didn't have to wait for her to supervise our activities. I was more than capable of handling three second-rate shits by myself. Hmm... How to approach this?

"I want to get them inside before they wake." I'd topped up the sedatives on the journey, and they'd slept through the whole trip. "Once they're secured to the chairs, we can let them come round. Should I take the head or the feet?"

"Relax, I've got this." Alex slung Moscow over one shoulder effortlessly. "I don't know what macramé is, but I look forward to finding out."

Relax? I couldn't relax, but at least I didn't have to carry two hundred pounds of dead weight. Wait... Was that a good thing? Or did Alex think I was incapable of doing my own job? Rad would have told me to take the feet. Having someone take the load off me—both physically and metaphorically— was a strange concept.

Hold on a second... This wasn't my fucking job anymore. Was it?

Today, I'd make an exception. Getting a man to talk was always a challenge I enjoyed.

And every man—or woman—*would* talk. I merely had to phrase the questions in the right way and provide a suitable incentive to answer... But what *were* those questions? The obvious one was who did these *mudaki* work for? And what did Ottie have that they needed? It would be useful to find out their future plans, but if Moscow was a hired gun, he wouldn't know the details. Or where the weapon was. If I were his boss, I wouldn't have told him.

The men hadn't been carrying much. Just the burner phones, weapons, and in Moscow's case, three syringes—one empty and two filled with a milky liquid. Had he planned to use the contents on Ottie? To knock her out? I suspected not. These men had spent enough time in the hospital to know she was scheduled for tests this morning, so they must have been aware she was unconscious.

No, the syringes were part of the distraction. Inject as many innocent victims as it took to get the staff out of the way, and then Moscow and his team would have a clear run to Ottie. What was in them? From the colour, I suspected a cocktail of propofol and something else. Potassium chloride? Calcium gluconate? I'd use the latter—the electrolyte imbalances it caused would slow the heart, but in a hospital setting, they could probably fix the problem by giving extra fluids or even using dialysis. Depending on the dose, of course. In that situation, I'd be conservative. Keep the staff busy. There was simply no challenge for them if the patient died right away. But would Moscow take the same approach?

I studied the man slumped in front of me as he twitched. *The Mule.* Did he get the same nightmares that I did? About the things he'd done? I hadn't shared Vik's relaxed attitude when it came to collateral damage, but sometimes, I'd had to weigh one life against the greater good.

What about Moscow? How much of an asshole was he? They *were* big syringes...

Maybe he'd gone for the potassium chloride?

Or something more dramatic?

Only time would tell...

Hallie peered into the back of the ambulance. "Emmy says she's turning down the driveway and not to shoot her."

Spoilsport.

"Maybe I'll just take out a tyre."

"Uh..."

How amusing that she thought I might be serious. I picked up the driver and followed Alex as he hefted the Mule onto a waiting chair in the cabin, then I ensured all three of the men were tied securely. You never could be too careful. Alex had put on one of the surgical masks, as had I—no point in letting these men get a better look at our faces. The Mule had his eyes open now, and the driver was drooling. Nothing from Moscow. I checked his pulse—strong and steady. Yes, he'd be awake soon.

The low rumble of a car engine sounded through the trees, and Emmy's SUV came into view. Somehow, she managed to look almost as elegant as Romi as she stepped out of the driver's side.

"How's it going?"

"They're still sleepy. Maybe ten more minutes until they can speak. Alex is watching them."

"Good. That gives everyone time for breakfast. I got the concierge at the hotel to pack coffee and muffins to go." Perhaps she wasn't so bad after all. "Well, green tea for Alex."

Green tea? Urgh.

"What did he do to upset you?"

"Nothing; he prefers it. I think his taste buds are wired up wrong." Her SUV had cupholders galore, and she handed me a giant paper cup with a plastic lid. "It's probably lukewarm by now, but caffeine is caffeine. Do you want milk? I brought some of those sachets."

"I don't take milk."

Hallie trotted over, relief that Emmy was here to save her from the Big Bad Russian Bitch written all over her face. This was the downside of being myself. People generally disliked me. On occasion, I'd considered making an effort to be nicer, *smilier*, but I was an introvert by nature and having to be sociable left me drained. Sometimes, Darla exhausted me.

Emmy held out a cup. "Decaf cappuccino, one sugar. Chocolate muffin?"

"I love you."

"Don't let Ford hear you say that. Do we have a plan?"

Hallie looked to me.

"I always have a plan. Hallie is looking through the confiscated phones, and I'm going to ask questions."

I narrowed my eyes at Emmy, daring her to try and take over, but she didn't.

"After you. Got a spare mask?"

"In the ambulance."

Now, how should I play this?

26

NINE

Go in hard, show them who's in charge, that's what Zacharov had always told me. And because I was female, I had to be twice as tough as the men.

Or twice as devious.

The prisoners were awake now, and I could tell by their expressions that they were worried but not *too* worried. They thought I'd gotten lucky at the hospital, that they were smarter than me, and ultimately, testosterone would prevail.

It was a look I'd seen a hundred times before, usually before the life faded from a man's eyes and all that was left was an empty shell and the belated realisation that they'd fucked up.

I started with a smile. Maybe they couldn't see my mouth, but it would show in my eyes.

"Good afternoon, gentlemen. Do you have a preference for English or *Russkiy*?"

All these little puzzle pieces to put together...

A weapon had been stolen. A Russian connection. Markovich's government must be involved because they'd okayed the raid on the internet café in St. Petersburg. And on the way to the hospital, Ana had told me that guarding Ottie was only a temporary arrangement, a few hours at most until a bigger team arrived and she could step down. *Step down.* Emmy had mentioned the powers that be. So this new team, they weren't from Blackwood. And who was more powerful than Blackwood? The US government.

Harrison and Markovich.

The past three years had marked a new era in relations between America and Russia. From what I'd seen on the news, Harrison had proven to be a more competent negotiator than his predecessor, while Markovich understood that more could be achieved by cooperation than through war. Every time a new treaty was announced, or a pact, or an agreement, I'd chuckled into my horilka because I knew Zacharov would hate it. Hopefully, he was turning in his grave. Hole. Whatever.

How had Zacharov fit in politically? Well, he was all for globalism, as long as Russia was at the head of the table, and he'd used every trick in the book to get us there. Did he want to *sit* at the table? No, no, not in the slightest. He preferred to remain in the shadows. Everybody knew that was where the real power was.

Would Zacharov have stolen the weapon Ottie had helped to develop? In a heartbeat. If he hadn't been dead, he'd have been at the top of my suspect list. But Alex assured me he *was* dead, so who was left? Not Markovich or Harrison, because they appeared to be working together to retrieve the weapon. So...their opposition? And let's go with the Russian side because that was where Moscow had come from.

Ivan Bornik had a following, but he was an idealist. A dreamer. He'd been in legal trouble before, but for stupid things like vandalising an oil tanker. It made him a hero in the eyes of some, a fool in the eyes of others. Anton Stepanov was the snake. A protégé of former president Lagunov, he was a hardline nationalist. More than once, I'd seen him at Base 13, and he shared many of Zacharov's ideals, but not his love of darkness. No, Stepanov preferred the limelight.

If I was a betting woman—and I'd once been a damn good poker player—I'd put money on him being involved somehow.

When the trio remained silent, I continued in English.

"This is an awkward situation we find ourselves in. Your boss didn't warn you Ottie had protection?" I shook my head. "Oh dear. But now that you're here, I do have a question or two. You see, we want our property back."

"We give you nothing." The driver spat at me, but the glob fell woefully short. "American bitch."

I suppose I needed to take that as a compliment. I had put a *lot* of work into my accents over the years.

"*Américaine? Non, je suis française.*" Oh, that puzzled him. "Just a little joke."

"We know nothing," the Mule tried, and perhaps it was true. He was a lackey, a sidekick.

"I thought that might be so, in which case, you're disposable." I shrugged, nonchalant. "Easier to dig a hole out here than transport you somewhere else, especially if you have no useful information to give us. Isn't it nice in the forest? So peaceful. Not another living soul for miles, rats excepted. But maybe you could satisfy my curiosity on one thing before we part ways?"

I drew two syringes from my pocket, and the milky-white contents gleamed in the afternoon sun that sliced through the window. Someone had cleaned the glass since I last came here. The police, probably. They'd have needed all the light they could get during their time in the cabin. Out of the corner of my eye, I noticed Emmy lean forward an inch. She was curious too.

"What's in these?" I asked. "Let's find out, shall we?"

I took a step forward, and I saw it. The flash of fear in

Moscow's eyes. He knew exactly what was in the syringes, and he didn't like the idea of being a test subject.

"You think you can threaten us?" the driver snapped with the arrogant pride typical of a low-level foot soldier. All brawn and no brain. "I won't talk. Never!"

"Suit yourself." I leaned in close. "And I don't make threats. I make promises."

He struggled, but I found a vein, drew the plunger back until I saw blood, and then injected. Out like a fucking light.

"Oops. Guess it wasn't a vitamin shot." I held up the remaining syringe and uncapped it. "Who's next? I only need one of you, so..." The driver twitched, and I turned to Alex. "Would you mind taking out the trash? We don't need him anymore."

Alex hadn't so much as flinched, and I was impressed. "We'll need a spade."

"Or maybe we could leave him for the vultures? Do they have vultures in Oregon?"

"Turkey vultures," Emmy supplied. "But is leaving him out a good idea? We don't want to poison the wildlife."

An excellent point, I had to grudgingly admit. "Burial would be the better option."

Alex lifted the chair, and the driver's head flopped to the side. Perfect.

"I'll deal with it," he said.

Yes, I really did like that man.

As Alex lugged the driver out the door, I centred a chair opposite Moscow and the Mule and took a seat. They knew I was serious now. The question was, would they be more scared of me or of whoever they were working for?

"Is he paying you enough to die?"

What was the going rate for assassination nowadays? My pay had been pitiful. Room and board and as much training as I could handle, plus a weekly stipend that I'd mostly frittered away on clothes. Occasionally, I'd wondered if I should save the money, but now I was glad I hadn't. Even with Zacharov gone, someone would be monitoring my old bank account.

The Mule glanced sideways, a silent plea for help. This was a new situation for him, wasn't it? And he hadn't expected an interrogation quite like this. Maybe he'd been prepared for pain, for the good-cop-bad-cop Reid technique, for the empathetic approach some preferred to take. Me? I liked to keep people unsettled.

"You'll kill us anyway." Moscow spoke for the first time. "There's no reason to keep us alive."

"Talk, and I'll let you live." I reminded myself to relax. "We're just freelancers doing a job, but I'm better at mine than you are at yours."

"Why should I believe you?"

"Because you're here and Ottie Marquette's still in the hospital."

"I meant about letting us live."

"Well... I hate digging, so there's that. Can you be certain I'll keep my word? No, but would you rather have a shot at living or a shot in the arm?"

The syringe lay in my lap, more threatening than any gun. Neither of them spoke, but the Mule fidgeted within the confines of his bounds, and a bead of sweat ran down Moscow's temple. Even as de facto team leader, he was out of his depth.

"Time's ticking, gentlemen. Shall I just pick someone? Eeny...meeny...miny...moe."

My finger landed on the Mule, and I took another step forward, syringe at the ready.

"Wait! I'll talk."

"Excellent."

I pivoted and jabbed the needle into Moscow's arm, no hesitation, and his eyes saucered.

"*Pizdets*! I'll talk, I'll talk! What do you want to know? They hardly told us anything."

See? Wasn't that easy? If we'd turned them straight over to the authorities, those fools would have taken days to get this far. Rules, so many damn rules. I kept my thumb over the plunger, and Moscow stilled, watching anxiously as I slid the needle out of his biceps, his breathing shallow.

"Let's start with an easy question. Which of you beat Ottie Marquette?"

Call it a test—I already knew the answer. When I searched the three men in the ambulance, I'd found the weeping dog bite on the Mule's left calf, and now I owed Scooby Weaver a package of sausages.

Moscow jerked his head to the side. "He did."

Nothing like dropping a buddy in it, was there? But at least he'd told the truth.

"Which means you searched her room. What were you looking for?"

"I don't know exactly."

"Aah-aah." I made a game-show buzzer noise and reached for the syringe again. "Wrong answer."

"Don't! Some kind of code, okay? They just said to bring electronic shit. Phones, laptops, any flash drives or memory cards we could find."

Now we were getting somewhere.

"And? What *did* you find?"

"There was only one laptop, and I think it belonged to the friend. They told us we had to try again."

"And who is 'they'?"

"A guy."

"You're gonna have to be more specific."

"Some guy I did work for in the past. Fedor, he calls himself."

"Fedor what?"

"Just Fedor."

"And how did you come to work for Fedor?"

"He was with another guy I know, and he asked if I'd be interested in making some money. This was back in Moscow. But fuck, man, he doesn't pay me enough to deal with you people."

"How do you contact him?"

"By phone, but most of the time, he calls me. He changes his number every month."

"When you took the laptop from Ottie's room, who did you give it to?"

"A guy I never saw before. A courier."

"You..." I pointed the syringe at the Mule. "Did you recognise him?"

"I wasn't there."

"You were still busy beating Ottie unconscious?"

I kept my tone light, but if we hadn't been trying to get information, if I'd just run into this motherfucker alone in the forest one dark night, I'd have turned him into a vulture's breakfast.

"All she had to do was tell me where the code was." A huff. "Why do women have to be so stubborn? My ex-girlfriend, she was the same."

This guy really was begging to get catheterised with a garden hose.

"Describe the courier," I instructed Moscow.

"Brown hair. Young, maybe twenty? Ah, he was wearing a Dodgers cap. You know, the baseball team?"

"Height? Build?"

"He stayed in the car. Just rolled down the window, so I didn't see anything but his face."

So there was a vehicle.

"Tell me about the car."

"A BMW import, the 5-series M-Sport in white. Tinted windows and six-spoke alloy wheels."

So he'd been looking at the car rather than the person. A gearhead? Planning how to spend his paycheck?

"What about Fedor?"

"I don't know what he drives."

Was Moscow being deliberately obtuse? "What does he look like?"

"He's older—more like fifty, but his hair's been grey for years. He dresses expensive—always the good suits. And he's missing a finger on his left hand. He told me it got blown off when he was in the army."

"What's his face shape?"

"Round, and he has a...a cleft in his chin."

"Build?"

"Fedor, he likes to go to the gym."

Right. But explosives accident, my ass—Valery Fedorov had lost that finger when his ex-wife went at him with a carving knife. Rumour said she'd been aiming for his mistress at the time and missed. Valery Fedorov was also an associate of Yuma Loslov, a hustler-turned-entrepreneur who'd become Anton Stepanov's right-hand man. Or rather, his left-hand man, seeing as Stepanov was a southpaw.

So, we had a new lead now. But where *was* Fedorov? Nearby? Probably not if he'd sent a courier, but did this team of fools have additional help in Coos Bay?

"Tell me, where did the ambulance come from?" I waved a hand at the vehicle parked in the clearing. "You managed to find it at short notice."

The Mule answered that one. "Is easy to get an ambulance. You just call 911 and they send one."

Fuck, these assholes had stolen an ambulance in the middle of an emergency visit? Where were the crew?

"What did you do with the EMTs?"

"Left them at the house."

"What house?"

"The house we borrowed."

"Give me the address."

He rattled off the name of a street on the outskirts of Coos Bay, and the number told me the house was right on the edge of town. Away from the prying eyes of nosy neighbours.

"Where are the people who own the house?"

"Who knows? It was empty."

"And the EMTs—are they alive?"

"Maybe alive, maybe dead." He shrugged as far as his bonds would let him. "Does it matter?"

Collateral damage. Yes, it mattered. Killing EMTs would have been senseless and completely unnecessary. That's what tranquillisers, handcuffs, and duct tape were for. Then you did the polite thing and called in their location later.

I turned back to Moscow. He seemed the more professional of the two.

"Where did you get this one?" I gestured toward the Mule. "The meat aisle at Walmart?"

Moscow gave a small groan. "He's my brother-in-law."

"And when the priest asked if anyone objected, nobody raised a hand? *Khui.*"

"My sister is headstrong. What could I do?"

He carried a gun. Did I really have to spell it out? Seemed I'd credited him with fifty percent more brain cells than he actually possessed.

"When you visited the hospital this morning, how did you know Ottie would be going for tests?"

"Two nurses were talking about it in the parking lot yesterday. I called Fedor, and he said we should take her."

We went back and forth for another fifteen minutes, but the men offered nothing else useful. They hadn't been hired for their ingenuity, more for their loyalty, but even that seemed to be in short supply. Fedor had paid as little as he thought he could get away with, a mistake that made my job a piece of cake. The good kind with sprinkles. A few roubles might buy unspeakable acts, but unwavering silence cost extra.

In spite of their ignorance, we had more information now than when we'd started, and it wasn't even lunchtime. If I left right now, I could still make the afternoon shift at the Craft Cabin.

I motioned toward the door, and Emmy joined me outside. Where was the driver? Alex had put him back into the ambulance, still tied to the chair, and I checked his pulse. His heart beat strongly, and there was no sign of anaphylaxis.

"What did you give him?" Emmy asked.

"Saline, ketamine, and milk."

"*Milk*?"

"I needed something white, and I didn't have propofol."

"You should have said—I'd have brought a bottle."

"Well, I'm used to working alone. Wherever he goes, he'll need some supportive therapy—fluids, antibiotics, that type of thing. The milk was pasteurised, but the proteins won't be good for him."

"I'll let the team know."

"The man they're looking for is Valery Fedorov, who in turn works with Yuma Loslov, who works for Anton Stepanov. Stepanov is—"

"Markovich's nemesis."

"Precisely."

Emmy studied me with a sudden intensity, and if I hadn't had Nine's spirit running through my veins, maybe I'd have stepped back.

"You're good, Darya. Really fucking good at what you do. Are you really gonna spend the rest of your life knitting?"

"I'm also good at knitting."

"That doesn't answer the question."

"At least here I have a life. Before, I only had an existence."

"But knitting?"

"I have no choice. Never again will I be a man's tool, and I'm not going to run the gauntlet as an assassin for hire either."

"You're the Bad Samaritan. You must miss your old life, if only a little."

Who had told her about the Bad Samaritan? *Nico.* It must have been Nico. Colt or Luca wouldn't have mentioned that in this morning's interview.

"There's a difference between taking a taste every now and again and disappearing for weeks to gorge myself. I have responsibilities now. Staff. Customers. A cat. And an excellent cover I can't afford to ruin. Can I get a ride back to Baldwin's Shore?"

"Sure. What about vacation time?"

"Two weeks a year?"

"You're the boss, and you're obviously still training hard. Why not take a month?"

"Because I'd have to pay an extra assistant, and we're not all made of money."

"How much does working in a craft store pay? Forty grand a year? Fifty? You could make that in a week and spend the rest of your time on the beach. Hell, you could take a decent break with what you earned this morning."

"What I earned? What are you talking about?"

"You think we're doing this for free?"

Emmy definitely took after her father, however unpalatable she might find that fact. Both had the unique ability to make me feel like the village idiot.

"In case you didn't notice, my mind was on other things."

"Understandably, but we're working as a team here, whether you like it or not. Blackwood will be billing the client for our time, and since you did a chunk of the work, you get a chunk of the money. Just tell me where you want it wired."

Wired? Darla banked at the credit union in Coos Bay. I couldn't have hundreds of bucks deposited there because they prided themselves on a personal service and everyone would want to know where the money came from.

Turned out there were some eventualities I hadn't been prepared for after all.

Luckily, Emmy misinterpreted my hesitation.

"If you don't trust me with your account details, I can just send over a big ol' bag of cash, okay? But you should still consider taking more vacations."

"Maybe I'd like to take an actual break that doesn't involve killing people?"

Although if I went to Virginia to see Alex, I might get tempted to murder *her*.

"Suit yourself. I need to call this in and get these assholes put on ice. Alex can drive you back to Baldwin's Shore. Plus you should call Luca—when I spoke with him earlier, he was worried about how you were holding up."

See? People cared.

"Make sure you get someone out to the house with the EMTs."

"It's top of the list." She shook her head as she walked away. "Fucking *milk*."

27

EMMY

I t was bloody freezing, but despite the chill, I had to appreciate the wild beauty of Baldwin's Shore. I'd persuaded the leader of the off-the-books task force who'd picked up the three Moscowteers to drop me off half a mile from the Peninsula, and now I was waiting for James to call. The beach wasn't as good as a SCIF, but between the biting wind and the desolate surroundings, I figured it was unlikely anyone would be eavesdropping on my conversation. *Hurry the fuck up, James.* My fingers were turning blue.

I'd spoken to his chief of staff earlier, a whip-thin guy named Martin O'Connor—who everyone just called Irish on account of his grandma having hailed from the Emerald Isle— and he'd put me in touch with the right people. Grudgingly, because he liked to do everything by the book and I most certainly didn't, so we'd butted heads on more than one occasion. But he'd done as James instructed, and now the prisoners were safely tucked away at a location unknown. Separately, so they couldn't finesse their stories, and also because we didn't want to reveal Darya's sleight of hand with the driver.

Fucking milk.

The task force leader, a guy named Slug I'd met once or twice before, had chortled about that little switcheroo but agreed they'd get a doctor to take a look at him. Both of us were of the opinion that the driver had brought the misfortune on himself. Slug's team—and incidentally, he'd gotten the nickname for being good in a fight, not for being slow—would keep an eye on Ottie Marquette and also begin working the Stepanov angle. They already had him on their list of suspects, somewhere near the top, apparently. The burner phones would go to an unnamed agency for analysis, so probably the NSA, and Slug would start the fun process of tracking their connections.

But he was already a step behind.

How did I know that?

Because Mack was on the hunt too, and at one minute past noon, those connections had started blinking out. There must have been a check-in requirement, and when the team leader—Darya called him Moscow—didn't get in touch with an update by the appointed time, whoever controlled him had shut that branch of the burner network down. Perhaps we should have guessed, but even if we had, we wouldn't have let Moscow make the call. It would have been all too easy for him to slip in a warning, an innocent-sounding phrase that in reality meant "we fucked up, run."

So, the burners had disappeared like dust motes in the dark, but not before Mack had gotten a lock on the first one —the phone Moscow had called this morning, right before his ill-fated trip to the hospital. It had been moving around downtown LA, taking in the sights before stopping at a coffee shop named Brewed Awakening for a while, presumably for brunch. Bet its owner paid cash. But while he was nibbling on a bagel or whatever, our man—or possibly woman because, hey, I was the last person to judge—made a mistake. Or rather, they made a call. To another burner, and where was that device located? At the Russian embassy's Orange County field office in Huntington Beach. Wasn't that interesting?

I thought it was interesting.

I also thought there was a good chance I'd be visiting California in the near future.

My phone rang.

"Hey."

James's voice was soft, a little husky as if he'd just woken up. But Irish said he'd been meeting with a group of Gold Star families this morning, so probably he was hoarse from speaking. James was far better at offering sympathy than me. I preferred action to talk.

"Hey. How was your breakfast meeting?"

"Probably not as exciting as yours. You really caught three guys?"

"Not personally, because I was doing damage control at another location. But the team caught three guys."

I gave James a quick summary, leaving out Darya's name and credentials. That information was on a need-to-know basis, and at this stage, James didn't need to know.

"The Russian embassy? Fuck. Markovich isn't going to be happy about that."

"Then maybe he should vet his people better?"

"Vetting can only tell you what a person's done, not what they plan to do. Ideology shifts. Allegiances change."

"Money talks."

"That too."

"We both know there's no chance in hell the Russians will give us a bona fide list of embassy personnel, no matter how pally Markovich appears to be, which means you need to speak with the NSA or Slug's buddies or whoever the hell eavesdrops on the Orange County field office."

"Are you suggesting the United States government might be spying on another country's embassy?"

"Dude, have you forgotten who you're talking to? The cleaner's probably on your payroll. I'm not dumb enough to believe the FBI really spends fifty thousand bucks on an umbrella stand and twenty thousand bucks on a soap dispenser. Somebody's watching that building."

"If the soap dispenser has a bug built into it, then it might cost twenty thousand dollars. Interesting things happen in bathrooms. Remember that evening at the country club in Chesapeake?"

Yes, I remembered. I remembered sneaking into the men's bathroom with James while he was a mere state senator, trying not to moan as he fucked me against the wall in a stall while a congressman and a well-known televangelist compared mistresses right outside the door.

"Stop changing the subject. And if the soap dispenser is bugged, then isn't that proving my point?"

James sighed. "Fine, I'll ask. Does that mean you're going to California?"

"Sure, if you pay me the big bucks."

Another sigh. "Just send the fucking invoice."

"Three hundred grand for a potted palm?"

This time, he groaned.

"And I need pictures of this Marshmallow thing. If we're searching for the weapon, we need to know what it looks like. Send the files on Fedorov, Loslov, and Stepanov too."

"Anything else?"

"Yeah, I'm desperate for coffee. Plus we have to talk about the Marquette angle. She was running, James, and she has some kind of code that the Russians want. Is that needed to activate the weapon? Like a password?"

"I don't recall hearing about a code, but I can check."

"Well, be bloody careful who you check with because if she wasn't the mole at the lab, then somebody else was. Who worked on the project with her? Are you digging into their backgrounds?"

"Of course we are."

"And?"

"The team has identified two possible suspects. A materials engineer with a significant amount of gambling debt, and a software tech from Ottie's team who dropped off the map three days ago."

"Gambling debt? How did they get a security clearance with gambling debt?"

"It wasn't an issue at his last renewal. As far as we can tell, he developed a problem after he split from his fiancée two years ago."

"Any problems with the software tech?"

"Not that we can find. Ottie's boyfriend said all three of them worked closely together, and Project Marshmallow wasn't their first collaboration."

"How would the boyfriend know? I thought the whole shebang was top secret?"

"He also works at Sandy Peake."

"On Project Marshmallow?"

"No, he led a different team."

"But I bet he knew what she was working on. Whether it was pillow talk, or he heard whispers at the lab, or he had access to the details as part of his job, I bet he knew. And he's just devastated, right?"

"I heard he's upset, but isn't that to be expected?"

"And he's been *super* cooperative?"

"Everyone who works there wants the weapon found."

"James, she *ran*. She saw or heard something that scared her, and she ran rather than voicing her concerns to the one person she should have trusted more than anyone. And somehow, the Russians found her in Oregon with a friend she hadn't seen since high school."

"Fuck."

"If voters could hear you now..." James was always so damned polite in public. "But you get where I'm coming from?"

"They found her because somebody guessed where to look."

"Exactly. And who better to guess than her nearest and dearest? Send me his file too. What's his name?"

"Stern. Timothy Stern."

"My plane's on its way to Oregon. I'll be in California by nightfall, but I need that data."

"You want help from the task force too?"

"No, I want you to keep those guys out of our way for now. Let them carry on with whatever it is they're doing. Better to have them bumbling around in daylight while we work in the shadows."

"You don't have a high opinion of them."

"Dude, they work for the government."

"*I* work for the government."

"Well, we can't all be perfect. Slug's team can take over later."

To clean up the mess, because I had no doubt this was gonna get untidy. Russian diplomats, a weapon that cooked people, fools like Moscow and his incompetent sidekick as muscle... If only Bradley hadn't gone to that bloody craft store.

James merely sighed for the millionth time. "Stay safe, Linny."

"Can't make any promises."

I hung up before he could protest or pull me off the job or roll me in bubble wrap. James got weirdly overprotective sometimes, despite knowing full well that I could look after myself.

So, California... Who did I have? Who did I want? Who did I need? Black was there already, thank fuck, and he'd stick around for a few extra days. Alex might come in useful, and when Bradley heard we were going to Malibu, he'd be first on the jet. If Hallie wanted to join us, it would be good experience for her, and I could pair her up with a more seasoned investigator from the LA office. Ana would help out, but the one person I really wanted was Darya. She was sneaky, tough, and well-trained, plus her memory for faces was uncanny. The problem? She didn't much like me.

But she did seem to have a weird affection for Alex.

Alexei.

Alexei and Darya... What were the chances?

He hadn't dated seriously since his divorce, nobody that lasted longer than a couple of months anyway. And who could blame him? His ex-wife was such a pain in the arse that I figured she'd put him off relationships for life. But Darya wasn't a needy little airhead like Colette. No, she was smart and independent and dammit, she lived in fucking *Oregon*. I didn't want to lose Alex from my team.

But what if I could gain Nine?

I tapped out a message.

Me: Next stop: Huntington Beach. What would it take for Darya to join us?

Then I headed for the Peninsula to wait for Ana.

28

NINE

Alex had made me coffee. He'd actually made me coffee while I took a shower, and not only that, now he was standing at the kitchen counter with a knife in his hand. Instinct made me reach for the blade I'd slipped into my bra, but when he turned, I froze with my hand halfway to my chest. He was...cooking? There was a frying pan on the stove and a pile of fresh fruit on the chopping board in front of him. Well, this was weird. In my old world, equal opportunities had extended to the battlefield but not quite as far as the kitchen.

"What are you doing?"

"I thought you might be hungry."

Ravenous, but I'd planned to take a sandwich and a banana to the Craft Cabin when I went to relieve Bradley. I'd spoken to Brooke as soon as I got back home, and she'd assured me everything was fine, just a little busy and she didn't mind staying around to assist, but I was still annoyed that circumstances meant I'd had to ask for a favour. At least Bradley was helping rather than hindering—Brooke reported that he was assisting Paulo with his painting class and all the ladies adored him.

"I need to get to work."

Alex scooped fruit into two bowls. "Really? And how does that fit with your cover story?"

"I'll tell them the painkillers kicked in."

"You can let Bradley fulfil his dream of working in a craft store for another half hour and eat breakfast."

Next, Alex scooped slices of French toast onto two plates and drizzled honey over the top, and okay, my mouth watered. Maybe I could take fifteen minutes.

"It's more like lunch."

"We can compromise on brunch." He waved a hand toward the dining area that opened off the kitchen. "Please, sit."

He'd made me breakfast.

Part of me wanted to take a picture of the food the way Paulo always did, but then my brain switched back on and I told myself not to be so fucking stupid. Who would I show, anyway?

But I sat, and Alex set fruit and French toast and coffee in front of me, then fetched his own plate and slid onto the seat opposite. This was way, way out of my comfort zone. In fact, I half wished we were back at the cabin in the woods. I knew how to deal with assholes. I'd become somewhat of an expert, seeing as I'd spent my whole life practising. Yes, I'd become adept at fitting into different social situations too, at faking my way through whatever I needed to do to survive, at wearing many, many different masks, but somehow, this was different. This was just me and the man who'd saved me from hypothermia half a lifetime ago, and for some reason that I didn't quite understand, I didn't want to lie to him.

A novel concept, and a foreign one.

But what should I do? Was it better to bullshit or to say nothing at all?

I took a bite of the French toast, and it was unexpectedly edible.

"This is good."

"Don't sound so surprised."

"Historically, the men in my life have struggled to open a can of fish."

General Zacharov hadn't placed much emphasis on culinary skills, and at Base 13, we'd had a cook, a miserable woman named Olga who put cabbage in every single dish. Even Vik, who was good at everything, had set fire to the kitchen once.

"Want me to make you a fish salad?"

Alex was joking, but I still shook my head.

"I never want to eat another fish salad as long as I live. Or anything containing cabbage."

"No cabbage? Damn, I was planning to make shchi for dinner."

Another joke, but my heart still threw out a palpitation. "You're staying for dinner?"

Now his smile faded. "I don't know yet. But if I can't, then when I come back, I'll cook you something with no fish or cabbage."

Alex's phone vibrated its way across the table, and he glanced at the screen.

"They found the EMTs."

"And?"

"One is okay, the other is in bad shape but alive. Our three friends clocked them and barricaded them inside a closet."

"Makes me wish I'd killed those *mudaki* when I had the chance."

"You played it right." He smiled, more to himself than for me, it seemed. "You played it *perfectly*."

I nearly smiled too. "Thanks for standing at the back and looking menacing."

"Anytime, *vertolet devushka*."

Helicopter girl. Okay, I finally did smile, but I quickly hid it by taking a bite of French toast because I was Nine and being sappy wasn't part of life's plan for me. In my experience, the small joys were always followed by greater sorrows, so even if Alexei said he'd come back, there was no point in getting my hopes up. Happiness was dust on the breeze—all around me but impossible to catch. Instead, I made do with small doses of satisfaction. As the Bad Samaritan, I took pride in a job well done, and dishing out a little vigilante justice in my adopted home town was well within my capabilities.

"So, how did you end up in Oregon?" Alex asked, and I choked on the toast I'd been about to swallow. "You glossed over the story before."

"What business is that of yours?"

He passed me a glass of water, calm as always. "If you don't want to tell me, that's okay, but I'm trying to get to know you here."

"Why?"

"Because I like you."

Oh.

"Why?" I asked.

"Why do I like you?"

"*Da*."

"There has to be a reason?"

"There's a reason for everything."

"I guess there is." Alex took a sip of coffee. "Words aren't my forte, but...the night we first met, you fascinated me. A girl, barely more than a child, not only living in a man's world but ruling it. One of the guys you were with complained about the job being tough, and the glare you gave him...that *withering* glare. I knew then who had done most of the work.

And now we meet again, and I find there's more to you than the tough shell. You're a *matryoshka*..." He referred to the nesting dolls so beloved of Russia, not that I'd ever owned one. "So many layers, each with a different face, a different facet of personality. And although it's a cliché, I've felt more alive with you this weekend than I have in years."

That was quite the speech. "Even when I threatened to shoot you?"

"I like that you keep me on my toes. With you, life is never boring."

Okay. *Okay*. When I thought things through logically, the question about Oregon was a perfectly reasonable one to ask —hadn't he already told me why he moved to Virginia?—but it had caught me by surprise. So I did something I rarely did and apologised.

"I'm sorry I snapped. I just... I just..."

"You're off balance."

"Yes. That." How much should I tell him? He knew I'd quit my job, but not the circumstances. Usually, I went with a story about leaving a troublesome ex, which wasn't that far from the truth, but Alex deserved more than smoke and mirrors. Could I trust him? I thought that maybe I could. And more than that— I liked him back. "Oregon... The short version is that I stole a car and kept driving until I couldn't go any farther."

"And the long version."

"I hate to threaten you, but..."

"If I breathe a word, you'll cut out my tongue?"

My turn to shrug. "Something like that."

"I'll keep your secrets, Dasha. They're yours to share, not mine."

Where to start... "I wanted to quit for a long time, but it wasn't the kind of job where you could hand in a resignation letter."

"As I said, I saw what Zacharov put Ana through when she tried to leave."

"*Da*, so I knew that when I went, I'd have to burn every bridge and then vanish. But it wasn't so easy. Before, I told you that one of my colleagues died, but he was more than that to me. We were...involved."

"Involved? As in romantically?"

"I suppose. What little romance was possible in a situation like ours. We cared for each other, but we had to keep that aspect of our relationship secret. The general wouldn't have approved. He didn't tolerate distractions. But Rad and I used to work together often, so with care, we managed to keep things quiet for two years."

"How did he feel about quitting?"

"The same as me, but slightly more risk-averse. He said Zacharov would send the dream team of Ana and Vik after us."

"You really believed Ana would kill you?"

"Zacharov had a way of fucking with your head, of making you think the worst. And Vik already took out Artem when he tried to leave, so yes, I believed it. But with Rad, I could cope. We held each other up."

"So what went wrong?"

"Everything." I pushed the plate away, the French toast half-eaten. My appetite had vanished. "*Everything*. That final job... We were sent to the US to eliminate three high-value targets. Two businessmen, one politician. They had security in place, of course they did, but we were used to that. And it should have been a simple undertaking, especially when we realised they'd all be in the same place. One of the businessmen owned a pad in the countryside, the American version of a dacha, and they planned to meet there to discuss their latest attempts at bribery and corruption or whatever it is those assholes do. A little plastic explosive, and boom... Problem solved."

"I think I saw that on TV—the place in Vermont?"

"If anyone asks, I'll deny everything."

Besides, I'd only killed one person that night—I hesitated to call him a man—and I'd framed someone else for the job.

"I know you have no reason to trust me right now, but I'm not going to tell anyone. You think I haven't kept Emmy's secrets over the years? Bet she has more skeletons in her closet than you do."

I wouldn't be so sure, but let Alex assume that if he wanted to.

"So maybe it was Vermont. The geography isn't important, but history was. It's hard to keep your humanity in the job I did, but I always tried. So did Rad, but Pavel had lost his entirely, and he was on the team with us that night." I shuddered, not out of fear but because by the end, Pavel had repulsed me. "He was Team Zacharov all the way. *Pizdets*, I need a drink."

Hell, I needed to drown myself in horilka. These days, it was the only thing that took the pain away.

29

NINE

Alex moved to the faucet to refill my glass, but I ignored the offer of water and found the bottle of horilka stashed inside the knitted motherfucking chicken I'd made when I was bored out of my mind one evening, watching TV with East Baldwin. He'd been fond of farming shows.

"Dasha, it's one p.m." Alex caught my hand before I could take a swallow.

"And it's eleven p.m. in Moscow."

"Alcohol won't fix this."

No, but it took the edge off the hurt.

"Nothing can fix this."

"Share the load first, and if you still want a drink afterward, I won't stop you."

"You couldn't stop me anyway."

He cracked half a smile. "This is true."

But he would judge me, and in that moment, I realised Alex's opinion mattered. When had that happened? Before, I'd never cared what anyone else thought of me. Reluctantly, I put the bottle down and sipped the water instead.

"You were in Vermont?" Alex prompted.

"*Da*. And I had the overwatch while Rad and Pav headed for the cabin. The *cabin*. That's what they called it, but it was a mansion built out of logs."

I'd been three hundred yards away, up on a hill with my favourite sniper rifle, a customised Lobaev prototype that cost half what I earned in a year working at the Craft Cabin. I rarely fired it nowadays—Darla's budget didn't run to 408 CheyTac. General Zacharov might have had few redeeming features, but he'd never skimped on the weapons budget. We'd had the best toys, and in those days, I'd gone through ammo like Darla went through embroidery floss, and she used way too much of that shit.

"The news showed the smoking remains."

"I didn't watch. Seeing it once was enough." Plus I'd relived those final moments a hundred times over in my nightmares. "The meeting was a last-minute arrangement, and the targets got there before we did. Rad went inside to plant the device while Pav dealt with a nosy guard or two on the perimeter. Fifteen minutes, that's all we needed. But then... Fuck, there were kids there. Rad radioed through. One of the targets had brought his family, and he wanted to abort."

I'd never forget his urgent whisper: *two little girls asleep in bed, pulling out.* It had been the right call. Yes, completing the job would have been more difficult if we'd waited—kill one guy, and his buddies would ramp up their security—but we still had two more weeks per the general's timetable. And we had to consider public perception. The average citizen didn't much care for rich businessmen who shirked paying their taxes, and politicians weren't too popular either. But bring kids into the equation, maybe a pretty wife too, and suddenly you had uproar. Zacharov had told us to send a message, but a car bomb or a bullet to the head would have worked just as well.

"Let me guess—Pavel didn't want to back off."

"Five seconds later, the place blew. Rad always said that karma would get him, but in the end, it was Pav. Pav told me Rad must have made a mistake, but there's no way that happened. Pav built the device. He was a *mudak*, but he knew electronics, and he was fond of including a backup trigger. Did he think I'd forget that?"

I paced the kitchen, the anger I'd felt that night rushing back as I recalled his smug face. Rad was careless, he told me. He'd let his standards slip and become complacent. And to be fair, Rad had made a grave error in thinking that Pav was anything but a callous psychopath, but I'd still shot that asshole. Funny how he didn't look so pompous with half his brain missing.

"So you killed Pav?" Alex asked.

"I put a bullet in his head, and then I ran."

Not before I'd put my unregistered gun into the hand of one of the dead guards, checked all sides of the building in case a miracle had happened and Rad had escaped the inferno, and dug the tracking chip out of my back, but I'd been out of there before the first sirens sounded in the distance. Our vehicle had been parked a kilometre away, a battered SUV we'd picked up for cash in Pennsylvania with licence plates we'd borrowed in New Hampshire. That night, a Friday, with the remnants of smoke still searing my lungs, I'd let myself into a building company's compound and borrowed a cargo van—they wouldn't miss it over the weekend, and by then, I planned to be halfway across the country. Seeing as I wore a reflective vest and stuffed my hair under a ball cap, nobody had given me a second glance.

I'd let my anger at Pav and the fear of getting caught fuel me, along with liberal amounts of caffeine, and I'd made it to Vegas before daybreak on Monday. Why Vegas, you ask?

Because that's where Darla Lewis was buried.

More of Pavel's handiwork, of course, although he'd roped

in Rad and me to dispose of her remains. That poor, stupid woman. To Pav, anything with breasts had been disposable, a commodity to be used and then thrown away. Honestly, my only regret in shooting him was that I hadn't been able to cut off his dick and ram it down his throat first. See how *he* liked it.

Darla—the real Darla—had believed his bullshit about being a property developer in town to meet investors, and she'd giggled constantly as she hung on to his every word. He'd brought her out for dinner with us, mainly so he could toy with her. *Here's my new pet, see how dumb she is.* At three a.m., Rad and I had received the inevitable call—could we help to move the body?

I'd nearly told Pav to shove it, but Rad sighed and climbed out of bed because we were meant to be a *team*. Many years ago, we'd tried reporting Pav's proclivities to the general. He'd just shrugged, and then Vik had rolled his eyes and told us Zacharov was Pavel's role model in *every* way.

Anyhow, we'd left Darla in a shallow grave in the Mojave Desert, and as I'd tucked her wallet beside her lifeless form, Pav had made a joke about the two of us being twins. Rad had told him to shut the fuck up, but I couldn't deny there were similarities. Darla was thinner, bordering on scrawny, but our faces were the same shape. If I dyed my hair brown and pencilled in bushier eyebrows... Yes, I decided it would work. Her eyes had been on the grey side, but her driver's licence said they were blue, so I avoided the hassle of wearing coloured contacts. And the best part? During that ill-fated dinner, she'd told us she had no family. Her mom had died three years previously, and she was all alone in the world.

Nobody would look for her.

So nobody would find me.

Darla had mummified in the dry heat, papery skin stretched across brittle bones. I hadn't lingered as I retrieved her ID, and half a day later, I was on my way with a new vehicle and a little more breathing space.

"And you ran all the way to Oregon?" Alex asked.

"*Da*. I didn't stop until I reached the ocean. Then I found a job here, and so I stayed."

"That was one hell of a goodbye. People don't often leave Blackwood, but when they do, we buy them a gift and Bradley usually throws a party."

Even as a strangled laugh escaped, I felt the tears prickling at my eyes. "Don't you make me fucking cry again, you asshole."

His turn to laugh. "Still want that horilka?"

Did I? The talking, it was strangely cathartic. Was this why people went to confession? To unload their secrets onto a stranger so they could feel lighter inside? Hmm. If I told a priest that I'd pushed a man out of a seventeenth-floor window, would he inform the police? I could just imagine how that conversation with Colt and Luca would go. *Well, it should have been a straightforward* splat, *but he landed on an ornamental lamp post and the spike at the top pierced right through his chest.*

"I'm undecided."

But a traitorous tear rolled down my cheek, and I cursed under my breath as Alex wiped it away with a thumb.

"This is embarrassing," I muttered.

"It's normal. Dasha, you couldn't even grieve properly. You've been bottling all this up inside for four years."

And Alex was making everything spill out.

"I hate you," I mumbled, but I still let him wrap me up in his arms, and it felt weirdly nice. Like being hugged by a wall. Safe. Which was dumb because I kept myself safe. Trust no one, that was my motto, but maybe I could stay here just for a minute or two?

Or not. Alex's pants vibrated, and he cursed too.

"Somebody wants you," I said.

Somebody other than me.

He loosened his grip and pulled the phone out of his pocket. Sighed when he saw the message, so presumably it was from Emmy. That was the type of reaction she tended to elicit.

"You have to leave?"

"Yes."

"Where are you going?"

"California. Huntington Beach."

"I went there once."

Not with Rad, but with Vik and Artem. One of the rare jobs that had actually been fun. We'd stayed in a nice hotel, and one day, Vik decided we'd all take surfing lessons. He'd fallen off the board more than Art, which had irked him to no end. Then we'd kidnapped our target—a troublesome politician's equally problematic son—and returned him to the fatherland, and the fun had been over.

"Emmy wants you to go there again."

"What?"

"She thinks you'd be an asset on this job."

I wriggled free of Alex's embrace. "Well, she can't just order me around. I have a life here. Obligations."

Alex let me go, but he kept hold of my hand. "What if I said *I* wanted you to come?"

I began to stiffen, then quickly forced myself to relax. To wear my poker face.

"*Do* you want me to come?"

"I do." When I didn't answer, he continued, "If work's a problem, Bradley could probably cover at the store."

My first instinct was to say "no way," but that was based on my feelings toward Emmy. I considered the offer. A chance to get away for some winter sun, a temporary staff member for the Craft Cabin, a few days with Alex, and presumably Emmy would pay for a hotel room. All I'd have to do was kill someone—why else would she want me there?—and if that person was the *mudak* responsible for the damage to Ottie Marquette's face, I wouldn't much mind eliminating them. Perhaps I could leverage this to my advantage?

"Emmy mentioned paying me for the work I already did this weekend. Do you think she meant it?"

"If she said it, then she meant it."

Hmm.

Okay, I'd play.

"Then tell her I'll go to Huntington Beach, but my rate is five thousand dollars a day plus wages for my replacement at the Craft Cabin. Brooke and Paulo will probably work extra hours if Bradley can't help."

How long would I be in California? Five days? A week? Twenty-five thousand bucks would buy me two new rifles with plenty left over for my emergency fund. Paulo would be happy to teach my arm-knitting class later. He loved making those giant blankets.

A smile spread across Alex's face, and thank goodness I wasn't in his arms anymore because he'd have felt my heart thumping against my ribcage.

"I'll tell her." And he did. Well, kind of. Emmy must have picked up quickly because a second later, he spoke into the phone. "Dasha will come, but her rate is eight thousand a day plus expenses. ... Yes... Yes... I'll get back to you on that."

What the fuck?

Alex tucked the phone back into his pocket. "We need to leave in half an hour. Do you want to drive yourself to Medford or ride with us?"

"I... Eight thousand dollars a day?"

"You undervalued yourself."

"And Emmy *agreed* to it?"

I'd thought I was pushing it with five, but I didn't particularly want to do the job, so...

"She pays people what they're worth. You already have a bag packed? Plan on being there for a week."

"Of course I have a bag packed."

"And the transport?"

"I'll drive myself."

For fifty thousand bucks, I'd walk to Medford if necessary.

30

NINE

The loss of control was unnerving.

Four hours after my awkward conversation with Alex, as I settled into a plush leather seat on Emmy's private jet, I realised why I'd grown so comfortable in Baldwin's Shore. Not the easy job or even the people but the fact that for the first time in my entire life, I'd been the mistress of my own destiny. Until the unfortunate incident with stepfather number four, my mama had been in charge, and then I'd relinquished my entire existence to General Zacharov.

Now, Emmy had taken over.

Or rather, Emmy's team had because Emmy herself didn't deal with the mundanities. As Nine, I'd had zero say in the jobs I undertook, but I'd still been tasked with arranging the logistics myself. Transport, accommodation, food… In those days, I'd felt a tiny rush of pleasure if I managed to reserve an exit-row seat with six inches of extra legroom, but now all of that was out of my hands. When I'd asked Alex if I should arrange a rental car, he'd just waved a hand dismissively and told me Blackwood had people who did these things.

"Drink?" a blonde in a white shirt and tailored black pants

asked. "We also have snacks if you're hungry. I'm Marte, by the way. Are you new to the team? I don't recall seeing you before."

"A bottle of water would be good."

"Darya is a contractor," Alex added when I failed to expand on my answer. "Yes, she's new."

Didn't he understand the concept of privacy?

"Why did you tell her that?" I hissed once Marte had vanished toward the galley.

"Because it's polite?"

"I don't like people knowing my name. Not my real name."

"You don't trust us."

He said it as a statement, and I detected a hint of disappointment.

"I don't trust anyone, and cabin crew aren't exactly famed for their discretion."

"Marte's the co-pilot," Emmy said from behind me. "She spent four years in the Swedish Air Force, and her father is Director of Operations at Blackwood's Stockholm office." Oh. "She's not going to gossip. But if you want to come up with a fake name, then by all means do so and we'll be sure to use it."

Ana glided up silently. "Everyone's vetted. I used to worry too, but..." She gave a one-shouldered shrug. "Now I don't."

Marte returned, holding out a bottle of water with a smile. "Here you go. Can I get you folks anything else?"

When everyone shook their heads, she disappeared again, this time to the cockpit. Yes, I was still very much off balance, and I wasn't sure I'd find my footing until I returned to Baldwin's Shore. But at least I'd return thousands of dollars richer. Mental note: open a new bank account.

"I came over to ask if you have any dietary preferences," Emmy said. "It'll be time for a late dinner when we arrive, and my husband offered to pick up food."

Her husband? He was also going to be there? This just got worse and worse.

"The hotel doesn't have a restaurant?"

"We're staying at our place in Malibu, but if you've got a burning desire for room service, someone can chuck a croissant outside your door in the morning."

Their place? I had to stay in a house with her? It was official: I was trapped in a new nightmare. *You can cope, Dasha.* If the job lasted a week, then I could afford to put a new roof on my cabin, and I'd survived worse—every single job I'd done with Pavel, for example. At least Emmy was unlikely to strangle a prostitute.

"I can make my own breakfast."

"Super. What do you want for dinner? It's California— you're legally required to have at least one food intolerance."

"Well, I don't, and I'll eat anything."

"Noted."

She headed for the table at the front of the cabin, and I closed my eyes. This would all be over soon. And at least one person was happy. When I'd called Brooke with a tale of woe involving a fictitious sister and her scummy boyfriend— thankfully, I'd had the forethought to invent a sibling in case an emergency such as this arose—she'd volunteered herself and Paulo to step in for a week just as I'd known she would. She'd also mentioned that if I needed to stay away for longer, one of the ladies in her Thrive group loved crafts and had a background in retail. Brooke said Everly needed extra money, and if there was enough cash in the kitty to pay her, she'd be thrilled to pick up some shifts. Since Emmy was footing the bill, I'd told Brooke to invite Everly in for a trial this afternoon. Bradley would stick around for a day in case there was a problem, but I trusted Brooke's judgment.

I didn't have to worry about the Craft Cabin while I was away, just everything else.

"I asked Emmy to give you a room in the guest villa by the ocean," Ana said as we stood in the hallway of Skywater House. "I thought you might want some space."

"From her? Yes."

Right now, I was just trying not to gape. Once or twice, when the job called for it, the general had reluctantly funded accommodation in a five-star hotel, so I was no stranger to luxury. Emmy's house fit that definition. And it *was* a house, not a home. The place was too perfect for anybody to actually live there.

"Give her a chance," Ana said.

"I *am* giving her a chance. I'm here, aren't I?"

And so was a giant. He stepped out of a doorway ahead of us, and the man was even bigger than Alex.

"Emmy's husband," Ana whispered as his gaze locked onto me.

It was like having my soul sucked out, which probably explained a lot if he looked at Emmy that way too. He paused to kiss her on the forehead, then headed in my direction.

"You must be Darya."

"Yes."

He offered a hand. "Black."

"Is that your first name or your last name?"

"Consider it both. You did a nice job on Emmy's nose."

Was he expecting an apology or something? Because he wasn't getting one.

"Yes, I did."

One corner of his lips twitched. "How's your arm?"

"Better than it was yesterday."

"Do you need further medical attention? We know a

plastic surgeon who'll exercise an appropriate degree of discretion."

"My budget doesn't run to cosmetic repairs."

Might as well get that out there.

But my statement seemed to amuse him. "I wasn't suggesting that you should pay for it. Let me know if you need an appointment, but in the meantime, we have work to do." He looked past me. "Ana, Quinn's online."

"I need to show Dasha the guest villa first," she said.

"Alex can do that since he's staying there as well."

He was? Well, that was...an interesting development. One I couldn't say I hated. The jury was still out on Black. He was certainly courteous, but darkness lurked around the edges, and instinct told me he was dangerous.

Ana glanced my way, and I gave her the merest nod, letting her know I was okay with the situation. *Think of the money.* She didn't seem fazed by Black, so I had to take that as a good sign.

"What's first on the agenda?" I asked.

"We'll meet in the dining room when you've stowed your luggage. Does anything need to go in the weapons locker?"

"I prefer easy access."

"As you wish."

Emmy had already vanished, and Black walked away too, followed by Ana. Alex picked up my bag.

"Okay?"

Nothing can be as bad as Pavel.

"*Da.*" I kept my tone light. "Why wouldn't I be?"

Maybe I deserved the "Do you think I'm stupid?" look.

"The guest house is this way."

He led me through a cavernous living room, past a trio of couches that clearly weren't designed to be sat on and out a sliding door at the back of the house. A covered terrace played host to a bunch more seating, this stuff made from wicker, and an outdoor kitchen at the far end looked as unused as the rest of the property. Beyond the terrace lay a pool, the rippling water bathed in the soft glow of a thousand fairy lights strung overhead. A twinkling waterfall tumbled at one end, but even over the splashes, I could hear waves breaking against the shore nearby.

Alex skirted the pool and stopped next to a two-storey building on the far side. Tropical gardens stretched toward the ocean, blanketed by a sky full of stars, and I caught a glimpse of water sparkling between waving palm fronds. The guest house matched the main building—starkly modern, all white walls and metal and glass. Too much glass. Were Emmy and Black insane, owning a place like this?

"Don't worry; the glass is bulletproof," Alex explained, as if he could read my mind. "And also..." He fiddled with a panel beside the front door, and the nearest wall frosted. "Magic. Black's a paranoid son of a bitch."

Downstairs was open plan with a sitting area that overlooked the pool and a dining table at the ocean end. A small but functional kitchen sat against the back wall, and an open door in the corner led to a bathroom so guests could go for a swim and then shower with ease. A twisted glass-and-steel spiral staircase led skyward under a glass ceiling, a piece of art in its own right that shimmered under the spotlights Alex flipped on.

Okay, I could grudgingly admit the place was nice.

"If I lived here, I'd never leave."

The words just slipped out, and Alex smiled. "It's the staircase, isn't it? Everybody loves the staircase."

And maybe the company too. He still had my bag, and we headed for the second floor.

"Ladies first."

"Because you're a gentleman or so you can admire my ass?"

Okay, I'd been planning to do the same to his. In my situation, I had to make the most of the small pleasures in life.

Alex's smile grew wider. "One of those."

Upstairs, two bedrooms opened off a central landing, each with an en-suite bathroom and dressing area. They called this the guest house, but it was bigger than my regular house.

"Pool view or ocean view?" Alex asked.

Decisions, decisions... I'd never had to make choices like this before. The ocean-view room had a balcony with steps that led down to a beachside terrace—a good escape route if I needed one, but conversely, a method of ingress for any undesirables who might pay me a visit. The view on the pool side wasn't so good, but I still didn't trust Emmy completely, and at least I'd be able to see her coming.

"What's perimeter security like?"

"The property is covered by motion sensors and cameras."

"How do we find out if there's been a breach?"

"The LA control room monitors the place twenty-four-seven, and they'll send an alert."

"To who?"

"To the Blackwood team. Want me to get you added to the list?"

"Yes."

"So... Which room?"

"I..."

Alex tucked a stray lock of hair behind my ear. "Are you okay with sharing this place? I can stay in the main house if it makes you more comfortable."

My whole miserable existence, I'd steeled myself not to react against all the shit that got flung my way. But somehow, the kindness had a way of seeping through the cracks and kicking me right in the feelings. Where had that lump in my throat come from? I tried to swallow it, but it seemed to be stuck.

"It's fine. Just pick a room, and I'll take the other one."

Alex put his bag in the pool room and mine in the ocean room. Well, that turned out to be easier than I thought. Then he held out a hand, and call it intuition or sixth sense or whatever, but I knew that if I took it, my life wouldn't be the same going forward.

Everything would change.

"Time for work," he said.

I put my hand into his and let him lead me out the door.

"How many people did you think we were feeding?"

"I didn't know what everyone wanted." Black shrugged. "So I just called the restaurant and ordered seven of everything."

"The delivery guy probably got a hernia."

"I tipped him thirty percent."

There was a mountain of food. A literal mountain. At times like this, I really missed Bradley. He'd have emailed a menu and hounded everyone until they provided their choices.

"You didn't even know what *you* wanted to eat?"

Black considered that for a moment. "Maybe we can reheat the leftovers for lunch tomorrow?"

"Yeah, and then we can invite every homeless person in Los Angeles County in for a filling meal, and we'll still have enough left for dinner."

The delivery guy was probably off to the Maldives to celebrate his windfall, and tomorrow morning, we'd read about a state-wide shortage of olives and passata.

Hallie appeared in the doorway and gaped. "How many people are we expecting?"

"Just the six of us plus Vance." Vance's work on the Pinchy-slash-Mike case had been solid, and he was one of the best investigators in Blackwood's LA office, so we'd recruited him onto the team. Black had given him a basic briefing earlier. "I hope you're hungry."

"I'm hungry, but I'm not planning to take up competitive eating anytime soon. Should I go find Ana?"

"If you wouldn't mind." The intercom by the door buzzed. "Could you let Vance in too?"

"Sure."

From the corner of my eye, I saw Alex and Darya exit the guest house, hand in hand. Black didn't miss that little factoid either, I could tell by his expression.

"Told you they had some weird connection."

"You think it'll go anywhere?" he asked.

"Yeah, I do."

"Does that worry you?"

"A little." I'd be lying if I said it didn't. Darya was still something of an unknown quantity, and she lived on the other side of the country. "Will Alex want to move to Oregon? It's a possibility, and one I don't much like, but he enjoys his job. Darya might say she's settled in Baldwin's Shore, and true, she has a business there, but I'm sensing she's got itchy feet."

"And you decided to tickle them by bringing her here?"

"If she's as good as Ana says, and I think she is, then she'd be a useful addition to the team."

Yesterday, she'd come damn close to doing me a serious injury. Too close for comfort, if I was honest, which made her a great candidate for the Special Projects division.

"You think she'd work for Blackwood?"

"Honestly? No. But she's not rolling in money, and I think she might freelance if the conditions were right."

"One of those conditions being Alex?"

"Exactly. If I'd asked her to come here, she'd have told me to go to hell, but he persuaded her to join us."

"Shame you got off on the wrong foot."

Black stroked a finger down the side of my nose, lightly enough that it didn't send fire shooting through my face. I'd felt the cartilage crack, but the swelling was subsiding and it didn't seem too wonky this time. Perhaps I'd had a lucky escape.

"Yeah, it is a shame. But what's done is done, and all I can do now is try to fix things. Darya's had one hell of a life. Maybe not as bad as Ana's, but still shitty."

In those rare unguarded moments, I'd seen the pain in her eyes, and fuck knew what she was discussing with Alex in their private chats. He certainly seemed protective of Satan's little sister.

And speaking of the devil...

She'd dropped his hand, and the hard mask was firmly back in place when she appeared in the doorway.

"I thought it was just us? How big is this team?"

"It is just us."

"Then who is all this food for?"

"Us. Black miscalculated the quantities slightly."

"*Slightly.*"

She walked past the table, more interested in the whiteboards Black had lined up on one side of the room, backs to the windows so nobody looking in could see what was written on them. Or taped to them. James's spies had been busy, and Black had printed out pictures of the players from the embassy, ready for us to add notes. Several had names written underneath, and another group had question marks, as yet unidentified.

Darya tapped one of the question marks with a fingernail. "That man is trouble."

I wanted to smile, but I suppressed it. This was what I'd hoped would happen, that she'd fill in some of the blanks, but no point in showing her how happy I was. I had a reputation as a bitch, and I quite liked it. Plus she'd probably realise she'd undervalued herself at eight grand a day—I'd been expecting to pay at least ten.

"Who is he?"

"Maxim Agapov. Junior spy and all-around *mudak*." She tilted her head to one side. "But I think not your kind of trouble. He makes mistakes with drugs and women and then others have to clean up after him."

"How does he still have a job?"

"His father is the minister of culture, and I'm ninety percent sure his wife doesn't know about Maxim or Maxim's mother or any of the other mistresses. The woman has the brains of a cabbage."

"Does Maxim take after her?"

"He's not smart, but he is sly."

She picked up the pen and wrote Maxim's name under his picture as Quinn's voice came from behind us.

"Sounds as if I'm not needed here."

Ana set her tablet on the table. "This is Quinn."

Darya turned to peer at him, and I couldn't blame her for being curious. She might have tried to hide it, but I hadn't missed her shock when she found out Ana had a daughter, and it stood to reason that she'd been wondering about Tabby's father.

Quinn had obviously been briefed. "You're Ana's old roommate, right?"

"*Da*. Darya."

"Good to meet you. Sorry I can't be there, but Tabby has a parent-teacher conference at school tomorrow and one of us needs to go."

"Did she call that kid a jackass again?" I asked.

Ana had spun some story about Tabby overhearing the word and not understanding what it meant, but she knew exactly what it meant.

"No, this time she called him a cockwomble, and I think we all know where she picked that up."

Oops.

"Look on the bright side—she's got great vocabulary for a four-year-old."

Before Quinn could go full *Dad* on me, the screen mounted on the wall came to life and Naz appeared. Another Russian who'd left his former job under a cloud, but he'd been intelligence rather than clean-up crew. Naz was a partner at Sirius Consulting alongside Alaric, one of my exes, and I valued his thoughts on the problem at hand. Blackwood had a small presence in Moscow, but we were far from experts on the region, so we needed all the help we could get.

I made the introductions. "Darya, this is Naz. Naz is former SVR"—Sluzhba Vneshney Razvedki Rossiyskoy Federatsii, also known as Russia's foreign intelligence service—"but now he's moved to the private sector. Naz, this is Darya, an old comrade of Ana's."

Officially, Naz no longer existed, and his current passport said he was Norwegian, as did his carefully cultivated accent. But he couldn't change his past, and his sharp intake of breath told me when he'd put two and Seven together and made Nine.

"Sorry I'm not able to greet you in person, but I don't like funerals, especially when they're my own."

"Coward," I said.

"No, I just have a healthy sense of self-preservation. So, why am I involved here? Alaric mentioned embassy personnel?"

"Somebody's high-school science project went missing, and the US government wants it back. There's reason to believe that one of the culprits involved has a connection to the Russian Consulate Field Office in Huntington Beach. Our job is to work out who, and then relieve them of the goods." I waved a hand towards the wall of whiteboards behind me. "Uncle Sam has kindly shared whatever information they have on the folks who came and went from the building today. We need to identify them and either rule them out of any involvement or dig into their lives further until we find what we're looking for. Any assistance you can provide would be much appreciated."

"Okay, I understand. We're waiting for more people before we begin?"

Hallie and Vance had just walked in, and Vance had headed straight for the breadsticks.

"No, everyone's here."

"Then who is all the food for?"

"We're going to freeze it and defrost it in batches for the rest of our lives."

"Your arteries will hate you."

"Tell me something I don't know."

Like who these mystery men were.

We'd actually had one small stroke of luck—today was a Sunday, and the field office ran a skeleton staff at the weekends. That left us with seventeen faces on the boards, and twelve of them had already been identified by the watchers as diplomatic staff, security personnel, or regular visitors. Four were suspected of being spies, and they must have kissed serious ass to get this gig. Year-round sunshine, hobnobbing with the Hollywood set, and a political landscape that was virtually flat compared with DC. The logs backed up my initial thoughts that this was a cushy little job—few of these guys were early risers. Maxim Agapov rarely showed up before eleven thirty a.m., and the notes said he often looked worse for wear. Now that Darya had identified him, that left us with four unknowns.

I helped myself to a slice of pizza as our quartet of Russia experts took centre stage—Ana, Darya, Naz, and Quinn. Quinn wasn't Russian himself, but he'd lived there for years, spying for the US, and although he mainly trained newbies at the CIA now, he still kept his finger on the pulse.

Naz and Ana both picked out a sour-faced chap as a career diplomat, a man who'd once been an aide to Pushkin, the former president. Quinn was eighty percent sure the sole woman on the list was Miroslava Novikova, a bottle blonde in her late twenties who'd worked under the former energy minister, quite literally if rumours were to be believed. That left two men who'd arrived together in the afternoon and stayed for less than half an hour. Both in their early thirties at a guess, one in a suit, no tie, and the other wearing slim-fitting khakis and a sweater with a quirky pattern of criss-crossing stripes in varying shades of blue. Darya stepped closer and studied the faces. The dude in the stripy sweater was looking down at the phone in his hand, so we didn't have a great view of him.

"I don't know the man on the right. And the other…" She traced Suit Guy's features with a fingertip. "I haven't seen him before either, but still, he's familiar. The eyes, the set of his chin, the shape of his face… He reminds me of Arseny Timonenko."

"Didn't he have a son?" Naz asked. "There was talk of one."

"Yes." Quinn snapped his fingers. "The son was Marat, and Arseny divorced his wife and married Marat's mother."

Who was Arseny Timonenko? "Could somebody enlighten those of us who aren't fluent in Kremlin?"

Ana did the honours. "He worked for Pushkin. Officially, he was a special advisor, but in reality, he was Mr. Fix It."

"So it's possible that this guy..." I pointed at maybe-Marat's picture. "...is another connection to Markovich's old opposition? How do we feel about Pushkin? Could he be involved?"

Darya held up both hands. "I've been out of the loop for four years."

"You must have watched the news."

Pushkin had come to power after his predecessor, Krupin, fell down the stairs in the Kremlin. *Fell.* Not many people thought it was an accident. Pushkin had started off as a proponent of Marxism-Leninism, but after years of sanctions first implemented under Krupin left the Russian economy crumbling, Pushkin had become more open to the idea of a social democracy. At least, that's what he claimed. Nobody had believed him. He just wanted the sanctions removed, so he said what the West wanted to hear, culminating in the mistake of agreeing to democratic elections monitored by an international team. By that point, the Russian people had been sick of queueing for bread and potatoes, and when a right-wing nutjob named Lagunov had promised them better things, they'd fallen for his spiel.

Oh, Lagunov had spearheaded a clever campaign, which was to say, he'd manipulated people by playing on their fears. Plus he'd coerced a thirty-seven-year-old oligarch's son, who also happened to be rather easy on the eye and the star of popular Russian cop show *Detektivy*, into running alongside him as prime minister. Gennady Nizhegorodov, known professionally as Gennady Markovich because nobody at the Screen Actors Guild could pronounce his actual surname, knew fuck all about governing, but that didn't matter. His role was to woo the female voters, post nice things about Lagunov on social media, and make the occasional speech.

Then Lagunov's plane had crashed two days after he was sworn in, and suddenly Markovich had a country to run.

The younger generations liked him. Women liked him. But Pushkin's people and Lagunov's people and Krupin's people were united in their hatred of him. Making meaningful change when his peers hampered him at every opportunity wasn't easy, but he was trying.

"Yes, I watch the news." Darya shrugged. "Four years ago, I'd have said that Puskin was a wannabe communist keen to maintain his grip on power, but he also had health issues."

That seemed to surprise everyone else.

"What health issues?" Quinn asked.

"Blocked arteries. Too much salo. He had an operation to fix the problem, but I doubt he changed his diet."

Ah, salo. The little chunks of salted pork fat Russians were so fond of snacking on, often chased with vodka. By birth, I was half-Russian and half-English, and although British cuisine was nothing to write home about—jellied eels, anyone?—I was glad I'd grown up eating beans on toast and fish and chips rather than fish soup and dumplings.

"Pushkin always was set in his ways," Quinn said. "Big on Russian culture and history, and resistant to change until the sanctions got too much to bear. But he's indicated no desire to run for a government position again. In fact, he's more or less disappeared from public life in favour of spending time with his family."

"So Anton Stepanov is still the more likely candidate for the theft of the Marshmallow," I concluded.

I'd been reading up on Russian politics, and Stepanov had been tapped by Lagunov to become Minister of Defence. Markovich had dumped Stepanov out on his arse.

"The Marshmallow?" Naz asked.

"The science project. Who else do we have here with a Stepanov connection?"

We ran down the list provided by the watchers, and when I read out the fifth name, Sergey Novak, Darya spoke up.

"Nobody calls him Sergey. He's Blok Novak."

The nickname fit. He was a fireplug of a man, as wide as he was high with the bulk coming mostly from muscle by the look of it. His dark hair was thinning on top, but I suspected most of it had fallen through his head and come out in his eyebrows, which were impressively bushy. In the picture we had, he was grinning, and his dimples were big enough to hide M&Ms in.

Now Quinn chimed in. "There's a name from the past. When Anton Stepanov was mayor of Moscow, Blok Novak worked with his right-hand man. What was that guy's name?"

Naz supplied the answer. "Kobylkin. Semyon Kobylkin. But he died in a hunting 'accident'"—Naz used air quotes around the word—"and got replaced by..."

Ooh, I knew this one. "Yuma Loslov."

"That's right."

"We have a file on him, and there's no mention of Blok Novak. Doesn't mean there isn't a connection, though."

"Stepanov likes to compartmentalise. It's why nobody's been able to pin anything on him in the past. Apart from a small core team, he outsources the dirty work, and none of his minions ever see the full picture."

I went through the rest of the names on the list, but nobody was aware of any specific connection to Stepanov. Right now, Novak seemed to be the most likely candidate, and he was simply noted as an attaché, which covered a multitude of sins.

"Let's focus on Novak first. We need to know where he lives, what he does in his spare time, and who he associates with." I checked my watch—we were closing in on one a.m. "Assuming he's planning to work tomorrow, the watchers will give us a heads-up when he arrives at the consulate. And while we're waiting, we can dig into his background. I'll have the cyber team in Virginia get started overnight." Some of those guys were practically nocturnal. "When we locate him, we can start surveillance."

"Want me to arrange a team for that?" Vance asked.

"No, I actually have a different project for you and Hallie. The Marshmallow went missing from Sandy Peake Defense Research Laboratory, and everyone assumed the inside person was Ottie Marquette. But recent events are leading us to question that belief. And if it wasn't her, then who was it? Somebody else working there betrayed the US, either for ideals or for money, and we need to find out who."

"Any leads so far?"

"Ottie was involved with one of her colleagues, although he didn't work on the same project. Plus there's a materials engineer with a gambling problem who could have sold out for money, and a missing software engineer. I'll send the files over. Use whatever resources you need—the budget for this project is comfortable."

"Should we work from here?"

"That would be ideal. And it goes without saying—not a whisper of this job can get out."

"Understood."

"If you need a bed for the night, feel free to take the guest room at the top of the stairs, but when Bradley arrives, you'll have to share or take the couch."

"The couch sounds good to me."

Darya gave a quiet laugh, and I hoped that maybe she was thawing a little.

"We'll catch up at eight tomorrow. Let's get some sleep."

NINE

Blok Novak had aged in the years since I'd last seen him, but his taste in women had gone the other way. His companion today couldn't have been more than twenty, and she towered over him in a pair of platform wedges that would leave her crippled if she stumbled off a kerb.

He'd also taken up golf.

Which was both a good thing and a bad thing.

Good because a substantial amount of business got done on the golf course, and for some reason, men felt free to run their mouths as long as they were knocking tiny balls around a patch of grass.

Bad because I'd picked up a golf club precisely once in my life, and that had been to rearrange the skull of a Polish shipping magnate who'd somehow ended up on the general's bad side. Golf wasn't big in Siberia.

Oh, and the Northlake Club was a private golf course, which meant we couldn't simply walk in there anyway.

When Novak turned into the club, I carried on past, then pulled our Porsche over a short distance down the road. Yes, our Porsche. I'd discovered another perk of working for

Blackwood this morning—the accessories. Since this was a last-minute gig, Emmy had requested three pool cars from the LA office, but when they got stuck behind a pile-up on the freeway, she'd offered the keys to the 911 in the garage instead. Alex had reluctantly folded himself into the passenger seat while I slid behind the wheel, trying to look indifferent about the situation. Grinning like an idiot would have done my reputation no good whatsoever.

And the car wasn't the only bonus. Ana said that if I needed more clothes, I should take anything I needed from the closets in the house. Apparently, they were communal, a repository for the overspill from Bradley's all-too-frequent shopping sprees. Plus Emmy and I were roughly the same build, and most of the outfits had been bought with her in mind. Sure, I was two inches taller, but when the label said Ishmael, I could make do. Back in the old days, whenever I'd swung by a mall, Rad had said I was trying to buy happiness, but that wasn't the reason. I'd always known happiness was an unachievable goal. My designer habit...it was more of a reaction to circumstance. Growing up on Base 13, I'd only ever been allowed to wear practical clothes, cargo pants and T-shirts and thick, drab coats, and putting on a pair of well-cut jeans and a silk top was my way of giving General Zacharov the middle finger.

And as for Darla's fashion sense... Urgh. But there was a reason I dressed her in outlandish muumuus. Not only could I hide all sorts of goodies underneath, but people also tended to remember her flowing outfits rather than the person wearing them. They were a modern-day invisibility cloak.

But today, I'd picked out a pair of navy-blue capri pants and a pale-pink cashmere sweater that would be warm enough for the California winter and fit in well with Novak's middle-to-upper-class cohorts. Alex had gone with chinos and a grey polo shirt that strained across his biceps.

"We should find somewhere we can see the course," I said. "I brought binoculars."

"But we won't be able to hear what goes on."

"No, but if we can see who he meets, that's better than nothing."

"Let me make a call."

We found a parking space that overlooked one corner of the course, and I wanted to climb over the fence, but there was a steady stream of people meandering past. Damn joggers. Alex said we should sit tight, and thirty minutes later, an SUV pulled up beside us. A grey-haired man got out carrying what looked like...two pairs of sneakers?

When Emmy said she'd find a solution, I'd expected somebody to deliver a parabolic microphone or a James Bond-style drone, not fucking shoes. And even though she'd told us the guy's name was Gerald and his daughter worked as an admin assistant at Blackwood's LA office, I still slipped a gun under a folded jacket on my lap while Alex wound down the window.

"Are you Gerald?"

Alex's American accent wasn't perfect, but when he put his mind to it, he managed to sound as if he hadn't just taken a wrong turn out of downtown Moscow.

"Indeed I am. And you're a friend of Emmy's?" He didn't wait for an answer. "I understand you and your wife want to play a round of golf at Northlake?" He held out the shoes. "You might want to borrow these."

"Do you have clubs?"

"In the trunk. How are you enjoying your vacation?"

"It's been pleasurable so far."

"Good, good. Follow me, and I'll sign you in."

As the stranger walked back to his vehicle, Alex passed me the shoes, but before I put them on and started the engine, I had a hundred questions.

"Golf? We're meant to play golf?" I glanced down at the shoes, and they weren't even my size. "Doesn't Blackwood have tiny drones?"

"Yes, but it's too windy for those to fly today. Also not good for golf, but..." He shrugged. "It doesn't matter if we're over par."

"Do you even know how to play golf? These shoes are too big."

"Mine are too small. And I used to play golf most weekends." A grimace. "My ex-wife wanted to join a country club, so we joined a country club. You can play?"

I shook my head. "In Siberia, the balls would get lost in the snow."

"Then I guess I'm giving you a golf lesson."

I'd spent a lifetime learning. From a young age, I'd been expected to pick up new skills every week. Medical training taught me how to save a life if I felt so inclined, though that was rare. Sniper training meant I could put a bullet through a man's medulla oblongata from a thousand yards. Masters had drilled me through hand-to-hand combat skills, and I'd developed mental stamina as well as physical. Games of chess had taught me strategy and patience, while psychology lectures gave me clues as to what my opponents were thinking. I knew how to fly a plane and parachute out of one if necessary, and I'd conquered any hints of claustrophobia when I spent a month on a submarine. I could ride a horse, handle a dog sled, and track a wolf through a frozen forest. I hadn't enjoyed all of the lessons, not by a long shot, but I'd understood why they were necessary.

Which brought us to golf.

There was a ball.

There was a hole.

And rarely the two did meet.

There was also walking, but the walking was interrupted at regular intervals by frustration. People paid money to do this? I thwacked another clump of grass out of the fairway and cursed, but only in my head. Out loud, I giggled like the vapid idiot I was pretending to be.

"Straighten your left leg a little," Alex said.

"If I straighten it any more, my knee will bend the wrong way."

"Like this..."

That was another thing nobody had told me about golf. It involved a lot of touching. Alex moved my shoulders, adjusted my hands, corrected my feet, and nudged my hips into a position he deemed to be suitable, which felt exactly the same as the position I'd been in before he started. To me, this whole...rearrangement was foreign, but it must have been normal because ahead of us at the tee, Blok Novak and his companion didn't bat an eyelid. No, they just carried on with their conversation as I strained to hear.

I didn't recognise the other man. His accent was American, and he spoke with a Texas twang, mainly, it seemed, about women. First, he bitched about his wife, and then he bitched about his girlfriend. Blok made sympathetic noises in the right places, subservient, which meant the Texan was in charge, or at least, Blok was giving him that illusion.

But who was he?

We still didn't know, but he sure played golf better than I did. And yes, that annoyed me. I hated being second best—something Rad had called a flaw, but I didn't understand why. What was wrong with wanting to be good at things?

The Texan had already teed off, his ball sailing into the air in the direction of the green. Blok followed suit, and the two of them ambled out of earshot while I was still carving up turf.

"I think this thing is faulty."

Gerald had lent me his wife's golf clubs, which came in a baffling array of woods and irons and were apparently designed specifically for women. Men required longer, stiffer shafts, according to Alex. Surely there was a metaphor in there somewhere? Or maybe they just liked tucking their egos away in their golf bags.

"You're too tense. Relax."

"You realise that when you tell somebody to relax, it has the opposite effect?"

He wrapped his arms around my body and closed his hands over mine, engulfing me. And, okay, I had to admit that his shaft felt reasonably impressive against my ass.

"Relax." The word whispered across my ear, followed by a brush of his lips, and I ended up tenser than I'd been before. But then he raised my arms, and *thwack*, the ball finally got off the mark.

"I detest golf," I muttered as I speed-walked after it, taking long strides so it didn't look as if I was in too much of a hurry. At least Alex was tall. He only had to stroll.

"Really?" His smile was more of a smirk. "I'm beginning to feel the benefits myself."

If any other man had tried that stunt, they'd have lost body parts. But this was Alexei, and I found I didn't hate the liberties he took. An unfamiliar weight settled in my stomach. Was that guilt? I thought it might be. Guilt that I liked the way Alex felt around me. Which was completely irrational. Rad was gone, and he was never coming back. What was I meant to do? Stay celibate for the rest of my life? My dry spell had already lasted four years, which had to be a long enough mourning period by societal standards, didn't it?

And in those four years, I'd had time to think. To observe.

To learn. I'd always believed that I'd been in love with Rad, and when he died, my world had certainly fallen apart. Everything changed in an instant. I'd lost my home, my job, and my partner. But our relationship had been far from conventional, and now that I'd seen how Brooke and Luca acted around each other, and Colt and Brie, and Aaron and Romi, I realised that what was between Rad and me had fallen short of the all-consuming love they shared. Oh, we'd liked each other well enough, but we'd only ended up together because there was no other option.

Yes, the heaviness was definitely guilt.

Guilt that whenever Alex touched me, my blood heated. And we were in the middle of a job, for fuck's sake.

"We need to find out who that guy is."

"The cyber team is running him through their facial recognition program."

Were they? Well, I wasn't about to get beaten by a computer. I located my ball in a clump of grass and knocked it back onto the fairway while I pondered the best way to approach the problem.

"You're not meant to kick it," Alex told me.

"Nobody was looking."

If I'd had better aim, I could have thwacked the ball into the Texan—when the EMTs arrived, Blok would have to give them the man's name. But since this was America, Gerald would probably get sued for my "mishap," and I didn't need a lecture from Emmy. So I decided to go with plan B.

As we approached the next tee, I swapped the plain silver ring I wore from my right hand to my left. It had been a gift from Rad, a trinket he'd picked up on a trip to Italy, but bought with practicality in mind rather than romance. Sometimes, it was advantageous to pretend I was married. In this environment, a wedding band would earn me a modicum of respect by telling people that a man had deemed me worthy of investment. At the country club, wives trumped girlfriends.

Which was yet another reason I disliked golf.

The Texan parked his electric caddy and set to work selecting a club. Why did people wear a single glove for golf? So they'd only leave half the amount of fingerprints? Screw tradition—I was wearing two gloves, the pair I carried with me everywhere in case of emergencies.

His spatial awareness needed improvement—when I approached, he didn't look up until I was more or less on top of him, although Blok did whip his head around as I got close.

"I'm soooo sorry to interrupt your game, but could you tell me, were you in that movie with Will Smith? My husband says I'm being silly, but..." I tapped my head. "I never forget a face."

"Then I'm sorry to disappoint ya, darlin', but I never was in that movie."

"Maybe I got confused? A different movie?" I thrust one gloved hand at him. "Oh, hark at me being rude—I'm Marlie Baldwin, and this is my husband, Alan. We just moved here from Idaho."

I waited, expectant, and he didn't disappoint. Texans had a tendency to be polite. "Well, I'm Joe Deaver, and I haven't been in any movies."

"You're not in showbiz at all? You look so...so distinguished."

His grin widened. "No, darlin', I'm in the oil business."

Score.

"Darn, then I must've been thinking of somebody else. I'm real sorry to have disturbed you."

Deaver was still holding on to my hand. "No need to apologise. And if you're in the clubhouse later, why don't you join us for a drink? It's always a pleasure to talk with a pretty lady."

I acted coy and giggled, made my cheeks turn red by thinking about Pavel and his murderous final act. Perhaps I'd take Deaver up on his offer—it all depended on what Emmy's team managed to dig up while we finished this round of golf. *Round.* That made it sound so innocuous. It was a *chore* of golf.

"Aw, that's real kind of you. We might just do that."

Blok didn't look happy about that idea, but he wasn't the boss, so who cared? Alex didn't seem thrilled either, which was...interesting. I gave my hand a gentle tug.

"So, uh..."

Finally, Deaver let go.

"A pleasure to meet you, Marlie."

"You too, Joe." Another giggle. "Enjoy your game."

Because I was enjoying mine, and it had nothing to do with golf.

So, Blok Novak was meeting with a Texan oil baron. What did that mean? How did it fit with our case? *Did* it fit with our case? Mack and her team were busy digging through his life, but I still posed the question to James when we caught up ten minutes later. He was in the Situation Room at the White House while I was on a secure line in a soundproof room on the ground floor of Skywater House, a room I'd carefully swept for bugs before we started the conversation. Just in case. One never could be too careful.

"Joseph Deaver?" I couldn't see James's face, but I didn't miss the scowl in his voice. "He's a pain in everyone's ass."

"In what way?"

"Climate 2050 is a cornerstone of my agenda, and Deaver and his buddies in the fossil fuel industry are trying to derail it at every turn. You say a Russian attaché is meeting with him?"

Every country in the world had agreed to sign the Climate 2050 treaty, a global attempt to reverse climate change by the midpoint of the century. Plans included cutting emissions, reducing the use of plastics, giving tax breaks for green energy, and setting ambitious recycling targets. James was one of the leading proponents, and he was determined for the US to not just comply with the targets but to smash them. I'd never understood why saving the planet was such a contentious issue —it was the only home we had, after all. But too many people valued profits over leaving the world habitable for the next generation.

"Yup. Novak and Deaver are around about the fifteenth hole at the Northlake Club."

"Shit. And I'm certain Markovich is feeling the pressure from the fossil fuel lobbyists too. It took a lot for him to get on board with the plan, and Anton Stepanov receives a significant amount of funding from the oil and gas industry."

"How close do you want us to get? Deaver invited two of our team members to join him for drinks at the nineteenth hole. Well, he actually invited one of our team members, but her fake husband can tag along."

"Who did he invite? Dan? She used to play golf, didn't she?"

"For about three weeks when she was screwing around with some guy who said he was a golf pro, but then it turned out he just worked in the club shop, so she quit. No, Darya is playing golf."

"Darya? Do I know her?"

"Nope. She's sort of new, sort of old."

"What do you mean by that?"

"Ana's worked with her before."

The meaning of that took about three seconds to filter in. James knew a reasonable amount of Ana's history, not all the details, but he was aware of her Base 13 escapades. And now he groaned.

"Tell me she isn't one of Zacharov's minions."

"Former minions. And I could tell you that, but I'd be lying."

"For heaven's sake, Emmy…"

"If you want me to dig you out of this hole, then you'll have to trust my judgment, okay? And you never answered my question about Deaver."

Was a sigh better or worse than a groan?

"I'll have to consult with a few people."

"You've got roughly twenty minutes to do that."

Which gave me enough time to visit the dining room. Not because I was hungry, although Vance *had* loaded the table with snacks, but to see what progress had been made in the last half hour. Ana was on the phone while Black, Hallie, and Vance sat in front of their laptops. If Vance typed any more furiously, he'd break a finger.

"Is there news?"

Black glanced up for a fraction of a second. "Maybe."

"Maybe? That's all I get?"

"Loslov's daughter studied in the UK. At Oriel College, Oxford," Ana announced. "She's a paediatrician in Moscow now."

"Darn it, I thought…" Hallie shook her head. "Never mind."

"What did you think?"

"Ford likes football. It's still kinda growing on me, but he often has a game on TV, and last year, we were watching the Stanford Cardinal versus the Washington State Cougars. The Cougars have a cool mascot, a…well, obviously it's a cougar. Makes sense, right? But the Cardinal have a tree. And there isn't even a cardinal sitting in it. Anyhow, Ford said it's not a cardinal bird that the name refers to, it's the colour cardinal. And the tree started out as a joke, but then it stuck."

"All very interesting, but what does that have to do with our missing device?"

"We dug up some pictures of Yuma Loslov, and in one of them, he's wearing a Cardinal cap. The Cardinal are from

Stanford. And when we entered that data into Providence, we found that Marat Timonenko studied for a master's degree in international relations there."

Providence was Blackwood's data analysis program. Think Google on steroids with extra bells and whistles. Once you'd entered the information you had on a subject, it ferreted out more from the internet, from Blackwood's internal databases, and from other sources we weren't really meant to have access to, and then it worked to link all of those little snippets together. Mack was the architect, and she'd built the Taj Mahal of programs.

And now we had a possible connection between Yuma Loslov and a member of the consulate staff?

"The two of them are linked?"

Hallie shook her head again. "Loslov didn't go to college in the US, plus he's twenty years older than Timonenko, so we figured that maybe he had a kid who got educated here. But I guess not."

"Loslov probably met his comrades in a bar in Tverskoy," Ana muttered. "A deal done in a back room."

Quite possibly, but a Cardinal hat? I'd have to ask Naz if he knew of a connection. He always came up with fascinating snippets of what he called intelligence and what any woman would call gossip.

"Yuma Loslov only had one kid? One wife? Every other fucker in politics seems to have a mistress. I mean, Joe Deaver's hitting on Darya right in front of Alex."

Ana grimaced. "And he's still alive?"

"Apparently, she has more self-control than you do."

"Is Deaver a politician?" Hallie asked. "I thought he was a businessman?"

"He hangs out with politicians. Bad habits are contagious."

"What's happening with Novak?" Black asked.

"Right now, we're in a holding pattern. Deaver's a problem, but it's unclear if he's *our* problem. In the meantime, we carry on looking at everyone else."

34

NINE

When I was fifteen, I'd made it a goal in life to learn something new every day. Mostly, I managed it, even if lately that knowledge had come in the form of a more complicated crochet stitch or the difference between pony beads and perlers.

Today, I'd learned three things.

Firstly, I'd learned that golf sucked.

Secondly, I'd learned that when Alex touched me, I went into atrial fibrillation.

Thirdly, and perhaps most interestingly, I'd learned that Blok Novak wasn't just an asshole, he was likely to be a double agent too.

At some point between the eighth and eighteenth holes, Emmy had gone through "channels," and due to the exceptional circumstances and President Harrison's improving relationship with President Markovich, the Russians were apparently offering unprecedented levels of cooperation in this matter. Word had come back quickly: do not touch Blok Novak. The Russians hadn't gone into detail, but a bunch of analysts sitting in a bunker somewhere had come to the conclusion that Novak was working for Markovich, spying on the opposition and feeding information back.

Of course, there was still the possibility that he was a triple agent, but my ex-colleagues could deal with that. Let them clean their own house if it was dirty. I felt no loyalty to my country now, not after the way I'd been treated by those in power. The only person I trusted was myself, and the only people I cared to help were the handful of friends I'd made in my new life. And perhaps Ana. And Alexei. And I guess I didn't particularly want to see hundreds of civilians roasted by an experimental weapon either.

Seemed I'd grown a conscience in my old age.

And maybe a heart too.

Damn.

But in this game of snakes and ladders, our roll of the dice had landed us back at the bottom of the board, and worse, the slithery little suckers were poisonous.

"Anyhow..." Emmy continued. "At least we've worked out what Ottie's code is for. The weapon has an electronic operating system, and she was the software's main architect. Current thinking is that she got wind of the plot to steal it, wiped the memory clean, and then ran. Took care of all the current backups too."

"So she has the only copy?" Ana asked.

"Given what Loslov's crew did to her, that seems likely."

"Could somebody rewrite it?"

"That's possible, and they might even have an old copy of the code, but it would take time and ability to get it up to scratch. So either they don't have anyone with that skill set, or they're planning to use the thing in a hurry."

Fantasticheskiy. Nothing like a little added pressure, was there?

"So, what's next?"

"Next, we have to—"

The front door slammed and I reached for my gun on instinct, but nobody else moved, which made me think that either they were asleep on the job or they knew something I didn't. And Emmy was probably an insomniac.

She glanced across at me and saw where my hand was. "Bradley's back in three, two, one..."

Half a second later, he skidded into the doorway. "Did you miss me?"

"No."

"I have gifts."

"We don't need gifts, and you've only been gone for a day."

"Yes, but it seems like so much longer." No, it didn't, and his neon-orange sweater was hurting my eyes. "Here, I brought cookies from Mary's Coffee House for everyone."

"Cookies? Okay, then perhaps I missed you a tiny bit." Emmy abandoned the slice of cold pizza she'd been eating and held out her hand for the bag. "Gimme."

"Did you solve the case yet? I hear Ottie's still unconscious, but that poor pooch should make a full recovery. We made him a gift basket with doggy treats and toys, and Paulo promised to send me updates."

"The case is still a work in progress, and you're interrupting the 'work' part."

Of course, Bradley completely ignored that complaint. "All these whiteboards are blocking out the light."

"It's dark outdoors."

"Yes, but in the morning it won't be. Maybe we could just move them to the side a bit?"

Now Black stepped in. "The whiteboards stay where they are."

"Okay, okay, it was only a suggestion." Bradley jabbed a finger at the photo of Marat Timonenko. We'd confirmed his identity now, but his friend was still an unknown. The facial recognition program had scored a big fat zero, unsurprising given the awkward angle the photo had been taken at. "This guy needs a haircut. The style he has is too long and all wrong for his bone structure."

"If I ever speak to him in person, I'll be sure to tell him that."

"You'd be doing him a favour, trust me. Who's his friend? He dresses better."

"That, dear Bradley, is the big question. If you find out, let us know."

"If I find out, can we have a Valentine's party this year?"

"If you find out, I'll dress up as the Queen of bloody Hearts."

"Boy, somebody needs to take a chill pill this evening."

Black's lips twitched as Emmy sucked in a calming breath. "I'm perfectly cool, thank you. Don't you have places to go, people to see?"

"My friend Barnaby *is* having a small get-together. Maybe I could drop by for a few minutes?"

"Great idea—off you go."

Once Bradley had swished out the door in a flourish of tangerine, I whispered to Alex, "Are they always like that?"

"They love each other really."

"How long has Bradley worked for her?"

"Over a decade."

Wow. I had to admire his perseverance. And maybe, just maybe, I had to give Emmy points for patience.

We plotted out a course of action for the next day, but with Blok removed from the picture, we were starting from scratch. While Alex was feeling me up on the golf course, Vance and Hallie had been running background checks on the rest of the consulate staff. Emmy's government contacts had provided the basics, but there were plenty of blanks to fill in.

We had a list, a ranked list, and with the elimination of

Blok, there were sixteen names left. At the top? We had a three-way tie for first place. Maxim Agapov wasn't smart enough to pull off the theft on his own, in my opinion, but he certainly had the ethics, and if he'd found himself a partner with a brain... Yes, he was a possibility. Then there was Marat Timonenko. His father was smart, ruthless, and connected, and if his son had inherited a fraction of those traits, then he might be a problem. Finally, we had a new player. Ruslan Smirnov—almost like Smirnoff vodka, Vance joked, which was ironic because the vodka had also been called Smirnov until the Smirnov family was forced to flee Russia in the October Revolution.

A new name, a new start.

Darya. Darla.

Anyhow, Ruslan Smirnov was a middle-aged security guard at the consulate, and he'd recently come into some money if his social media feed was anything to go by. A lottery win, he said, but how many lottery millionaires kept working a minimum-wage job? Not many. Ruslan drove to work in a Toyota Camry, but on his days off, he cruised the streets of LA in a shiny new Ferrari. Something didn't add up.

With any luck, we'd find out what it was tomorrow. Or even later today—midnight had come and gone. At least, I thought it had. The clock on the wall was some weird abstract thing consisting of a waterfall of coloured blobs, curved hands, and no numbers. But Emmy yawned and stood, so I figured it was time to sleep. In the surveillance sweepstakes, Alex and I had drawn Timonenko, and a tired spy was a shitty spy.

Alex took my hand in his as we walked to the guest house, as had become his habit. One I quite liked. I'd never be the type of woman to *need* a man, but sometimes in the past, it had been nice to share parts of my life with Rad. To feel as if I wasn't quite so alone. And at least with Alex, unlike in

Baldwin's Shore, I could be my true self. He hadn't run screaming yet, which I had to take as a good sign.

In his other hand, he held our gifts from Bradley. Socks for Alex and a box of hot chocolate bombs for me, round spheres of chocolate filled with marshmallows, which made me smile because bombs hadn't been spherical since the eighteenth century. Unless of course you counted the time I'd packed plastic explosive into a target's antique globe and detonated it as he relaxed with a snifter of brandy.

"You want one of these chocolate things tonight?" Alex asked.

"We need to sleep."

"You'll sleep better if you unwind first. Don't roll your eyes."

Did I do that? Okay, maybe I did.

"Unwinding is a luxury I don't have time for."

"When I took the job with Blackwood, the brief was to push Emmy when required but keep her in optimum shape, physically and mentally. At first, Black didn't give her enough downtime, and when we increased her rest periods, her performance actually improved. Clearly, there's a point where too much R & R is also detrimental, but what I'm trying to say is that there's a balance to be reached. And I know from working with Ana that General Zacharov didn't respect that balance."

"He liked to squeeze the last drop of blood out of the workhorse."

"At Blackwood, we take a different approach. Yes, there will be times when rest is impossible, but longevity is the goal." Alex held up the bag. Bradley had even tied ribbon around the handles. "Sit down, and I'll make the drinks."

Ten minutes less sleep wouldn't hurt, would it?

"Just don't tell me to start meditating."

"Meditation has health benefits."

"Paulo gave me one of those CD sets for my fake birthday, and it left me more stressed than I was when I started. I..." I sighed. Alex had a way of digging into my psyche, of making me confront truths I'd rather avoid. "I guess I don't find it easy to relax."

"Then we'll start slow, I promise. One drink."

Ten minutes turned into half an hour. Half an hour of staring at the stars and listening to the waves and talking softly about our lives. Alex had bought a house in Richmond a decade ago, a fixer-upper, and now it was fixed up, but he didn't spend much time there. Mostly he hung out at Emmy and Black's home, a sprawling estate with three houses, a lake, some horses, and an airstrip that doubled as a shooting range. Plus there were indoor and outdoor pools and a gym with top-of-the-line equipment.

"I miss swimming," I confessed. "We had an indoor pool at the base, a heated one, although the general thought it was fun to drop us into Lake Baikal and see if we drowned."

One time, he'd even blasted a hole through the ice so we could dive there in winter. Our guide had gotten frostbite and lost three toes, and Ilya had tormented me with stories about the Lake Baikal monster, although in those days, getting eaten alive had been the least of my worries.

"There's no pool in Baldwin's Shore?" Alex asked.

The Peninsula resort had two pools, but Nico's domain was off limits for obvious reasons. Not that I could swim there anyway.

"I have scars, and I can't afford to have people ask questions about where they came from. And Darla isn't the type to pull on a wetsuit and dive into the sea."

"The pool here is warm. Black turned the heater on when he arrived, so the water's up to temperature now."

I already knew that because I'd seen Hallie take a dip before dinner. She'd stroked smoothly up and down for fifteen minutes, then checked her watch and hurried back inside again.

"I don't have a bathing suit."

"Bradley will find you one. Or we could always go skinny-dipping at midnight."

"Oh, you think?"

There were two lounge chairs on the balcony outside my bedroom, but somehow, we'd both ended up squashed onto one of them. Purely for practical reasons, you understand—sharing body heat was the best way to ward off hypothermia.

"I won't stare at your ass, I swear."

"Why not? I have nothing to be ashamed of. I do a lot of squats."

Alex's arm tightened around my shoulders, and he stroked my cheek with a fingertip.

"Dasha..."

The word came out thick and hoarse, and I thought that maybe he was going to kiss me. And even though it was soon, so soon, and he lived on the other side of the country, and my whole life was a fucking shitshow, I wanted him to.

His breathing hitched as his lips brushed against mine, a whispered promise of what was to come. There were those damned palpitations again. Was his heart skipping too? I pressed a hand to his chest, felt the hammering against his ribcage.

"You're okay with this?" Alex murmured.

"If I wasn't, you'd have lost the ability to father children by now."

He cursed under his breath, and I instantly regretted my words. This kind of relationship was new to me, romance a concept I'd seen and read about but didn't quite understand.

"That was meant to be a joke."

Probably. I mean, if I hadn't liked him so much, he'd definitely be missing his balls.

"I know. My fucking phone is ringing." He fished it out of his pants pocket. "Emmy."

Suggesting he ignore it wasn't an option, and besides, I was curious. There had to be news. Otherwise she wouldn't be calling this late at night, would she?

"Well, answer it."

Alex did, and after he'd listened for a few moments, his mouth creased into a grin.

"No, I'll tell her. We'll be there in five."

See? News.

"What?" I asked the instant he hung up. "What happened?"

"Next month, Emmy will be dressing up as the Queen of Hearts."

35

NINE

In the kitchen, Emmy fought with the coffee machine while Black leaned against the counter, watching her with a vague look of amusement. They were dressed identically now, in boxer shorts and supersized T-shirts. Emmy's came to her knees while Black's was a little tight across the chest. Suddenly, I felt self-conscious in my day clothes. Everyone else had gone to bed, and it was evident that Alex and I had stayed up together. Still, it could have been worse—if things had escalated between us, if that heat had kept building, Alex's shirt would have been missing its buttons in another ten minutes. Would my borrowed sweater have survived? He didn't strike me as the clothes-shredding type. Oh, he sure knew how to fight—I'd learned that in our training session— but off duty, he was a gentle giant.

"You're drinking coffee at this time of night?" I asked.

"No, I'm trying to sober Bradley up."

"He found our mystery man?"

"So he claims."

Black gave a soft chuckle. "What actually happened was that he staggered in, announced our Valentine's ball would have an Alice in Wonderland theme, puked into a decorative bowl, and passed out. So we're assuming he found the mystery man, but that fact is far from certain."

The general might have been a brutal son of a bitch, but at least nobody had thrown up during his briefings. Blackwood's unorthodox ways bordered on crazy at times. In the living room, Ana had put Bradley into the recovery position, and since I couldn't see any bowl or smell any vomit, I had to conclude that somebody had dealt with that part of the problem.

"He's still breathing?" I asked, just to check.

Emmy nodded. "Right now, I'm not sure whether that's a good thing or a bad thing."

Hallie meandered in wearing a faint look of disgust, her slender nose crinkled, so I figured she'd been tasked with clean-up duty. Vance followed and gave a shrug.

"Who the hell knows where his shoes ended up—they're not in the driveway."

"How did he get back here?"

"No idea."

Hallie gave Bradley a gentle shake. "Are you okay?"

"Mmm-mmm."

What did that mean? Yes or no?

"I think maybe we should sit him up now."

She tried to lift his arms, and when he flopped to the floor again, Ana obliged and hauled him into an armchair. How much had he drunk? He'd only been gone for a few hours.

"What did he do? Pour vodka down his throat?"

Emmy spoke from behind me. "There was probably free champagne, and this is the result of two or three glasses, most of which he chucked up. He's a lightweight." She gave him a harder shake. "But fortunately, the effects soon wear off. Dude, wake up."

"Mmm-mmm."

"What does that mean?"

Everybody shrugged, and somebody had to do something or we'd be here all night. So I stepped forward and slapped him.

"You heard her—wake up."

Now his eyes flickered open.

"I don't like you very much."

"Then you can join the club. What happened tonight? Who is the man?"

Emmy thrust a mug of coffee toward him. "Drink this and talk."

"Is it organic?"

"How the fuck should I know?"

"You read the package, duh."

"There was no package. You told me the bag was 'too drab' and dumped the contents into a canister decorated with butterflies, remember?"

"They're hummingbirds."

"Whatever. Talk."

"I need Tylenol."

Emmy rolled her eyes. "For crying out loud, someone find him a painkiller."

Ana slipped out of the room, and I wouldn't have been surprised if she didn't come back, but at least Bradley started speaking.

"You didn't think I could do it, did you? Find the man's name?" He giggled. "But it was soooo easy."

"Go on then, tell us how great you are."

"In the picture, he was wearing a Jacobi Wykoff sweater. They're very distinctive."

"Is that supposed to mean something to me?"

Bradley looked her up and down, taking in the boxer shorts and giant T-shirt.

"Probably not. Why can't you wear silk pyjamas like a normal person?"

"Normal? How many people here do you think wear silk pyjamas?"

At least one, but I wasn't about to admit that in front of Emmy. They were one of the few luxuries I still allowed myself, okay? Plus they were practical. I always bought mine in black or navy blue, and I could run and jump and kick while wearing them.

Surprisingly, Ana reappeared with a bottle of pills, and Bradley swallowed a couple, then complained the coffee was too hot. If I were in Emmy's position, he would have been wearing it by now. Hmm. I wondered for a moment whether Moscow's burns were healing. His skin had been peeling nicely by the time Emmy's contacts took him away.

"So, the man was wearing a Jacobi Wykoff sweater—which means he has excellent taste, by the way—and you can't simply walk into a store and buy one off the rack."

"Then how did he get it?"

"You book a consultation with Jacobi, and he makes you a custom piece tailored to your aura."

"Are you serious?"

"Jacobi's a genius at picking out personality traits. The sweater he made for me is pink and yellow to represent both my feminine side and my sunny disposition."

"And how much did I pay for that?"

"Trust me, it was worth every cent. Anyhow, I can tell you that the man you're looking for projects a friendly image, but he also has a dark side. See the way the cobalt stripes cross under the cornflower ones? Those are the parts of his psyche he keeps hidden."

Sheesh. Who knew knitwear could be so revealing? Luckily, my budget didn't run to a personalised sweater, and there was no way any designer would be analysing *my* aura.

"Fantastic. So you're saying we need to speak to this Jacobi guy?"

"You think I didn't already do that? I had Barnaby call him up and invite him over."

"Tell me you didn't mention the case?"

Bradley narrowed his eyes, indignant. "Do you think I'm a numbskull?"

Keep your mouth shut, Dasha.

"No, but you've been drinking," Emmy reminded him.

"Yes, but only *after* the conversation with Jacobi. Barnaby opened a crate of champagne—what was I meant to do, turn it down?"

"That might've been a sensible option."

"It was Laurent-Perrier rosé," Bradley said, as if that explained everything. "And I didn't mention the case at all. I told Jacobi that a rude man wearing one of his sweaters drove into my car and refused to give me his insurance details."

"And Jacobi knew who you were talking about?"

"All I had to do was describe the pattern. So now I have the name, and Jacobi promised not to make him any more knitwear."

"And what's the name?"

"Bryant Angelou." Bradley fumbled through half a dozen pockets and finally found his phone. "Here—I had Jacobi check the spelling. Bryant is a movie producer, but not a very good one. Should I order cases of Laurent-Perrier for the Valentine's ball? We could have matching wine-glass charms for each couple." He turned to me. "Do you have an online tutorial for those? Could you source the materials?"

"Paulo could probably put something together. He's the best at beadwork." A sale was a sale, and next week, I'd be Darla again. A prospect I wasn't particularly looking forward to. "Why don't you message him?"

"Maybe...maybe I'll do that in the morning."

Bradley's eyes began to close, and ten seconds later, he was dead to the world again. But by a miracle, we had our name. Bryant Angelou.

"Is he right?" Ana asked.

Black had already looked the guy up on his tablet. "I believe he is, and he's also correct about Angelou being second rate. He's listed as executive producer on three infomercials and five movies, all of which were low-budget affairs that went nowhere. A sixth is in post-production. The photo from the embassy isn't the best, but this looks like the same man to me."

Angelou's publicity shot was an artsy setup that showed him half-hidden in shadow, but there were also a dozen candid pictures that caught him from varying angles, plus several that looked as if they'd been taken at red-carpet affairs. And yes, there were definite similarities. When put together with Bradley's information, I considered it ninety-five percent likely that we'd identified our unknown subject.

The question was how, if at all, did he link to the stolen weapon?

"Hallie, Vance, your priority in the morning is to find out everything you can about Angelou and Timonenko. Once we have more information, we'll make a decision on how to proceed." Emmy threw Bradley over one shoulder and headed for the door. "Get some sleep, everyone. Again."

Back in the guest house, Alex followed me up the stairs, but instead of heading into his bedroom, he stopped outside mine and wrapped one arm around my waist.

"We *will* finish what we started, but not tonight." He ghosted another barely-there kiss across my lips. "Not when we both need to rest."

A part of me wanted to crawl into bed beside him. I'd always slept better when Rad was next to me—his presence had kept the nightmares away, and I wondered if Alexei possessed the same superpower. Only time would tell, and we had precious little of that.

"At least kiss me properly before you go."

"Is that a good idea?"

"No, it's a terrible idea, but just fucking do it."

First, he smiled, and then he obeyed. He had to dip his head and I had to stand on tiptoes, but we made it work, and as he deepened the kiss, I felt the first stirrings of his cock against my stomach. Heat burned through me, and hell yes, this was the worst idea in the history of bad ideas because now I longed to push him onto the nearest horizontal surface and drink my fill of him.

But we couldn't always have what we wanted, could we? The general had taught me that important lesson.

Alex wrapped my hair around his hand and tilted my head back, giving himself access to my throat. Feather-soft kisses along my jaw and down my neck sent my pulse racing before he stepped back.

"Sleep well, Dashenka."

And then he was gone.

36

NINE

In my past life, I'd spent some time around embassies, studying their layouts, watching the activity nearby, occasionally slipping inside for a closer look. Visit Embassy Row in DC or Kensington Palace Gardens in London, and you'd find yourself immersed in a world of quiet wealth and privilege where loitering unnoticed was difficult. I'd had to get creative—dress up as a tourist with a different disguise every day, skulk around at night avoiding the watchful eyes of security cameras, that kind of thing... Once, I'd reinvented myself as a landscaper just to spend time in the area. Nobody questioned a woman with pruning shears.

The Russian Consulate Field Office in Huntington Beach presented a different set of challenges. It perched above the Big Break Surf Store, a stone's throw from the ocean, and there were people everywhere. Locals in a hurry, tourists wandering in the way, kids on skateboards, a woman arguing on the phone with her boyfriend, and a pickpocket scoping out potential marks. On a different day, maybe I'd have treated him to a dose of his own medicine, but this morning, I had other priorities.

I knew now where the "watchers" were. The Surfside Hotel overlooked the entrance, a nondescript door sandwiched between Big Break and the Matrixx nightclub. Guess the diplomats liked to be in the heart of the community. I'd bet my Remington CSR that the US government occupied one of the hotel rooms on a long-term rental, and even as Alex and I ate a late breakfast at the café opposite Big Break, an agent would be sitting above our heads, studying the comings and goings. We'd considered renting a room ourselves, but if somebody left and we needed to follow, they'd have disappeared into the crowds by the time we made it down to the lobby.

So for now, our brief was simple: play tourist. At this moment, our three main targets—Timonenko, Smirnov, and Agapov—were all inside, and after we'd taken our time eating, Emmy and Black would relieve us. By then, we hoped to have a location for our new friend, Bryant Angelou. It was possible the meeting between him and Timonenko had been entirely innocent—one role of diplomats was to promote the culture of their homeland, after all, and Angelou's latest venture was an action thriller being shot on location in both Moscow and California—but he was still a loose end.

I didn't care for loose ends.

"Want more coffee?" Alex asked.

"Not yet. After we've eaten."

Which wouldn't be anytime soon, I suspected. The couple next to us had ordered before we arrived, and they were still waiting, the woman tutting and looking at her watch. Twice, she'd asked her boyfriend to *go and say something*, but he didn't seem to share her impatience, a response that only left her more peeved. She'd never worked in hospitality, that much was clear, as was the fact that the café was short-staffed. One server rushed around trying to keep everyone happy, and a "Help Wanted" card in the window had "flexible shifts, free meals" handwritten at the bottom as an afterthought.

If we needed to watch the office long-term, Emmy could have an agent hire on as waitstaff, but for us today, the place was almost perfect. The server could take as much time as she wanted, and I'd make sure to leave her a nice tip from Emmy's expense budget when we left.

I say "almost perfect" because the tables had been set out with one chair back-to-the-window, one chair back-to-the-street. Far from ideal as one of us would have to face away from the consulate. Rad and I would have flipped a coin for the window seat, but when we arrived, Alex had taken the street side for himself without asking. That tiny gesture had left me with a lump in my throat.

A stack of guidebooks sat between us, and I flipped through the pages, jotting down notes. I'd done this dozens of times in the past—worked a surveillance detail, planning an itinerary for a vacation I'd never take, but this time, something felt different. Not just the company but the tiny bud of hope in my chest. A real vacation was out of the question, but I wasn't beholden to an unreasonable master now. If Alex didn't need to rush back to Virginia, maybe we could spend a day together by the ocean?

"You okay?" he asked.

"Huh?"

"You looked kind of...glazed?"

"I..." *Pizdets.* I'd never zoned out like that before, not in the middle of a job. A lapse in concentration could result in death, either mine or someone else's. "I'm fine. I don't... I don't think anyone left."

"They didn't," he said, his voice so quiet I had to strain to hear. "I was watching in the glass."

"Sorry. I'm just...just..."

Off balance. Usually, I didn't apologise for getting things wrong because I made sure I got them right.

Alex reached across the table and took my hand in his. Good. That was good. We needed to stick to our cover story, and a regular couple would demonstrate affection.

"We're a team, Dashenka. We hold each other up."

I nodded because that stupid golf ball wedged in my throat made it difficult to speak. The general had told us the Ten were a team, but in reality, it had been every assassin for themselves. Pavel wouldn't have pissed on me if I'd been on fire, not unless it benefitted him in some way, and if Ilya had been drowning, I'd have pushed him under if nobody had been looking. Sure, I'd have saved Ana or Rad, maybe even Vik or Artem, but the others? No.

I'd only been involved with Blackwood for a few days, but I already knew these people were different. A real team filled with genuine friendships.

"I'm still getting used to this," I whispered.

"I understand. And if you stumble, we'll all be here to hold you up."

"You think I'll stumble? Because I'm good at my job. I—"

A squeeze of my hand quickly shut me up. In this moment, I was being anything but professional.

"I know you're good at your job. But you're also dealing with a lifetime of trauma, whether you want to admit it or not."

How dare he judge me, this man who'd only met me properly four days ago? He thought I was weak? That I hadn't put my past to rest? That every so often, the pain got so intense that it threatened to overwhelm me? That memories plagued me like suffocating shadows in the night? That some days, I drove to the middle of the forest just to scream? That I buried my feelings and focused on training because it was the only way I could cope? That every time I killed a man, I imagined it was Oleg Zacharov in the vain hope that my demons would finally be exorcised?

Because if Alex did think those things, he'd be absolutely right.

Nine was the shield I used to hide the real Darya from the world and sometimes even from myself.

Today would be no different.

"I'm fine," I repeated, then the server finally brought our food, and I turned my attention to a plate of waffles with fresh fruit on the side so I wouldn't have to face Alex.

So I wouldn't have to face the truth.

The carbs sat in my stomach like buckshot, and I spent the next hour studiously reading the guidebooks. Alex chipped in every so often with a suggestion, and I jotted everything down when all I wanted was to be alone. On my own, I could cope. I was in control. Alex took over the watch while I went for a bathroom break, necessary after three cups of coffee, but when I got back, he'd dropped a hundred-dollar bill on the table and packed up our stuff.

"What happened?"

"Timonenko just left."

Now I saw him, strolling along the street, and I took up the tail while Alex headed for the car as we'd parked nearby. Had Timonenko left to buy lunch? Or was he going somewhere else?

I stayed at a safe distance as he stopped at a deli two blocks away and ordered...well, everything, it seemed like. Food for the whole office? When he emerged with three bulging paper carrier bags, I figured he was the designated lunch gopher, but then he turned left out the door instead of right, and a tiny buzz ran through me when he continued to a parking garage, one of those upscale places that would detail your car inside and out while you worked. The valet didn't ask for his ticket, so I had to assume he was a regular.

"It's a go," I told Alex, holding my phone to my ear but speaking into my watch.

I didn't have to give him the address because Blackwood had provided me with the watch earlier, which doubled as an all-in-one communication and tracking device. I didn't much like the latter feature, but apparently it was standard operating procedure, and at least Black had shown enough decency to explain the features to me instead of just implanting it into my body while I was unconscious. So I'd agreed to wear it. I could always toss it if I decided I didn't want them checking up on me anymore.

Two minutes later, the valet pulled up in an emerald-green Mercedes convertible, and Timonenko climbed behind the wheel, checking his hair in the mirror while the top folded down.

"He's mobile."

"Twenty seconds."

Alex appeared from a side street in the Porsche, and as soon as I closed the passenger door, he pulled out into traffic.

"Emmy and Black will take over at the consulate, and Ana's going to follow us in case we need to switch out."

Timonenko didn't act like a man in a hurry. When we got stuck in traffic, he tapped his fingers on the edge of the door, but in time to the music blasting from his stereo rather than out of impatience. At least if he vanished from sight, we'd only have to listen to find him again. He'd also be deaf before he hit forty.

"Didn't have him pegged for a country fan," Alex said.

"Sometimes, people surprise us."

Alex glanced across at me, then reached out and twined his fingers through mine.

"Yes, they do."

The screen on the dash showed a map overlaid with our tracking data, and I watched as our blue blob turned onto the Pacific Coast Highway. Had the general sat like this in his office, studying us from afar as we played our deadly games? The thought lit a spark of anger in me, but I tamped it down. *That was the past. Dead. Gone. There's only one tiny piece of my old life left—Ana—and the rest is history.* Instead, I focused on the present. The white blob by the consulate must have been —ironically—the Blacks, and Ana's red dot was a mile behind us, keeping pace.

"Who's green?" I tapped a blob in Long Beach. "Hallie?"

"Hallie and Vance. They went to check out Bryant Angelou's place in Naples. They say it's nice."

"Nice" was an understatement. We found that out a little later when Timonenko slowed to turn into the driveway. He had to wait a moment for a truck to leave first. Ella's Catering Supplies. Angelou was planning a party?

Maybe we had this all wrong—diplomats spent half their lives going to events, and it wouldn't be unusual if Timonenko attended a get-together. A showcase for Russian cinema, perhaps? A fundraiser for theatre students back home in Moscow? Like the rest of the arts, the Russian film industry was underfunded.

Alex slowed as we rolled past, and I peered through the open gates to the mansion behind, a monstrosity of giant terracotta cubes stacked haphazardly on top of each other. The architect had taken the "bigger is better" approach and stuffed the home onto an undersized lot with a perfectly manicured square of lawn out front. Or was it AstroTurf? Hard to tell from that distance. Another truck was parked to the side, this one filled with those tall round tables people put their drinks on at parties. Loading or unloading? Two men in coveralls walked out of the house empty-handed. Ah, unloading. A third man followed, and I only caught a glimpse of him before we were past the house and out of sight, but it was enough to make my breath hitch.

Because in that instant, I knew we hadn't been wrong.

Timonenko and Angelou were up to their eyeballs in dirt.

I knew where the weapon was.

And I'd never, ever be able to escape my past.

37

EMMY

I t was one of those good news, bad news days.

The good news? There was an excellent chance we'd pinpointed exactly who at the embassy was fucking around with Project Marshmallow, and quite possibly, we'd identified the rough location of the weapon itself.

The bad news? Two key members of the team were benched.

I'd thought Darya might be a little happier about being sidelined seeing as (a) she wasn't my biggest fan and (b) she preferred to bore people to death with macramé classes nowadays, but she looked just as sick as Ana about the situation.

"Nothing is certain yet," Black said from his perch on the edge of the dining table. I'd never understood how he could stay so still when faced with a massive bloody problem. I paced constantly. It helped me to think. "How sure are you that the man you saw was Six?"

Six. Also known as Ilya Molotov, a fitting name if I'd ever heard one. Darya's voice had been flat when she called through

282

with the news, but now that she was back at Skywater House, you couldn't miss the tension in her frame.

"Eighty percent? Maybe eighty-five? I didn't see him for more than a second. But there's only one reason a man like Ilya would be hanging around a house in Long Beach, and that's if there's something valuable inside."

Black remained emotionless, as usual. "Playing devil's advocate, we don't know that he's guarding the weapon. He could have been hired as a bodyguard. The thing of value could be his principal."

Darya snorted at that. "Ilya wouldn't last twenty-four hours as a bodyguard. He's offence, not defence."

"He'd get bored," Ana agreed. "One of his many flaws is that he has the attention span of a toddler. Another is that he actually enjoys his work."

I had to agree with both of them. Ana had described Ilya as an arrogant son of a bitch, even as a teenager, and as a member of the Ten, he undoubtedly had skills. So he'd be charging a fee commensurate with those skills, and it would be in excess of Darya's eight grand a day. No sane person would pay that for a bodyguard, not when they could hire a perfectly competent one from, say, Blackwood for a fraction of that amount.

And Darya's hypothesis that the weapon was located at the Long Beach house was an interesting one.

"Why would the weapon still be here? If Stepanov's crew stole it, why wouldn't they have put it on the nearest plane or boat and shipped it home to the fatherland? They'd only need to fire it at a few folks in Moscow, then blame Markovich for being too soft on the Americans."

"They tried that before, remember?" Darya said. "Five years ago, when Pushkin was still in power, one of the deputy prime ministers was shot on his way to work, and Lagunov tried to blame that on the Americans—wrongly, of course.

But the state controls most of the Russian media, which meant Pushkin could shape the narrative, so the effort was wasted."

Curious that Darya seemed so certain the USA hadn't been involved in that little episode. Had she?

"So you think they'll try some shit here instead?"

"Strategically, it could work," Ana said. "A Russian target in the US."

"Like a Russian businessman? Or a politician?"

"Or a group of politicians. Mass murder with an experimental weapon would be big news, and Harrison's opposition would put their weight behind the story too."

There could be no good outcome for James in that scenario. Either he'd look like a lunatic for attacking Russians on his own soil, or if he somehow managed to blame the situation on the true culprits, he'd appear weak for not preventing it. The news would trickle into Russia through social media, and if Markovich attempted to quash the story, there'd be cries of a cover-up. The fragile US-Russia relationship would be shattered. Trust would be destroyed as everyone tried to unravel the true story. Conspiracy theories would spring up left, right, and centre, and too many people believed the bullshit they read on the internet nowadays.

"How accurate is the weapon?" Darya asked.

"I'm not totally sure."

"Because if a number of innocents happened to get caught in the field of fire, the media would lose their collective minds."

"Are you insane?"

"Just saying." She shrugged. "There's a good reason I retired. I was sick of being forced to follow orders I didn't agree with."

"Would Ilya do it?"

"Sure, if somebody paid him enough money."

Fucking hell. Okay, I had to admit that Darya's hypothesis made a certain amount of sense. Why steal a weapon if you weren't going to use it? And where better to use it than the home state of Facebook, Twitter, and whatever other social media platform was popular these days?

"So, what's the target?"

Bradley bustled in with a tray. "Drinks? Snacks? I went to the new patisserie and picked up cannoli, but don't tell Toby." Toby was my nutritionist. "What target?"

Darya narrowed her eyes. "Should he be here?"

"It's fine."

Bradley beamed at her, utterly oblivious to the daggers shooting in his direction. "Chill out; I'm excellent at keeping secrets. Confess your sins, yada yada yada. I'm like a priest, except better dressed, obviously." He turned to Ana. "Is she always this uptight?"

"Yes."

"I'll pick up some essential oils this afternoon. Lavender, sandalwood, and clary sage." He patted Darya on the shoulder, then took a hasty step back when she snarled at him. "Those'll help you to relax in no time."

Alex was trying to suppress a smile, and she focused that sharp gaze on him.

"It's not funny."

"Maybe a massage would help?"

"From who?"

"Alex is a qualified sports massage therapist," I told her. "He can help you to work out the kinks later, but for now, can we get back to the slightly more pressing issue?"

Ah, now I got the glare.

"Look for an event on this side of the country with both a Russian and US presence," Darya said. "Probably not political because nobody's going to get upset if there are a few less politicians in the world, are they?"

"Like a movie premiere? Timonenko's hobnobbing with the Hollywood set."

"Or an awards ceremony. Those also have cameras everywhere."

"What about a soccer match?" Bradley suggested. "Russia and the US are playing at the stadium in Exposition Park to raise money for penguins. It's been all over the TV, which you'd know if you ever took any time off."

On the rare occasions I did take time off, I still didn't watch TV, but a soccer match... Yeah, that was another possibility.

"Penguins?"

"They're building a joint nature preserve in the Antarctic. James told us about it over dinner one time, remember? Or it might be the Arctic. Let me check..." Bradley pulled out his phone. "It's definitely the Antarctic."

Darya raised an eyebrow. "James?"

"President Harrison."

"I went to school with him," Black added, fixing Bradley with a stare before he managed to tell Darya that I used to date James too. Bradley actually was good at keeping important secrets from strangers, but he'd run his mouth amongst the Blackwood team, and Darya only had one foot in the camp at the moment. Until she made up her mind about her future, she didn't need to know everything.

"We'll research possible targets, but ideally, we want to retrieve the weapon before it gets that far. And if they're lining up targets, they'll need the thing to work. Which means that either they'll have another try for Ottie, or they've found an alternative way to get the code they need." An alternative way... I thought back to the missing software technician. Had he shown up yet? I needed to speak with James. "When's the soccer match?"

Again, Bradley consulted his phone. "March ninth."

"So if that's the target, they have over a month to get ready. Let's look into showbiz events as well."

"No further out than March," Darya said. "Ilya won't need that much time to prepare. And you should move Marquette. If Ilya decides to visit her himself, he won't make the same mistakes as Fedorov's lackeys."

"Okay, so we have action points." I moved over to the nearest empty whiteboard. "Number one: warn the team with Ottie of a potential new threat. Number two: confirm Ilya's identity. We'll need you or Ana to do that."

I wrote notes on the board as the two of them looked at each other. Neither of them volunteered right away, but finally, Darya nodded.

"It should be me. I've spent more time with him in recent years."

"We can change your appearance. Bradley?"

"I'll get right onto that. You won't even recognise yourself by the time I'm finished with you."

Darya looked kind of dubious, and who could blame her? Bradley was wearing a pair of pink skinny jeans with sky-blue boat shoes—no socks—and a matching blue sweater with fluffy clouds stuck to it. No sunshine today, probably because he was still hung-over.

"I can put together my own disguise," she said. "Do you have a wig I can borrow?"

"Yes, but I'll help because I'm the *expert*."

Before she could argue, my phone rang. Naz. I beamed him through to the screen on the wall.

"Is this a good time?" he asked.

"Depends. If you've got a lead for us, then it's a good time. If you're calling to shoot the breeze, then no, it definitely isn't."

"It might be a lead, or it might be a dead end." He sipped something turquoise from a glass and grimaced. Another fad diet? "You asked me to take a look at Yuma Loslov? For connections to California?"

"You found one?"

"I'm sending a photo to your encrypted mailbox. I don't have a name yet, but there are rumours the girl is a daughter."

"And how is she connected to California?"

"You'll see."

Thirty seconds later, I did indeed see. We all saw. We saw Yuma Loslov grinning for the camera beside the Golden Gate Bridge, his arm around a pretty blonde. In this picture, he was a decade or so younger, the furrows that creased his forehead less pronounced than in the mugshots Mack had dug out for us.

"She must have inherited her mama's looks." Naz chuckled to himself. "My source believes the girl's mother is American. Want me to keep digging for the name?"

"No need. Her name is Miroslava Novikova, and she works at the Russian Consulate Field Office in Huntington Beach." Finally, we had our link between Timonenko and Loslov. "But I do want you to keep digging into a man named Ilya Molotov. Also known as Six, probably known by a hundred other aliases too."

"You won't find him under his real name," Darya muttered. "Just like you won't find me under mine."

"But he's still active, and he has to be touting for business somehow. He doesn't have Zacharov pimping him out anymore. Which means there's a trail back to him, although I don't doubt it's well-hidden."

"Six? How many of these people are left?"

"Only one more, but his name hasn't come up in connection with this case."

Yet. Right now, I was ruling nothing out.

"Sure, I'll ask around, but very carefully."

"I appreciate it."

Naz's pale face faded to a black dot in the middle of the screen, and I felt the familiar buzz as I saw the pieces slotting into place. *This* was why I did this job. Because of the rush that came from solving puzzles and conquering challenges and generally achieving the difficult if not downright impossible. We were getting closer to the Marshmallow. I could practically smell the s'mores.

But we were also at a disadvantage. If Ana and Darya had to back off, I'd need more manpower, but in what form? That depended on our next steps.

"Where were we? Point number three: assuming Ilya is at the property, we need to set up a surveillance post, which leads us to point four: work out who else is in the house in Naples."

"Would they really plan a party if the weapon was in there?" Alex asked. "Wouldn't that be a risk?"

Darya picked up one of the glasses of OJ that Bradley had brought in and took a tentative sip. What, did she think he'd drugged it? The worst thing he'd do would be to add extra vitamins, and he'd only do that if Toby put him up to it.

"Yes, it's a risk, but absolutely Ilya would take it. Hell, he'd probably get a kick out of it too. He assumes that he's smarter than those around him, and usually, he's correct. He's arrogant, but he isn't stupid. And as long as he monitors the guests, it's also a shrewd move. Who on earth would look for a secret weapon at a party full of luvvies?"

"And besides," Ana continued, "it makes it easier for him to move the weapon if he needs to. All he has to do is load it into a truck for Ilya's Party Supplies and drive it wherever he pleases."

They were both right. Unfortunately.

"Which brings us nicely to point five: if we conclude the weapon could be at the house, we'll have to find a way to get in there and search for it and—point six—retrieve it."

I expected a snarky comment from Darya, but it didn't

come. She understood the stakes, didn't she? We couldn't let the Marshmallow stay in the wrong hands. Together, the six of us came up with a plan—Bradley would give Darya a makeover, and she'd spend a few hours in Long Beach with Alex, scouting out the area, although we weren't expecting much to come from the evening. It was too dark. But maybe we'd get lucky and Ilya would decide to head out for pizza. Stranger things had happened.

As Darya followed Bradley out the door, she leaned in close.

"I should have charged ten thousand a day."

"Yeah, you should. I'd have paid it."

38

NINE

"Y ou okay?"

It was peculiar, having people ask me that. Rad rarely had, because even if my answer had been "no," there wasn't a hell of a lot either of us could have done about it. But standing here on the guest house balcony with my hands on the railing as I looked out over the water in the distance, a shiver ran up my spine at Alex's whispered words. Not a warning shiver or a cold shiver, but an oddly pleasant shiver.

He stepped up close behind me and placed his hands either side of mine, his body heat warming me even though we were barely touching.

"Do you want my regular answer or my honest answer?"

"Always the honest answer."

"I'm not okay, and I never have been. Not once in my entire life. So for me, it's SNAFU."

Status Nominal: All Fucked Up.

At least tonight, I was an hour away from Ilya. And we knew it *was* Ilya. He hadn't obliged us by going out for dinner, but a little after eight p.m., he'd escorted a blonde woman and a small, yappy dog along the street. It barked at everything, which meant it would also bark at us if we ventured inside the terracotta house. Just one more problem to deal with. Anyhow, Ilya had walked right past the Porsche, now complete with false plates, and peered in at us. But his gaze hadn't lingered. There was no need—Alex cupped my cheek in his hand and leaned in to kiss me, and Bradley hadn't been kidding when he said I wouldn't recognise myself. At first, I'd resisted his offer to help, but Alex had told me it was easier to just go along with things and assured me that Bradley knew what he was doing. So I'd gritted my teeth while he turned me into a redhead with a mass of unruly curls, changed the contours of my face with cheek pads and clever make-up, and completed the look with a pair of wire-rimmed glasses. And I had to concede that Alex had been right. Ilya had no idea who I was. No, we weren't a threat to him, and he carried on at a steady amble, pausing every time the dog stopped to pee on something.

But I'd seen enough.

It was definitely Six.

The woman? I hadn't crossed paths with her before, but she was pretty. Poised. She looked around her as she walked, but not in the same way Ilya did. He was *aware*. She was more...hopeful. As though she thought she should be recognised and was almost disappointed when nobody gave her a second glance.

Too short for a model, so...a singer or an actress. In this town, everyone wanted to be one of the three. Ironically, the one bona fide supermodel I knew, Brooke's soon-to-be sister-in-law, hated to be recognised and went about her business with her head down.

Why was Ilya with the blonde? He wouldn't lower himself to bodyguard work, and he didn't do the girlfriend thing.

Were there trust issues? Did he want to keep an eye on where she was going and who she was speaking with? Yes, that was a possibility.

When we got back to Skywater House, I'd checked out Bryant Angelou's most recent movie, the one in production. The leading lady was Svetlana Oliskaya, and now I had a name to go with the face. She was shacked up with her producer? How cosy. I'd always wondered whether stories of the casting couch were true, and perhaps now I knew the answer.

Alex kissed my hair. My real hair. "One day, I'm going to ask you that question again, and you're going to tell me you're okay and mean it. I promise."

"Somehow, I doubt that. After tomorrow, I don't even know when I'll see you again."

If I'd see him again.

Nobody ever kept the promises they made to me. When I was a child with dreams of becoming a figure skater, my mama promised that one day, she'd cheer me on in the national championships. Then she'd died. The woman with the tight smile and the big leather briefcase who'd visited me during my temporary stay in jail had promised everything would be okay. Agreed that I'd acted in self-defence and sworn she'd get everything straightened out. She'd lied. Nine's first victim had promised I'd enjoy what was to come as he unbuckled his belt, and even he'd let me down.

Promises were nothing but wasted words.

"Tomorrow's Wednesday, so after that, you'll see me on Thursday."

"Emmy's hardly going to keep paying me if I can't do my job, so I'll need to head home."

Because I wouldn't earn as much as I'd hoped, which meant I couldn't afford to fund a third assistant at the Craft Cabin. Although I'd pay Everly until the end of the week.

When I checked in with Brooke earlier, she'd said Everly was doing a great job, so I owed her that much.

"Emmy will find something for you to do, even if it's surveillance."

"Eight thousand bucks a day to watch a house through binoculars? Are you serious?"

Although surveillance would prove challenging in that particular location. If we could find a suitable vehicle, then monitoring the rear of the property might be possible. The terracotta house backed onto the water, and across the channel in Belmont Shore, a road ran along the edge of the water. If we parked there in a small RV or a cargo van, we could keep an eye. I bet the back of the house would have plenty of windows. Folks in Naples liked to enjoy their multimillion-dollar views.

Or maybe we could sneak onto a yacht moored at one of the private docks that lined the edges of the shore, the boats squashed in like very expensive sardines? It was winter—some of those floating palaces would be closed up until the weather got better. Although "better" was of course a relative term. Dump these people in Siberia and they wouldn't survive twenty-four hours, even in summer.

"Emmy will have a plan. She always has a plan." Alex let go of the railing, and a second later, his thumbs dug into my shoulders. "You're too tense. Your muscles are full of knots."

"Darla's budget doesn't run to spa days." Alex kneaded and smoothed, and fuck, that felt good. "Are you really a trained massage therapist? I thought Emmy was kidding."

"Blackwood encourages staff to develop their skills. I also have a bachelor's degree in kinesiology, and I'm learning acupuncture."

I could speak seven languages, put a bullet through a man's eye at twelve hundred metres, and fly everything from a Cessna to a commercial jet to a MiG, but I didn't have a piece of paper to say so. My "qualifications" were useless in the civilian world.

Alex's definitely weren't. He hit exactly the right spots, and a sound that wasn't even human slipped from my lips. A cross between a moan and a purr? I'd lost my damn mind.

Which was probably why I didn't say a word when he led me back into my bedroom. When he peeled my sweater over my head and unsnapped my bra. When he...lowered me face-first onto the bed?

"You don't even want to look at me when you fuck me?"

I thought I'd exhausted the capacity to be hurt in my life, but it seemed I'd been wrong.

Alex's laughter was unexpected.

"I'm not going to fuck you. Not tonight, anyway."

"You're not?"

"No, I'm going to work the kinks out of your back."

Cool splashes hit my skin—massage oil? Where had that come from?—swiftly followed by the sweep of Alex's hands, and those hands were impressive. No wonder Emmy funded his continuing education if this was what she got out of it. All those little tight spots magically disappeared, pummelled into submission by a man who knew precisely what he was doing.

Every so often, his fingers would slow, and I knew he was studying my scars. Was he wondering where each one came from? Some were obvious—the thin slice of a knife, the pucker of a bullet hole. Others less so, such as the zipper-like tear I'd gotten when I jumped out of a building and caught the back of my shoulder on a sharp nail as I fell. Art had been the one to sew me up that day, his stitches neat and precise, so the evidence wasn't as glaringly obvious as it might have been.

Alex's fingers paused between my shoulder blades, stroking over the bump that remained there.

"This is where you cut out the tracker?"

"I didn't have time to finesse the job."

No, I'd just gritted my teeth against the pain as I hacked away, desperate to get that last part of my past out of me. Blood had still been oozing from the wound when I reached Las Vegas.

"Does it still hurt?"

"Sometimes the muscles underneath feel tender, especially when it's cold."

"Then I'll skip that spot." Instead, he leaned forward and pressed his lips to the lumpy scar. "I hate that you went through that."

"It's over," I whispered.

But was it? Ilya was back...

Alex raised my hips to unfasten my jeans, then slid them off over my feet before starting on my legs. Even though I was nearly naked, there was nothing sleazy about his touch, although when he turned me over, the enormous bulge in his pants told me he wasn't quite as unaffected by the situation as he'd made out.

"Tell me that's not an occupational hazard?"

"Only with you."

"Are you sure you don't want to...?"

Wasn't everything in life a trade? And okay, I was a tiny bit hot and bothered too.

"Tonight, I want you to sleep well, nothing more. Close your eyes."

I'd always prided myself on being prepared. On staying alert and ready to react to any threat. But by the time Alex had finished with me, I was nothing but a limp heap of dopamine and thoroughly unknotted muscles, my skin slick with oil and my eyes barely able to focus.

He leaned in and pressed a soft kiss to my lips.

"I'll see you in the morning."

"Wait...wait..."

He stared down at me, expectant.

"You can't leave me here like this."

"Like what?"

Alone. I didn't want to be alone, not tonight. For the first time, I felt vulnerable, not just physically but emotionally too. Alex was slowly breaking down all the barriers I'd erected to keep myself safe.

But I couldn't admit that.

Never would I admit that.

"I need pyjamas."

"Where are they?"

"In the closet." Dammit, now I sounded needy, like one of those simpering fools who couldn't function without a man. "I'll get them."

"You don't have to—"

But I was already out of bed, cursing as I stumbled across the room. What was wrong with my stupid legs? I snatched my nightclothes off the shelf and tugged them on, only to find Alex watching me with an amused smile.

"Silk pyjamas?"

"Don't you dare say a word to Emmy, or I'll...I'll..."

"You'll cut off my balls? That would be counterproductive, don't you think? You might need them later."

"No other man would dare to speak to me the way you do."

"Then it's a good thing there's no other man, isn't it?"

Alex caught me with an arm around my waist, and just because I could, I dumped him backward onto the bed. Still, he smiled.

"Is this a subtle hint that you want me to stay here tonight?"

"I..." Hmm. Was my subconscious trying to tell me something? "Maybe."

He held out a hand. "Come to bed, Dashenka. Just to sleep."

So I did. I climbed into bed and Alex curled around me, and that night, I slept better than I'd ever slept in my life.

39

NINE

"**H**as she lost her fucking mind?"

This morning, I'd woken in Alex's arms, fully prepared to pack and return to Baldwin's Shore after breakfast. To go back to my life of lies, changed by the experience I'd had this week. To try to reconcile the old me with the new me.

To work out how and when I'd be able to see Alex again.

But after I arrived in the dining room, Emmy acted as if it was business as usual. She had a plan, she said, exactly as Alex had predicted. Ana and I would steer clear of Ilya, and Blackwood would bring in additional team members to assist with surveillance at the terracotta house. In two hours, we'd have a briefing at the new base of operations, farther to the south, so I did find myself leaving Skywater House, albeit for a different reason. And maybe I was even a tiny bit happy, although the feeling was so foreign that I couldn't be sure.

And then we'd arrived in Naples.

"I'm sure she knows what she's doing," Alex assured me.

Our new base was another mansion, an even bigger one, complete with a spacious terrace and a swimming pool and a damned putting green because we clearly hadn't had enough of golf this week. Fuck only knew where the yacht had come from, but Black looked perfectly cool as he nudged it closer to the private dock on the other side of the road.

And less than fifty metres away across the all-too-narrow channel of water, I saw Ilya monitoring Black's efforts from the rear terrace of the terracotta house and ducked back behind the curtain.

"*Feelin' Nauti*? The boat is called *Feelin' Nauti*? That's hardly subtle."

"Until this morning, she was called the *Black Opal*."

Ana appeared behind me, her approach silent. But I'd known it was her. You didn't spend three years living as a person's sister without learning to read their energy.

"Subtle is the wrong approach with Ilya," she said. "He's like us—too sensitive to things that are out of place. If we parked a vehicle on a nearby street or ran patrols past the place, he'd notice."

Ever felt as if you were being watched, then turned in time to see somebody look away? Ilya was a hundred times more perceptive. Once, he'd picked out a sniper dressed in a ghillie suit eight hundred yards away, right before we walked into his field of fire. Said he *felt* him. We used to kid that he was psychic, but his abilities had saved us on more than one occasion.

Now they were working against us.

We'd already had to ditch the Porsche because he'd seen it —that was back at Skywater House along with my red wig and possibly the last of my sanity. We'd driven here in a black SUV with a jelly bean air freshener stuck to the dash and an "I Love Vegas" bumper sticker. I had to admire Emmy's attention to detail in that respect. If anyone ever had to describe the vehicle, those were the two things people would remember, both of which could be easily removed.

"So we're hiding in plain sight?"

"It'll mess with his perceptions."

Hmm. Okay, I saw where Emmy was coming from, but her plan was a gamble. Ilya would be able to see our faces. Not mine or Ana's because we'd stay out of sight, but everyone else's. Following him would become more difficult, and I had a sudden fear that I'd been wrong about the location of the weapon. Yesterday, I'd been so certain, but Emmy had put a huge amount of trust in me and now I was second-guessing my theory. Why? I'd never doubted myself in the past.

Because in the past, I had nothing to lose.

If my light had blinked out, nobody would have missed me except maybe Rad during that brief time we were together. And I'd had no future to worry about. No hope had led to no fear.

But in this new life, I had everything to lose.

Alexei. Ana. My friends back in Baldwin's Shore.

Focus, Dasha. I had to trust my own judgment. I knew Ilya, and that weapon was somewhere close to him. It had to be. And by running an unconventional surveillance pattern, there was less chance of arousing his suspicions. So no, Emmy hadn't lost her mind, but there was a fine line between genius and insanity.

A door slammed, and a moment later, Emmy and Black walked into the great room.

"Everyone making themselves at home?" Emmy's phone pinged, and she glanced at the screen. "Ah, the first of the reinforcements are here."

The newcomer was a delicate-looking dark-haired woman who hugged Black, kissed Emmy on the lips, and then waved at everyone else. Hmm.

"Vance and Hallie are five minutes out. Fia, meet Darya. Darya, this is Fia. If she offers to make you dinner, decline."

"Why? Is she that bad of a cook?"

"No, because she poisons *everyone*." Bradley rolled his eyes as he set a tray of snacks onto the table. "It's her schtick."

"Not everyone. I haven't poisoned you. Yet," Fia added under her breath, then turned to me. "So, what's your schtick?"

"I'm a jack of all trades."

"Jack of all trades, master of none?"

Bitch. Yes, I understood why she was friends with Emmy.

"Master of all."

"She can even crochet," Bradley put in, and Fia's face creased in laughter.

I fixed him with a stare. "Did you know that with a midsized Tunisian crochet hook, you can pull a man's brain out through his nose?"

He backed away in a hurry. "I'll just go make coffee."

Fia jerked a thumb toward me. "Yes, I like her. Are those red velvet cupcakes?"

Emmy nodded. "Yup."

"Who are we waiting for? Hallie and Vance and who else?"

"Alaric and Ravi are on their way from the East Coast, plus Pale's bringing a few friends over to add some atmosphere and lend a hand with...stuff."

"Is anyone watching the front of the house?" I asked. Because by my count, the whole team would be here, which left a gaping hole in our net.

"Yup." Emmy used the exact same tone as when she'd answered about the cupcake.

"Who?"

She pointed at the ceiling. "Eye in the sky."

A satellite? A drone? She didn't elaborate, and I didn't push because in her position, I wouldn't have told me either. Emmy had been surprisingly open in many regards, but I didn't doubt she was holding back in some areas. We were still virtual strangers, after all. Only my past relationship with Ana and a shared hatred of General Zacharov had bought me a seat at this table.

Hallie and Vance arrived and quickly dug into the snacks, and they were followed by an older guy in a Hawaiian shirt, board shorts, and flip-flops with a bimbo on each arm, one blonde, one brunette. This was what Emmy had meant by "add some atmosphere"?

The blonde giggled and gave a finger wave. "Hi! I'm Barbie."

Had he picked the pair of them up on the corner of Hollywood Boulevard?

The brunette would have been shorter if she'd worn shoes she could walk in, and she clung to the surfer dude as if she might overbalance at any moment. How she stayed upright when she tossed back her hair was a mystery.

"Spider."

Spider? Surely that couldn't be her birth name?

Emmy looked them up and down. "Good to meet you. Help yourself to snacks, and then we'll start the briefing."

"Oh my gosh, are those salted caramel cupcakes?" Barbie took a step forward and her dangerously short skirt rode up an inch, but as she leaned over the table, her jacket tightened across her back and I saw the telltale bulge of a gun. Fuck. These two were also operatives? Given my Darla escapades, I should have been the last person to judge a woman by her appearance, but females were still such a minority in this game that I'd made a poor assumption. Lesson learned.

Emmy gave a quick rundown of events, and by the time she'd covered the developments to date, I'd eaten two cupcakes. Which wasn't ideal, but these were exceptional circumstances.

"So," she continued, "the good news is that I spoke to James, and Ottie Marquette's been moved to a more secure location. If Ilya planned to pay her a visit, that's just got a whole lot harder for him. And the better news is that we asked around, and Bryant Angelou is looking for funding for his next movie. That's what the party on Saturday night is about. It's not a birthday celebration or a family get-together—he's invited a whole bunch of people he barely knows in the hope that they'll give him money."

"And Ilya's okay with this?" I asked.

"I'm not certain what the arrangement is with the house, but the rental contract is in Angelou's name."

"How did he get tangled up with Timonenko? Do we know?"

"Not for certain, but they're both Stanford alumni— Angelou and Timonenko, plus Novikova too."

"Their studies overlapped," Vance added. "Timonenko graduated first, a year before the others, and they were all members of the chess club, so there's a good chance their paths crossed even before the two Russians began working at the consulate."

"Ilya plays chess. He was reasonable, but Vik used to beat him three times out of four."

Which had been a sore point for Ilya, and their games had gone from semi-frequent to almost never.

"So he enjoys games of strategy? Interesting. I do too, but Cards Against Humanity is more my thing when it comes to board games."

"Cards Against Humanity doesn't use a board," Fia pointed out.

"Whatever. Anyhow, Angelou's scratching around for a backer."

"Any idea what the project is?" Surfer Dude asked. Nobody had introduced him yet, but since Emmy appeared to be meeting the two women for the first time, I had to conclude that he was an old acquaintance because there had to be a connection somewhere.

Vance grinned. "Yeah, it's a spy thriller." Did Angelou plan to write Ilya's fees off as research? "Rumour says Bryant's dating Svetlana and he wants her to star in it, but she needs a co-star and he wants a big name to attach to the project. Making a blockbuster doesn't come cheap."

Black took a sip of coffee and then spoke up. "He's put out feelers all over Hollywood, but we understand there's been little interest. Unsurprising, since he's out of his depth. But desperate men do stupid things, which should benefit us."

"Ilya isn't stupid." Arrogant, yes, but not stupid.

"Ilya Molotov has spent his life in the shadows, and that's where he expects any threat to come from." Black smiled, the first time I'd seen him do so. "But why sneak through the back door when you can waltz in the front?"

"You plan to crash the party?"

"No, I plan to get an invitation."

"How? We only have three days."

"We have several possible routes to pursue. Firstly, we'll scatter a little bait around here and see if he takes it. Secondly, Emmy and I own shares in a movie production company, silent partners of course, but we've had the CEO request the treatment. Thirdly, Blackwood has a number of celebrity clients, and over the years, some have become friends. One or two are willing to do us favours. Speaking of which... Bradley, we'll need brunch on the terrace tomorrow, enough food for four people." His grin stretched wider. "Everyone's an actor now."

Emmy swallowed a mouthful of cake. "Fia, we have another project for you. This is our main avenue of investigation, but we still have two loose ends at the embassy— Maxim Agapov and Ruslan Smirnov. It doesn't look as if they're involved, but we need to be sure. Can you tackle that angle?"

Fia gave a one-shouldered shrug. "No problem."

I caught Alex's eye. I wouldn't be eating brunch on the terrace with Emmy and Black, that was for sure.

"What about Ana and Dasha?" he asked.

"We still need to find the traitor at Sandy Peake. The government team seems to be at an impasse, and a fresh set of eyes could help."

"Don't they have exterior cameras at this place?" I asked. "I thought the weapon was the size of a sniper rifle? Can't they look for someone exiting with a large bag?"

"This is a simplified version, but as best the investigators can ascertain, an inside person placed the weapon into a box that once contained a flat-packed desk chair and marked it as trash. The janitor took it outside, and trash pickup came through as usual. Then fifteen minutes later, trash pickup came through again."

Sheesh, that was some lapse in security. At Base 13, we'd had an incinerator for waste disposal, so none of it ever crossed the perimeter. But the distinctive smell of burning human flesh was one I'd never forget.

"Emmy mentioned there were three suspects with Ottie Marquette out of the picture?"

"That's right," Black said. "Her boyfriend, Timothy Stern, a software technician named José Santoro, and Mark Fitz, a materials engineer with a hidden gambling problem. Santoro's AWOL, and Fitz and Stern have both been placed on leave pending further investigation."

"I don't suppose any of them went to Stanford?"

Vance spoke up. "They graduated from Harvard, NYU, and UC Berkeley respectively. Santoro did his undergrad at Syracuse before transferring."

"You say he vanished—any indication he left the country?"

"He left his passport in his apartment."

"His home's been searched?"

"The day after he left, and he didn't pack for a long trip. He told his roommate he was meeting a buddy for a drink and promised to pick up a pizza on the way home."

"Any family nearby?"

"An estranged wife. There's a child too, a four-year-old girl."

"Do we know why the Santoros split?" Emmy asked.

"Yeah. He was—according to the wife's statement— married to his job."

"Dedicated to the pursuit of research, or hanging in there for a pay-off?"

"That's the key question, isn't it?"

"Any other family?"

"His mom still lives in Mexico, and she hasn't heard from him either, not since he called to wish her a happy birthday. But he was too early because her birthday isn't until next month."

"She didn't think that was strange?"

"Apparently, he has a terrible memory when it comes to dates."

"He doesn't have a calendar?"

"A calendar is only as good as the man adding the events."

The way Vance said that, I knew he'd forgotten a birthday at some point or another.

But back to Santoro... It wouldn't be the first time a man had run away from his problems, and he could have acquired a second passport, especially if Ilya's crew had deep pockets. But it was equally possible he'd gotten in the way or seen something he shouldn't and was lying in a shallow grave somewhere. Or perhaps they'd tried to recruit him, and he'd refused to cooperate?

"What about Stern?" I asked.

"Sticking to his story—he doesn't know anything about

anything, he cared deeply for Ottie, and he would never do anything to hurt her."

Yet when she was in trouble, she'd turned elsewhere for help.

"Fitz?"

"Embarrassed that his addiction came to light, but swears he had nothing to do with the weapon's disappearance."

"He needed money—has he acquired any recently?"

"Apart from his salary, there's only been one significant payment made into his bank account in the last two months, and that came from a casino. He took a trip to Vegas the weekend after the weapon vanished and won big, but according to the file the Feds put together, he gambled half the winnings away before he got escorted out of the Zodiac for being inappropriate with one of the waitresses."

"The Zodiac?" Spider made a face. "He must've taken a heck of a lot of liberties to get kicked out of that place. It ain't exactly the Bellagio."

Mentally, I added "asshole" to Fitz's list of attributes.

"Didn't you get married there once?" Black asked Hawaiian-Shirt Guy.

"Apparently I did." He shrugged. "Don't remember much of it."

"Was that the cocktail waitress?" Spider asked.

"No, that was the frozen-foods heiress."

"What frozen-foods heiress?"

"We were only hitched long enough for her daddy's lawyer to draw up the annulment papers." He settled an arm over Spider's shoulders. "Hardly worth mentioning. And you, my lovely, need to stop asking questions and work out how you're going to get into our target house. We have three days, and the clock's ticking."

Three days, and with every hour that passed, Ilya's team got closer to having an operational weapon. Yes, they'd failed with Ottie, but I couldn't believe they didn't have a backup plan in place. A man like Ilya *always* had alternatives.

Not only that, I couldn't stay away from Baldwin's Shore forever, and nor did I want to. Yes, this trip had turned out to be less unpleasant than I'd feared, but Baldwin's Shore was my home, and I'd already had three messages from Brooke and six from Paulo asking how my imaginary sister was. At least the new girl at the Craft Cabin—Everly—was working out okay.

And so was my relationship with Alex. Wait, relationship? Did we have a relationship? I thought that maybe things were heading that way. Spending more time with him would be a challenge, though. I didn't want the whole town asking questions that might ruin my cover, but I was an excellent liar, which gave me a small advantage at least.

Three days, and the clock was ticking...

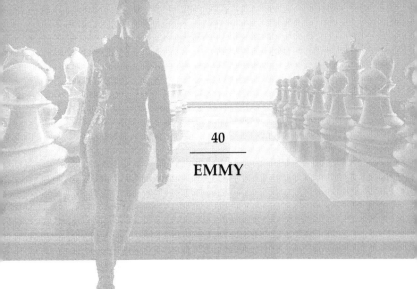

Objectively speaking, Scott Lowes was a dreamboat, but no need to take my word for it. Ask any woman from Antarctica to Zagazig and they'd confirm that indisputable fact. Shiny brown hair with a hint of curl, dreamy blue-green eyes, a movie-poster smile... Oh, and he was rich too. According to Bradley, who knew these things, Lowes had been paid twenty-five million bucks for his most recent leading role. Women swooned over him; guys wanted to be him. Last year, he'd single-handedly started a trend for tweed kilts when he wore one to an award show.

Scott Lowes also made excellent bait.

"You decided to wear trousers today?" I asked as he took a seat opposite Black and me. The sun was shining, the smog was barely noticeable, and jet skis hummed in the distance. What better way to celebrate this glorious day than with brunch on the terrace? And what better guests than an A-list actor and his lovely wife?

Callie Lowes giggled. "He only wore the kilt because he lost a bet with Connor."

Ah, Connor... The other Lowes brother. Also hot, but a

pain in the ass. Although I had to concede that he'd settled down over the past few years. Both men had hooked up with English girls within months of each other, and by some miracle, both of those girls had turned out to be remarkably normal. Callie used to be a schoolteacher, and now she ran a not-for-profit raising awareness of missing women worldwide.

We'd known the Lowes brothers for years, ever since Scott got targeted by a deranged female fan and hired Blackwood to track her down before she succeeded in her plan to burn his life to the ground, quite literally. Fortunately, the fuel tank on his Porsche had been full when she tossed the match in, so there wasn't enough vapour to ignite. Rule number one of being an arsonist: understand the fire triangle. But the woman was still dangerous, and we'd caught her before she did any lasting damage. Scott had become quite chummy with one of the other Blackwood directors too, which meant that when Nick called to ask him for a small favour, he'd been happy to oblige.

"How is Connor these days?" Black asked.

"Still on the straight and narrow. He's filming in Budapest at the moment."

"You must be relieved you don't have to worry about him anymore."

"Well, he volunteered to do his own stunts, so..."

"So you'll always be a big brother."

"Exactly. Can you tell us why we're here? Nick said you needed help with something, but he was hazy on the details."

"Just your presence here is enough," I said. We'd discussed how much to tell Scott and Callie, and decided to go with a vague version of the truth rather than lying outright. Firstly, we counted them as friends and we didn't lie to friends, and secondly, it was possible we might need Scott to add another layer to our cover story later. "We can't say much for obvious reasons, but one of our neighbours is holding a party this weekend, and we'd like an invite. Apparently, he's involved in the movie business as well as some other shady stuff, so you're basically here to up our street cred."

My phrasing was deliberate. The reasons weren't obvious at all, but who wanted to look like a fool by admitting they didn't know that? Not Scott or Callie.

"It's not dangerous?" he asked, his arm tightening around Callie's shoulders.

"The only danger might come from Bradley's cooking, but I think we convinced him to order in."

Black turned to click his fingers at Alex, who'd taken on the role of butler, and as he did so, his gaze swept over the house opposite. Today's seating arrangements were awkward. Normally, Black and I would have bagged primo position at the table—backs to the house, looking out across the water—but we needed Scott and Callie on show, so we'd been forced to give up those spots. At least the reflection in the windows meant we weren't completely blind. A blur of movement caught my eye, and Alex gave me the slightest nod.

Someone was watching us.

Good.

Callie giggled. "Brunch with a side of mystery? This is quite exciting. Was there a murder?"

"Sorry to disappoint."

"Being involved in one murder mystery was enough, babe," Scott told her. "But while we're here, there's something else we want to speak with you about."

"The charity thing? Nick mentioned that."

"Callie's made it her mission in life to publicise the plight of missing women whose cases aren't getting enough attention. We have the social media side of things dialled in, but there are times when a lead needs to be followed up locally and the cops either can't or won't help. Since Blackwood has offices all over the world, we were wondering if there's anything you could do?"

"You mean provide boots on the ground?"

Scott nodded. "I'm willing to put money behind the project, but I'm hoping we can negotiate a favourable rate."

Black and I had already anticipated that, and we'd agree to the proposal, but we'd also go further. Callie Lowes had put her heart into the project and had several successes so far. With a little extra resource, her efforts could have even more impact.

"How about this—we'll offer a bank of one hundred pro bono hours, with a fifty percent discount off subsequent time, in exchange for Blackwood being credited for our part of the work in any write-ups?"

When Scott said they had the social media side of the project cracked, he meant it. Callie had a new-generation digital army at her disposal now, and some of those kids would one day grow into decision makers. Budget holders. If they ever needed to hire a security firm, we wanted Blackwood to be the first name they thought of.

"Really? Wow." Callie beamed at us, then glanced at Scott. "That's a good deal, right?"

"It's a good deal."

The marketing department would be so proud of us. Quite honestly, the business side of things bored me to death, but it was a necessary evil.

Bradley must have been listening from the wings because he practically ran over with a bottle of champagne in an ice bucket and five glasses.

"Fantabulous! We should all celebrate."

I groaned. Black groaned. Even Scott groaned because he'd visited Riverley with Nick a time or two, and once you met Bradley, you never forgot him.

"We're technically working here," I tried, but Bradley ignored me completely and popped the cork.

"You can have one drink." He shoved a champagne flute at me. "It's an excellent vintage."

"No can do, champ. Today, I'm embracing sobriety."

"Fine." Bradley passed the champagne to Callie instead. "If someone had warned me, I could've picked up a bottle of Nozeco. I hope everyone likes waffles? And poached eggs? And smoked salmon bagels? Hash browns with bacon? Avocado toast? Pancakes with fresh fruit?"

How much food had he bought?

The answer: all of it. He sent the Loweses home with a fucking doggy bag. Scott rolled his eyes, but Callie was polite enough to take it. I figured we could palm the rest off onto the folks who'd stayed inside—Alaric, Ravi, Pale, Barbie, Spider, Hallie, and Vance—but oh no, Bradley had thought of that. Alaric's face still bore traces of powdered sugar when we went inside to view the surveillance tapes.

"Waffle?" he offered, holding a piece out on a fork.

"I never want to eat carbs again."

"Next week when you're sneaking out for a cheeseburger, I'll remind you of that."

"Please don't." I nodded towards the laptop beside him. "Did we get anything?"

Under cover of darkness, we'd set up miniaturised cameras on the boat, on the terrace, and in an upstairs window. Combined with the drone overhead, we now had eyes on the house twenty-four-seven, and our remote teams could take some of the surveillance burden.

"Svetlana spotted Lowes, I guarantee it. One moment she was reading a book on the terrace, the next, she ran inside and came back with Angelou."

"Scott walked right up to the back railing with Callie midway through the meal. Spent a few minutes looking across the water and pointing at shit, just to give them an eyeful."

"Good sport."

He was, but possibly not as good a sport as Armand Taylor. Armand was another A-lister who used Blackwood's services, and over the years, he'd grown tight with Dan. When she asked him nicely, he'd put out feelers via his own network in an attempt to get tickets to the party.

"It was a fruitful meeting all around."

"What's the plan now?"

"Now? Now, we wait."

Shortly after two p.m., Bryant and Svetlana walked across the footbridge to their dock and climbed into a boat—a medium-sized RIB, nothing too flashy—with Ilya following. As soon as Svetlana had settled herself onto a seat at the rear, Ilya fired up the engine. He didn't look happy.

Good.

I popped another marshmallow into my mouth and offered the bag to Black. He shook his head, jaw clenched. James had come through with the care package, and now I had six kinds of gourmet marshmallows, two kinds of coffee, and a box of artisan chocolates. Well, half a box of artisan chocolates. They were moreish, okay?

To give Team Ilya their credit, they made an effort. We watched discreetly as the trio puttered around with the engine on tickover, visiting five other houses before they reached ours. Aw, how sweet. They'd come up with their own cover story.

An hour later, they drew up at our dock, and when Bryant and Svetlana crossed the road and rang the intercom at the back gate, Alex headed out to meet them. Five minutes passed before he returned with a card.

"You have an invitation." He broke into a rare grin. "Dress code is semi-formal."

"Does that mean I should take my gold-plated revolvers?"

"Beats me. Ask Bradley."

Shit, did I have to?

"What did they say?"

"That they're having a get-together on Saturday evening, and they're looking forward to meeting their new neighbours."

"I bet they are."

But in just two short days, their grand plan would backfire. We'd make sure of that.

NINE

"**D**on't you think this is weird?"

Ana glanced at me, chopsticks in hand, a sushi roll halfway to her mouth.

"Our whole life is weird. Which particular part are you talking about? Being back together again?"

"Being so far behind the front lines."

While Emmy and her people planned their entry into the terracotta eyesore, Ana and I had been exiled to Santa Clarita, with nights spent at Skywater House. Instead of plotting to retrieve a deadly weapon from under the nose of our former colleague, we were puzzling over a much less significant problem. The weapon was already gone. Getting it back was the priority, not working out which scientist betrayed their country. ARU—Acronyms R Us—could do that later.

But Ana only shrugged. "Operationally, it makes sense for us to stay out of Ilya's way."

"I know. It's just...weird."

Plus I was being paid eight thousand bucks a day for breaking and entering, which, let's face it, was child's play. Even weirder.

The ARU file had described Timothy Stern as "peeved yet cooperative," but having spent the afternoon listening to him via the bugs I'd installed while Ana followed him to his lawyer's office this morning, I was inclined to go with "indignant." His sister had visited with her son this afternoon, a boy of seven or eight years old, and Stern had spent the whole time complaining while the kid played video games in the background.

His suspension from work was *so* unfair. Those assholes wouldn't let him see Ottie. Only a monster would betray his country, and he was a gosh-darned-patriot, didn't they understand that? *Beep-beep-boop.* Rinse and repeat when his brother got home from work in the evening—the brother appeared to be sleeping on the couch—minus the video game soundtrack.

A case of a man who doth protest too much?

Or was he just a whiner?

Either way, I couldn't understand what Ottie Marquette saw in him. In any normal situation, her taste in men—or the lack of it—would be *her* problem, but thanks to Anton Stepanov's desire for power, now it was our problem too. A Blackwood team would continue to monitor the Stern bugs tomorrow while we tackled the next candidate. Santoro. Or rather, his estranged wife.

Laurie Santoro was referred to by ARU as both "hostile" and "cagey." I'd add "quiet" to the list. So far, she'd spoken only with her daughter, a pony-obsessed four-year-old named Esme. I'd paid a visit to their apartment while they stocked up on groceries—it had been a busy morning—and there were toys lying everywhere, most of them of the equine variety. Housekeeping wasn't one of Laurie's strengths, or maybe she'd just been distracted lately?

Either way, she'd sounded slightly teary when she promised Esme they could go to the Jumbo Jungle tomorrow afternoon, so perhaps José's disappearance had left her more stressed than she'd originally let on. The Jumbo Jungle Bounce-n-Play was neutral territory and potentially a good place to get to know Laurie better, but there was a slight technical hitch—it was a kids' play centre. Sure, there was a café too, but the café was themed with chairs shaped like ladybugs and giraffes and tables modelled on giant lily pads. Not a place where adults went alone.

Ana's phone vibrated its way across the table, and she checked the screen.

"They're coming. Sam isn't happy, but they're coming."

Fantastic. Our surveillance team had just doubled in size, and tomorrow, I was going to become Aunt Dede.

"We can't make a habit of this. She's missing kindergarten."

Quinn—Ana was the only person who called him Sam, apparently—folded his arms as he watched his dearly beloved help Tabby into a new sweater. We'd bought it last night at Walmart, along with fabric paints and yarn, and after dinner, I'd painted a pair of multicoloured ponies on the front, then made them swishy little tails. Tabby was distinctly unimpressed. The way she curled her lip was all Ana.

"We're only taking her to a play centre," Ana told Quinn.

"Today, it's a play centre. This is a slippery slope. Next thing we know, she'll be twelve years old and jumping out of an airplane with an MP5."

"If she's jumping out of a plane, an Uzi Model B Carbine would be more appropriate."

Ana was correct—the Uzi Model B had a higher tolerance for rough handling. At twelve years old, Tabby would still be a relatively inexperienced skydiver, and nobody wanted a hard landing to ruin a carefully planned operation.

"That wasn't the point I was trying to make. We agreed to let her be a normal kid."

"Normal kids bounce around on inflatables. If it wasn't totally safe, I wouldn't be taking her."

Tabby rolled her big brown eyes and looked up at me. The kid had Ana as a mom and Emmy as an aunt; normal was relative.

"Aunt Dede, can I have a juice box?"

Quinn crouched beside her. "You have to use the magic word, *kotyonak*."

"Aunt Dede, can I have a fucking juice box?"

I knew I shouldn't laugh, but a snort escaped. I might not have spent much time around kids, but I'd put money on Tabitha Quinn following in her mother's oh-so-silent footsteps.

Quinn tore both hands through his hair. "I'm fighting a losing battle here."

"We're on the same side," Ana reminded him, and he took a calming breath.

"Tabby, you shouldn't say 'fucking.' The magic word is 'please,' remember?"

"Aunt Dede, *please* can I have a juice box?"

"Sure. Want me to take a picture of you guys? Tabby's first undercover job is one for the memory book."

"What did I do to deserve this?" Quinn muttered, but he was smiling as he said it.

Because he cared.

He cared about Ana and about Tabby.

And that...that left me with...feelings. A little envy, but also hope. Quinn was such a regular guy. Not the type of man I'd ever have imagined Ana ending up with. They had a relationship I'd always assumed would be impossible—Quinn knew Ana's past and her present, and still he loved her.

What if I could have that too?

Alex had called me last night. My first instinct had been to ask, "What's wrong?" but nothing was wrong. He just wanted to talk. Not about work, but about things of no consequence. My favourite movie (I didn't have one), places we'd been on vacation (what was a vacation?), how we'd spent Christmas (Alex had wrapped gifts for underprivileged kids while I'd dressed up as a Shadow Trooper to extract a confession from a murderer), that kind of thing. Which was weird, but in the same way that Brooke showing up with cupcakes on her first day at work had been weird. *Nice* weird.

And that left me even more mixed up.

Outside the Jumbo Jungle, Ana showed Tabby a photo of Esme Santoro.

"You need to find this kid, make friends, and bring her to us, okay?"

"What if she doesn't wanna be friends?"

"You'll find a way to make her."

"The thing you said? The manpi... The manpu..."

"Manipulate. Yes, that thing. We believe in you, *kotyonak*."

"Okay." Tabby clenched small fists by her sides. "Okay. I do this."

Laurie Santoro was sitting alone at a table overlooking the ball pool, and she didn't look good. Haggard, chewed ragged around the edges. She stared into a steaming mug shaped like a hippopotamus as painfully enthusiastic "fun managers" shepherded kids around an inflatable obstacle course. *Fuck, the noise.* Ana grimaced faintly as we headed for the café's counter, and I began to yearn for the brutal isolation of Base 13.

"Are kids always this loud?"

"When you get a bunch of them together, yes." She

opened her purse and offered me a tiny package. "You want earplugs?"

"Thanks."

Our mugs were shaped like an owl and a penguin, neither of which lived in a jungle, so I figured the staff had decided to use poetic licence. What I needed was horilka, but we had to make do with coffee and cupcakes. The cupcakes had cat ears and whiskers. Paulo would have been in heaven here.

Tabby waded gamely into the melee, and although Ana's expression was one of bored resignation, she didn't take her eyes off her daughter. We'd selected a table near the back (a) because it was quieter and (b) so we could watch Laurie without her noticing us.

"All these years we dreamed of a normal life," Ana said. "And then normal turns out to be watching two kids beating the shit out of each other with inflatable flamingos."

"I still can't believe you have a child."

"Some days, *I* can't believe I have a child. But I wouldn't change things."

"Not even the soundtrack? What *is* this?"

"It's the Baby Shark song."

"Now there are sharks in the jungle?"

We stared at each other for a beat and then began laughing. What else could we do? This situation was entirely absurd. If General Zacharov could see us now, he'd give himself an aneurysm, which, quite frankly, would have been far too kind an end for him.

Ana reached across the table and squeezed my hand. "I know we've had a hard week, but I'm glad you're back in my life."

"Same."

The word fell out of my mouth, an instinctive response, even though Ana's reappearance had turned my life upside down. Life in Baldwin's Shore had been safe. Far from perfect, but safe. Now my future was filled with difficult decisions.

"So, you and Alexei?"

I choked on my coffee. "You can't ask me that."

"Why not?"

"Because...because we didn't cover meaningful human interactions in our training."

"So you're saying you don't know what you're doing?"

"No, I'm not saying that at all."

I'd spent my entire life learning how to be good at *everything*. Admitting I was clueless would be outing myself as a failure. And I *hated* failing.

"Liar."

"I...I... Fine. *Fine*, I could use a few pointers on the whole thing."

"He likes you, and you like him. Just let it happen."

"How? How can I 'just let it happen'? We live in different states. And not even Oregon and Idaho. We're talking Oregon and *Virginia*. A logistical nightmare, and fifty percent of the variables are outside of my control."

"So what are your other options? You knock Alex back, return to Baldwin's Shore, hook up with a local, and keep very, very quiet about your basement? And Alex meets another version of his ex-wife, who everyone ends up hating? And then you both end up miserable and alone?"

"Well—"

"Do you know where Bradley's boyfriend lives right now?"

"How the hell would I know that?"

"Egypt. He lives in Egypt. And they've managed to have a healthy relationship for the past decade, even though they spend most of their time apart."

"How?"

"Don't ask him unless you want to hear about the phone sex. And the Skype sex. And the—"

"Okay, okay, I get it."

And I didn't want another woman to get Alex. Somehow, we'd have to make it work. If I could sneak onto a nuclear submarine, then surely I could manage Skype sex. But how safe was Skype? Was it encrypted? What if somebody hacked my phone? I'd need some kind of secure line, and—

"Mom, this is Esme."

"Can we play in the fish pond?" Esme asked.

"They's not real fish," Tabby pointed out, just in case we weren't sure.

Ana rarely smiled, but one corner of her lip twitched.

"You can go in the fish pond if Esme's mom says it's okay. Or her pop?"

Esme pointed at Laurie. "That's my mom."

Perfect. Okay, I'd concede there was one small benefit in having a child. And I strongly suspected General Zacharov had been one step ahead of me, which was the only reason Ana had been allowed to keep her daughter. Did she realise that? Of course she did. She was too smart not to.

Laurie looked up as we approached, her mind clearly elsewhere.

"You're Esme's mom?"

"What did she do?"

"Nothing at all. She just asked to play in the fish pond with my daughter, and I wanted to check that was okay with you. According to the website, this place has one fun manager for every six children and an excellent safety record."

"Oh, sure, the staff here are real good."

"Off you go, girls."

But Esme didn't move.

"Mom, can I have a sweater like that one?" she asked,

pointing at the ponies on Tabby's chest. I'd added glitter, and they twinkled under the strip lights.

"You have to use the magic word," Tabby told her.

"Huh?"

"The magic word is"—*Fuck*—"please."

We all owed Quinn a debt of thanks.

"Your little girl is so polite." Laurie gave us a shaky smile. "Where did you buy the sweater? It's Esme's birthday soon, and I haven't... I need to get her a gift."

Ana nodded toward me. "My sister made it. Not the actual sweater, but she painted the picture."

"Oh." Now Laurie's lips quivered. "You're real talented."

"When's her birthday? If you buy a plain sweater, then maybe I could make her one similar?"

"Really? You'd do that?"

"Sure. I mean, I'm not a professional artist, though. Painting's just a hobby."

Shit, why was she crying? A tear rolled down her cheek, and she wiped it away, but another soon took its place. Ana nudged Tabby with her foot, and the kid took the hint.

"Let's go play." She tugged Esme's hand. "I wanna meet Sammy the Shark."

Okay, we could work with this... I slid into the seat beside Laurie and channelled Brooke. I'd learned a lot from watching her over the past year. Brooke was the sweetest person I knew, one who listed kindness as her superpower.

"Hey, are you okay?"

A dumb question, in my opinion, but apparently the correct one in these situations.

"I...I..."

"Is there someone we can call for you?" Time to push another button. "Esme's pop, maybe?"

She cried harder. Excellent. I tucked an arm around her shoulder and squeezed as Ana held out a tissue.

"Th-th-thanks. I'm s-s-sorry. Everything just... Stuff's been so hard lately, and when you said something nice, it... Well, I guess it just tipped me over the edge."

"Is there anything we can do to help?"

"We b-b-barely know each other."

"Momma always told us not to turn the other cheek. Would it help to talk things through?"

"Dede's a good listener," Ana put in. "I've lost count of the number of times I've called her to vent."

"I'm not even allowed to talk about most of it."

"Not allowed? By who?"

"The cops. At least, I think they were cops."

Ana took a step back and glanced toward the fish pool. The fish were made from foam, fifteen varieties in total, each with the name of the species printed on it. Fun *and* educational, or so the website claimed.

"Cops? Uh..."

"I didn't do anything illegal, I swear. But they had questions about my h-h-husband, and..."

"Did he hurt you? Your husband?"

"No! No, never. Not physically, anyway. Only in here." She placed a hand over her heart. "They said that he stole something from work, but they wouldn't even tell me what, and I just... I can't..."

"Did you ask him about it? Maybe he could clear all this up?"

"I can't. He's gone."

"Gone?" I kept my face blank. "Gone where?"

"I don't freaking know! Just gone."

"Did you file a report? Like, a missing persons report?"

Laurie shook her head. "The cops knew he was gone before I did. And he...he left a note."

This was new. "A note?"

"In the mailbox. I found it after the cops left."

"Did it say where he went? Leave a number?"

"It only said that he needed space and not to worry."

Ana sighed. "Why do men do that? Of course we're going to worry."

"We've had some problems recently." Laurie sighed. "He... I think he cheated on me, so I made him move out, pushed him away, and now he's disappeared. What if he...if he...?"

José had cheated? That was something else Laurie hadn't told the ARU team. She obviously wanted to talk—*needed* to talk—but not to a group of investigators who made her uncomfortable. Plus the worry in her voice said she still cared for José, whether or not he'd done the dirty on her, and now she thought there was a possibility he'd taken his own life.

"I'm sure he wouldn't have told you not to worry if he was going to do something drastic. He hasn't gotten in touch since?"

Another shake of the head. "Even after he moved out, he still came every weekend to see Esme, but last week, he didn't show up, and I have no idea what to tell her."

"You think that maybe he's with the other woman?"

"At first, that *is* what I thought. But the cops said she's in the h-h-hospital, and he's still m-m-missing." Ottie? Was she talking about Ottie Marquette? José and Ottie had been having an affair? "They said he was mixed up in some big conspiracy at work, but I don't believe it. His job meant everything to him." Laurie wiped away more tears. "Even more than I did."

"Did he admit to cheating?"

"No! And that just made it even worse. My friend saw him and a redhead coming out of a hotel room together. A freaking *hotel room*. Why else would they have been there? Oh, he said that she was his boss and they were only working, but does he think I'm stupid?"

A redhead—yes, she was definitely talking about Ottie

Marquette. But now Laurie's voice had risen, and people began to stare at us. Time to dial this back a notch.

"Maybe he went to stay with a friend for a few weeks? To get his head straight?"

"José doesn't have many friends, and I called all of them. He spent most of his time at work. Some important project, he said, and maybe I should have guessed that the project was his boss, but I was so busy trying to be a good mom, and...and..."

"Hey, it's okay. You're a great mom. Esme looks so happy, and I'll be sure to make that sweater for her birthday. Don't even worry about buying a plain one—I can do that. Just let me know where to mail it."

"You're such a kind person." Laurie gripped my hand. "You have a good heart."

Oh, if only she knew.

"And Esme's lucky to have you as her mom. You want a fresh coffee? Our treat. That one must be cold by now."

Ana didn't wait for an answer. "I'll get it. Cream? Sugar?"

"One sugar. Thank you. Uh, what do you think I should do about José?"

An interesting question. José Santoro had aligned himself with Ottie Marquette, for reasons as yet unknown. *Had* they been having an affair? Or was José telling the truth when he said they'd simply been colleagues with a close working relationship? Or worse, had he cosied up to her for more nefarious reasons? Only time would tell. As for where José was... It was possible he was hanging out with Stepanov's team of bad actors, but I considered it more likely that he was six feet under. Or three feet, if the calibre of our opposition was anything to go by—I couldn't imagine Moscow or the Mule doing more than a half-assed job. If Santoro had gotten in the way, if he'd seen something he shouldn't, none of Stepanov's hirelings would have risked him talking.

"Difficult as it might be, I think you should stop worrying about things you can't control."

"Trying to ignore what's happening is hard. I think... I think that even after everything that's happened, I still love him. Is that crazy?"

"Love is the part that's crazy. We can't control it, no matter how much we might want to." Thanks to Alex, I understood that now. "All we can do is sit back, buckle up, and try to enjoy the ride."

We were halfway to the car when Tabby asked, "Mom, can I have a shark?"

"A toy shark?"

"No, a real shark."

Ana glared at me when I snorted, but how could I keep a straight face?

"That isn't a good idea."

"Why?"

"Because sharks bite."

"Dogs bite, and we have a dog."

"Sharks need to live in water."

"Daddy said we can have a swimming pool."

"Oh, he did, did he?"

Either Quinn hadn't discussed that particular plan with Ana, or Tabby was trying her luck. She was a smart kid—I wouldn't have put it past her.

"Aunt Dede, can you make me a sweater with a shark on it?"

"Sure, but what if he gets lonely? You should have two sharks."

"Don't encourage her." Ana took a calming breath. "For fu—fudge's sake, don't encourage her."

"But—"

"*Don't.*"

Okay, I'd leave the "Mom" stuff to Ana.

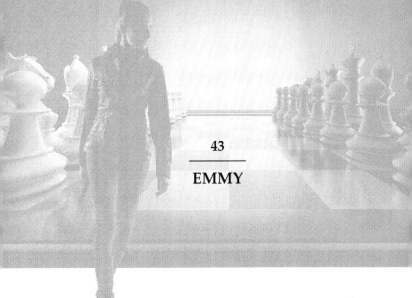

"No, no, a thousand times no. Is he crazy?"

The good news was that Armand Taylor had procured us two more tickets to Bryant Angelou's party. The bad news? Armand thought that achievement entitled him to use one of them.

And frustratingly, Dan was taking his side.

"It's not the absolute worst idea. If he shows up, nobody's going to be paying attention to anything we're doing."

"But we can't guarantee his safety. Ilya Molotov is a highly trained Russian assassin. Having gone up against one of his former comrades last week, I can assure you that he's not a man to mess around with."

Without thinking, I touched a finger to my nose. The swelling had gone down now, but the bridge was still tender. Ilya had six inches and seventy pounds on Darya—if he'd been in the forest in Baldwin's Shore that day, I'd have needed to get my entire face reconstructed.

"It's a covert operation," Dan said, as if I might have forgotten that fact.

"Exactly. *Covert*. Softly-softly, fly under the radar. The last thing we need is the Armand Taylor circus."

"He's landed the lead role in a new spy thriller, and he sees this as a research opportunity. There'll be other guests there too."

"Who will also be in danger."

"He'll sign a waiver."

"Oh, hurrah, a waiver. Like that'll help if his ugly mug gets splattered across the deck. The media will have a field day."

"So, here's the thing—I don't think we can stop him. He says he could use a little excitement in his life."

"Excitement? *Excitement*? He's a Hollywood actor. In his last movie, he base-jumped off a mountain and waterskied behind a helicopter."

Even I hadn't waterskied behind a helicopter, probably because I didn't want to get chopped to pieces by the tail rotor.

"That was CGI."

"He was still involved. If he wants excitement, why doesn't he take a vacation? He's loaded—he could go anywhere in the world."

Dan rolled her eyes. She'd flown in this morning and swung by Armand's place before she drove down to Naples, and by a miracle, she'd got here without putting any dents in Armand's Mercedes. He was a brave man, lending it to her. Brave or monumentally stupid. In light of our current conversation, I was inclined to go with the latter.

"You think I didn't suggest that?" Dan asked.

"Can't Hans talk some sense into him?"

Hans was Armand's boyfriend, not that the rest of the world knew that. America's heartthrob was so far in the closet that if he fished around, he'd probably find the pink spangled catsuit Bradley had misplaced four years ago and still reminisced about to this day.

"Hans tried and failed. Armand is coming, whether we like it or not—all we can do is give him stage directions."

Bloody fucking hell. Anything else want to go wrong? This job had been jinxed from the start.

"You'd better keep him on a damn short leash. And next time he wants to hire a bodyguard, give him a penknife and a water pistol and tell him to do the job himself."

At least we'd had more luck with the third pair of tickets. Several years ago, Black and I had invested in a production company for some kind of tax break. Our finance manager thought it would be a good idea, and for the most part, he'd been right. Apart from a zombie movie that bombed at the box office, Black Hole Entertainment had turned a steady profit. And tomorrow night, Alaric and Hallie would be representing BHE at Angelou's party. The two of them would position themselves on the back terrace, ready to sound the alarm to Ravi and Spider if they attracted any unwanted attention. The party planners had been kind enough to set up tables at the rear already, so we knew the terrace would be in use.

This close to the water, a hidden basement was unlikely, so if the weapon was in the house as Dasha believed, then upstairs seemed the most probable location. It would be easy enough for Angelou to position a man at the bottom of the staircase to keep guests out of the way, which was why Ravi and Spider planned to go in via the balcony. That would take masterful timing and a distraction, which was where Barbie came in. Alex would play boat captain, and Pale would stay in our rental house with Vance to monitor operations and step in if the shit hit the fan.

"Emmy, we have to choose your outfit." Bradley bustled in with an armful of garment bags. "I've gone with pants and shorter dresses just in case you need to kick anything, and plenty of draped fabric to hide your weapons."

He knew me so well.

"Okay, champ, what've you got?"

"How many guns are you planning to take?"

"Only one."

If I needed more than that, I'd take a spare from one of my victims. Not that I was planning to shoot anyone. If all went smoothly, Ilya's crew wouldn't even know we'd breached their defences until the weapon turned up missing.

"Can you put the gun in your purse?"

Nobody was going to search a bunch of rich folks arriving at a cocktail party.

"No, I need to keep it close."

"Then my favourite is this jumpsuit with a pair of kitten heels and a jacket. The deep-sea blue will complement your fake eye colour."

Bradley might have been a pain in the ass, but I had to give him credit for always picking the perfect outfit for parties. He reserved the most outlandish creations for himself, like the turquoise suit he was wearing today, complete with silver brogues.

"Okay, we'll go with the jumpsuit. Did you find something for Hallie?"

"She's wearing a longline jacket and a minidress in slate grey."

"What about Dan?"

"No need to trouble yourself." Dan waved a hand. "I already have the perfect outfit. Semi-formal, right?"

Bradley's grimace said it all. Heaven help us.

NINE

The ARU files described Mark Fitz as "sheepish" and "compliant." He knew he should have informed his superiors about his gambling problem, but he'd carried on hiding it in the hope that the next big win would pay off his debts. Now that he'd been found out, he seemed more relieved than anything else, and he'd begun attending Gamblers Anonymous meetings.

That was where he'd gone this evening.

His rented bachelor pad was a strange mix of minimalism and sentimentality. Light wood floors, a neutral colour scheme, big windows with gauzy drapes. Framed pictures covered the walls, photos mainly, but the living room lacked a couch. A desk in the bedroom held a laptop, but there was no TV. A shelving unit was home to an ornate glass chess set, several tennis trophies, and a bunch of books, mostly memoirs with the occasional reference text. I flipped through the pages of each, but there were no hidden notes and no hollowed-out centres.

"Think he sold his furniture?" Ana asked as she unscrewed the cover plate of the electrical outlet beside the bed.

I unearthed a pile of receipts in the desk drawer. "Pawned it."

Did that mean he was still hoping to hit the jackpot and get it back? Tsk-tsk-tsk.

"Doesn't he realise the house always wins?"

"Not always. Anatoli the Bear didn't win."

The former Bratva boss had fallen to his death from the seventeenth floor of his casino in Atlantic City during a late-night tryst with a hooker. Someone had filmed the landing, and the video of his insides dripping off the roof of a Lexus had racked up over half a million views online before it finally got taken down.

"That was you?"

In my early twenties, I hadn't been burdened with so many scars, which made that type of undercover work much easier. Especially with a man like the Bear, who, in his later years, had developed a tendency to drink too much vodka and think with his dick.

"He didn't see eye to eye with the general. You think the light fitting in the living room belongs to the landlord?" It was fancy, designed more for decoration than illumination. "I don't want Fitz to accidentally pawn a bug."

"It was pictured in the rental listing."

I glanced at my watch. Fitz's GA meeting was scheduled to go on for another fifty minutes, and then he had a twenty-minute drive back home. Quinn was keeping an eye on him—the group met in a community centre, and he'd taken Tabby for burgers at the fast-food joint opposite.

"Then I'll work with it."

Installing the bug took less than five minutes—I'd had plenty of experience, and the hardware supplied by Blackwood was designed for ease of use—and then I checked on Fitz's laptop. The data was halfway to being copied. Cracking the encryption would be somebody else's problem—I broke people, not codes.

A young Fitz looked down on me from the walls as I worked. The photos were arranged in chronological order from birth to the present day or close to it. What kind of person documented their life like that for all to see? The idea made me shudder. Baby Fitz in a crib, toddler Fitz playing under a lawn sprinkler, junior Fitz playing chess with an older man who might have been his grandfather. There was a facial resemblance.

Hmm.

Chess. *The chess set...*

I scanned the other pictures, now with a goal in mind. There he was again—teenage Fitz, playing in a chess tournament, his face tense with concentration. And then near the end of the timeline...

"Ana?"

"*Da?*"

"Look at this." A second later, she was at my side. "Fitz plays chess, quite seriously, it seems. Timonenko, Novikova, and Angelou also play chess."

"You think they met at some chess tournament? That Fitz is our guy?"

"Blackwood has people who can research this?"

"I'll contact them."

"While you're putting in the request, ask about this boat too." I tapped the picture of grown-up Fitz posing on the swim platform of a yacht. "The *Balestra M*."

"Why? Isn't the balestra a fencing move?"

"I believe it is, but back in Russia, I used to play chess with Vik sometimes." At first, I'd always lost, which irked me, but I'd gotten better with practice. "The Balestra Mate is a chess move. The queen cuts off the king's escape both diagonally and vertically while a bishop delivers the checkmate. Balestra *M*. Whoever owns that boat is also a player."

"And rich."

"Stinking." The photo only showed the rear of the *Balestra M*, but it was bigger than the yacht Emmy and Black had parked outside the rental house in Naples, and vessels that size cost a small—and often dubiously obtained—fortune. "If someone bribed Fitz, then we've just found a candidate with the funds to do so."

Ana snapped a photo of the ass-end of the *Balestra M* for reference. We'd put in the research request once we'd left the apartment—no point in pinging a cell tower to record our presence, even if she was using a burner. The rest of the visit turned up nothing of interest—no bundles of cash, no coded notes, no hidden flash drives or memory cards, although it was possible we'd missed something tiny due to the nature of our search, namely fast and non-destructive. We were back in our borrowed SUV before Fitz was halfway home.

Which left us with the boat.

"Ten bucks says the *Balestra M* is registered to a shell company."

"Pass," Ana said. "But Mack will find the true owner eventually."

Eventually. Who knew where I'd be at that point? My sense of pride hated the idea of leaving a job unfinished. I was driving so Ana could send her messages, and part of me itched to turn toward Naples. The party would be starting now, but all the two of us could do was wait for the chips to fall where they may.

"Maybe we could track down the boat itself? That photo isn't more than a couple of years old. If we find out where Fitz travelled during that period, he might lead us to the *Balestra*'s home port. Deckhands talk—someone there would know who the owner is."

A rare smile spread over Ana's face. "You know, there could be an easier way. How big do you think that yacht is?"

"At a guess, thirty metres long? Forty?"

"Yachts with a gross tonnage of three hundred or more that travel internationally should have an AIS—an Automatic Identification System—installed."

"You're an expert in yachts now?"

I was annoyed that I wasn't.

"Emmy has an AIS on the *Black Opal*. I know this because she showed me how to disable it, but most people don't do that for safety reasons. Nobody wants to get run down by a container ship in the middle of the night."

"Okay, and how do we track the AIS?"

Ana's smile turned into a grin. It looked weird on her.

"There's an app for that. Give me a minute."

A minute was literally all it took. We were sitting at a stop light when Ana burst out laughing.

"What? What's funny?"

"Guess where the boat is?"

"Where?"

"Guess."

"Just tell me, for fuck's sake. You know I hate guessing."

"One clue: it rhymes with Cuntington Peach."

"Are you joking?"

"When do I ever joke?"

A valid point. "How do we get to Huntington Beach from here?"

It wasn't so late. We could just take a quick look and be home in time for dinner. And maybe we'd find another piece of the puzzle? I couldn't deny I was disappointed with our work in Santa Clarita—three days of nosing around, and we still didn't know for certain who the traitor was. Right now, I was edging toward Fitz, but the evidence was circumstantial and Santoro was still a big fat question mark.

"I'll program the satnav," Ana said, reaching out to do precisely that. "And I guess I should let Sam know we'll be late."

"We can pick up food on the way back. A pizza or something."

Once a liar, always a liar. I just couldn't help it. Because the way things turned out, even returning in time for breakfast would be a challenge.

*O*h, *for crying out loud.*

"That's Dan's idea of semi-formal?" Black murmured.

Well, technically, she wasn't wrong. Dan had paired a tuxedo jacket with matching micro shorts and black leather ankle boots.

"I didn't realise she planned to take it literally."

"At least nobody's looking at the terrace."

No, half of Ilya's lapdogs were studying Dan's ass, and the other half were staring at her boobs. We'd counted seven men so far, including one guy positioned at the bottom of the stairs in the hall, just in case the velvet rope and the "Please refrain from passing this point" sign weren't enough of a deterrent. Every single woman in the room was checking out Armand, Miroslava Novikova included. She'd shown up with Timonenko, and he didn't look happy about the situation.

The inside of the house wasn't quite as ugly as the outside, although let's face it, that wasn't much of an achievement. An archway led from the large living room into an open-plan kitchen and dining area where a chef prepped canapés with a flair that was more theatre than cooking. Angelou had expensive taste. From Mack's research, he appeared to be struggling with his finances, though. He'd maxed out three credit cards, and parties like this didn't come cheap. What was his grand plan for paying off the debt?

Folding doors at the back of the house led to the terrace, and another henchman had positioned himself just inside to monitor the rear. Ilya himself was standing at the front door, giving each guest the once-over as they walked in. Alaric and Hallie had passed muster, and now they were out on the terrace, sipping drinks and making small talk with a bunch of industry types. A guy in a dinner suit played bland tunes on a grand piano in the corner, although his efforts couldn't drown out the sound of Svetlana's dog barking upstairs.

Ilya had missed me and Black, though. We'd come in through the back. Angelou only had one small boat, and there was plenty of space at his dock, so Alex had shuttled us over in the tender from the *Black Opal*. Now he was playing the bored chauffeur, reading a paperback in the light spilling over from the terrace as he waited to take us back. And of course, he was also providing us with quiet commentary through hidden earpieces.

"Ravi and Spider are in place."

By "in place," he meant waiting farther along the beach, dressed in the same style of plain black uniform the waitstaff were wearing. When the time was right, they'd hop onto the terrace, pick up trays, and make their way to the side of the house, where they'd have an easy climb to the second-floor balcony. Ravi was basically a mountain goat in human skin, and Pale assured us that Spider could scale a wall in seconds. Was that where she'd got her nickname?

Angelou approached with Svetlana, and I put on my "trophy wife" face. Slightly imperious, a little bored.

"We're so glad you could make it tonight. You're from

across the water, right? Our new neighbours?" He held out a hand. "Bryant Angelou, and this is my partner, Svetlana."

Black shook hands with Angelou and kissed Svetlana on the cheek.

"Chuck Brown."

I followed suit. The diamond on my ring finger left no illusion as to our relationship, but just in case Angelou was a complete idiot—he had gotten involved with Ilya Molotov and Marat Timonenko, after all—I made things clear.

"And I'm Emily, Chuck's wife."

Svetlana's bio claimed she was twenty-three, but up close, she looked younger. There was an air of naivety about her. The way she kept sneaking glances at Armand as if she couldn't quite believe he was real said she still played in the minor leagues, and now she was staring up at Black with the same fascination. I'd half watched one of her movies earlier while Bradley was doing my hair—she'd be all right in a romcom if she could sort out her accent, and she might do a half-decent job as the damsel in distress-slash-sidekick in an action flick, but she didn't have the acting chops for a serious dramatic role.

"Have you been in Naples for long?" Angelou asked.

Black pretended to sip from his glass of champagne. "A week or so. We're only here for a change of scene—the weather on the East Coast hasn't been too kind lately."

"That's where you're based? The East Coast?"

"New York, but we have friends in California, plus I do some business here."

"What line of work are you in?"

"I have fingers in various pies. Mostly, I invest in things that interest me. And what do you do, Bryant?"

"I'm a movie producer."

"Oh, really? What genre?"

Alaric spoke in our ears. "Good to go?"

Confirmations followed from Barbie, Ravi, and Spider, and when nobody raised any objections, Pale—who'd been nominated as director of tonight's production—gave the okay. He was viewing proceedings from the terrace of the rental house, where he'd settled in with a beer he wasn't drinking, a cigar he wasn't smoking, and a book he wasn't reading.

"My next project is an action thriller. We plan to film on location in the US and Russia." Angelou spread his arms wide. "Picture a female James Bond."

Black gave a quiet snort. "A female James Bond? That's not very realistic, is it?"

"We believe there's a market for it. Think back to the early days of Sarah Connor—some would argue that she was the true star of the Terminator movies. And now we have Tomb Raider, Charlie's Angels, Wonder Woman... The genre is growing, but it's still a short list of titles compared to the number of male-dominated action movies."

"So will you have Bond guys?" I asked. "Men in tight shirts and swimming trunks?"

"Nothing so clichéd, but there will be a romantic subplot. We're looking for the right male lead to attach to the project."

Angelou glanced towards Armand as he spoke. Good luck with that.

Black nodded. "So you have the female lead cast already?"

"Svetlana will be taking on that role."

Svetlana didn't have the upper body strength to manage five pull-ups, let alone climb a forty-foot rope into a moving helicopter or haul the remains of a corpse out of the ocean or wrestle with a three-hundred-pound meth head, all of which were things I'd had to do in the past. She looked as if she'd snap in half if the wind blew wrong.

"When does production start?" Black asked.

"We're still in the process of securing investment. You mentioned that you—"

The screech of brakes from outside made everyone's heads snap to the front of the house. The screech was followed by the unmistakable crunch of metal on metal, and Angelou ran past Ilya and out the front door. *Perfect timing.*

"You okay?" Pale asked over the radio.

Barbie's voice came through loud and clear. "Oh, I'm just fine. Do I get paid extra for being a crash-test dummy?"

"Ravi, Spider, you're clear. The rear guard's stepped away from the door."

I risked a look myself. Yup, he was as nosy as everyone else. There had to be sixty people at the party so far, and half of them had rushed outside at the first sign of excitement, camera phones at the ready. Even Ilya had headed in that direction to see what was going on, but now he was back.

"Does anyone here own a black Mercedes-AMG coupe?"

Armand raised a hand. "I do."

"You should come outside."

Well, Armand was the one who'd insisted on joining us, and with Dan driving the car this week, that Mercedes had been on borrowed time anyway. Barbie had only planned to damage one corner, so Armand probably got off lightly, all things considered. He trailed Ilya out the door, his expression the perfect mix of annoyance and trepidation. Okay, there were certain advantages to having an actual actor on the team. Dan went with him, a glass of wine in her hand. She'd find somewhere to pour the contents while Ilya was looking the other way.

Dan was also equipped with an earpiece, which meant we all heard Barbie's squeal when she pretended to realise just whose car she'd accidentally-on-purpose driven into.

"OMG, OMG! You're Armand Taylor! This is your car? I'm so, so sorry I hit it. Like, I didn't mean to swerve, but this cat ran out in front of me, and well..."

She burst into tears. Give the woman an Oscar.

"Do you realise how much a car like this costs?" Dan was playing the drunk bitch tonight. "Why didn't you just hit the cat?"

"The car doesn't matter." Armand was always a gentleman, in public and in private. "Are you hurt? Do you need medical attention?"

"It was probably a stray," Dan muttered.

"I'm fine. I mean, my neck's a little stiff, but I don't need an ambulance. Can I get your number?"

"My phone number?"

"For the insurance. We're meant to swap details, right?"

"My assistant handles that for me."

"Oh, of course. Do you think the damage is fixable?"

"I really have no idea."

"Uh, do you think I could get your autograph? My friends totally aren't gonna believe this."

Ilya had a short attention span. From my vantage point by the window, I saw him motion one of his men to keep an eye on the situation outside, and then he retook his position by the front door. But it was too late. The damage was done.

Ravi and Spider were already inside the house.

46

EMMY

Patience wasn't one of my strong suits. Oh, I knew how to bide my time—I could hunker down for days in the jungle, getting bitten to fuck by mosquitoes, and I could squirrel myself away on a rooftop for hours in order to deliver the perfect shot, and I could even bite my tongue and wait an extra day for a package to be delivered when I'd specifically paid extra for express shipping, but I really, really hated having to do it.

It was far worse when I had the most boring job of the evening. Chatting, eating canapés, pretending to be interested in some male model's fitness regimen as he explained the advantages of six different types of squats to Black in excruciating detail.

How were Ravi and Spider getting on? We hadn't heard a word from them, but that was understandable. They wouldn't want to draw attention to themselves as they moved through the house. So far, I was working on the theory that no news was good news—at least they hadn't got caught. Svetlana's dog was still yapping away upstairs, but it had also been making a racket before Ravi and Spider arrived, so I had to assume that was its normal behaviour. Certainly nobody else seemed fazed, and at least the barking would cover up any accidental noise from our team.

Was the dog locked in a bedroom? Ravi was carrying chicken pieces laced with a sedative, but the drugs would take time to work.

Damn, I hated waiting...

And waiting...

And waiting...

Finally, a whisper from Spider.

"The weapon is here."

Shit, I was mid-conversation with some lawyer from San Bernardino.

"Excuse me a moment. I need to go use the little girls' room."

"Can you get it out?" Pale asked as I headed to the bathroom off the hall. Since most of the guests had arrived now, Ilya had taken up position in the living room and left a minion to watch the front door.

"A man's working on it. Santoro, we think. It's hooked up to a computer."

Santoro. So that's who the mole is.

"Can you incapacitate him?"

"Yes, but he's chained to a radiator." Ah, fuck. They'd *kidnapped* Santoro? Guess he'd been more straightforward to round up than Ottie Marquette. Or had Ilya done that job himself? "And there's a guard up here."

"Are you safe talking to us? Where are you now?"

"On the roof. Santoro's in the walk-in closet in the east-facing bedroom, and the guard is lying on the bed, watching TV. I can deal with him, but I can't guarantee it won't be noisy."

"What about the dog?" It had finally shut up. "Did you drug it?"

"No, it seems to have barked itself hoarse."

Which meant another distraction was required. Barbie was done now, back at the rental house with her dented car and ready to assist Vance with the electronic surveillance. We needed to keep Alaric's and Hallie's hands free so they could help with the egress if necessary. Ditto for Alex. Which left me, Dan, and Black.

"How long do you need?" I asked Spider.

"Ten minutes to get into position, and probably another ten to get out. We're not sure how the chain's attached."

Ten minutes? Gee, she wasn't asking for much. But as leader of the Special Projects team, I specialised in achieving the impossible, so it was my job to make it happen.

"Dan, are you ready to do your worst?"

"Mm-hmm."

I outlined my plan and silently kissed goodbye to Emily Brown's dignity in the process. When this was over, I'd take a vacation. An actual vacation where I didn't accidentally find a corpse, which had happened to me more times than you might imagine. A week on the private island Black owned, or maybe a few days on the ski slopes in France. Hell, we could even disappear on the *Black Opal*.

But first, I had to play my part in retrieving the fucking Marshmallow.

"You lookin' at my man?" Dan poked me in the chest harder than was strictly necessary. "Staring's rude."

"I wasn't staring at him."

"You think I'm blind?" Champagne slopped over the rim of Dan's glass as she prodded me again. "Find your own."

I shoved my diamond ring in her face. "You're the one who's blind. I'm married."

"Ring, schming. I know what I saw."

"Look, lady, you're drunk. Do us all a favour and call a cab."

I took a step back and half turned, but Dan grabbed my arm and spun me around. "Hey! You walkin' away while I'm talkin' to ya?"

"Get your hand off." I looked around for help. Would one of the goons step in? "Can someone get this woman away from me? She's crazy."

"Who're you calling crazy?"

Dan shoved me, and I stumbled backwards, arms windmilling until I hit the buffet table. But she still wasn't done. No, the whole lot crashed to the ground as she piled into me, pulling at my hair. Was this enough of a distraction for Spider? My ass was in a fucking trifle. I grabbed a cream cheese bagel and smushed it against the side of Dan's head, and she scooped a glob of mousse out of a bowl and threw it over me. *For crying out loud, avoid my nose.*

For the first few moments, everyone stood frozen. Partygoers, guards, waitstaff, even Ilya. Guess it wasn't every day they got front-row seats to a food fight. Dan straddled me as she whacked me with a bread basket, and I had to admit that the shorts had been a good choice of outfit—at least I didn't have to deal with a faceful of her crotch as well.

"Help me! She's lost her freaking mind!"

Ilya reacted first—mainly because Black was trying not to laugh—and hauled Dan to her feet. She managed to elbow him in the guts before he wrapped her up in a bear hug and threw her at Armand.

"She needs to go. This woman is trouble."

Armand, for his part, appeared suitably horrified. Possibly

he was realising that undercover work wasn't as much fun as it looked in the movies.

"Honey, you need to calm down, okay?"

"Don't you tell me to calm down!"

"Sorry." He addressed the room in general. "Sorry, I thought we were past her anger issues, but... I'll call Dr. Wallberger again. Uh, I'd appreciate if we could keep this quiet."

Ilya glared at the partygoers. "No pictures." He nodded at one of his minions, who removed a phone from a woman's hand. Guess what? Now she wasn't happy either.

"Hey, that's my property. Give it back."

"He said no pictures."

This was going swimmingly so far. Two minutes down, eight to go. I licked at the mousse smeared across my lips and found it didn't taste too bad. Maybe it wasn't mousse at all? Maybe it was Key lime pie?

"Are you okay?" Black handed me a pile of napkins. "Did that woman hit you?"

"Do I look okay?"

"What kind of a party is this? Call yourself security? Why didn't anyone stop this sooner?"

I wiped at my face and probably made the mess worse. At least I'd landed in the desserts instead of the smoked salmon.

"Do I have a bruise on my cheek?"

"Hard to tell with the..." Black made a swirling motion with his hand. "That."

Bryant Angelou looked all kinds of sick. His face had turned quite ashen. "Do you want to clean up? Take a shower? Svetlana has clothes upstairs, and—"

"Nobody goes upstairs," Ilya snapped.

"This is my home, not yours."

Interesting little power struggle there. Who was actually in charge? We'd have to work that out later, and I definitely didn't want anyone poking around upstairs.

"I just want to get out of here. Where's my purse?"

Black held it up. "Right here, sweetheart."

"You should vet your guests better, Mr. Angelou." I mopped more gloop out of my hair. "This evening has been —" I froze. "Where's my earring? It's gone. My earring's gone!"

"Are those the ones your mom gave you?" Black asked.

"Yes!" I let fake panic show as I ran back to the buffet table. "I have to find it."

"I can replace the earring," Armand offered.

"It's irreplaceable, you imbecile. They used to belong to my grandma. She wore them on her wedding day."

What the hell was happening upstairs? We needed a sitrep. The earring was safe in Black's pocket, but how long did we have to spend fishing through the remains of dinner while we pretended to look for it?

Well, the update came, but it wasn't what I hoped for.

"We might have an issue," Pale informed us.

What sort of an issue? Did the guard fight back? Was Santoro causing problems? Had someone blocked the exit route? Of course, I couldn't ask, but thankfully Spider voiced the question.

"What issue?"

"The drone team is reporting police activity nearby. Four cars. They're forming up for some type of operation."

"Where?"

"From the positioning, we think it might be at your location."

What the fuck? Who called the cops? Why? Tell me this wasn't a bullshit drugs bust. I'd seen traces of coke on the bathroom counter, but half the fucking world did coke at parties.

"Why?"

"Vance is trying to find out. How long until you're done?"

"A couple of minutes. Ravi's working on Santoro's padlock while I pack the weapon into its case. This thing is *heavy*. Do we have a route out?"

"Clear on the terrace," Alaric told us.

"Engine's idling," Alex added.

Five minutes. For five fucking minutes, the operation would be balanced on a knife-edge, and all I could do was dig through trifle with a teaspoon. Why did Angelou even have a trifle? It was a British dessert, not American, so I wasn't surprised when I dug in and found blueberries, chocolate chips, and a bunch of other stuff that wasn't supposed to be there. Nice try, guys. Fail.

"Let me help with that," Armand said, rolling up his sleeves. Dan glowered from a couch in the corner, arms folded as one of Ilya's men stood over her. Svetlana and Bryant grabbed spoons too, presumably trying to salvage something from an evening they'd clearly put a lot of effort into planning.

The good news? We only had to do the trifle thing for two minutes.

The bad news? A guard from the front of the house whispered to Ilya, and he switched from grouchy boredom to high alert in the blink of an eye. I'd seen that change before—in Black, in Ana, hell, in myself—and I knew exactly what it meant. Shit was about to hit the fan, and we were talking elephant doo-doo.

"They're spooked," I murmured, not that it mattered if anyone heard me now. The other guests didn't have a clue what was going on, and Ilya was running towards the stairs with two men in tow. Another guy headed for the dock.

"Spider, Ravi, incoming. You too, Alex."

A fourth guard ran for the stairs, and Dan stuck out a foot. Oh, ouch. Before he could get up, she belted him with her purse, and what on earth did she have in there? A dumb-bell? Because he didn't get up again.

Where were the others?

Spider had presumably taken out the guard upstairs, and we'd seen seven men besides Ilya standing around down here. That left three. Two had moved into the hallway, curious about the commotion by the buffet, and one was unaccounted for. Where had he gone?

"We're missing a guard. I last saw him heading for the kitchen."

The atmosphere in the room had changed. Guests inside were beginning to realise there was something very wrong—the sober ones at least—and they started whispering amongst themselves. *Where did those security guys go? What's happening outside? Is someone trying to break in?*

"We can't get out," Spider said. "We'll have to hide."

My operations rarely went wrong, but when they did... This was the runaway freight train of fuck-ups. Could it get any worse?

Yes, of course it could.

The cops hammered on the door. "Long Beach PD."

The guards in the hallway formed up on either side of the entrance, and one of them drew out a gun. Terrific. If we weren't careful, we were about to have dead police on our hands, and I really didn't want to be on the national news. We had to act now. In ten seconds, it would be too late.

"Uh, excuse me?" I covered the ground quickly, and I didn't need to look to know Black was at my side. "What the hell is happening?"

"Get back in there." The nearest goon jerked his head towards the living room.

"How dare you speak to me like that?"

As he swung the gun around, I forced his arm upwards. In close quarters, I almost preferred to face a gun over a knife.

Knock the muzzle by a few degrees and a bullet would miss, but try that trick with a knife, and you'd get cut. I took a leaf out of Nine's playbook and headbutted the asshole, kneed him in the balls at the same time, and then clocked him with a handy-dandy statue from a nearby side table. Black took his guy out with a single punch. Show-off.

At least now I had a Glock. Thanks, dude.

A burst of static sounded in my ear. No, not static. Splashing.

"Alex is in the water," Pale told us.

Fan-fucking-tastic.

Then shouting, from the rear this time.

"Everybody get over there!"

"Hostile on the rear terrace," Pale announced as Alaric told Hallie to stay down. They were both outside—how much danger were they in? "Looks like Timonenko."

Another bang on the front door. "Long Beach PD. Open up."

Then the gunfire started.

One shot, then a pause, followed by an answering volley. Screams. A muttered curse that could have been Alaric or Pale, but was probably Alaric because Pale's words would have been more colourful. Another single shot.

"Two down. One's terminal. Alex is still swimming."

A whisper. "Ilya didn't look in the shower. He left."

Left and went where?

The runaway train was speeding up. Adrenaline flowed as Black and I swivelled towards the stairs, borrowed weapons in our hands. Was Ilya about to come flying in our direction? Dan had Armand on his feet, and he didn't have to fake his terror as she shoved him into the downstairs bathroom. I had a feeling he wouldn't try to invite himself along on any more ops in the future.

Stairs made a terrible meeting place, especially when you

had the disadvantage of being below the enemy. Better to wait in the hallway and catch the incoming team by surprise. Out the back, guests continued to scream and cry, and from Alaric's hasty orders, I gathered he was treating a gunshot victim. He had medical training—we all did—but he'd need first aid supplies ASAP.

And then I heard music. Was that... Was that "Never Gonna Give You Up"? Seriously? We'd just been Rickrolled in the middle of a gunfight?

"Son of a flaming sphincter."

Ah, that was Pale.

"What is it?"

"It's a boat. A fucking party boat."

And now the cops had a battering ram, but that door was solid. They had one, two, three tries before it began to splinter. My radio blipped again, and this time, the words made my chest seize.

"Let me go!"

Shit, that was Hallie. And Hallie wasn't trained in the same way the rest of us were. She was an investigator with good instincts and great observational skills, which was why we'd brought her along tonight, but she wasn't a fighter. Sure, she'd had basic defence training, even killed a man recently, but against Ilya's crew, she stood no chance on her own.

"Move!" a man barked.

"Go," Black told me as the front door finally gave up its stubborn hold.

I went.

47

NINE

"Where did I go wrong in life?"

Instead of opening a craft store, I should have become a criminal. It was a career path I could have excelled at if I'd put my mind to it. And crime really did pay. The *Balestra M* occupied a slip at Sunrise Harbor, a private marina offering laundry facilities, showers, slip-side electric, secure storage, a clubhouse, and a night-time courtesy patrol, although that last item didn't add much value. The single guard we'd spotted was sitting in a prefab cabin watching TV. A sitcom, judging by the laughter.

The owner of the *Balestra M* had clearly come to the same conclusion regarding the guard's abilities because they'd hired their own security. A heavyset guy dressed in black sat on the steps leading down to the swim platform, smoking. Occasionally, he checked his phone, but he was at least partially engaged with his surroundings.

The presence of private security as well as an array of lights in the windows suggested the owner could be on board, so we settled in to watch for signs of activity. Sunrise Harbor was bracketed by an ecological reserve to the north and a development of new-looking homes to the south. A tree in the reserve offered reasonable cover, and a pair of binoculars gave us a good view. Occasionally, a crew member in a black-and-white uniform walked past a window on the third out of the four decks, and once, he brought a plate of food to the guy at the stern, but there was no sign of anyone more senior.

"You grew a conscience," Ana told me. "Don't try to deny it."

I opened my mouth to do just that because my morals were warped by any normal standards—I wasn't so blind that I didn't realise that—but at the same time, I was no Ilya. I didn't sell my deadly services to the highest bidder.

"Half a conscience."

"Two-thirds. Want to see if we can find an office? If the *Balestra* has a slip, there must be paperwork."

"I bet it's rented by a corporate shill. We need whoever is on board to show their face so we can take a look at them. Maybe we could encourage them to come out?"

"You want to light a firework display?"

"Something like that." Although creating a suitable distraction could prove difficult. The road was too far away, so staging a car crash wouldn't work. A simple argument between two passers-by wouldn't be powerful enough. A dumpster fire might have the desired effect, but the dumpsters were kept in a wooden enclosure, so we'd risk the blaze spreading. The boats themselves were moored close together, and if one caught alight... Although, hmm... Yes, they were *very* close together. "Or we could just climb on board and poke around."

It was the quickest way to find the answers we needed, and probably the easiest too. Those boats were like giant stepping stones.

Ana shrugged. "Okay. Should I ask Sam to cook dinner for Tabby?"

"I guess we might be a little late back." I studied the boat as Ana typed out a message. "If the owner's on board, where do you think he'd be?"

"At this time of the evening? On one of the middle two decks. Cabins will be on the lower deck, and nobody's going to use the sun deck in the dark."

The marina guard didn't stir as we tiptoed past the office. Was he asleep? I thought he might be. None of the other boat owners felt the need to hire their own heavies, and I linked arms with Ana as we strolled along the jetty and boarded the *Lady Jean*, a smaller sailboat berthed four slips away from the *Balestra M*. The guy on the swim platform looked up from his dinner to give us a bored once-over, and I waved. Emmy was right—sometimes, hiding in plain sight was the easiest way to achieve our goal.

After that, it was child's play to hop from one boat to the next, and two minutes later, we landed silently on the walkway that ran around the edge of our target vessel. This sure beat an evening of crocheting.

Using hand signals to communicate, we worked our way around the yacht, and when we reached the starboard deck, we found the owner's desire for security only went so far. The crew entrance was unlocked, and when we slipped inside, I heard dishes clanking through a doorway. The galley? The smell of steak cooking suggested it was. A staircase lay to our left, another door to our right. If a chef was serving up steak, the big boss was probably eating dinner, and logic said the dining area would be close to the galley. Which meant our target was on the other side of that door, but we couldn't simply walk through it. Not without the risk of revealing ourselves. And on this deck, the crew had pulled blinds over the windows for privacy.

Ana motioned to the stairs. Perhaps we could go up and around and find a different way in?

The stairs brought us to the bridge, and in the quiet, a soft snore told me somebody was nearby. Ana jerked her head toward the glow from a doorway behind the captain's chair. A cabin. A man was sleeping on the bed, dressed in black pants and a white shirt. The captain? A small nightstand held a cap with the boat's name embroidered in gold, a semi-automatic handgun, and an open bottle of Russian vodka. Great combination.

I crept backward and rolled my eyes, miming lifting a bottle to my lips and then forming my fingers into a gun. Ana smiled and shook her head, incredulous. But a drunk could still be dangerous, especially if that drunk found intruders in his bedroom.

Ana headed out the door on the far side of the bridge. That led us past the top of a spiral staircase and into an empty lounge, which featured a wet bar and giant TV. An outdoor dining area beyond lay in darkness. So far, we'd identified three people on the yacht—the guard, the captain, and a chef. If the crew member who'd taken the guard dinner wasn't the chef, then we had four. Plus the owner and any guests they might have. Seeing as the captain was armed, there was a good chance the other staff carried weapons too, but I still liked the odds. Two versus five or six or seven. No problem.

Not that we wanted to get into a confrontation, obviously, but I'd be remiss if I didn't consider these things.

I slipped past Ana and stepped onto the stairs. Given that our goal tonight was identification rather than elimination, it made sense for me to go first. I always had been good with faces. A gift, the general had said, and one he hadn't hesitated to exploit.

Have you ever been surprised with a gift? Until I moved to Baldwin's Shore, I'd been able to count the number of presents I'd received on one hand, but now I knew this random giving of unnecessary items to be a common occurrence. Only last week, Paulo had handed me a musical sunflower because he said it reminded him of yours truly. I'd shrugged off the insult and focused on the intent—his aim had been to make me happy, and it *was* thoughtful of him.

But tonight? Tonight I got the best surprise *ever*.

Because Anton Stepanov and Yuma Loslov were sharing a cosy steak dinner and a bottle of red wine on board the *Balestra M*.

The sense of joy lasted approximately ten seconds.

Long enough for me to retreat a few steps and mouth their names to Ana.

Then Loslov's phone rang, and although I couldn't hear every word, the sentiment was clear—Loslov was furious. What was going on? Something to do with the raid on the house? Did that mean Emmy's team had been successful? I heard Ilya's name, and a minute later, Stepanov strode in our direction, yelling for the captain. With little other choice, we were forced to retreat through a door to our rear and found ourselves trapped in the luxuriously appointed master cabin.

"Bathroom," Ana muttered.

Good plan, because surely no one would take a bubble bath in the middle of an unfolding crisis?

"What do you think is happening?" she whispered.

"I think they fucked around and now they're realising there are consequences. Any word from Emmy?"

Ana checked her phone. "Not yet, but her priority is the operation at the house."

"We should stay with Stepanov. See if we overhear anything else."

A vibration ran through the *Balestra M* as her massive engines rumbled into life.

Ana gave a wry laugh. "Good thing Sam's putting Tabby to bed."

"It's not every day we get to ride on a luxury yacht." Then

I remembered the *Black Opal*. "Okay, it's not every day *I* get to ride on a luxury yacht. How many guns did you bring?"

"Only one, but we can just borrow more if we need them. I need to update Emmy."

Ah, yes, the teamwork thing.

But before Ana could send a message to Emmy, Emmy got in first.

48

EMMY

Well, tonight had to rank high amongst the most spectacular balls-ups of my career.

Yes, we'd achieved our initial objective—in the chaotic aftermath of the police raid, Ravi and Spider had escaped along the beach with the weapon and a shocked Santoro. Barbie had picked them up, and they were all safely back at the rental house, watching the drama from across the water as we tried to unpick how everything had gone so, so wrong.

Black, Dan, Alaric, Armand, and I had been herded into the living room with everyone else while the cops searched the property and an ambulance crew did their stuff on the terrace. Revealing our true reasons for being at the party didn't seem wise at this point because that would only lead to more questions we didn't have time to answer. At least someone had found me a towel and a packet of wet wipes to clean the worst of the trifle off myself.

As best we could work out, Timonenko had tried to clear a route through the partygoers by waving a gun and shouting, and when the guests didn't move fast enough, he'd fired a warning shot overhead. At which point, a property magnate from Texas had drawn his own gun—afterwards, he proudly told us that he never left home unarmed—and attempted to bring the situation under control. Can you guess how that went? Luckily, or unluckily depending on how you looked at it, only one civilian had been wounded before Pale took out Timonenko with a headshot.

Alaric had attempted to staunch the blood flowing from the woman's chest wound, and at that point, Rick Astley had joined the party, blasting from the speakers of a yacht filled with drunk coeds as it sailed merrily through the middle of a gunfight, the passengers completely oblivious to the danger.

And while everyone was losing their heads, Ilya and two of his men had exited via the rear balcony and run to the dock. Alex had surfaced from drowning the guy he'd tackled in time to see Angelou's RIB speed off, and Ilya had thoughtfully knifed ours so Alex couldn't give chase. Worse, Ilya had grabbed Hallie on the way. Alaric had pushed her behind an oversized concrete plant pot beside the walkway to the dock and told her to stay there, and it seemed Ilya had figured a hostage would come in handy.

Fuck, the girl couldn't catch a break. This was the fourth time she'd been kidnapped, and now I felt sick to my stomach. Finding her wouldn't be a problem—after the previous incidents, she wore a tracker at all times, so we knew exactly where she was—but retrieving her promised to be a headache. Currently, she was speeding south in the RIB. Not only did Ilya have a head start, but we had no idea of his destination.

Spider was busy stitching up a knife wound on Alex's arm while Ravi babysat Santoro. Vance was still trying to find out what the fuck was going on with the Long Beach PD because they weren't telling us anything, while Pale and Barbie loaded hardware onto the *Black Opal* and manoeuvred her into place for a pickup. At her top speed, we'd be able to keep pace with Ilya but not overtake him, which wasn't the disaster it sounded—our boat had a pair of modified Waverunners on board that would go significantly faster when the need arose.

But while catching Ilya was certainly possible, retrieving Hallie presented a far greater challenge. We couldn't have a shoot-out on the water. No, we'd have to wait for him to come ashore and take things from there. He wouldn't dispose of her, not yet. Not while she still had a use. Maybe he'd try to trade her for the weapon?

"Two minutes," Pale said.

"We need to get out of here," I murmured to Black.

Across the room, Armand had an arm around Dan's shoulders, but he was the one who was shaking. Turned out there was a big difference between playing an undercover agent in the movies and actually being one. Still, at least he could write his torn suit off as a bona fide business expense. Alaric would need new clothes, too. His were covered in blood, which meant everyone else in the room was giving their little huddle a wide berth.

Miroslava Novikova glanced in our direction. She'd abandoned her beau, and now she was sitting with a group of women by the grand piano, trying her utmost to look innocent. I didn't believe the act for a moment. She was buried in this from the tips of her Jimmy Choos to her ruby earrings, but we'd deal with her later.

"The police are looking for Charlotte McGuinn," Vance told us. "She was abducted on her way home from school last week."

What the actual fuck? A kidnapped schoolgirl? "Why the hell would they think she was here?"

"They got a tip-off."

"From who?"

"I don't know, but if they see the padlock and chain upstairs..."

Oh, bloody marvellous. If we stuck around, we'd be

answering questions forever. Fuck it, we were getting out of here.

"Ma'am, please sit down."

I almost felt sorry for the cop. He was barely more than a kid and clearly way out of his depth tonight.

"Sorry, but no."

"You can't just leave."

"Actually, the Fourth Amendment says I can."

"Uh..."

"Don't blame me; I didn't write it."

"You're a witness to a crime. We need to take a statement."

"Exactly. A witness, not a perpetrator." For once. "Here's my card, and I've jotted my lawyer's number on the back. I'll make a statement tomorrow, but tonight, I'm feeling sick, and so I'm going home."

"But the captain..."

"The captain can call me tomorrow."

The cop craned his neck back to look up at Black, presumably hoping for a little help in dealing with this unreasonable female. But Black just shrugged.

"You heard what she said. God bless the Constitution."

Alaric and Dan would stay, Dan to keep Armand out of trouble and Alaric to control the narrative around events on the terrace and keep an eye on Novikova. But that left us short of manpower. Or rather, womanpower. Where were Ana and Darya? Probably at Skywater House, eating pizza and planning their next B&E excursion. But tonight, I needed their help. If anyone could predict what Ilya was likely to do, it was those two. As we waited for Pale to pick us up, I fired off an SOS text to Ana, then checked on Hallie's whereabouts again. She was still heading south at a rate of knots, her heart rate elevated but otherwise strong. As long as she was still alive, we could fix this.

Just hold on, Hallie. We're coming.

Ana showed me her phone screen.

Emmy: All hands on deck. The Long Beach PD decided to join the festivities, and Ilya got away in a RIB with two men and Hallie. We're tracking her, and they're heading south. Where are you?

Ana: South. Can't talk right now.

Ilya had escaped? On a boat? Realisation dawned. The horrible truth. He was heading south, and because Ilya was Ilya, he undoubtedly had a plan. Did that plan involve a rendezvous with the *Balestra M*?

"*Pizdets*," Ana muttered.

"He's coming to meet the *Balestra*."

"*Da.*"

Emmy: How far south? Need to intercept him when he comes ashore. We're following, but he's got a head start.

Ana: He's not coming ashore. He's coming to Stepanov's boat, and we're on board.

Emmy: Fuck.

Ana: Track us and provide an ETA. We'll need a pickup. Does he have the weapon?

Emmy: We have the weapon.

Well, that was one small mercy. We still had to face one highly trained assassin and two others of questionable quality, but at least we wouldn't get boiled alive in our own skin.

Ana: Loslov also here. How many pieces do you want them in?

Emmy: Wait one minute...

"It had better be one minute," I muttered. "Time is a luxury we no longer have."

"Let's do a weapons check."

Ana had gone for stopping power with a Glock 20, while I'd opted for stealth with a suppressed Ruger Mark IV Tactical. Between us, we had three knives, a variety of syrettes filled with sedatives and fast-acting poisons, a garrotte, flex-cuffs, a Kobotan, pepper spray disguised as a lipstick, two-way comms units, and a stun gun. Which of those items we used would depend on Emmy's answer.

Which did indeed arrive within a minute.

Emmy: No pieces would be preferable.

Message received, loud and clear.

"What about the staff?" Ana asked.

In the old days, that wouldn't even have been a question. General Zacharov's approach in this situation would have been scorched earth, not surgical removal. But I was playing for a different team now, so we had to give the matter due consideration.

"We could dump them into a life raft."

"Yes, if they're not involved in the shady side of Stepanov's business." Did he have an un-shady side? "But the captain has a gun. How many yacht captains carry guns?"

"We're in America," I pointed out. "Everyone carries a gun."

"The *Balestra M* is flagged in the Cayman Islands, and the

captain is likely to be Russian. Stepanov wouldn't trust an American."

This was true. "So we drug them, and when we have breathing space, we can make a better assessment."

Another message popped up in Blackwood's encrypted app, this time from Blackwood HQ. Ten minutes. If Ilya and the *Balestra* held their current courses and speeds, his ETA was ten minutes. Which meant we had ten minutes to neutralise Stepanov and his crew and take control of the boat. Ten minutes to come up with a plan to rescue Hallie. Ten minutes until we faced a man whose body count was higher than both of ours combined.

"Stepanov and Loslov first?" Ana asked as she set a timer for nine minutes on her phone. I did the same.

"Ideally. Better to cut the head off the snake. The chef will be in the galley, and Loslov is probably still eating. Why waste a good steak? The captain's on the bridge, and Stepanov could be in either place."

"So our unknowns are the guy acting as waiter and the guard."

"The waiter will be near the galley, but the guard could be anywhere." I took a deep breath and let calm settle over me. "When Ilya arrives, I'll face him alone. You have too much to lose now. A daughter, a boyfriend..."

"You also have a boyfriend."

"Do I?"

Ana just rolled her eyes. "We should face him together."

"Somebody needs to drive the boat, and you have more experience at that."

"A boat like this will have an autopilot." Ana touched my arm. "We started this as a team, and we'll end it as a team. Ilya won't be expecting both of us."

"He won't even be expecting one of us."

Ana cracked a smile. "True. Seven and Nine, back from the dead."

Another minute, and we'd formed a plan of attack, and then it was time to move. I paused at the bedroom door, not so much listening as *feeling*. Instincts had saved my skin more than once over the years. Was there anyone out there?

No.

Seven minutes to go, and we crept back to the main staircase. Was Stepanov back in the saloon? Or had he lost his appetite and decided to stay on the bridge?

The plan called for me to clear the remainder of this deck first. Saloon, dining area, and galley. We wore tiny earpieces to communicate, and once I'd dealt with Loslov, the chef, and anyone else I found, Ana would make her move.

At the beginning of my career, a massive adrenaline kick would send my heart racing at the start of this kind of job. Sweat used to trickle down my back as I desperately hid my nerves from the other six. These days, fear was a servant, not a master. Adrenaline provided not so much a kick as a mild jolt, and I harnessed it to heighten my senses.

This evening, the kick came from the fucking waiter.

Oh, the first part of the task went smoothly, almost surprisingly so. I should have realised that was a bad omen. Stepanov barely looked up as I put two bullets into his head. The small calibre meant they didn't exit, just rattled around in there, turning his brain into Swiss cheese. Loslov turned with his mouth open, his face frozen in a question he'd never ask. They were both dead before Stepanov's glass of red hit the plush grey carpet. A Château Lafite Rothschild. Fancy. I recognised the label because General Zacharov used to spend his ill-gotten gains on the stuff.

Then the waiter entered from stage left like the karate kid. His foot caught my shoulder as I ducked out of the way, and I guess that at least resolved our earlier concern about whether the staff were innocent bystanders.

"Scorched earth," I told Ana as I regained my balance and blocked another kick.

"Copy."

Fortunately, the guy had more style than substance, and when I threw a chair at him, it knocked him down long enough for me to aim for his centre mass. Two rounds slowed him considerably, just in time for the chef to pop out of the galley and go full Steven Seagal. A knife flew past my ear, but you know the old saying about bringing a knife to a gunfight? So, so true. A double-tap pushed him back, but adrenaline let him fight on even as blood bubbled out of his chest. He was a big guy, too. Over six feet tall and fond of his own cooking. Above, I heard Ana's 10mm join the party, and either the captain or the guard was history. Probably the captain. Which meant we still had an unknown somewhere on the boat, plus these two assholes to finish.

The waiter had found a pistol, so he got priority. Two to the head, and the gun fell from his fingers. That left me with one round in my Ruger and an irate chef waving a meat cleaver. With little choice, I went for a headshot and missed—fuck—and perhaps spending my days crocheting wasn't so bad after all? At least yarn didn't try to kill you. I vaulted backward over another wet bar, a twin of the one upstairs—how much did these assholes drink?—and the cleaver splintered the wood half an inch from my hand.

A hurled cocktail shaker was met with a grunt of, "*Suka*," which was accurate if not very polite. I needed a moment to change my magazine, but I wasn't going to get it, so I grabbed the switchblade from my belt instead. The next time the cleaver embedded itself in what had once been a nice piece of polished walnut, I thrust upward and slashed through the chef's carotid artery. Blood sprayed everywhere, including on me, and I cursed under my breath because now I'd have to clean up before Ilya arrived. At least I'd worn black today. It was such a practical colour. Although Paulo told me it wasn't a colour at all, it was a shade, because he liked to nitpick over these things.

But first things first. I switched out my magazine for a fresh one and retrieved the waiter's gun too. A 9mm Makarov, well-maintained by the look of it. I tested it by firing a round into the chef's head. Not bad, and at least he stopped groaning.

"Sitrep?" I asked Ana.

She didn't answer, but I heard two barely audible taps. Our code for "okay, but can't talk." Since she'd eliminated one target, that had to mean she was closing in on the second. Was he coming to investigate the noise? How long did we have left? Just under five minutes, but the saloon looked like the scene of a massacre, probably because it was, and where was the first place on the boat Ilya would go? That's right: the fucking saloon. Even if I dragged the bodies out of the way, there wasn't much I could do about the arterial spray. Although Stepanov did have some bizarre pieces of modern art. Maybe Ilya—who had zero appreciation of culture—might mistake the scarlet spatter for personal expression?

Okay, that was wishful thinking. I hauled Stepanov and Loslov into the galley, then heard a gunshot as I dumped the waiter on top of them.

"Target eliminated, going to the bridge."

The chef just about fit behind the bar, and as I wedged his feet in place with a stool, I caught sight of my reflection in the mirrored shelves. *Pizdets.*

"I need to clean my face."

"It was messy?"

"*Da*, it was fucking messy."

"*Der'mo*, Ilya is radioing the captain. He wants a position."

"Can't he use the AIS?"

"If nobody answers, he'll be suspicious."

Of course he would. "Then we have to answer."

"I have a voice-changing app on my phone."

"Remember to sound drunk."

I paid another visit to the bathroom while Ana reported in, slurring, pissed off, and convincingly male, and told Ilya we'd cut the engines while we waited, but to hurry the fuck up.

Two minutes, and I scrubbed at my face with a wet towel, desperately trying to get the blood out of my eyebrows. At least I had Darla's brown hair today instead of my old ice-blonde. Ilya would question the suppressed Ruger in these circumstances, so I tucked the Makarov into my holster instead. It still had seven rounds in the magazine, and if I needed more than that, I'd be dead anyway.

"Thirty seconds," Ana told me.

I ran to the stern, and although I wasn't religious, I said a little prayer.

And there they were.

50

NINE

One small boat, four occupants, and I recognised Hallie's blonde hair streaming in the wind.

Ilya and his men came closer...closer... I couldn't open fire at them in the boat, not with Hallie there. There was too much movement for a clean shot. I'd need to wait until they were all on board the *Balestra*, the closest thing to solid ground five miles offshore. I hadn't bothered to hide the Makarov. Ilya would be more surprised if I didn't have a weapon strapped to my hip than if I did.

Aaaaaand here he was...

I saw the moment of recognition. Ilya's first instinct was to grab his sidearm, just as I'd expected.

"*S vozvrashcheniyem, tovarishch.*" Welcome back, comrade. I spread my arms wide. "It's been a long time."

"What the hell are you doing here?"

If you act like you belong, then you will.

"Apparently, I'm saving your sorry ass."

I held out a hand, but Ilya didn't make a move to pass me the painter. Suspicion clouded his gaze, and he was right to be cautious. He didn't know it yet, but he was a dead man. Hallie was ashen under the yacht's spotlight, and she looked as if she was about to vomit. Fear or seasickness? Or both? Whatever, the only thing that mattered was that she didn't give my loyalties away. So far, she'd kept her mouth shut, and I had to trust that Emmy had trained her well enough for it to stay that way.

"Suit yourself." I hated to turn my back on Ilya, but I had to do it. "Anton is waiting in the saloon."

"He hired you? He didn't tell me."

"You think he tells either of us everything?" I said over my shoulder. Stepanov compartmentalised; that was what Naz had said. The left hand never knew what the right hand was doing. "All I know is that the B-team and C-team both failed, so now the A-team is required to clean up the mess."

"And you think you're the A-team?"

"I wasn't the one who screwed up, was I? Are you coming aboard? Or shall I tell Anton you changed your mind about needing a ride?" When Ilya hesitated, I yelled, "Let's go."

The two other men on the RIB looked at each other. Followers, not leaders. Nothing but foot soldiers, hired muscle, but they were armed and therefore dangerous if I lost control of the situation. *Hurry up.* To assist with Ilya's decision-making process, Ana fired up the engine, and he threw the painter at me, scowling.

"Zacharov said you were dead."

"Do I look dead to you?"

"Where have you been for the past four years?"

If you become him, then you can destroy him.

"Doing the same thing that you are now—earning more money than Zacharov ever paid us. Why did you stay with him for so long?"

Ilya must have deemed that answer acceptable because he jumped on board. Up close, he was still as bulky as he'd ever been, a wall of muscle and bad attitude.

"My only mistake was not getting out sooner."

"Your *only* mistake?" The first minion clambered aboard with considerably less grace than Ilya had managed. "What went wrong tonight?"

I needed to keep Ilya talking. Keep him here with us. If he walked into the saloon too soon and saw the blood, we were all in trouble. The second minion pushed Hallie toward the front of the boat, and she reached for me, her expression a mix of puzzlement and sheer terror. She didn't know what I was doing here. Couldn't work out whether I'd switched sides and become the enemy.

Should I be pleased or disappointed by that?

Arms straining, she pulled herself out of the boat, and at that precarious moment, that instant when her balance was at its most vulnerable, I let her go, then gave her a shove for good measure so she fell clear of the propeller.

"Hey!" Ilya shouted. "Why did you do that?"

"Oh, Ilya." My tone was mocking. "Have you finally grown a conscience?" I grabbed a life ring from its hook and tossed it after Hallie. It landed with a splash, and she grabbed for it, spluttering. "There, are you happy now?"

"She was a bargaining chip."

"She was baggage."

And now she was safe.

The yacht began to increase its speed, putting distance between us and Hallie. The water might have been cold, but she was a good swimmer, and Emmy would be on her way in the *Black Opal* or *Feelin' Nauti* or whatever the fuck it was called today.

"Are you joining us?" I asked the second minion. "Or do you prefer a rough ride?"

He scrambled on board, and I steeled myself for what was to come. Years had passed since I'd trained properly with Ana. Two decades ago, we'd been able to anticipate each other's movements, to react as one, to read each other's minds. But now? Now, there was enough room for error that a bead of sweat rolled down my spine. Three men, two of us, one chance.

"After you," I said to Ilya, motioning toward the saloon. "Good luck explaining your screw-up."

To your maker.

In person.

"No, after you."

He used his semi-automatic to gesture me forward. I started up the stairs, hairs prickling on the back of my neck. Would he shoot me? If I made one wrong move, the answer was most definitely yes.

"Always so suspicious, Ilya."

"Someone tipped off the cops."

"And you think it was me?"

"You wouldn't be here if my operation had succeeded."

"No, I'd be back in DC, doing the job I was hired to do before your shit hit the fan. Don't let your trigger finger slip. Anton's in a foul enough mood already."

"If you didn't call the cops, then who did?"

"How the hell should I know?"

"They will regret it. They'll be sorry they ever crossed me."

It was the last promise he'd ever break.

I dropped to a crouch as Ana stepped out, twisting as I ducked. Ilya reacted in a heartbeat, tracking me with his gun, and a bullet whizzed past my ear and embedded itself in the deck. *Close, but not close enough.* He didn't get a second chance. Ana's first shot went straight through his medulla oblongata. I'd drawn the Makarov as I pivoted, sending silent thanks to General Zacharov for the hundreds of times he'd made me rehearse that move, for the endless drills he'd forced me through. *You can always be faster, Nine. There's no such thing as too much practice.* As Ilya crumpled, I fired a round between the first minion's eyes before he got his gun out of his holster, and the third died with a mask of horrified shock on his face and the bridge of his nose missing.

Ilya's gun hit the deck with a *clunk*, followed by his body. Sightless eyes stared up at us.

"You're still an arrogant fuck, Six."

The endgame had taken less than ten seconds, quick and relatively clean. General Zacharov would have been so proud.

Ana came closer and stared down at Ilya before poking him with a foot. "And then there were three."

The two of us plus Vik, somewhere.

"I only wish Rad was still here."

Ana wrapped her arms around me, and I did the same to her, guns still in our hands, and then I kissed her hair the way I always used to when we were scared kids.

"We still make a good team," she whispered.

"*Da*, I guess we do."

And I had some big decisions to make about my future.

"We should go back for Hallie."

"I'll take the RIB."

"Then we need to dispose of..." Ana looked around and wrinkled her nose. "Everything."

"How deep is the ocean floor around here?"

"I'll check the charts and turn off the AIS."

It was a pleasant evening for a sail. A cloudless sky, a sumptuous yacht I'd never be able to afford in a million years, and good company. Hallie stayed quiet after we retrieved her, but I suppose that was understandable after getting kidnapped yet again. Ana said this was her fourth abduction in as many years. Someone needed to teach that girl how to watch her back.

The gravesite we identified lay a hundred and fifty miles offshore, a nice spot with no submarine cables where the ocean floor dropped to thirteen thousand feet. The trip would take five hours or so. Once we'd sunk the yacht—a tragic waste but also a necessity—we'd set off toward the shore in the RIB, and Emmy's team would pick us up.

"How can you eat?" Hallie asked from the corner of the saloon. We'd found her a blanket, and now she was huddled up in a chair, wearing a minidress that had looked black when I hauled her onto the *Balestra*, but which had dried to a dark grey. Her jacket was gone, stripped off in the water. "There are bodies everywhere."

"Relax, they're all dead."

"That was kind of my point."

"Why waste the food? Sure you're not hungry?"

She shook her head.

Before he died, the chef had been proficient at his craft. There were chilled crème brûlées in the refrigerator, so I'd caramelised the tops before using the blowtorch in the IED I was building. Along with the blowtorch, I'd used fuel I'd siphoned from the jet skis in the hold, a bunch of lithium batteries, cans of hairspray, several bottles of vodka, a remote-control toy Ferrari, superglue, a Zippo lighter, dental floss, the cocktail shaker I'd thrown at the chef, and a variety of other useful objects.

Ana was driving the boat, so I took her a plate of sandwiches.

"Did you finish the device?" she asked.

I nodded. "And I searched the boat. The laptops are ready to go, but I couldn't get the safe open, so we'll have to take the whole thing with us."

Complete with the piece of wall it was still attached to. I'd borrowed the chef's meat cleaver and chopped through the wood. I'd also gathered over a hundred thousand bucks in cash, the same in rubles, and a number of other electronic devices.

"Thirty-five minutes until we reach the dumpsite." Ana

covered her yawn with a hand. "I hope Tabby went to sleep okay."

The yawn was contagious. In our old life, showing signs of tiredness had been punishable by even more training—another of the general's favourite mottoes was "better dead than lazy"—but in this new-found freedom, we could do whatever the hell we wanted. For good measure, I stretched my arms above my head too.

"I'm sure she's fine. You need another drink?"

"A coffee would be good. How is Hallie?"

"Quiet."

"At least she doesn't get in the way."

An hour later, the hard part was over. We heaved the safe into the RIB, loaded the rest of the goodies on board with it, and retreated to a safe distance. According to the toy car's box, the remote had a range of a hundred metres, and I was pleased to report the manufacturer hadn't been exaggerating. The IED blew with a satisfying *boom*, and it wasn't long before the *Balestra M* began to sink beneath the murky waves. I hummed the Russian national anthem and gave a salute as she submerged.

"*Do svidaniya, mudaki.*"

"And good riddance," Ana added.

Then we set off for home.

51

NINE

Hammering on the door woke me.

Shit, shit, shit! Where was my gun? There were arms around me. In bed... *Can't get found like this...* Then my brain caught up and I realised they were Alex's arms, not Rad's, and Blackwood didn't have the same ban on fraternisation that General Zacharov had insisted upon.

But who was at the door?

"Are you awake?"

Bradley.

"What do you want?"

I checked the clock; it was ten a.m.

"I picked up breakfast from the patisserie. And while you were out saving the world yesterday, you missed the flash sale at Macy's, but fortunately you had *moi* to do the hard work. They had a fantastic pair of boots that are soooo you, and a darling scarf with—"

"I was asleep," I growled.

"Okay, so I guess I can just leave the bags outside. Emmy says there's a debrief in an hour."

Ana and I had slept for most of the trip back last

night, and I still had so many questions. But at the same time, I wanted to curl up and close my eyes again. How long would it take me to throw on some clothes? Five minutes? So I could spend another fifty-five minutes in bed.

Alex nuzzled my neck. "How are you feeling this morning?"

"Fine. Why would I be anything else?"

"Hmm... Let me think... Maybe because you spent the night saving the world?"

"There were only nine men on the boat. It wasn't difficult."

He groaned into my hair. "Help me. I've fallen in love with Superwoman."

"Superwoman is a Hollywood construct. My operational capabilities are down to years of training and experience, not special effects and—" Wait, what? "Can you say that again?"

"I've fallen in love with Superwoman?"

Yes, that was what I thought he'd said. I twisted in Alex's arms, and his skin scratched against mine.

"You *love* me? How can you love me?"

"Because you're the most amazing woman I've ever met. I don't expect you to say it back, not yet, but I know how I feel."

"But..." Hold on a second... Why was Alex's skin scratchy? I unpeeled his arm and held it up to the light to see a row of neat stitches, three inches long. "You got hurt? Who did this? How did it happen?"

"I was involved in an altercation last night."

"At the terracotta house?"

"Yes."

"With one of Ilya's men?"

"Yes, but don't worry; I took care of the problem."

"Don't worry? How can you say that? Do you realise how

close this is to your brachial artery? If the blade had gone any deeper—"

"It didn't."

"I..." Was this what love was? Freaking out when somebody was injured? I'd stitched Rad back together plenty of times without feeling such overwhelming worry. "I *really* don't like it when you get hurt."

"Does that mean you're going to kiss me better?"

"I would have kissed you anyway, without the knife wound."

"In future, I'll remember that."

Alex rolled me underneath him and pinned my arms, his fingers twined with mine. I almost rolled him right back off again—old habits died hard—but I caught myself in time. This was exactly where I wanted to be. Our lips met, and he kissed me lazily as he nudged my legs apart with his feet.

"We don't have—"

"Shh."

Last night—this morning—Alex had carried me to my room and dressed me in one of his T-shirts, but now he sat me up and peeled me out of it. Being manhandled was still a strange experience, but I decided to go with it. So much of my life was changing—why not let someone else do the work for once? When his mouth closed over one breast, I let my head sag back onto the pillow and allowed the sensations to wash over me. The tickle of his tongue. The scrape of his teeth. The caress of his fingers. Not always gentle, but not rough either. I let my own gaze wander over his broad shoulders, watching the muscles ripple.

Sex with Rad had always been a hurried affair, pleasurable but tainted by an underlying fear that we'd be caught. In the early days with Ana, we'd both fumbled our way through things because neither of us had a clue what we were doing. And the one time I'd fucked Vik—something I'd never admit to Emmy or Ana and a mistake I'd tried to erase from my mind —he'd got me off, then got himself off, then left the hotel room without saying another word.

Other than those forbidden dalliances with colleagues, sex had been a chore. Work. A task I'd performed like a circus monkey when the job called for it. Oh, sure, I'd become technically proficient at it, just as I'd strived to master every skill, but I'd gained zero enjoyment from the act.

And now there was Alex...

We both knew what we were doing, and neither of us was going to get punished for doing it. He said he loved me. At some point, he would come to his senses, but for the moment, I could enjoy our time together. I twisted one hand out of his to check my watch. We had fifty-five minutes, although we should allow ten minutes for a shower because even if fraternisation wasn't banned, attending a debrief smelling of sex would be unprofessional.

"Am I taking too long?" Alex asked, and he didn't sound happy. Uh-oh.

"I'm just considering the logistics."

"Logistics?"

"Yes, assuming we're planning to have sex. Do you have a condom? Because my implant expired, so I removed it."

"Dashenka, the words 'sex' and 'logistics' don't belong in the same sentence."

"We only have forty-five minutes, so planning is—"

He covered my mouth with one hand, then reached for his phone with the other. What the hell? Who was he calling? This was only wasting time.

"Emmy? We'll be late for the debrief." A pause. "Why? Because we're having our own debrief first." Another pause. "Three hours should be enough." Alex looked down at me and smiled. "Actually, make it four."

For a whole five seconds, I was speechless.

"Did you just tell your boss"—and technically my boss too, for today at least—"that we're planning to sleep together?"

"Who said anything about sleeping?"

I grabbed his balls and gave them a little twist.

"Counterproductive, Dasha. You think Emmy doesn't already know what we're doing?"

"You didn't need to spell it out."

Alex settled his weight onto me, trapping my hand. "You're a top-tier assassin masquerading as a craft store owner, and your biggest concern is that people might find out you have a healthy sex life?"

I opened my mouth. Closed it again. When he put things like that, my little foible did sound slightly ridiculous.

"I'm still getting used to the new rules."

"In Emmy's Special Projects team, the only rule is 'don't fuck up the job.' Can you let go of my testicles now?"

"Sorry." I loosened my grip.

"Going back to your earlier question, yes, I have a condom. I have a whole box of condoms, and if you can't walk later, I'll carry you to Emmy's meeting. *Ladno*?"

"*Ladno*," I agreed.

Alex tossed the phone across the bed and ran a finger between my breasts, shaking his head. "Fucking logistics."

When he teased my nipple with his tongue again, I didn't check my watch. And when he moved lower and buried his head between my legs, I forgot about the concept of time entirely. Thank fuck I'd taken a shower on the *Black Opal* last night because otherwise, I'd taste like sweat and seawater, and — *Khui!* I arched off the bed as Alex hit precisely the right spot. If he intended to keep that up for the full four hours, I really wouldn't be able to walk by the end of it. Crawling might be possible, but— My brain misfired as he slid a finger inside me. His hands were a weapon in their own right—one touch, and they scrambled my mind. The first orgasm tore through me like a frag grenade, destroying any last remnants of coherent thought.

Was that such a bad thing? On another day, I'd have said yes—because remaining alert to potential danger was vital—but today, there was a whole houseful of trained operatives close by, and if an enemy appeared, Ana or Emmy could pick up the slack. Hmm. Maybe this teamwork thing had more benefits than I'd previously considered?

"You're overthinking things again," Alex warned.

"I'm barely thinking at all."

He grinned up at me. "Good. Then I'm doing something right."

"You're doing everything right." I sat up, forcing him onto his knees so I could kiss him again. "*Everything*. Where are the condoms?"

Alex leaned over me and opened the drawer in the nearest bedside table. He hadn't been kidding about having a whole box, but he had glossed over the size of it, and now he tipped them all over the bed.

"They didn't have a regular box?"

His cheeks reddened, which was weirdly sweet. "I delegated to Bradley."

"And that's why we have the variety pack of a hundred and fifty?"

"Exactly."

"Doesn't he realise these things have an expiry date?"

"Dasha?"

"Yes?"

"Stop talking."

When Alex sank into me, I couldn't help thinking back to the first night after we'd met. I'd lain there wrapped up in his coat, imagining a life I'd always thought was out of reach, and now here I was, wrapped up in his arms instead. Alexei tasted of hopes and dreams. When he tipped me over the edge for the second time and I choked out his name, I realised that life as I'd planned it would change yet again. A few snatched weekends with this man wouldn't be enough.

We both needed more.

And I was the one who'd have to give it.

52

EMMY

Alex and Darya had an interesting dynamic.

As evidenced when they walked out of the pool house, four and a half hours late. They exited holding hands, but as they rounded the pool, Darya pulled hers away. Words were exchanged. She folded her arms. Then she just sort of... gave in and let Alex tuck an arm around her waist. Somehow, he'd worked out how to tame the Siberian tiger, which basically made him a magician.

But would his charms be enough? I had a proposal for Darya, and I had a feeling Alex would be the deciding factor in whether she accepted it.

At least the extra four and a half hours hadn't been wasted. Ana and Sam had taken Tabby to see the La Brea Tar Pits as part of their losing battle to turn her into a normal almost-five-year-old child, Alaric and Ravi had taken Hallie and Dan out for lunch, and the rest of us had gone surfing in between calls with the various agencies tasked with sweeping last night's fun under the diplomatic carpet. The beach behind the house had decent waves, and what better way to unwind than face-planting in cold water?

"I *knew* those boots would suit you," Bradley told Darya when she walked through the door, and I had to agree. The four-inch spike heels made her look like even more of a bitch than usual. "Do you want the matching purse? I didn't buy it because it wasn't big enough for a gun, but I can go back to the store."

Was there even anything left in the store? "No more shopping, not today. Don't you have cookies to bake?"

Tabby grabbed his sleeve. "Yes, cookies."

As she dragged him to the kitchen, I raised an eyebrow. "Sleep well?"

Darya turned to face me, one hand on her hip. "No, but the sex was fantastic."

Alex made a choking sound and looked away, laughing, but Darya just stood there, chin jutting, almost as if she was daring me to complain. Why would I complain? Black had fucked me in the shower twice after we'd finished surfing, so I'd have been the biggest hypocrite ever.

"Glad to hear it. Any requests for dinner? We're about to order food."

"I'm taking Dasha out for dinner," Alex said.

"Need a ride? Bradley can arrange a car."

"Thanks, but I'll drive."

"Then let's get this discussion over with. Everyone's waiting in the living room."

Someone had found snacks, and I grabbed a handful of popcorn from the bowl in Dan's lap as I passed. Hallie was sitting next to her, legs curled onto the cushion. Pale was stretched out on the floor, and Barbie was lying on a couch with her head in Spider's lap and her legs across Vance's. Darya and Alex took half of the third couch beside Quinn and Ana, and I perched on the arm of Black's chair, partly because I loved him but mostly because he was holding a bowl of tortilla chips. The only people missing were Alaric and Ravi—they'd flown back to DC after lunch because Sirius was hella busy these days.

"First of all, I want to thank everyone for doing a great job under difficult circumstances last night. The shit might have hit the fan from several directions, but ultimately, we achieved our goals."

And more—the disposal of Stepanov had been a bonus, and I very much suspected that champagne corks were being popped in both DC and Moscow right now.

"Do we know who called the cops?" Vance asked. "That's what really screwed everything up."

"We do." That little snippet of information had been revealed in the last conference call. "It was Santoro. Kind of."

Last night, he'd barely said a word, which had been understandable. When the shooting started, he'd thought he was being abducted again, this time by a different set of people. So he'd clammed right up. Slug's team had collected him and the weapon while we'd sanitised the rental house and retrieved Ana, Hallie, and Darya.

"How?" Spider asked. "He was chained up, and I bet the laptop he was using didn't have internet access."

"It didn't. Timonenko's people removed the wireless card, but they probably didn't realise that the weapon has its own wireless network adapter."

"He used it to communicate? Why did it take him so long?"

"Because when Ottie wiped the software, she did a thorough job. Santoro had to rewrite half the program because the copy Timonenko obtained was months out of date. He couldn't talk because there was always a guard in the room, but as soon as he established an online connection, he submitted a tip to Crime Stoppers."

"The cops were looking for a kid, though? Charlotte McGuinn?"

"Yeah, he figured that trying to explain the logistics of a top-secret weapons program to whoever staffs the Crime Stoppers desk would be tricky, so he went with a story that he thought would get a better response."

"How did he know McGuinn was missing? He got snatched before she did."

"The guards in his room watched a lot of TV, and he saw the AMBER alert."

Black offered me a chip. "Have to give the man points for creativity."

"If he'd just waited for one more day..." Barbie said.

"Yeah, damn him for being too competent. But the guy was terrified. Ilya snatched him off the street and forced him to work by threatening his family. Nobody knew he was missing —Ilya made him write an 'I need space' note to Laurie—and he thought he was going to die. We got off lightly, I think. The only civilian injury was to the actress who got shot by one of her fellow guests, and thanks to Alaric, she'll live."

"What happened to the guy with the gun?"

"He's out on bail. Maybe he'll be found guilty of gross negligence, or maybe a high-priced lawyer will get him off, but either way, I expect the actress'll sue him into oblivion in the inevitable civil suit."

"Do we have any exposure for the other deaths?" Pale asked.

Black shook his head. "No. James Harrison conveys his thanks, as does President Markovich."

"How did the weapon end up with Angelou?" Alex asked. "Movie director to terrorist is a big leap."

It was a smaller leap when you were a fool desperate for money. "Angelou's talking to anyone who'll listen. He met Timonenko at Stanford, as we suspected, and they stayed in touch. Fitz was there too—he spent a semester at Stanford as part of an exchange program, but on his transcript, the credits registered against his home school." A discrepancy nobody had picked up. "Anyhow, Timonenko knew Angelou was having cash-flow problems, and he offered to rent some of the rooms at the terracotta house short-term to help out. Good buddy, huh? Angelou and Svetlana were elsewhere most of the time, and they both swear they didn't go into those rooms and knew nothing about the weapon or the prisoner or any other illegal shit."

"Do we believe them?"

"Honestly? I think they knew Timonenko was doing something shady, and Ilya, but Angelou also hoped to attract funding for the movie from Russia, and Timonenko's connected. So why not turn a blind eye? Anyhow, the FBI can deal with that rat's nest. We've done our part, and thanks to an absolute fucking masterstroke of timing by Ana and Darya, Hallie's back with us and Anton Stepanov can't wreak any more havoc."

"There's always another Stepanov," Ana muttered.

"True, so let's think ahead. I've spent some time training with Pale's crew lately, and I believe more joint exercises would be beneficial, perhaps with Sirius involved too. That way, if we need to work as one expanded team, we'll gel better."

Hallie raised a hand. "Uh, could I get some extra training too? Because I really hate being kidnapped, and I promised myself after the last time that I'd stop being a victim, and yesterday...yesterday..." She choked back a sob. "I didn't know what to do. I had a knife, but I dropped my purse with my gun, and there were three of them, and... I froze. I just froze."

Surprisingly, it was Darya who spoke up.

"You did exactly the right thing. You kept quiet and let your tracking device do the talking." Hallie had also recorded everything Ilya said to his men on the boat. She was a smart cookie, even if she lacked confidence at times. "I'm not saying that you shouldn't train harder, but if you'd tried making a move on Ilya, you'd have ended up as shark food."

"But I felt so...so helpless."

"Sometimes, passivity is what's needed. If you hadn't stayed calm, Ilya would have thrown you overboard and shown up on the *Balestra* without warning, and we'd all be dead. Do you feel better now? Good. Now erase him from your mind."

Darya Volkova was definitely an acquired taste, but I didn't find her quite so bitter anymore. Her heart was in the right place, even if she denied having one.

Hallie swallowed hard, but she nodded. "Is there any news on Ottie Marquette? She was the person who started this whole roller coaster, and it feels as if we've forgotten about her."

"We haven't forgotten. The latest update is that the doctors are planning to bring her out of her coma tomorrow. Her injuries have healed well enough to try."

"Has somebody spoken with Leona?"

"I've spoken with Nico, and he's keeping Leona updated."

Nico... I still owed him a favour. Kaylin La Rocca, the missing woman. Maybe I could put Hallie on that case? But after she'd taken a vacation. She'd had a tough few months, and she needed a break, preferably with Ford. I'd need to meet with Nico again, get more details. If all went according to plan, I'd be paying another visit to Baldwin's Shore anyway, so I could kill two birds with one stone.

Hopefully.

I'd need to have a conversation with Darya first, but coward that I was, I decided to put that little chat off until tomorrow.

53

NINE

"**G**ot a minute?"

I could hardly say no, could I? I was a guest in Emmy's home, and ignoring her would be rude. I opened the door of the pool house wide enough for her to enter and then walked back to the dining table.

"You're painting a sweater?" she asked. "Is that a gift for Tabby?"

"It's for Esme Santoro."

I lied when necessary, but I didn't break my word, and I wasn't going to disappoint a child on her birthday. Rad used to talk about balance, about kismet, and how we were both in negative equity when it came to building up karma points. More than once in the later years, we'd sabotaged a job—very, very carefully—but I was still so deep in the hole that I'd never dig my way out, no matter how many craft sessions I ran at the hospital, no matter how many cats I saved or sweaters I decorated.

And yet, somehow, I had Alex.

Last night, he'd taken me out to a Japanese Fusion restaurant—not just our first date, but my first real date ever.

Previous efforts had all been work-related, although I'd taken a certain comfort in knowing the endgame—usually death—and pre-planning the steps I needed to take in order to get there. At times with Alex, I'd felt as if I was falling into the dark.

But at least the landing had been pleasurable.

"That's nice of you," Emmy said.

"No, it's a self-serving endeavour. I'm trying to influence the gods of fate."

Emmy barked out a laugh. "You keep telling yourself that if it makes you feel bitchier."

"Is there an actual point to this conversation?"

"Yeah, there is." Emmy settled herself into a chair and leaned forward, elbows on the table. "I'd like to offer you a job."

"I—"

She held up a finger. "I'd like to, but I'm not going to."

I'd told myself I didn't want to work for Blackwood, didn't want to be at Emmy Black's beck and call, so why did I feel a pang of disappointment?

"Because I know that's not what you want," she continued. "You spent most of your life working for a despot, and one I unfortunately happen to be related to. You barely know me, and you don't much like me, and you've got no desire to let anyone have that much power over you again. Accurate?"

"Much of it is."

"But you want to spend more time with Alex."

"Yes."

"Alex gets five weeks of paid time off per year, and we're pretty flexible about the days he works. But that's not going to be enough for you. Maybe he loves you enough to move to Baldwin's Shore, although truthfully, I'm not sure he'd be happy there. He has a lot of friends in Virginia, and he enjoys his job."

"You think I don't know this?"

"No, I think you do. Which is why I have an alternative suggestion. Actually, it was Bradley's idea—I can't take all the credit."

The groan slipped out unintentionally. Bradley meant well, I understood that, and I had to concede that the boots he'd dumped outside my bedroom door yesterday were superb. But we were talking about my future happiness here, and I had enough glitter in my life already, courtesy of Paulo.

"Yeah, that was my first reaction too. But surprisingly, it wasn't as terrible as I thought it was going to be. You want a coffee? I need a coffee."

No, I wanted to get on with this conversation, but Emmy was already heading to the kitchen, leaving me with little choice but to follow.

"So, Bradley's always had this dream of owning a craft store. In reality, he'd get bored after a week because he'd hate sitting behind a register and ordering stock and having to answer the same questions over and over, but the key thing is that he likes the *idea* of owning a craft store, and we can use that to our advantage." *Our* advantage? "And when he spent the day helping out at the Craft Cabin, he talked to Brooke about her Thrive group. Empowering women has always been a cornerstone of the Blackwood Foundation's work—that's the charity Black and I started years ago, but his niece runs it now."

"I still don't understand what this has to do with me?"

"Bradley thinks you should open a whole chain of Craft Cabins, and he'd like to invest."

"You just said he'd grow bored after a week."

"Absolutely. But he'd get the project up and running, and that's where we could leverage Thrive."

"Thrive isn't a tool to be leveraged. It's a support group."

"Okay, poor word choice. Through the Blackwood Foundation, we work with various organisations, including several women's shelters. Many of the residents have fled from violence with nothing but the clothes on their backs, and finding employment is key to them getting back on their feet. A fair few of them enjoy crafts. Bradley's always taking wool and fabric and whatever over to the local centre for them to use, and Dan's a big supporter too. When I first met her..." Emmy closed her eyes for a moment. "When I first met her, she was in a refuge, miscarrying after her fucker of a boyfriend kicked her in the stomach. So, needless to say, this is the kind of project we could all get behind."

Now I understood where Emmy was going with this. "You want to open more branches of the Craft Cabin and use them to provide employment to survivors of domestic violence?"

"What do you think of the idea?"

What did I think? I thought Brooke would love it, and I could potentially earn an avalanche of karma points. But I wasn't sure it could work.

"The idea is good, but I've been running the Craft Cabin for over two years now. It makes enough money to employ three people, but half of the revenue comes from online sales, and those are national. We only need one location to service that part of the business, therefore a second branch wouldn't be profitable."

"That's what I figured."

Emmy spooned coffee grounds into the espresso machine, and I didn't miss the self-satisfied smile on her face. She had me exactly where she wanted me. The problem? I had no idea where that was.

"I refer you back to my earlier question. If you know it's a flawed idea, what's the point of having this conversation?"

"The point is threefold." She ticked off the items on her

fingers. "Number one, Bradley could live out his dream. Number two, we'd be able to give more women a step up, and number three, opening a Craft Cabin in Richmond with the Blackwood Foundation's backing would give you the perfect excuse to spend more time in Virginia."

I froze. Emmy's solution was the logistical equivalent of half the jigsaw pieces falling into place, of having my cake and eating it. Keeping my business *and* Alex? I'd been trying to work out a way to do that for days.

But it wasn't the whole story, was it? Because so far, all the upside came to me. What would Emmy get out of the deal? Yes, she'd be certain to retain Alex as her trainer, but that wouldn't be enough. She'd want more. Emmy Zacharova was all smiles on the surface, but underneath, she was ruthless like her father, and she'd want blood.

"What would you ask for in return?"

Ah, now that smile turned cunning.

"You. I'd want you on my team."

"But you said—"

"Part-time. Freelance. I'd take as much time as you'd give, but a minimum of three months in every twelve. The rest of the year, you could play happy families with Alex or vigilante in Baldwin's Shore or improve your crochet skills or whatever."

Three months. Three months at ten thousand a day— Emmy had told me I was worth that—and I could clear the best part of a million bucks a year before tax. Then who would care if the new Craft Cabin made a loss? I'd be able to cover it. Plus I could spend half my time with Alex and actually take a proper vacation. I'd see Ana, and Tabby, and hell, maybe I could even give Hallie a few pointers on how not to get kidnapped again.

It wasn't actually a bad deal.

"I'd need access to your training facilities."

"Absolutely."

"And a pay raise."

"Twenty-five percent?"

I nodded. "But I couldn't start right away. We'd need to break the idea to Brooke and Paulo gently."

Emmy grinned at me. "I'm the queen of bullshit, believe me. Do you need a fake sister? Because we can arrange one."

She held out a hand, and I stared at it. Was it really that easy? If I shook it, I'd get everything I'd ever wanted? An improved version of my old job, a man I loved—even if I hadn't said the words out loud yet—my soul sister, more money than I'd ever earned in my life, plus a safety net in Oregon just in case it all went pear-shaped? Oh, and kick-ass new boots.

"I won't do jobs I consider to be morally wrong. Not anymore."

"Good. Because I don't do those jobs either."

Some hockey player once said that you missed one hundred percent of the shots you didn't take, and that applied equally to assassination. If I didn't at least try this new life on for size, I'd forever regret it. What was the worst that could happen? That I'd crawl back to Baldwin's Shore with my tail between my legs? Yes, death was also possible, but I wouldn't be around in the aftermath, so...

I shook hands with Emmy.

"You got one thing wrong."

"What thing?"

"I didn't much like you to start with, but now I'm more ambivalent."

"Well, I suppose that's progress." Emmy's smartwatch pinged, and she checked the screen. "Black and Alex are running past the patisserie. Do we want anything?"

"I wouldn't mind an apple Danish."

I'd gone several rounds in the gym with Alex this morning,

practising moves again, again, again, and then I'd taken a swim with Ana. After an hour in the sea, I figured I'd earned a pastry.

Emmy dictated the message. "Pain au chocolate for me, apple Danish for Darya."

"You should probably start calling me Dasha now."

The corner of her lip twitched as she revised the message. "Progress indeed."

"Peace offering." Alex held up a bakery bag and raked a hand through sweaty hair. "How was your swim?"

"Fine. But why a peace offering?"

Wasn't it me who might need one of those? Because only after I'd accepted Emmy's offer had it occurred to me that perhaps I should have discussed it with Alex first. What if he thought it was too soon for me to rearrange my life? He'd mentioned coming to Baldwin's Shore, and I'd assumed that would involve staying at my place, but we hadn't actually discussed the details. Where would I live in Virginia? Should I rent an apartment? Or buy one? What were property prices like in Richmond?

"Because I pushed you hard this morning."

"Hard? You think that was hard? I had harder rest days on Base 13. Is that my Danish?"

"I brought you two." He wrapped an arm around me and pressed his lips to mine. "What's wrong?"

"Why would something be wrong?"

"Your frame is full of tension."

I'd intended to let him take a shower before we had the awkward discussion, but my mouth had other ideas.

"I'm going to rent an apartment in Richmond," I blurted.

His turn to stiffen. "That's a big commitment."

"Yes, but you like your job more than I like mine, so it makes sense for me to spend more time in Virginia. And when I say 'mine,' I mean my current job in Baldwin's Shore, not the one I just took with Emmy, although in—"

"Slow down, Dashenka." Alex rubbed small circles on my back. "What are you talking about? You took a job with Emmy?"

I gave him a brief summary. "And, yes, I realise I should have run it by you, but...but..."

"You were excited."

Hmm. Did that explain the weird bubbly feeling in my stomach? I'd just assumed I'd drunk too much coffee after swimming.

"Maybe."

"And now you're happy."

Again, I wasn't going to commit. "That's possible."

"You realise that staying at my place is an option, yes? You don't have to rent an apartment." Now it was Alex's turn to look unsure. "Unless you want to."

"It would be a big step."

Alex nodded. "So I'll ask a question. When I come to Baldwin's Shore, do you want me to stay in a hotel?"

"No."

"That's how I feel about you renting an apartment in Richmond." He brushed hair away from my face. "The nights when we're three thousand miles apart will be hard enough."

"So it looks as if we're moving in together. What's next? Matching slippers? His 'n' hers bathrobes?"

"You act as if Bradley isn't out buying all that crap already."

"Did I mention that I'm also proficient in arson?"

Alex plucked me off my feet and carried me toward the beautiful staircase. I didn't even fight him, probably because we still had one hundred and forty-three condoms left and only two years to use them. Although with me spending half my time in Richmond, they'd only last... Never mind. We could just buy more.

"I love you, Dashenka."

Fuck it.

"I love you too."

EPILOGUE - EMMY

"So, Dasha was right about Maxim Agapov."

Fia took a sip of the cocktail Bradley had made for her and trailed a hand in the pool. Two years ago, she'd never have sat this close to the water, but with a little help from a good man, she'd finally got over her aquaphobia.

"Dasha's right about a lot of things," I said.

Annoyingly right.

While the rest of us had been rolling around in trifle, crashing cars, swimming, and shooting people, Fia had been beavering away in the background, tying up loose ends, namely Agapov and Ruslan Smirnov. In Agapov's case, the tying-up part had been literal—once he'd exceeded his usefulness, she'd left him handcuffed to a bed in the Oceanview Inn.

He hadn't told her much, but he did let slip that he'd procured several dozen tickets to the USA versus Russia game on March ninth. Did Fia want to join him? They had a box with full hospitality, and everyone from the office was going. Miroslava Novikova wasn't talking, but it was a fair bet the soccer match had been the target. Now it would go ahead in the spirit in which it had been intended—one of friendly rivalry.

In contrast to Maxim Agapov, Ruslan Smirnov was a sweetheart.

"Ruslan really did win the lottery," Fia said. "And he tried giving up work, but after a month, he got bored and began missing his colleagues. I think he has a crush on the receptionist."

"So he basically goes to work for fun?"

"Yup. He likes chatting with new people every day, and he likes the way the girl in the café opposite the office makes his sandwiches each lunchtime, and he likes feeling as if he's making a difference. But he was upset about Marat Timonenko. They were friends, he said, even though Timonenko had changed in recent months. He wasn't the same after Novikova joined the team."

"He thinks she was the instigator? That she turned Timonenko?"

Fia nodded as she took another sip of her drink. "Yup. Until she showed up, he was politically neutral, maybe edging toward Pushkin's views because Pushkin and his papa were friends. But after Timonenko hooked up with Novikova, he switched his allegiance to Stepanov."

"Did Ruslan know why?"

"He said Novikova was a temptress." Fia laughed. "Ruslan's a nice old guy, but he does love to gossip."

"What story did you tell him?"

"He thinks I'm a journalist writing a piece on the evolving nature of the US-Russia relationship."

"And he was happy to talk?"

"Once he got started, I couldn't stop him. He's lonely, I think. After we'd discussed his colleagues, I showed him how to set up an online dating profile and helped him to take a bunch of good pictures. Hopefully someday, he'll find a girlfriend."

"The Ferrari'll help with that."

"He doesn't drive it much. The seats give him a backache, and he worries about parking such an expensive car on the street. Each to their own, huh?"

I nodded. "Yeah, each to their own."

Ottie Marquette gripped the arms of her wheelchair as Ana and I carried her down the steps of the Learjet. Hallie followed with Ottie's bag, and there was a strange sense of déjà vu as we walked across the tarmac at Portland International. The last time we'd made this journey, five long, long weeks ago, I hadn't realised I was about to get my nose broken yet again.

Bradley ran down the stairs behind us. "Hey, you forgot your hat."

No, I didn't forget it. I'd left it behind quite intentionally on account of it being pink. Paulo had knitted it for me—he and Bradley had become pen pals or phone friends or something, so he'd be thrilled when we popped in for a "surprise" visit later today.

"Can you make yourself useful and supervise the luggage?"

"Yes, but you still have to wear the hat."

We'd see about that.

Ottie was making steady progress, and although she was still frail, the doctors were hopeful she wouldn't have any long-term cognitive impairment. Now that she'd been discharged from the specialist facility James's chief of staff had stashed her in, she'd decided to spend a week or two in Baldwin's Shore to continue her recovery. A physiotherapist would travel from Coos Bay to help, and the medical staff at the hospital were on hand if needed. At first, Ottie had been apprehensive about coming back to Oregon, but once we'd assured her the town was safe from murderous treason weasels, she'd wanted to visit Leona and pick up her dog. The staff at the Peninsula had been taking care of Gidget while Ottie was otherwise indisposed.

Leona might have been an old friend, but she was a good friend, Ottie said. The best. And the feeling had been mutual. When Ottie graduated high school two years early, that was exactly what Leona had written in her yearbook. *I'll miss you, bestie, but someone has to go show the world how it's done.* And how did we know that? Because Slug's team had found the yearbook in the terracotta house along with various other items stolen from Ottie's home.

Loslov's men had violated her in so many ways.

But her ordeal was over.

Timothy Stern would fly up on the weekend to spend a few days with her too. Personally, I thought he was a bit of a dick, but Ottie liked him and he wasn't a traitor, and those were the only two things that mattered. We'd got to the bottom of that matter too. Why had Ottie run? Because the night the weapon disappeared, she'd been working late and overheard Mark Fitz discussing the theft on the phone—a burner, we now knew—and when he'd called his partner in crime "Tim," she'd assumed the worst. Believing she'd been betrayed by two close friends-slash-colleagues and unsure who to trust, she'd panicked, wiped the weapon's software, and run.

The "Tim" in question?

Timonenko.

It had taken some coaxing, but she'd finally agreed to show us where she'd hidden the memory card containing the code, and tomorrow, we'd deliver it back to Sandy Peake where it belonged.

Why weren't we leaving tonight?

Because tonight, Dasha planned to attend a salsa dancing class with a group of friends—Brooke and Paulo, of course, plus Brooke's fiancé and Aaron, her brother, and a couple of others whose names I'd forgotten—which was basically her worst nightmare. But while she was out, Ana and I had agreed to break into Aaron's apartment and leave a note from the Bad Samaritan, which was apparently what Dasha usually did, but this time, she'd have an alibi. It shouldn't be difficult—she'd provided us with a door key and the alarm code, plus she'd explained how to log into the security monitoring app to turn off the cameras temporarily.

A car was waiting for us near the plane, and Hallie helped Ottie into the front seat.

"Are you comfortable? Do you need a hand with the seat belt?"

Ottie managed a tight smile. "I'm okay."

Once again, Hallie had proven her resilience. Despite being abducted for a fourth time, she hadn't cracked from the pressure. In fact, she seemed to have become stronger. Every time she survived an episode that would have broken ninety-nine percent of other people, she grew in confidence. Three days after the fuck-up with Ilya, I'd been surprised to find her in the gym, smacking Dasha around under Alex's watchful gaze. I'd still insisted she take a break with Ford—they'd spent a week in the Bahamas, doing nothing but each other—but now she was back and ready for our next project: the search for Kaylin La Rocca. Investigating a hit-and-run couldn't be as dangerous as chasing down a secret weapon. Could it?

We set off for Baldwin's Shore.

"It's so good to see you."

Leona Curran flung her arms around Ottie, and they hugged for a long moment before Ottie took half a dozen shaky steps towards an armchair. Nico had arranged a sea-view suite on the ground floor, so Ottie didn't have to crash on a fold-up cot this time around. Gidget yipped around her feet like a caffeinated fluffball, now fully recovered from the poisoning incident and ecstatic to see her owner. Someone—Leona, probably—had thrown a blanket over the chair so Gidget wouldn't leave hair all over it, and when Ottie sat down, the mutt leapt up and snuggled into her lap. A happy ending.

Ottie fiddled with Gidget's collar, cursing under her breath until she finally detached the tags.

"Here you go."

I took the tags and turned them over in my hands. "Why do I need these?"

Ottie's name, Gidget's name, their address in Santa Clarita, phone numbers, proof of rabies vaccination, county licence number, a pretty little pendant with a paw print... The dog wore more jewellery than I did.

"Look closer."

I did as instructed, and then... Ah, clever girl. I began laughing. The paw print wasn't just a decoration; it was also a locket. The back unscrewed, and when I opened it, I found a tiny memory card inside.

"You entrusted the code to a *dog*?"

"Gidget runs faster than I do. Plus she doesn't much like men, so I figured she'd bite anyone who tried to take a closer look."

"She likes Nico," Leona said. "He bribes her with chicken."

"I thought she'd gotten fat."

"You'll be walking properly in no time, and then we can exercise her together."

"Tim can take her out when he gets here." Ottie smiled. "He bribes her with cheese. Don't let José mess with my code, okay? I'm almost certain I know what the problem is with the power consumption, and I'll fix it when I come back."

Yes, Ottie planned to go back to work. She believed in her job, and the idea of a non-lethal, non-contact weapon with near-instant stopping power was one that had grown on me. We didn't live in a utopia. There would always be bad actors who aspired to turn a peaceful gathering into a riot, always be assholes who turned to crime rather than doing an honest day's work. But was a bullet an appropriate punishment? Ottie's work opened up all kinds of other possibilities.

As long as it stopped boiling people alive.

"I'll tell José to keep his hands off."

He was too busy trying to repair his relationship with his wife to screw around with the code, anyway. Ottie swore they hadn't been having an affair, but José had become as engrossed in Project Marshmallow as she had. The day Laurie's friend saw them at the hotel, well, that had been a misunderstanding of epic proportions. Timothy Stern had been away in DC, presenting a progress report on his own project to the powers that be, when Ottie had seen a cockroach in her bedroom. And Ottie Marquette didn't do cockroaches. Rather than stay in Timothy's apartment—because his asshole brother had moved in "temporarily" after his own marital problems and showed no signs of leaving—she'd simply checked in to the nearest five-star hotel. Timothy had asked José to make sure she was okay and take her a can of roach spray, but Ottie refused to go home until the entire house had been fumigated.

The two of them had talked over several project-related issues, and when José arrived home, Laurie was crying and packing her stuff to move in with a friend. Then she'd refused to speak to him, and, well, you get the picture...

Anyhow, that was in the past. Laurie had agreed to try again, and José had promised to reform his workaholic tendencies.

Another happy ending.

Now we just needed to set up Dasha's new fake life for the win.

Dasha was back in her Darla outfit when we walked into the Craft Cabin, and she mustered up a vague look of recognition that morphed into barely disguised horror when Bradley hugged her.

"I love your dress! Did you make it?"

"Sure did, hun."

"How's your sister?"

"She's doing a little better now, thank you for asking."

Paulo rushed over with Brooke in tow, and there were more hugs and some squealing. I'd agreed to let Bradley do the talking—he liked to be a part of the team, and this subterfuge had been his brainwave, after all.

After the chit-chat, Paulo made everyone coffee, and then we got down to it. Black and I would provide a retail site at reduced rent. The Blackwood Foundation would offer financial support with the hope that in the future, the new Craft Cabin could stand on its own two feet as a social enterprise offering classes, craft supplies, and a small café. The details had been hashed out with Dasha and Cora, who oversaw the Foundation, over the past few weeks, and we even had two possible locations in mind. The staff at Crossroads, a local women's shelter Dan had ties with, were keeping an eye out for potential candidates for the job openings.

Bradley spread his arms wide. "The possibilities are endless —a whole network of Craft Cabins, each with their own Thrive group. Don't you love it?"

Brooke nodded enthusiastically. "More Thrive groups would be amazing. When I started this one in Baldwin's Shore, I never dreamed so many women would attend. In a way, it's been sickening. I mean, it's heartbreaking that domestic and sexual violence is so widespread."

Didn't I know it? I'd been a victim too, before I was old enough to defend myself. But my job today was to temper expectations.

"Let's start with one new store, champ. Then we can scale up if it works, okay?"

"Where?" Bradley asked. "In Oregon? What about Roseburg? Coquille?"

"That's too close to Darla's existing store. We don't want to split the customer base. How about Virginia? If we opened a branch in Richmond, you could oversee the fit-out."

Brooke and Paulo looked at each other.

"Virginia?" Oh, that dampened Brooke's enthusiasm. "But that's so far away. I have a dog, and Luca…"

"I guess I could spend some time there," Paulo said. "How far is Richmond from New York City?"

"An hour and twenty minutes from Richmond International to La Guardia."

The boyfriend Paulo pretended he didn't have lived in New York, so Dasha said. She'd thought he might volunteer.

And now she spoke up. "If anyone goes, it should be me. The Craft Cabin is my brand, and I'd want to make sure things were done right. Plus my sister lives in Maryland, and she sure could use some extra support at the moment. That boyfriend of hers..." Dasha shook her head and sighed.

"You'd really do that?" Brooke asked. "Go to Richmond?"

"Last month, he spent the rent money on new rims for his truck, and my sister just won't stand up for herself."

Brooke made a face. "Ouch. What does she see in him?"

"He can be very charming. *Too* charming, if you know what I mean."

"Red flags are waving?"

Dasha nodded. "And I don't have as many ties to Baldwin's Shore as you do. We'd have to sort through all the finances, but if that works out and you could take care of Pickle..."

"We could definitely take care of Pickle."

"And we'd need to keep Everly on if she's willing."

"Oh, she will be. She's already said that she loves working here."

Another problem solved. And once Dasha got to Richmond, she'd "meet" Alex in a way that didn't involve helicopters, stolen weapons, or assassination. We could send him into the craft store, or have them bump into each other in a coffee shop, or engineer a coordinated stroll through the park... As Bradley said, the possibilities were endless.

And finally, two of the Ten would be happy.

From time to time, I couldn't help wondering where Vik was. Would we ever cross paths? Did I even want to? But that was a question for another day. This afternoon, I had Nico to speak with and an apartment to break into, and Dasha had to put on her dancing shoes.

There was no rest for the wicked, and we were as wicked as they came.

WHAT'S NEXT?

My next book will be *Hydrogen*, a romance novel (with a hint of suspense) in the Blackwood Elements series...

If a man wants to date Leah Burgess, he'd better be rich, handsome, and dress to kill. Kevin ticks precisely none of those boxes, but when a surveillance operation goes wrong, Leah's forced to spend more time with him—and his unruly dog—than she'd like. Can Kevin convince Leah to take a chance on a regular guy?

For more details:
www.elise-noble.com/hydrogen

If you want to read more about the trip to Egypt that Emmy mentions in Chapter 1, you can find that story in *Copper*.

And if you'd like to read more about Scott and Callie, that tale is told in *Trouble in Paradise*.

If you enjoyed *Secret Weapon*, please consider leaving a review.

For an author, every review is incredibly important. Not only do they make us feel warm and fuzzy inside, readers consider them when making their decision whether or not to buy a book. Even a line saying you enjoyed the book or what your favourite part was helps a lot.

WANT TO STALK ME?

For updates on my new releases, giveaways, and other random stuff, you can sign up for my newsletter on my website: www.elise-noble.com

If you're on Facebook, you might also like to join Team Blackwood for exclusive giveaways, sneak previews, and book-related chat. Be the first to find out about new stories, and you might even see your name or one of your suggestions make it into print!

And if you'd like to read my books for FREE, you can also find details of how to join my advance review team.

Would you like to join Team Blackwood?

www.elise-noble.com/team-blackwood

facebook.com/EliseNobleAuthor

twitter.com/EliseANoble

instagram.com/elise_noble

END-OF-BOOK STUFF

I hope you enjoyed Nine's story! Ever since I wrote *Ultraviolet*, I've been wondering what happened to Ana's other comrades, and I thought it'd be fun to have her and Emmy run into a couple of them. And folks have been asking for Alex's story for a while, so it all worked out quite well.

Will we ever meet Vik? I'd like to think so.

While I was writing *Secret Weapon*, I decided to teach myself how to read the Cyrillic alphabet, which has definitely helped me to swear more proficiently in Russian, which in turn has been useful when watching the seemingly endless videos of Ukrainian troops blowing up what's left of the not-so-great Soviet army. Fuck, what a mess the world is in. When I sent Emmy and co. in to blow up Base 13, I thought I was pushing it a bit to have them destroy a whole military base, but now it doesn't seem quite so farfetched. *Slava Ukraini.*

I also realised that I should probably have spelled Zacharov as Zakharov, as the latter is far more common. Ah well. A good chunk of *Ultraviolet* was written while I was in Dahab, and I cribbed the name off a Russian guy I went diving with a few times. I considered going back to change the spelling, but I figured that would get too confusing as it appears in four other books. But I did sneak into *Platinum* to make Markovich a few years younger. My books are constantly evolving, and I often update them for pop culture references, etc. At some point, I'll probably rewrite *Ultraviolet* completely as my writing style has changed since it was published, hopefully for the better!

So, what's next for the Baldwin's Shore crew? Well, I want to write a story for Sara in the main series, but I'd also like to write another crossover book with Nico. Someone has to find out what happened to Kaylin La Rocca, right? But at the moment, I'm working on a new series—Blackstone House. As with Baldwin's Shore, there's going to be a bit of a crossover with Blackwood, and you may spot a familiar character from the Elements Series in *Hard Lines* :)

At the moment, I'm also trying to tame my jungle of a garden and grow some veggies, plus I have a big, goofy foster dog named Razor staying while he looks for a new home. He's a bit of a weirdo. A little growly, a lot cuddly, sometimes at the same time. This week, he's carrying (the remains of) a stuffed elephant everywhere. If he likes you, he'll bring the elephant to show you, but you're not allowed to touch it. Like so many rescues, he hasn't had the best of starts in life. Here's hoping that by the time *Hydrogen* comes out, he'll have found his forever home <3

Hope you have a great summer!
Elise

RUSSIAN TO ENGLISH GLOSSARY

Пиздец/Pizdets - Dammit

Гавно/Gavno - Shit

Сука/Suka - Bitch

Сучка/Suchka - Little bitch (also used as a term of endearment)

Мудак/Mudak - Asshole/Shithead

Иди на хуй / Idi na hui - Go fuck yourself

Хуй тебе тоже / Khui tebe tozhe - Fuck you too

Чёрт / Chyort - Damn

Дерьмо / Der'mo - Shit

Спасибо / Spasiba - Thanks

Снежинка / Snezhinka) - Snowflake

Нет / Nyet - No

Привет / Privyet - Hello

За победы / Za Pobedy - For victories

За нашу дружбу / Za Nashu druzhbu - For our friendship

Спокойной ночи сестра / Spokoynoy nochi, sestra - Good night, sister

Ладно / Ladno - Okay

С возвращением, товарищ / S vozvrashcheniyem, tovarishch - Welcome back, Comrade

До свидания / Do svidaniya - Goodbye

ALSO BY ELISE NOBLE

Secret Weapon (Crossover with Baldwin's Shore)

The Devil and the Deep Blue Sea (TBA)

Blackwood Elements

Oxygen

Lithium

Carbon

Rhodium

Platinum

Lead

Copper

Bronze

Nickel

Hydrogen (2022)

Blackwood UK

Joker in the Pack

Cherry on Top

Roses are Dead

Shallow Graves

Indigo Rain

Pass the Parcel (TBA)

Blackwood Casefiles

Stolen Hearts

Burning Love (TBA)

Baldwin's Shore

Dirty Little Secrets

Secrets, Lies, and Family Ties

Buried Secrets

Secret Weapon (Crossover with Blackwood Security)

A Secret to Die For (TBA)

Blackstone House

Hard Lines (2022)

Hard Tide (2022)

Hard Code (2023)

The Electi

Cursed

Spooked

Possessed

Demented

Judged

The Planes

A Vampire in Vegas

A Devil in the Dark (TBA)

The Trouble Series

Trouble in Paradise

Nothing but Trouble

24 Hours of Trouble

Standalone

Life

Coco du Ciel

A Very Happy Christmas (novella)

Twisted (short stories)

Books with clean versions available (no swearing and no on-the-page sex)

Pitch Black

Into the Black

Forever Black

Gold Rush

Gray is My Heart

Audiobooks

Black is My Heart (Diamond & Snow - Prequel)

Pitch Black

Into the Black

Forever Black

Gold Rush

Gray is My Heart

Neon (novella)

Printed in Great Britain
by Amazon